PRIMA'S OFFICIAL STRATEGY GUIDE

turn to a galaxy far, far away and relive the classics as LucasArts brings you flying and ;hting action in the midst of the civil war between the Empire and the Rebel Alliance. .ke Skywalker and Wedge Antilles are the principals, but you'll also guide Princess Leia d Han Solo through heroic adventures. Prima's Official Strategy Guide provides you mplete maps and strategies for every mission objective, plus details on how to unlock ips, earn tech upgrades and win the coveted gold medals.

'RIMA GAMES
A DIVISION OF
{ANDOM HOUSE, INC.

)00 LAVA RIDGE COURT
{OSEVILLE, CA 95661
1-800-733-3000
VW.PRIMAGAMES.COM

ISBN: 0-7615-4497-6
PRINTED IN THE UNITED STATES OF AMERICA

03 04 05 06 UU 10 9 8 7 6 5 4 3 2 1

TABLE OF CONTENTS

INTRODUCTION

LUKE SKYWALKER'S CAMPAIGN

WEDGE ANTILLES' CAMPAIGN

ENDOR CAMPAIGN

BONUS MISSIONS

TABLE OF CONTENTS

COOPERATIVE CAMPAIGN

VERSUS MODE

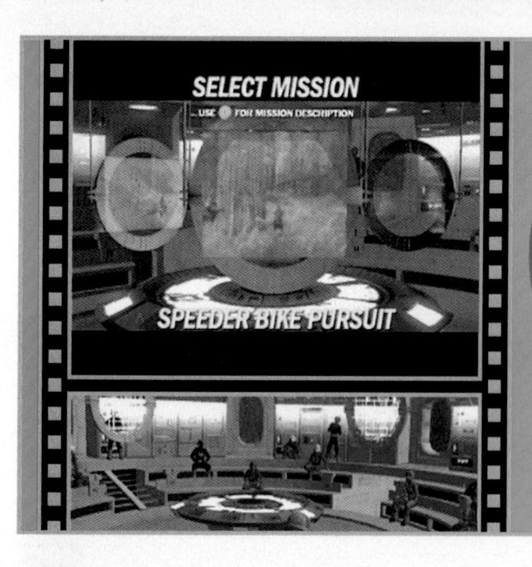

INTRODUCTION

GAME PLAY MODES

From the single-player campaigns to the cooperative missions and competitive scenarios, Star Wars™ Rogue Squadron™ III: Rebel Strike™ is a Force to be reckoned with. Jump in and join the struggle to save the Rebellion.

SINGLE-PLAYER CAMPAIGNS

LUKE SKYWALKER'S CAMPAIGN

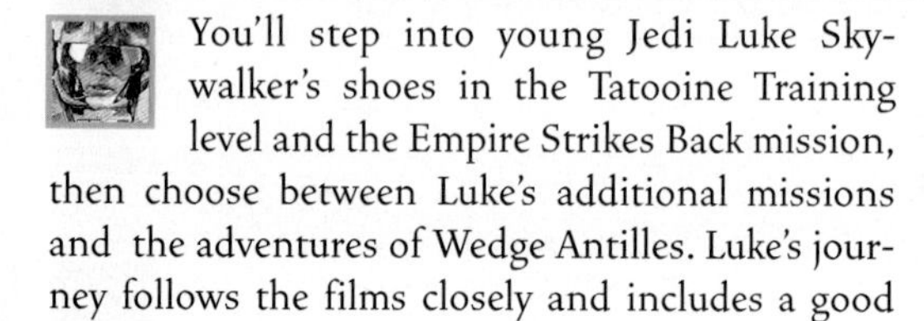

You'll step into young Jedi Luke Skywalker's shoes in the Tatooine Training level and the Empire Strikes Back mission, then choose between Luke's additional missions and the adventures of Wedge Antilles. Luke's journey follows the films closely and includes a good mix of vehicular battle and on-foot fighting.

WEDGE ANTILLES' CAMPAIGN

Ace pilot Wedge Antilles joined the Rebellion to lead squadrons against Imperial ships. His campaign focuses on battles that take place outside the events of the classic films—He'll often lead only a few Rebel ships against waves of TIEs and Star Destroyers.

Although Wedge Antilles does occasionally climb out of his X-wing, the bulk of his missions take place in space, reenacting devastating battles between the Empire and the Rebel Alliance.

ENDOR CAMPAIGN

Both Luke's and Wedge's campaigns funnel into missions that mirror the final conflicts of *Return of the Jedi*, with Luke, Chewbacca and Han Solo as the player-controlled characters. Your fate in the final battles will hinge on getting help from the forest-dwelling Ewoks.

BONUS MISSIONS

Your medal-earning performances in the single-player campaigns will give you the points you need to unlock a wide variety of bonus missions, many of which parallel key scenes from *A New Hope, The Empire Strikes Back* and *Return of the Jedi*. You'll see footage from the films between game sequences.

COOPERATIVE CAMPAIGN

The 10 core missions and three of the bonus missions from *Star Wars* Rogue Squadron II: Rogue Leader make up Rebel Strike's two-player cooperative campaign. The objectives are basically the same as they were originally, but their difficulty has been adjusted for two-player gaming. Partners can team up to accomplish objectives together or divide and conquer.

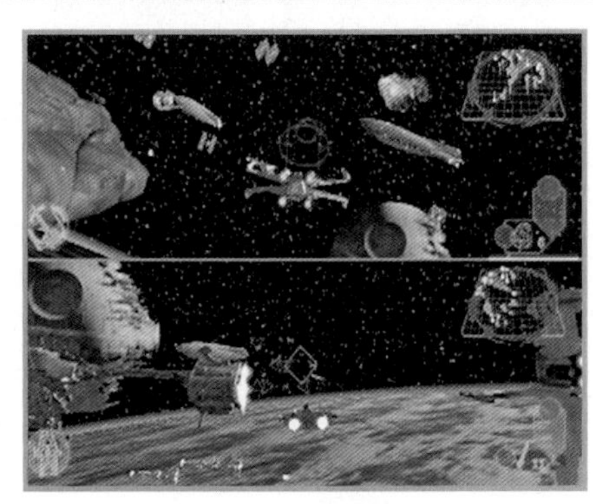

Rebel Strike's cooperative campaign covers the same territory as Rogue Leader, but adds enemies and tougher targets and displays the action in a split-screen format.

VERSUS MODE

Vehicular battle rules in Rebel Strike's split-screen two-player competitive scenarios. They include one-on-one dogfights, scenery-destroying rampage levels, tag-and-defend missions and races.

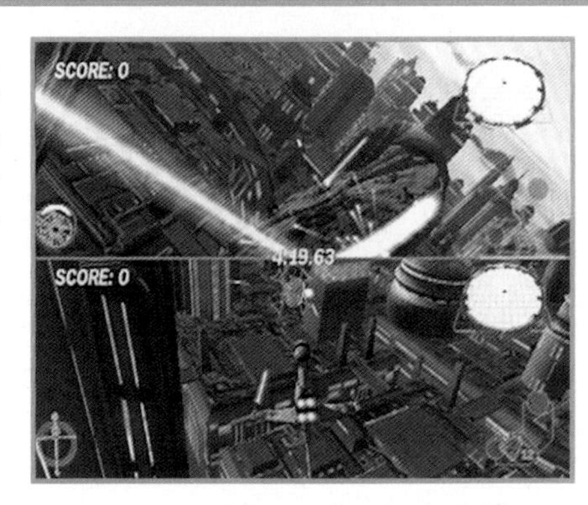

After you save the Rebellion with your partner, find out who rules the skies by entering any of several competitive scenarios.

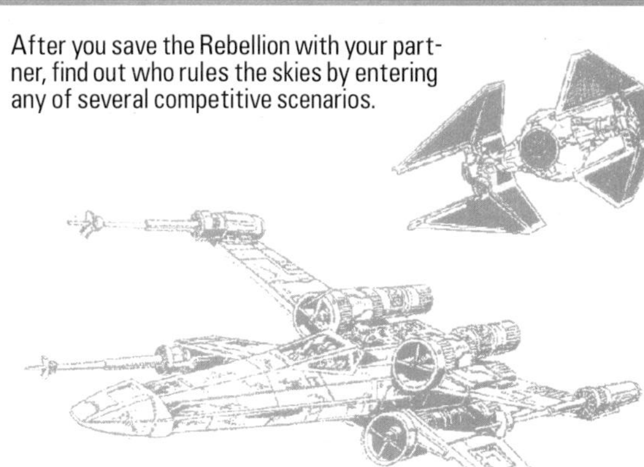

OPTIONS

Star Wars Rogue Squadron III: Rebel Strike uses progressive scan technology and supports Dolby Pro Logic II sound. You can adjust video, sound and game settings from the Options menu. You can also use the menu to check your rankings with those of the Rebel Strike elite, enter secret passcodes and check out special features.

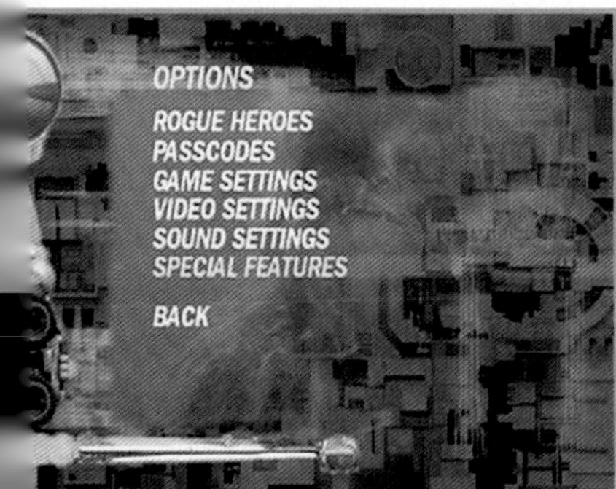

Your in-game heroics will unlock special features that take you behind the scenes to learn about the making of Rebel Strike. See page 22 to discover feature-unlocking conditions. Passcodes also unlock special options, along with game cheats. LucasArts will release passcodes in the months following the game's launch.

INTRODUCTION

FLIGHT CONTROL

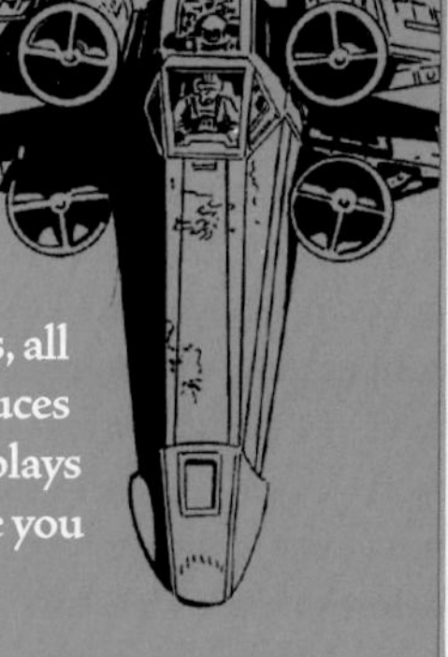

Although every Rebel and Imperial ship has its own qualities, all ships have controls in common. The following section introduces flight controls, navigation and weapon use and explains displays and upgrades. Familiarity with your craft's functions will take you a long way toward mission completion.

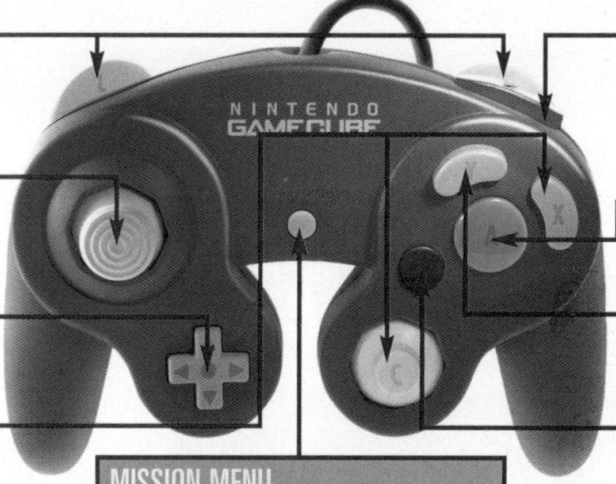

1 SPEED CONTROL

Press the L Button to slow your vehicle. Press the R Button to accelerate.

2 STEERING

The Control Stick adjusts your ship's attitude. Press Up to dive. Press Down to climb.

3 WINGMAN COMMUNICATIONS

Use the Control Pad to give orders to your computer-controlled squadmates.

4 CAMERA ADJUSTMENT

Press X to toggle between the chase camera and the cockpit view. Use the C Stick to move the camera in the cockpit view.

MISSION MENU

Press the Start Button to pause the action, view objectives and access mission options and game settings.

5 ROLL CONTROL

Hold Z and press Left or Right on the Control Stick to bank hard and roll.

6 PRIMARY WEAPON CONTROL

Press A to fire primary weapons.

7 TARGETING COMPUTER

Hold Y to view the targeting computer display.

8 SECONDARY WEAPON CONTROL

The B Button triggers secondary weapons. Press and hold the button to charge ion cannons or lock on to targets with homing missiles, then release the button to fire.

1 SPEED CONTROL

The L and R Buttons allow you to adjust your speed. Press the R Button to increase your speed, and press the L Button to decrease it. By pressing R until the button clicks, you'll activate a speed boost in most ships. By pressing L until it clicks, you'll activate the brakes and make it easier to execute tight turns.

The Rebel Alliance's X-wing and B-wing are both equipped with S-foils that close when you activate the ship's speed boost. You can't operate weapons when the S-foils are closed. Press the L Button until it clicks to slow the ship and open the foils.

2 STEERING

The Control Stick gives you the ability to bank, dive and climb. The more you tilt the stick in any direction, the sharper your craft will turn.

3 WINGMAN COMMUNICATIONS

The command cross appears automatically at times, and whenever you tap the Control Pad. It shows situation-specific commands, each associated with a Control Pad direction. Press the Control Pad in the command-associated direction to issue the order.

4 CAMERA ADJUSTMENT

The chase camera shows the default view of the action—behind and slightly above the player-controlled vehicle. The camera pans back to show enemy ships that are in hot pursuit of your craft.

The cockpit view allows you to see the action from the pilot's perspective. Manipulate the C Stick to turn the pilot's head. Press X to switch between the chase camera and the cockpit view on the fly.

5 ROLL CONTROL

By holding the Z Button and pressing Left or Right on the Control Stick, you can roll your ship, allowing it to make tight turns and slip through narrow openings.

6 PRIMARY WEAPON CONTROL

The primary weapons for all Rebel Alliance ships are lasers. Tap the A Button to release a single laser blast or hold the button to fire repeatedly. If you allow your laser to recharge between blasts, you will fire its strongest shots.

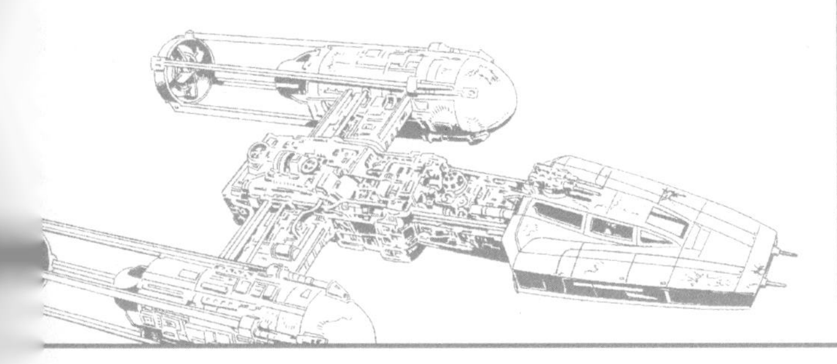

7 TARGETING COMPUTER

When you press and hold the Y Button, your view will switch to the cockpit automatically and the targeting computer will activate. In the computer's display, friendlies are shaded green, enemies that pose an immediate threat or are attached to a mission objective are shaded yellow and all other enemies are shaded purple.

After you've collected the advanced targeting computer tech upgrade, you can toggle the computer on and off by pressing the Y Button. If the display shows yellow-shaded targets, you can use the C Stick to select a target with a cursor. After you've identified a target, your wingmen will fire at it.

8 SECONDARY WEAPON CONTROL

Most ships are equipped with missiles, bombs or torpedoes. If a weapon is capable of firing multiple simultaneous shots, hold the B Button to paint your targets, then release the button to fire. If the weapon can home in on only one target at a time, press B once to switch to the homing reticle, then again to fire after you've identified a target.

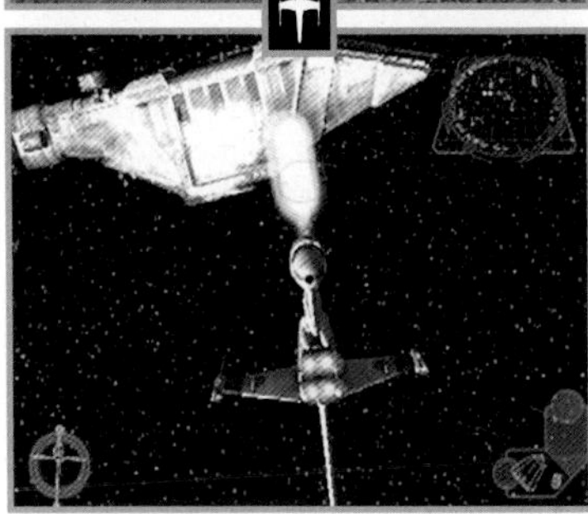

B-wings and Y-wings are equipped with ion cannons in addition to their proton torpedoes and proton bombs, respectively. Press and hold the B Button to charge the cannon, then release the button after the reticle turns blue to fire the shot.

! SHIELD REPAIR

REPAIR
REPAIR REPAIR
REPAIR

Some ships are equipped with droid units that fix shields on the fly. When your shields are damaged, your droid will work to regenerate them at a steady pace. If your shields are critical, your droid will let out a distressed beep and a command cross with repair instructions will appear. Tap the Control Pad to execute the one-time-only full repair.

ON-SCREEN DISPLAYS

Your ship's computer offers important information about ship status, weapons and enemy location in on-screen displays. If the cockpit view is on, you'll find the displays among the cockpit instruments.

SCANNER

Your ship is always at the center of the scanner. Enemies appear as red dots, and friendlies are shown as green dots. Lines that extend from the dots indicate the vehicle's vertical distance from your ship's horizontal plane. The scanner's orange-shaded wedge points to the current objective. Arrows in the corner of the scanner point to the objective if it is above or below your ship.

SHIELDS

The shields display shows a line drawing of your ship, surrounded by a graphic that starts as a green circle and becomes shrinking circle segments that change from green to yellow and red as your ship is damaged. The line drawing spins with increasing frequency after consecutive hits to your ship. The shields will regenerate over time for ships that are equipped with R2 units. The display also shows the ship's regenerating boost power.

WEAPONS DISPLAY

You'll get more power out of laser blasts if you wait for your lasers to recharge after every shot. The weapons display shows the power returning to your lasers in the area marked by the A Button icon. The secondary weapon area (marked by the B Button icon) shows your ship's current secondary weapon payload. Some secondary weapon supplies replenish automatically. Icons in the lower-right corner of the display appear if you have upgraded the weapons.

TECH UPGRADES

You'll find tech upgrades hidden in core campaign missions. After you collect an upgrade and complete the mission successfully, all player-controlled ships that can benefit from having the item will be equipped automatically. The single-player and cooperative missions do not share tech upgrades.

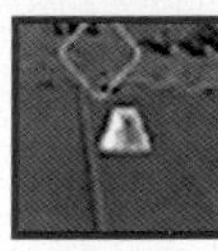

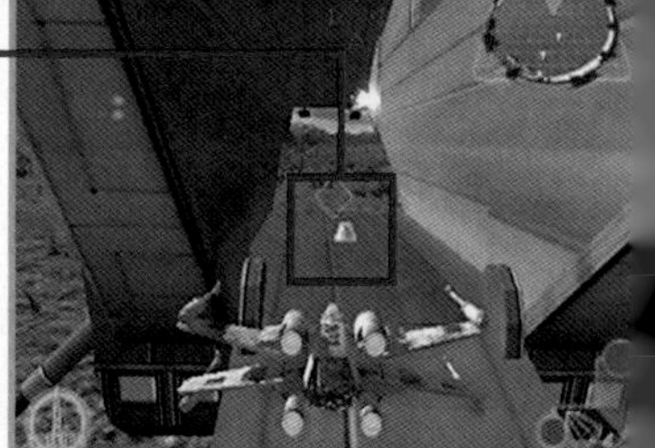

PROTON TORPEDOES

ADVANCED PROTON TORPEDOES

The initial upgrade for every secondary weapon increases the weapon's power. Advanced proton torpedoes allow you to destroy armored targets with speed and efficiency.

ADVANCED HOMING PROTON TORPEDOES

After you upgrade your proton torpedoes with homing capabilities, press B to switch to a locking cursor, then press B again to release a torpedo that will home in on your locked target.

CONCUSSION MISSILES

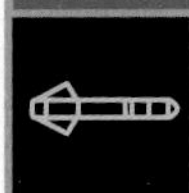

ADVANCED CONCUSSION MISSILES

Although standard concussion missiles are not very powerful, advanced concussion missiles pack a punch. They are also faster than their unmodified counterparts.

ADVANCED HOMING CONCUSSION MISSILES

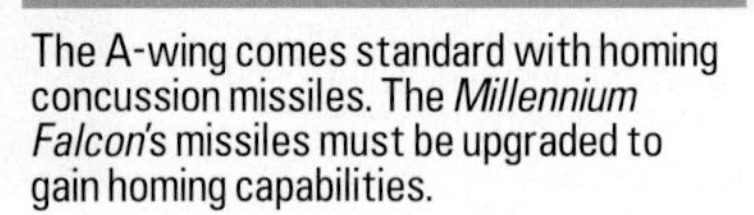

The A-wing comes standard with homing concussion missiles. The *Millennium Falcon*'s missiles must be upgraded to gain homing capabilities.

PROTON BOMBS

ADVANCED PROTON BOMBS

Advanced proton bombs have more explosive power than regular bombs. Press B once to make the bomb cursor appear. Press B again to drop a bomb.

ADVANCED SPREAD PROTON BOMBS

Advanced spread proton bombs drop like standard bombs, then they break into a spray of smaller bombs after they land to increase the area affected.

CLUSTER MISSILES

ADVANCED CLUSTER MISSILES

The scattershot quality of advanced cluster missiles makes them powerful, but difficult to aim. The missiles fire in groups of six.

ADVANCED HOMING CLUSTER MISSILES

By adding homing capabilities to cluster missiles, the upgrade makes the missiles among the strongest weapons in the game. They can lock on to several enemies at once.

ADVANCED TARGETING COMPUTER

The standard targeting computer disappears from the screen as soon as you release the Y Button; the advanced targeting computer stays on-screen until you press the Y Button a second time. Use it to identify targets for your wingmen to go after.

ADVANCED SHIELDS

Once you collect the more-powerful advanced shields tech upgrade, your shield display's default color will be blue

ADVANCED LASERS

Advanced lasers increase your chances of attaining better Completion Time and Enemies Destroyed ratings.

INTRODUCTION

STARFIGHTERS

Every flight-oriented mission places you in the hangar at launch time to select your ship from the mission's available craft. You can unlock some ships after reaching certain milestones (as detailed on the next five pages). You'll also switch to new ships in the middle of some missions.

STARFIGHTERS

 T-16 SKYHOPPER

Great for disposing of womp rats and for learning maneuvers, the T-16 skyhopper is a Tatooine Training mission vehicle. Its capabilities change on the fly, depending on the current training objective.

SECONDARY WEAPON
VARIABLE

The T-16's secondary weapon changes to demonstrate a variety of weapons during flight training exercises.

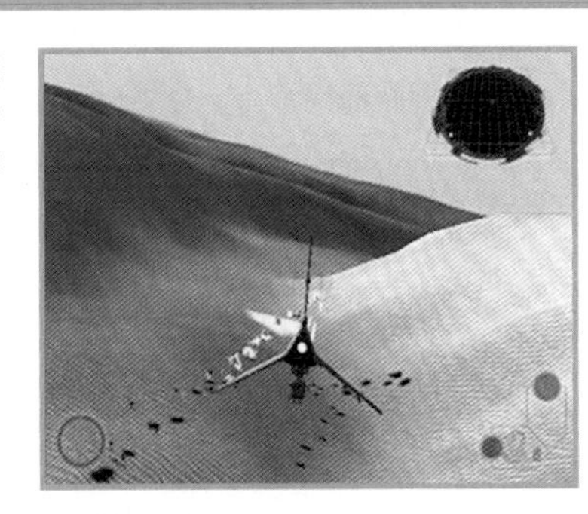

Equipped with a primary laser and a variety of secondary weapons, the Tatooine trainer is a serviceable sand skimmer, but it wouldn't last long in a real battle against Imperial ships. The craft's speed booster recharges after every use.

 X-WING

The Rebel dogfighter's weapon of choice will always be known as the ship that destroyed the Death Star to commemorate Luke Skywalker's fateful run. It offers a perfectly balanced mix of speed and maneuverability, with strong shields and impressive weapons. X marks the best all-around fighter in the fleet.

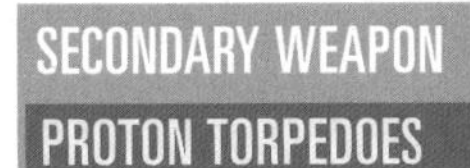

SECONDARY WEAPON
PROTON TORPEDOES

DROID REPAIR

The X-wing's four blasters fire in alternating double blasts. If you allow the blasters to recharge, all four will fire at once for a stinging single shot.

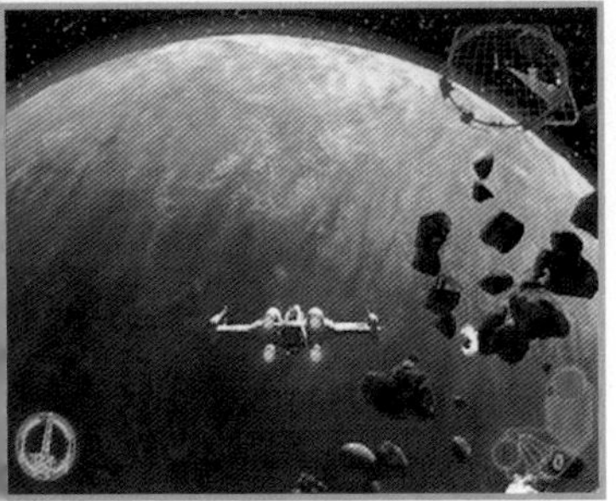

After you press the R Button until it clicks, the X-wing's S foils will close and the ship will take off like a rocket. The craft is unable to fire lasers when its foils are closed. Press L until the button clicks to open the foils. The X-wing's speed boost recharges after each use.

A-WING

The A-wing's light frame makes it the quickest ship in the Rebel fleet, but one of the easiest ships to destroy. A pair of laser cannons gives the A-wing a strong sting, and the ship's built-in homing concussion missiles add to the weapons package. It's a great ship for wily veterans.

SECONDARY WEAPON

HOMING CONCUSSION MISSILES

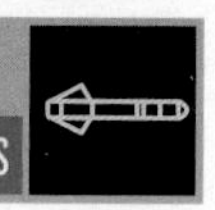

UNLOCKING CONDITIONS

Complete Deception at Destrillion.

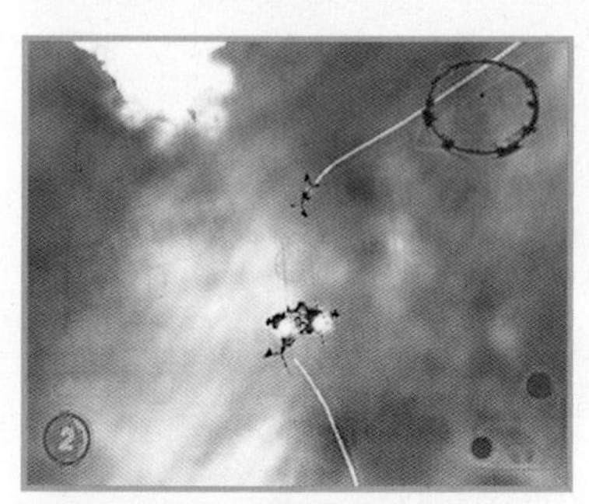

The A-wing is the only Rebel ship that starts with homing concussion missiles. Hold B to switch to the homing reticle, paint up to four targets, then release the button to let the missiles fly.

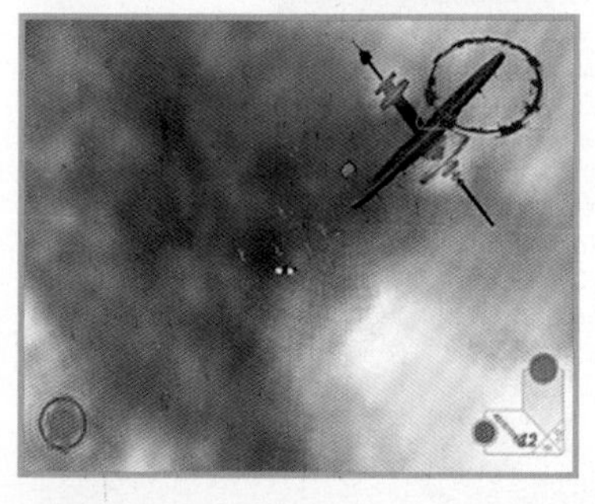

As fast and maneuverable as any ship that the Rebel Alliance or the Empire has to offer, the A-wing also offers a quickly rechargeable speed boost. The ship's only real weakness is that enemies can blast it out of the sky with only a handful of laser shots.

Y-WING

The Y-wing proves that speed and maneuverability aren't the only qualities that a pilot should look for in a fighting craft. Its strong armor, ion cannons and bombing capabilities make the ship a perfect choice for planet-based missions that have lots of ground targets. Just don't expect it to out-duel an X-wing.

SECONDARY WEAPONS

PROTON BOMBS

ION CANNON

UNLOCKING CONDITIONS

Complete Revenge of the Empire.

DROID REPAIR

Press B to switch to the bombing view. A targeting reticle will appear on the ground. Press B again to drop a bomb. The Y-wing's proton bomb supply replenishes automatically.

The Y-wing does not have speed-boost capabilities—its general lack of speed and poor maneuverability are significant disadvantages in dogfights, but strong shields guarantee that it will endure.

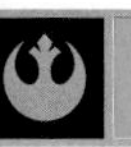

B-WING

An awkward-looking design and low speed rating put the B-wing between the X-wing and Y-wing in overall flight performance, but a strong arsenal that includes an electronics-disrupting ion cannon and surprisingly good mobility make it a wise choice in attacks on capital ships.

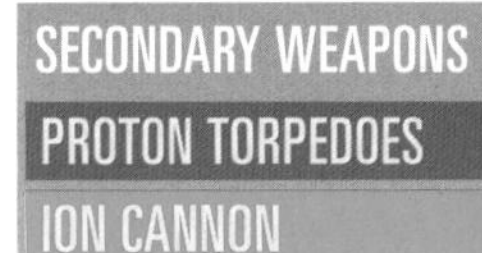

SECONDARY WEAPONS

PROTON TORPEDOES

ION CANNON

UNLOCKING CONDITIONS

Complete Raid at Bakura.

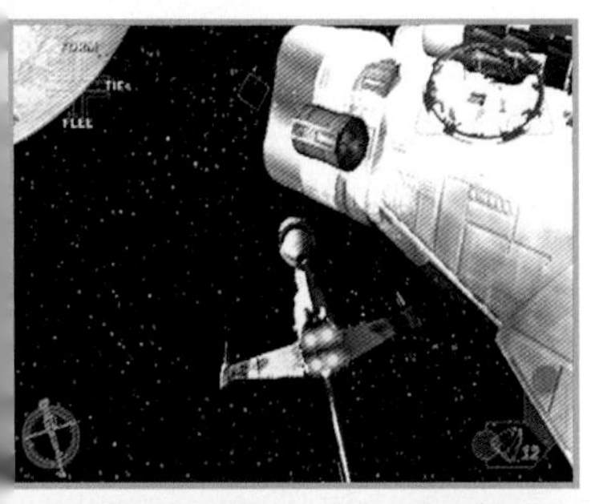

At first glance, the B-wing, with S-foils open, looks unwieldy. However, it proves to be more maneuverable than the X-wing in many situations, even if it is a little slow.

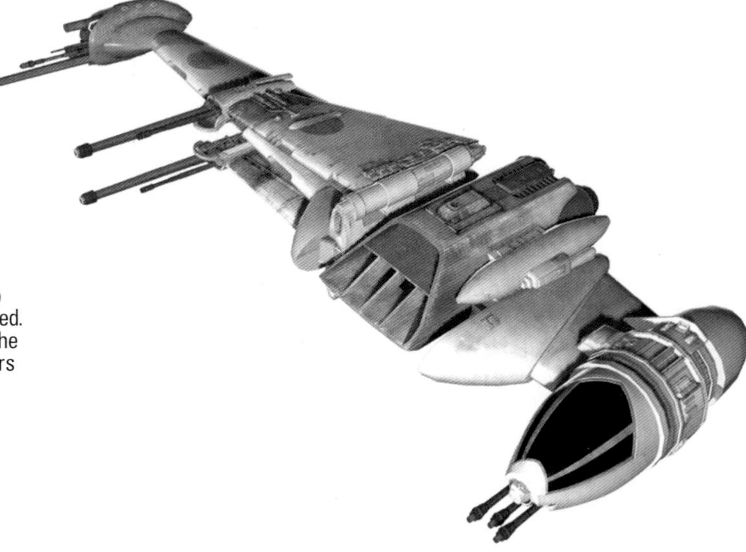

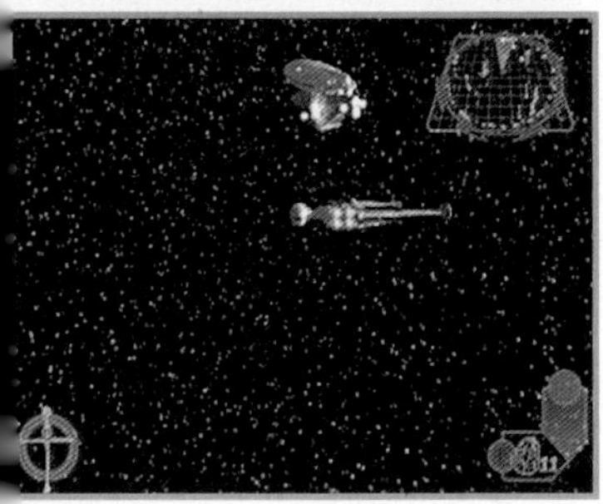

When you press R until the button clicks, the B-wing's S-foils will close and the ship will take off in a burst of speed. As is true with the X-wing, the B-wing cannot fire its blasters when its S-foils are closed.

SPEEDER

With no deflector shields and no conventional secondary weapon, the low-to-the-ground speeder is limited in its abilities as a fighter. However, good speed and an innovative tow cable make it lethal in the right situations. It can fly below an Imperial's radar and deliver a big surprise.

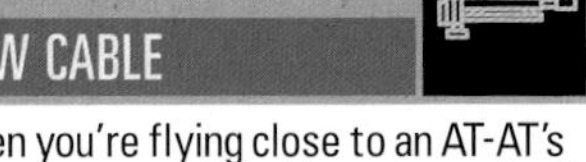

SECONDARY WEAPON

TOW CABLE

When you're flying close to an AT-AT's legs or any towable object, press the B Button to release the tow cable.

The speeder's quickness and maneuverability put it in a class with the A-wing. The vehicle's speed allows you to fly circles around an AT-AT, and you can use its tow cable to tie up the Imperial walker's legs.

Since the speeder is a repulsor craft—not technically a spacecraft—it cannot reach high altitudes, but it can hug the ground better than any ship in the fleet.

MILLENNIUM FALCON

Han Solo's modified Corellian freighter is famed for its speed and power. Although it's not a traditional starfighter, its reputation gives the pilot enough confidence to get through most situations.

SECONDARY WEAPONS
- CONCUSSION MISSILES
- QUAD CANNON

The *Falcon's* quad cannon helps give the ship coverage at all angles. Use the C Stick to fire the weapon.

UNLOCKING CONDITIONS

Earn bronze medals on all single-player missions, including bonus missions.

DROID REPAIR

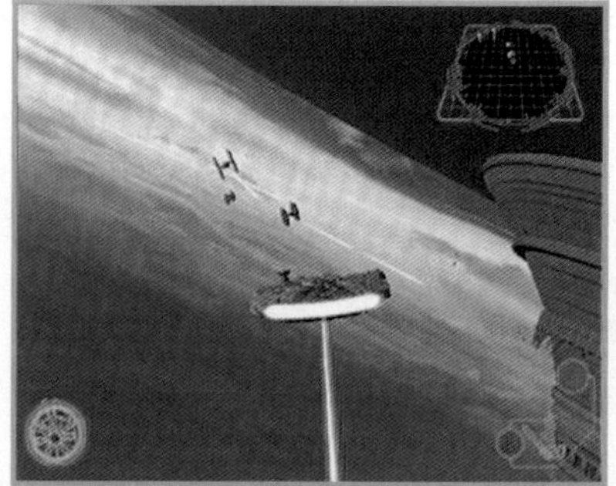

Don't let the *Millennium Falcon's* size fool you. It's fast and easy to maneuver. Since the ship is built like a freighter—wide and somewhat clunky—you'll discover that Z-Button-aided rolling turns are useful in dogfights. Once you get a ship in your sights, you can send it to the scrap heap using the *Falcon's* strong lasers and concussion missiles.

TIE BOMBER

The two-seat TIE bomber is an unlikely rescue vehicle in the Raid at Bakura mission. It's the least maneuverable of the TIEs, but it can take a lot of damage and its weapons payload is impressive. The ship's primary weapons are homing concussion missiles.

SECONDARY WEAPON
- PROTON BOMBS

UNLOCKING CONDITIONS

Destroy all of the ground turrets in the Raid at Bakura mission in missile-linked groups. The turrets in any cluster must detonate within a half-second of each other.

The TIE bomber looks like two TIEs fused together. It also has enough weapons for two TIEs—homing concussion missiles and proton bombs. The ship rivals the Y-wing in suitability for surface missions.

TIE HUNTER

The TIE equivalent of the X-wing is speedy, mobile and well-equipped. It even has S-foils that close when the ship is flying at top speeds. Like the X-wing, the hunter is unable to fire when the foils are closed.

SECONDARY WEAPONS
- PROTON TORPEDOES
- ION CANNON

UNLOCKING CONDITIONS

Earn gold medals on all single-player missions, including bonus missions.

The fastest TIE in the Imperial fleet is equipped with lasers and an ion cannon in addition to its proton torpedoes. The ship's only weakness is in its slight shields.

JEDI STARFIGHTER

The vintage Jedi starfighter, from the Clone Wars era, is the A-wing's predecessor. What the starfighter lacks in shield strength, it makes up for in speed, mobility and a strong secondary weapon.

SECONDARY WEAPON
- SONIC MINE

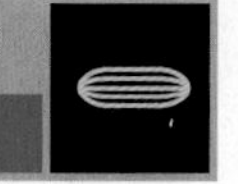

After a sonic mine rockets out into space, it will spread like fireworks and hit targets in a wide radius. Your mine supply regenerates over time.

UNLOCKING CONDITIONS

Earn silver medals in all single-player missions, including bonus missions.

DROID REPAIR

It may be old, but the Jedi starfighter is still a good choice in missions that require pure speed. Its sonic mine may be slightly unpredictable, but it is devastating when it hits.

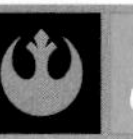

SLAVE I

Jango Fett's ship, passed down to Bobba Fett, wraps around the pilot, who is in a standing position. The ship is built for forceful forward attacks. Its shields are strong in the front but weak in the back.

SECONDARY WEAPON
SONIC MINE

UNLOCKING CONDITIONS—BOBA FETT VERSION

Earn bronze medals on all standard single-player missions.

UNLOCKING CONDITIONS—JANGO FETT VERSION

Jango's version appears in a Versus mode dogfight over Geonosis when the other player selects a Jedi Starfighter.

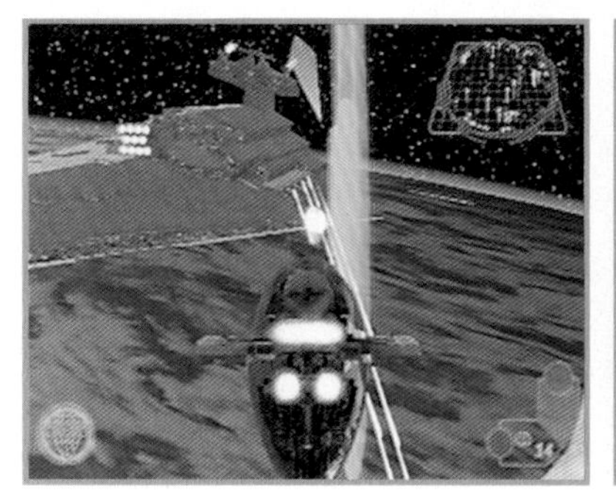

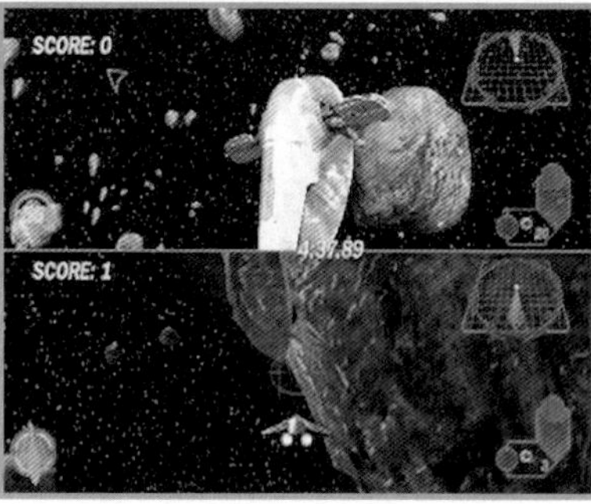

You can unlock two versions of the Fett family fighter. Bobba's *Slave I* is battle-scarred, but in good working condition. Jango's version still has that new-starfighter smell. The ship is relatively slow and its shields are unequally distributed, but its sonic mines and lasers make it a powerful force and the ship's overall performance has improved since Rogue Leader.

NABOO STARFIGHTER

The Old-style Naboo starfighter is outdated in the post-Clone War era, but it can still hold its own in battle. The ship's shields are mighty, and its big engines help it keep pace with most newer vehicles.

SECONDARY WEAPON
CLUSTER MISSILES

DROID REPAIR

UNLOCKING CONDITIONS

Complete Tatooine Training and collect hidden items during all four times of the day.

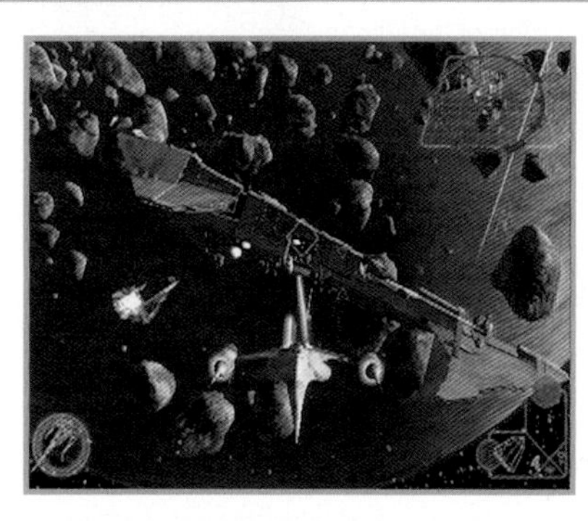

The Naboo starfighter's strong shields and shield-repairing droid unit have given it lasting power. While other ships have come and gone, the NSF is in the fleet to stay.

! MORE SHIPS IN THE MULTIPLAYER MODES

Most of the ships featured in the single-player campaigns are also available in the cooperative campaign and versus mode, and they accompany four multiplayer-only vehicles (shown here). See Page 89 for details on how to unlock ships in the cooperative campaign.

TIE ADVANCED

SECONDARY WEAPON
CLUSTER MISSILES

The TIE Advanced is a marked improvement over the original TIE fighter. Its rapid-firing laser cannon and cluster missiles give it a sharp bite, and its thick armor allows it to withstand a beating. Unlike the standard TIE fighter, the TIE Advanced could come out on the winning end in a showdown against an X-wing.

IMPERIAL SHUTTLE

Large and clumsy, the Imperial shuttle is not built to go up against dedicated starfighters, though its front- and rear-mounted lasers will do in a pinch.

SECONDARY WEAPON | QUAD CANNON

The cooperative Imperial Academy Heist mission puts both players in the same ship. While one player pilots the craft, the other player fires the quad cannons.

TIE FIGHTER

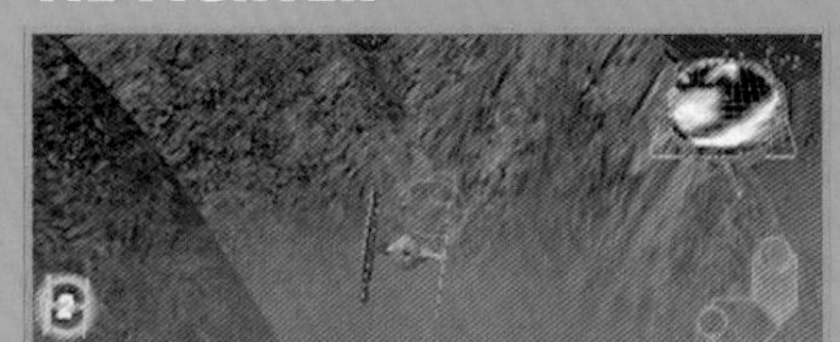

If you've shot down a TIE fighter using an X-wing's lasers, you might imagine what it's like to be on the receiving end of the blast. The ship is fast, but its shields are oh so weak.

CLOUD CAR

Like the speeder, the cloud car can lift a short distance from the ground. It's light and maneuverable, but its shields are weak. It appears in ground-bound Versus mode scenarios.

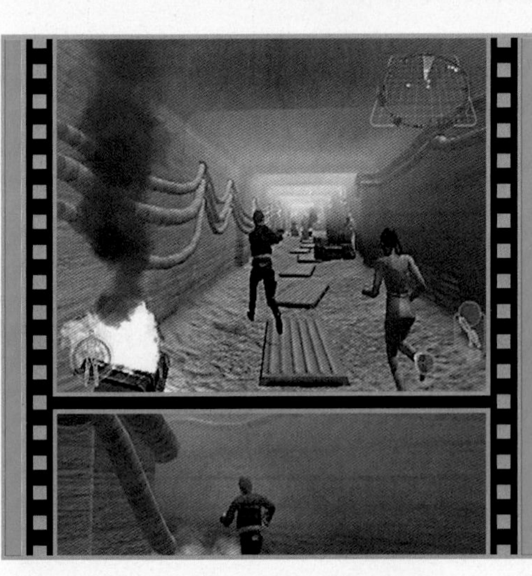

INTRODUCTION

CHARACTER CONTROL

Characters climb out of their starfighters and fight on foot in Rebel Strike. Luke Skywalker is the primary hero, but Princess Leia and Han Solo also step into action and several others tag along for support.

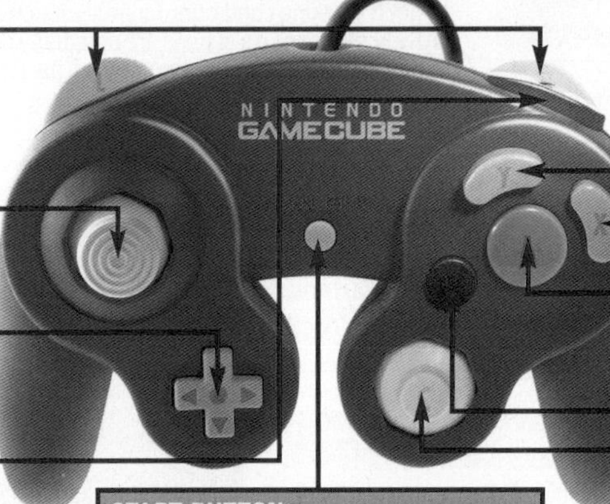

1 LOCK WEAPONS / CROUCH

Use the L Button to stay locked on to your current target. Press the R Button to crouch.

2 CHARACTER MOVEMENT

Use the Control Stick to move your character.

3 SUPPORT COMMUNICATIONS

Communicate with support forces by using the Control Pad to select instructions.

4 ROLL

Press the Z Button while your character is moving to trigger a running roll.

START BUTTON

The Start Button lets you pause the action, view objectives and access mission options and game settings.

5 ELECTRO-BINOCULARS

Press Y to view the scene from your character's perspective.

6 JUMP

Press X to make your character jump.

7 PRIMARY WEAPON

Fire your primary weapon by pressing A.

8 SECONDARY WEAPON

Press B to toss explosives or block shots.

9 CONTEXT-SENSITIVE ACTIONS

A C-Stick icon will appear to indicate that you can manipulate a nearby object. Tap the C Stick to carry out the interaction.

1 LOCK WEAPONS / CROUCH

When you're guiding a character on foot, the Controller's shoulder buttons trigger two unrelated actions. The L Button allows you to stayed locked on to your current target. Normally, green crosshairs switch automatically to the target that is closest to your character. When you press and hold the L Button, the crosshairs will turn red and stay attached to one target until you release the button or the target is destroyed. Pressing the R Button instructs your character to crouch. Hold R to keep the Rebel in a crouched position. If you manipulate the Control Stick while the fighter is crouching, he or she will roll.

2 CHARACTER MOVEMENT

The Control Stick facilitates character movement. The more you push the Control Stick in the desired direction, the faster your character will walk, then run. Movement direction is camera-relative. When the camera angle changes, you must make adjustments to continue on the same course.

3 SUPPORT COMMUNICATIONS

You can give orders to your computer-controlled allies by way of the Command Cross. Tap the Control Pad to bring up the cross, then tap it again in a command-related direction to issue the associated command.

4 ROLL

Use the Z Button in combination with the Control Stick to make your character roll from a standing position. If your timing is right, the maneuver will keep you from getting hit by enemy fire.

5 ELECTRO-BINOCULARS

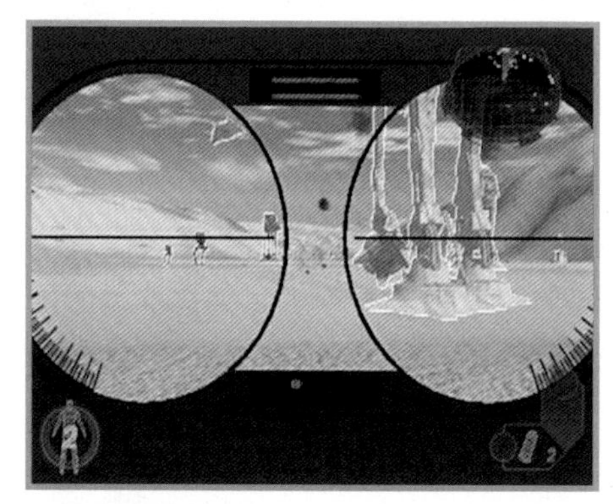

The on-foot equivalent of the targeting computer appears when you press and hold the Y Button. The Electro-Binoculars shade friendlies in a green hue. Enemies are yellow and purple.

6 JUMP

Jumping plays a part in a few of Luke's missions. Press X to make him leap. The Rebel will clear gaps and jump over obstacles.

7 PRIMARY WEAPON

In most missions, you'll use the A-Button-triggered blaster to fight for the Rebel Alliance. When Luke Skywalker is in Jedi form, the A Button will trigger his lightsaber.

BLASTER

Press A to release a blaster shot. After a few seconds, it will recharge to full power.

RIFLE

After you collect a laser rifle from a defeated enemy, hold A to trigger rapid-fire blasts.

LIGHTSABER

Press A to swing Luke's lightsaber.

8 SECONDARY WEAPON

In select missions, you'll use grenades as secondary weapons. Grenades have the explosive power to defeat more than one enemy at a time. When Luke is in Jedi form, you can summon the Force by pressing the B Button. Use it to deflect enemy shots.

9 CONTEXT-SENSITIVE ACTIONS

You can use the C Stick for a variety of situation-specific tasks. When the C Stick icon appears, tap the C Stick in any direction to perform the task. C-Stick functions include using a grappling device, mounting an E-Web blaster, opening doors and planting explosives.

! BACTA TANKS

When health is low, there's no better sight than the glimmering green light of a bacta tank. By picking up a tank, you'll get a health repair. Examine level maps for bacta tank locations and search fallen enemies for dropped tanks.

HEROIC TRIO

The three principal human characters from the classic film trilogy are the main characters whom you will guide through missions on foot in the single-player campaign and bonus missions. Luke Skywalker is the most frequently used member of the trio.

WEDGE ANTILLES

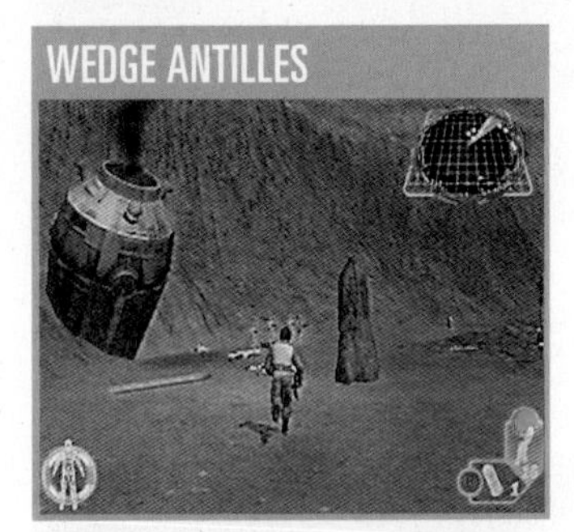

Wedge Antilles is a vehicle specialist, though you will control him on foot in the middle section of the Relics of Geonosis mission and in the hangar before space missions.

LUKE SKYWALKER

Luke spends as much time on foot as he does in vehicles over the course of his long campaign and bonus missions. He wears different uniforms, depending on the missions.

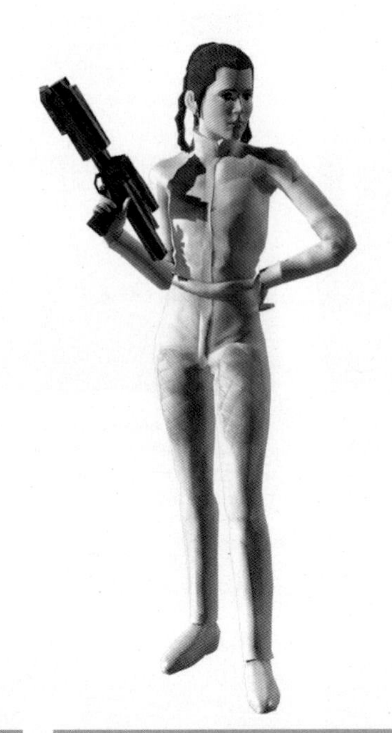

PRINCESS LEIA

Princess Leia is a support character in several missions and the player-controlled character in the Flight from Bespin bonus mission.

HAN SOLO

Never tell Han Solo the odds. He's the player-controlled character in the second half of campaign-closing Triumph of the Rebellion and the Escape from Hoth mission.

LUKE USES THE FORCE

In the Trials of a Jedi mission, Luke will learn to use the Force to deflect blaster shots and make midair jumps. He'll employ both skills in the Sarlacc Pit mission.

Face enemy blasts and hold the B Button to deflect the shots using the power of the Force. Press X to jump, then press the button again when Luke is in midair to leap higher.

A LITTLE HELP FROM YOUR FRIENDS

You will have allied characters on your side during many missions—especially those that are based on scenes from the films. In addition to Princess Leia and Han Solo, you'll encounter computer-controlled characters Lando Calrissian, R2-D2, Chewbacca and C-3PO.

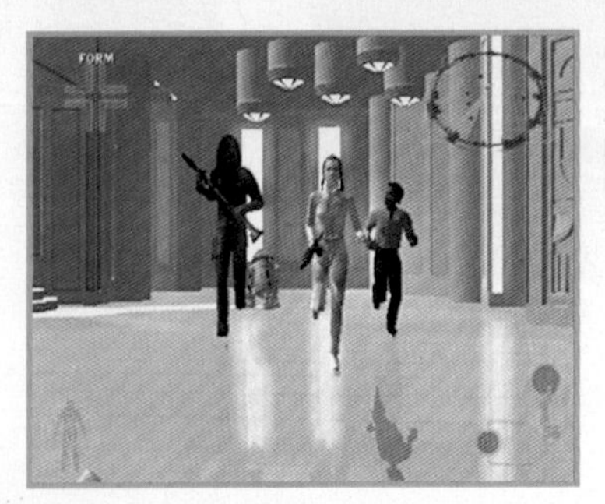

Support characters provide cover fire and occasionally perform other functions. In the Flight from Bespin mission, for example, R2-D2 connects with the complex's computer and unlocks doors.

INTRODUCTION

GROUND VEHICLES

Not only do you control Rebels on foot, but you also use them to take charge over several ground vehicles—speeder bikes and Imperial AT-STs among them. The vehicles offer the speed and power you need to fulfill many mission objectives.

LANDSPEEDER

Luke's landspeeder is a vintage vehicle from *A New Hope*. He sold it to pay for passage on the *Millennium Falcon*. You can return to Luke's home in the Tatooine Training mission and climb into the landspeeder for a fun, fast run.

By climbing into Luke's landspeeder during the Tatooine Training mission, you'll get a feel for flying low to the ground. Ground-skimming skills will come in handy when you pilot speeders and speeder bikes.

1 SPEED CONTROL

Press the L Button to brake and the R Button to accelerate.

2 STEERING

Use the Control Stick to turn left and right, and to adjust your altitude. The landspeeder can make short climbs and dives.

3 CAMERA ADJUSTMENT

Press X to toggle between the chase camera and first-person perspective.

4 CAMERA MOVEMENT

Use the C Stick to move the camera in first-person perspective.

CONTROLLER CALLOUT KEY

1 2 3 4 5
NINTENDO GAMECUBE

5 TARGETING COMPUTER

Press Y to activate the targeting computer.

AT-ST

Luke, Wedge and Chewbacca climb into AT-STs during the single-player campaign. Imperial chicken walker controls are a mix of the character and vehicle schemes.

SECONDARY WEAPON

HOMING CONCUSSION MISSILES

1 LOCK

Hold L to lock the AT-ST's head with its body.

2 WALK

Press R to make the vehicle walk. The longer the AT-ST walks, the faster it will move, until it reaches maximum speed.

3 PIVOT

Use the Control Stick to turn the AT-ST's head. The vehicle will pivot when its head is locked with its body.

4 COMMUNICATIONS DISPLAY

Tap the Control Pad to call commands for support forces, such as Ewoks on Endor.

5 TARGETING COMPUTER

Press Y to activate the targeting computer.

6 CAMERA ADJUSTMENT

Press X to toggle between the chase camera and the cockpit view.

7 PRIMARY WEAPON CONTROL

Press A to trigger the AT-ST's rapid-firing blasters. Let them recharge for more power.

8 SECONDARY WEAPON CONTROL

Hold B to activate the homing reticle. Release the button to launch a concussion missile once you've locked on to a target.

9 CAMERA MOVEMENT

Use the C Stick to look around and to move the camera in the cockpit view.

CONTROLLER CALLOUT KEY

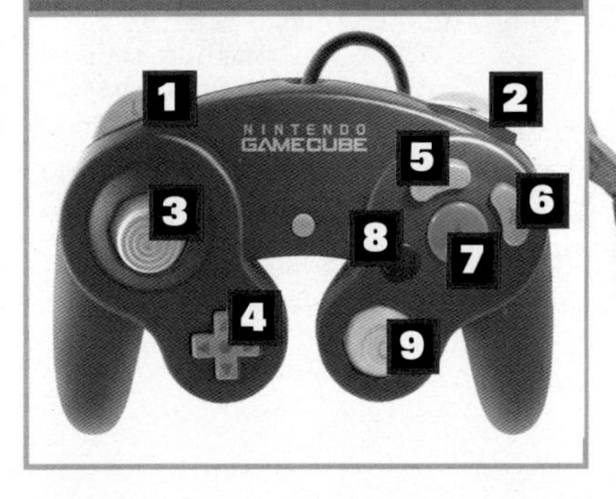

It's no wonder that the Imperials use the AT-ST for many ground missions. The vehicle is versatile and powerful. When you press the R Button, the AT-ST will move in the direction in which it is looking. You can have more direct control by using the L Button to lock the head to the body. The AT-ST is the only ground vehicle that is equipped with regenerating shields.

! AND THE LIST GOES ON . . .

TAUNTAUN

Controlling a tauntaun is much like controlling a character on foot, only the tauntaun runs faster. You'll make tracks on Hoth's frozen battlefield in a hurry after you hop onto a tauntaun's back.

1 LOCK WEAPONS

Hold the L Button to stay locked on to your current target.

2 CHARACTER MOVEMENT

Use the Control Stick to steer the swift beast.

3 GOGGLE TOGGLE

Press Y to switch to first-person view.

4 5 FIRE WEAPONS

Press A to fire forward. Use the C Stick to fire left or right.

CONTROLLER CALLOUT KEY

SWOOP BIKE

The hovering swoop bike is a must for exploring Tatooine. A swoop bik training ride will give you experienc for speeder bike rides in the campaign. The only difference is that th swoop bike is not laser-equipped.

SPEEDER BIKE

Luke rides a speeder bike in a pair of campaign missions. The quick vehicle also appears in a two-player competitive racing scenario. In a mission based on one of the most famous scenes in the film trilogy, you'll race scout troopers on speeder bikes through Endor's forest.

1 2 SPEED CONTROLS

The L Button slows the bike. Press it until it clicks to apply the brakes fully. The R Button increases your speed. Press it all the way to invoke a rechargeable speed boost.

3 STEERING

Use the Control Stick to steer the bike left and right. Press Up and Down to dive and climb.

4 TARGETING COMPUTER

Press the Y Button to activate the targeting computer.

5 CAMERA ADJUSTMENT

Press X to toggle between the chase camera and first-person perspective.

6 PRIMARY WEAPON

Press A to trigger the bike's rapid-firing blasters. The rate of fire slows as you hold the button without letting the weapons recharge.

CONTROLLER CALLOUT KEY

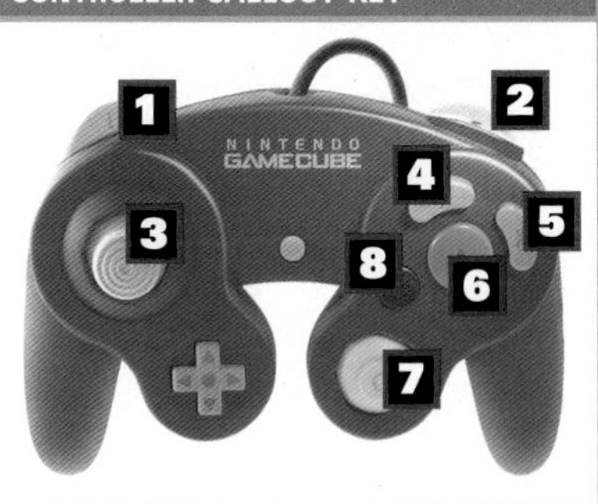

7 CAMERA MOVEMENT

Use the C Stick to move the camera in first-person perspective.

8 SIDE SLIDE

When competitors sidle up to your bike, you can give them a quick bump by pressing the B Button.

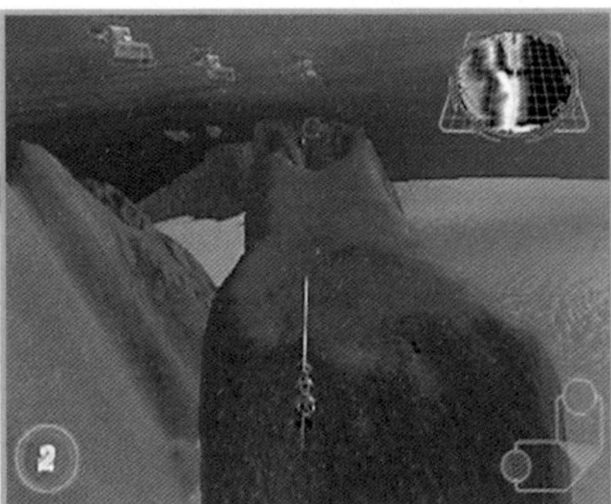

Controlling a speeder bike is one of the ultimate *Star Wars* experiences— incredibly fast and exciting. The bike can lift into the air, but it quickly reaches a ceiling. You can stay in the air longer by using a speed boost, but try to engineer a soft landing, or you could take damage. Let your blasters recharge between quick bursts for the most effective target-beating technique.

AT-AT

In the Guns of Dubrillion mission, you'll climb into a huge AT-AT Imperial walker and cause some serious damage. Your perspective is always from inside the walking tank.

1 2 3 FIRE WEAPONS

Press L, R or A to fire lasers at your target.

4 AIM

Use the Control Stick to move the targeting reticle.

CONTROLLER CALLOUT KEY

AT-PT

SCORE: 10
4:30.05
SCORE: 100

The AT-PT is available in selected Versus-mode scenarios. It is similar to the AT-ST (with identical controls), only it is faster and equipped with a more powerful laser. It does not carry a secondary weapon.

INTRODUCTION

CAMPAIGN BREAKDOWN

The single-player campaigns depict an epic struggle between the Rebel Alliance and the Empire. Check the campaign breakdown for a quick reference of what you can expect to find in each mission.

LUKE SKYWALKER'S CAMPAIGN

TATOOINE TRAINING — PLAYABLE
LUKE SKYWALKER
T-16 SKYHOPPER
LANDSPEEDER
AT-ST
SWOOP BIKE

TECH UPGRADE: ADVANCED SHIELDS
REVENGE OF THE EMPIRE — PLAYABLE
X-WING
LUKE SKYWALKER
Y-WING

TECH UPGRADE: ADVANCED LASERS
DEFIANCE ON DANTOOINE — PLAYABLE
SPEEDER BIKE
LUKE SKYWALKER

TECH UPGRADE: ADVANCED TARGETING COMPUTER
DEFENDERS OF RALLTIIR — PLAYABLE
SPEEDER

BONUS MISSION
UNLOCK WITH 10 POINTS
DEATH STAR RESCUE — PLAYABLE
LUKE SKYWALKER

WEDGE ANTILLES' CAMPAIGN

TECH UPGRADE: ADVANCED PROTON BOMBS
RAID AT BAKURA — PLAYABLE
B-WING
TIE BOMBER
Y-WING
TIE HUNTER

TECH UPGRADE: ADVANCED PROTON TORPEDOES
RELICS OF GEONOSIS — PLAYABLE
X-WING
WEDGE ANTILLES
JEDI STARFIGHTER
A-WING
B-WING
Y-WING
SLAVE I
MILLENNIUM FALCON
TIE HUNTER
NABOO STARFIGHTER

TECH UPGRADE: SPREAD PROTON BOMBS
DECEPTION AT DESTRILLION — PLAYABLE
A-WING
Y-WING
X-WING
B-WING
SLAVE I
MILLENNIUM FALCON
JEDI STARFIGHTER
TIE HUNTER
NABOO STARFIGHTER

BONUS MISSION
UNLOCK WITH 20 POINTS
FLIGHT FROM BESPIN — PLAYABLE
PRINCESS LEIA
MILLENNIUM FALCON

! CATCH A RIDE

After you press A to choose an entry in the Select Mission screen, the Available Craft screen will show 3-D line drawings of all vehicles that you will eventually be able to choose for the mission. Green vehicles are unlocked. Red vehicles are not yet available.

Before the action gets under way in each space-based mission, you'll find the mission's available craft in the Calamari cruiser's launch bay. Some ships, such as the Imperial TIEs, are tucked away in remote sections of the bay.

TECH UPGRADE: HOMING PROTON TORPEDOES

EXTRACTION FROM RALLTIIR — PLAYABLE
AT-ST
LUKE SKYWALKER

TECH UPGRADE: ADVANCED CLUSTER MISSILES

BATTLEFIELD HOTH — PLAYABLE
LUKE SKYWALKER
TAUNTAUN
X-WING

BONUS MISSION
UNLOCK WITH 30 POINTS

ESCAPE FROM HOTH — PLAYABLE
HAN SOLO
MILLENNIUM FALCON

TRIALS OF A JEDI — PLAYABLE
LUKE SKYWALKER

THE SARLACC PIT — PLAYABLE
LUKE SKYWALKER

ENDOR CAMPAIGN

TECH UPGRADE: HOMING CONCUSSION MISSILES

SPEEDER BIKE PURSUIT — PLAYABLE
SPEEDER BIKE
LUKE SKYWALKER

After you complete Speeder Bike Pursuit, Triumph of the Rebellion will be unlocked.

TECH UPGRADE: HOMING CLUSTER MISSILES

TRIUMPH OF THE REBELLION — PLAYABLE
AT-ST
HAN SOLO

BONUS MISSION
UNLOCK WITH 40 POINTS

ATTACK ON THE *EXECUTOR* — PLAYABLE
A-WING
X-WING
B-WING
Y-WING
SLAVE I
MILLENNIUM FALCON
JEDI STARFIGHTER
TIE HUNTER
NABOO STARFIGHTER

BONUS MISSION
UNLOCK WITH 20 POINTS

REBEL ENDURANCE — PLAYABLE
LUKE SKYWALKER

TECH UPGRADE: ADVANCED CONCUSSION MISSILES

GUNS OF DUBRILLION — PLAYABLE
AT-ST
AT-AT

FONDOR SHIPYARD ASSAULT — PLAYABLE
TIE HUNTER
A-WING
X-WING
B-WING
Y-WING
SLAVE I
MILLENNIUM FALCON
JEDI STARFIGHTER
NABOO STARFIGHTER

UNLOCKABLE STARFIGHTERS QUICK REFERENCE

Y-WING: Complete Revenge of the Empire.
B-WING: Complete Raid at Bakura.
A-WING: Complete Guns of Dubrillion.
NABOO STARFIGHTER: Complete Tatooine Training during all four time settings.
TIE BOMBER: Destroy all floor turrets using lock-on combos in the TIE bomber section of Raid at Bakura.
***SLAVE I*:** Earn bronze on all missions, excluding bonus missions.
***MILLENNIUM FALCON*:** Earn bronze on all missions, including bonus missions.
JEDI STARFIGHTER: Earn silver on all missions, including bonus missions.
TIE HUNTER: Earn gold on all missions, including bonus missions.
NOTE: **Starfighters unlocked in the single-player campaign are also available in Versus mode.**

GOLD AND GLORY

Your mission completion rating ranks you in six categories, including Completion Time and Enemies Destroyed. By meeting set criteria in each category, you'll earn one of three medals. Medals unlock ships and give you points that you can use to open bonus missions. You can earn a maximum of 10 points from any mission, even if you complete the mission multiple times.

BRONZE MEDAL	SILVER MEDAL	GOLD MEDAL

3 POINTS	6 POINTS	10 POINTS

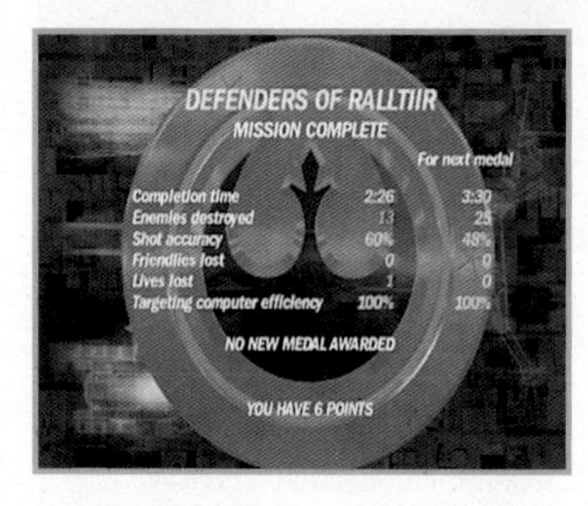

The Mission Complete screen breaks down the medal categories and shows the criteria that you must meet to earn the next medal. The statistics that did not meet the medal requirements will appear in red.

! THE ULTIMATE REWARD

When you meet the requirements for a gold medal in any mission, a new list of requirements will challenge you to rise to the level of the experts at LucasArts. See if you can out-ace the galaxy's best.

BRING ON THE BONUSES

In addition to ships and missions, you can unlock classic arcade games, videos and even running commentary. Look for the unlocked items in the Special Features section under the Options menu.

! WATCH FOR PASSCODES

Passcodes unlock missions, ships and special modes. LucasArts will reveal Rebel Strike's passcodes over the coming months. Check Nintendo Power's Classified Information section for the passcodes as they become available.

STAR WARS ARCADE GAME

By completing the Triumph of the Rebellion mission, you will unlock the original *Star Wars* arcade game, released by Atari in 1983. Relive the experience of taking down TIEs and blowing up the Death Star in one of the first 3-D games.

THE EMPIRE STRIKES BACK ARCADE GAME

Complete all standard single-player campaign missions.

THE RETURN OF THE JEDI ARCADE GAME

Enter a passcode to be revealed by LucasArts.

DOCUMENTARY

Complete Triumph of the Rebellion.

AUDIO COMMENTARY

Earn bronze medals in all standard single-player campaign missions to unlock developer comments that reveal details during game play.

CREDITS

Complete Triumph of the Rebellion.

ACE MODE

You'll unlock ultra-challenging Ace mode by earning gold medals in all single-player campaign missions, including bonus missions, and completing Tatooine Training during all four times of the day.

LUKE SKYWALKER'S CAMPAIGN

The farm boy destined to be a hero makes his mark in eight missions, starting with a training session in the Tatooine desert and ending with a daring rescue over Tatooine's Sarlacc Pit. Luke's missions interweave with the original *Star Wars* film trilogy, and they follow the discovery of a traitor to the Alliance.

LUKE SKYWALKER'S CAMPAIGN

TATOOINE TRAINING

Training is not required, but it's a good idea to spend some time on Luke's home planet to familiarize yourself with the controls. You'll start by guiding Luke through lessons on foot, then jump into your T-16 skyhopper or landspeeder.

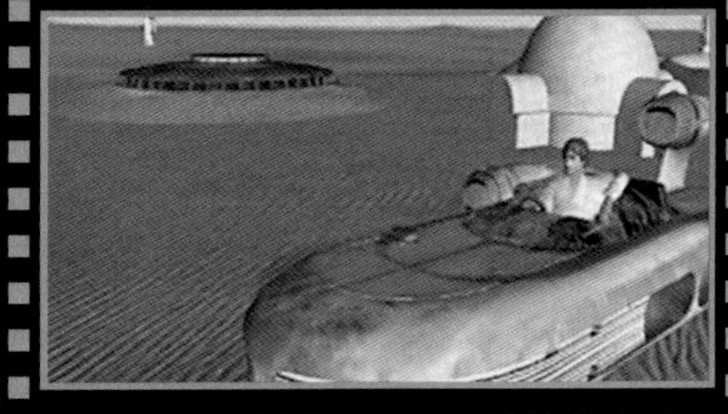

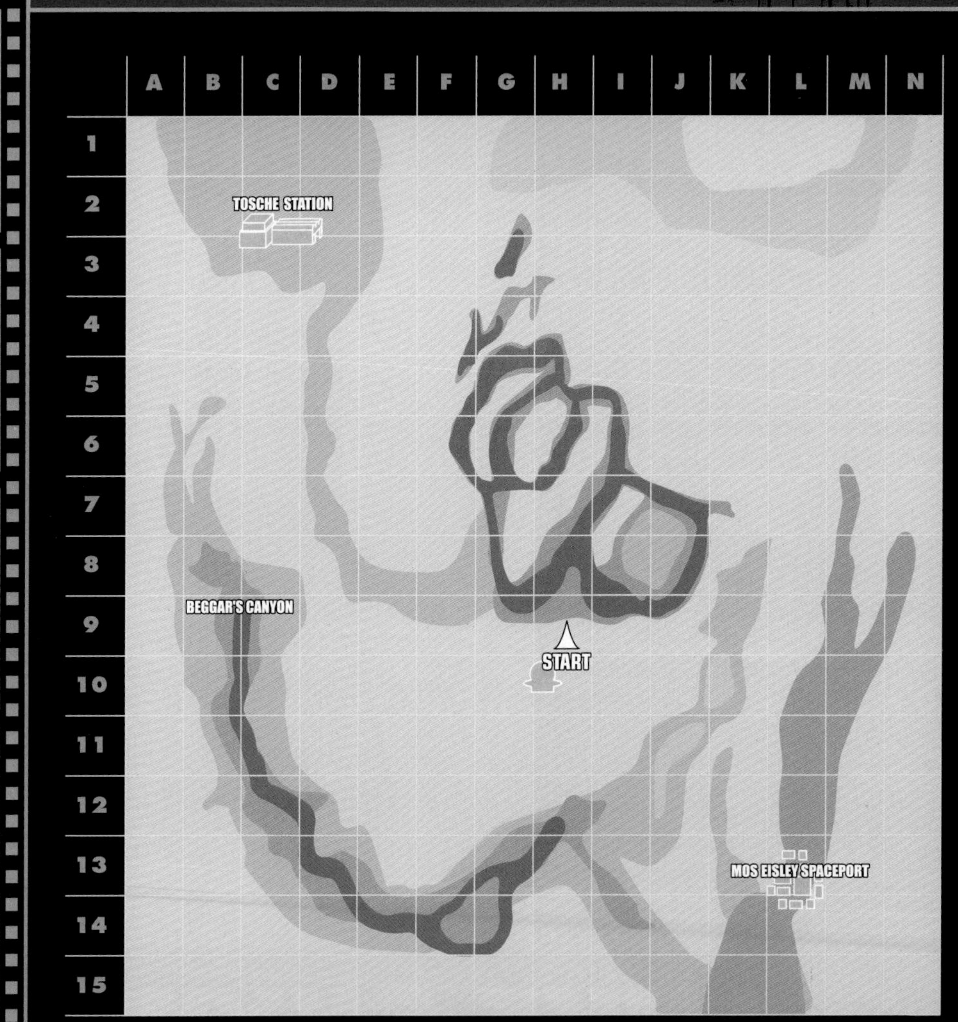

REVIEW YOUR ACCOMPLISHMENTS

TATOOINE TRAINING

Time:	20:06
Number Of Lessons Completed:	23/28
Number Of Bonus Items Found:	7/7
Beggar's Canyon Race	
Easy	COMPLETED
Medium	COMPLETED
Hard	COMPLETED
Droid Hunt	
Easy	COMPLETED
Medium	COMPLETED
Hard	COMPLETED
Craft Unlocked:	3/3

RESTART TRAINING
BACK TO MISSION SELECT

At the end of a training session, a recap screen will show the training duration, the number of lessons that you completed, the number of bonus items that you found and additional stats about your performance. You must accomplish all training goals in four times of the day to unlock the Naboo starfighter.

HOMESTEAD TUTORIAL

Rebel Strike presents a new emphasis on character control for the Rogue Squadron series, especially in Luke Skywalker's missions. You'll begin the training session by getting accustomed to character actions.

HOMESTEAD OBJECTIVES

1. COMPLETE ALL TUTORIAL LESSONS
2. FIND YOUR WAY TO THE TOP OF THE HOMESTEAD
3. USE THE AVAILABLE CRAFT TO ACCESS OTHER AREAS OF TATOOINE

1 COMPLETE ALL TUTORIAL LESSONS

The lessons begin at the homestead (point H10 on the map). As you walk into Rebel symbols, you will receive instructions on how to carry out basic tasks. After you successfully complete the first group of tasks, a symbol will appear in front of a door, allowing you to move on.

! TRAIN DAY AND NIGHT

Your Nintendo GameCube's time setting determines whether the training session will take place in the early morning, daytime, early evening or nighttime. The lighting scheme is different for each time of day. If you are attempting to unlock the Naboo starfighter by completing training at all times of day, you can reset the GCN clock for the desired times.

2 FIND YOUR WAY TO THE TOP OF THE HOMESTEAD

After you've completed the lesson that deals with context-sensitive actions, a door will open. Follow the path to the top of the homestead and the open desert.

3 USE THE AVAILABLE CRAFT TO ACCESS OTHER AREAS OF TATOOINE

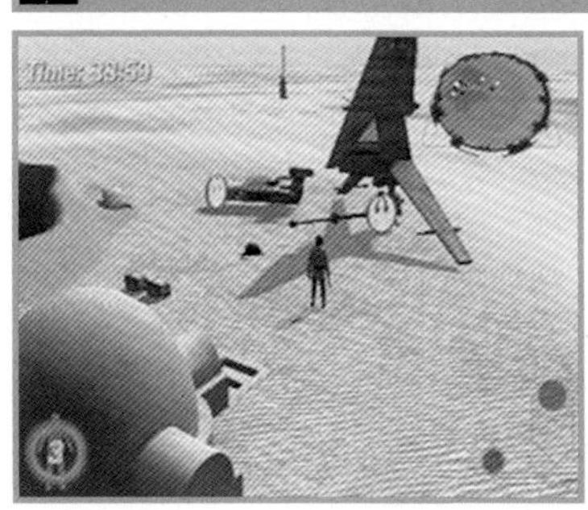

Exiting the homestead, you'll find two vehicles accompanied by Rebel symbols. By stepping into a symbol, you will hop onto the vehicle and continue your training en route.

T-16 SKYHOPPER TUTORIAL

The T-16 skyhopper's tutorial is similar to Rogue Leader's training session. It will acquaint you with flight control and point you to the bonus items. The skyhopper's secondary weapon changes to give you experience with every weapon type.

T-16 SKYHOPPER OBJECTIVES

1. COMPLETE ALL TUTORIAL LESSONS
2. WIN THE BEGGAR'S CANYON RACE ON ALL DIFFICULTIES
3. WIN THE DOGFIGHT AGAINST FIXER
4. FIND ALL BONUS ITEMS

1 COMPLETE ALL TUTORIAL LESSONS

The first task is to follow the wedge indicator to an orange Rebel symbol. After that, you'll get a new lesson every time you fly into an orange symbol. Once a lesson is complete, the associated symbol will turn green. Once you finish all of the flight lessons, you'll shuttle off to Beggar's Canyon for a race against Fixer.

2 WIN THE BEGGAR'S CANYON RACE ON ALL DIFFICULTIES

The Beggar's Canyon race begins at point B9 on page 24's map. Every time you race against Fixer at a more advanced difficulty level, your opponent will have a little more skill. Watch the boost thruster status indicator in the lower-left corner of the screen and press L to use it whenever it is available. Rise above the lower ridges of the canyon so you don't have to go around them and veer left at the fork in the path (F14) for a shorter route.

! UNLOCK THE SWOOP BIKE

By defeating Fixer in three races (easy, medium and hard), you'll unlock the swoop bike, a craft that is very similar to the speeder bikes that you'll pilot in the single-player campaign.

3 WIN THE DOGFIGHT AGAINST FIXER

Immediately following your first race against Fixer, your rival will challenge you to a friendly dogfight. Watch for a red dot on your scanner and fire at the ship as soon as you have a clean shot. If you're behind Fixer, slow down and keep firing. If he's behind you, speed up to create some distance between your ship and his, then turn around and head straight for him.

4 FIND ALL BONUS ITEMS

There are seven bonus items scattered throughout the Tatooine desert. Find them on the map to the right and by following your scanner's wedge indicator. Fly low to get credit for your finds. After you discover the sandcrawler, pass it, turn around then hit it with a fully charged laser blast. You'll expose R2-D2 in the rubble. There are two bantha herds. Together, they count as one bonus item. After you've raced and fought Fixer, and you've found all bonus items, fly into the blue Rebel symbol above the homestead to land.

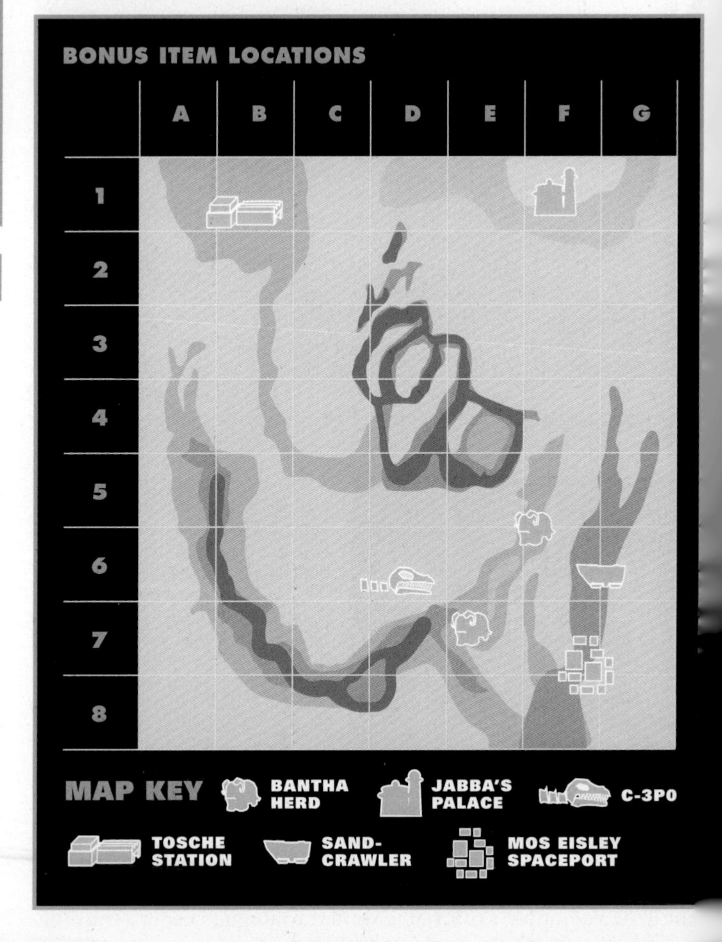

LANDSPEEDER TUTORIAL

You can catch a ride on the landspeeder at the homestead. The tutorial will give you practice in piloting a low-flying vehicle, such as the speeder or the speeder bike.

LANDSPEEDER OBJECTIVES

1. COMPLETE ALL TUTORIAL LESSONS
2. RACE TO TOSCHE STATION

1•2 COMPLETE ALL TUTORIAL LESSONS AND RACE TO TOSCHE STATION

The landspeeder tutorial takes you to Tosche statio On the way, you'll learn all c the complexities of control ling a land-skimming vehicle Pull back on the Control Stick and Press R for a spe boost to catch air and avoi hard scrapes.

AT-ST TUTORIAL

Imperial recruiters on Tatooine will give you a spin in an AT-ST after you reach Tosche station in the landspeeder. Little do they know that you will ultimately use hijacked chicken walkers in your fight against the Empire.

AT-ST OBJECTIVES

1. COMPLETE ALL TUTORIAL LESSONS
2. WIN THE DROID HUNT ON ALL DIFFICULTIES

1 COMPLETE ALL TUTORIAL LESSONS

The AT-ST tutorial offers basic control lessons and ends with the easy-difficulty droid hunt. After you complete the first hunt, walk into the blue Rebel symbol to continue to the swoop bike tutorial.

2 WIN THE DROID HUNT ON ALL DIFFICULTIES

By walking into the orange Rebel icon, you can move on to another droid hunt. The three levels of droid hunt difficulty vary in the amount of time you have to destroy 10 droids.

! UNLOCK THE LANDSPEEDER

By completing the droid hunt in all three difficulties, you will unlock the landspeeder for the duration of the training session.

SWOOP BIKE TUTORIAL

:ompletion of the AT-ST tutorial leads to the swoop bike tutorial. The speedy one-seater will give you a slightly wilder ride than the andspeeder. After you catch big air, pull back and apply the brake o avoid a headfirst crash into the sand.

SWOOP BIKE OBJECTIVES

1. COMPLETE ALL TUTORIAL LESSONS
2. CLEAR ALL JUMP SYMBOLS
3. RACE TO THE SANDCRAWLER

1 COMPLETE ALL TUTORIAL LESSONS

Since you've already completed the landspeeder tutorial, you'll have only one more maneuver to learn to become a veteran swoop bike pilot—flying off jumps. The lesson will prepare you for the your speeder bike runs through the Defiance on Dantooine mission and the Triumph of the Rebellion mission.

2•3 CLEAR ALL JUMP SYMBOLS AND RACE TO THE SANDCRAWLER

The swoop bike route from Tosche station to the sandcrawler features seven high-flying jumps into Rebel symbols. You may have to backtrack to hit all of the marks. You can launch from natural jumps on the surface to reach some symbols and take off from cliffs to reach others. Study the scanner's map to find paths to each ledge. After you've cleared all of the jumps, continue to the sandcrawler for your next set of lessons.

! UNLOCK THE T-16 SKYHOPPER

Successful completion of all swoop bike jump challenges will unlock the T-16 Skyhopper for all applicable Tatooine Training scenarios.

SANDCRAWLER TUTORIAL

our final set of lessons offers on-foot ombat training in a battle against nperials near the sandcrawler. Could ne stormtroopers be searching for a air of droids who escaped from a ebel transport?

ANDCRAWLER OBJECTIVES

1. COMPLETE ALL TUTORIAL LESSONS

1 COMPLETE ALL TUTORIAL LESSONS

The sandcrawler battle will give you experience in thinking and fighting on your feet. After you complete the lessons, you'll be ready for several challenges that await you over the course of Luke Skywalker's single-player campaign.

LUKE SKYWALKER'S CAMPAIGN

REVENGE OF THE EMPIRE

The Revenge of the Empire mission shows the Imperial reaction to the Death Star's demise. As Imperial forces descend on the Rebel base on Yavin 4, Luke and Wedge must buy time for an evacuation by fighting TIEs and troopers and saving key leaders.

OBJECTIVES

1. DESTROY THE IMPERIAL TRANSPORTS
2. DESTROY THE IMPERIAL LOADER SHUTTLES
3. DEFEND THE REBEL TRANSPORT
4. FIND THE GENERAL
5. ESCAPE WITH THE GENERAL

OBJECTIVES 1-3: YAVIN 4 SURFACE

A B C D E F G H I J K
1 2 3 4 5 6 7 8 9 10
REBEL BASE
OBJECTIVES 2-3 START
OBJECTIVE 1 START

OBJECTIVES 4-5: REBEL BASE

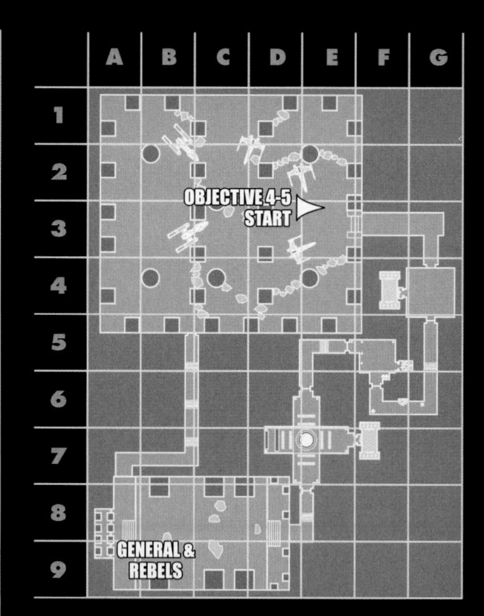

MAP KEY

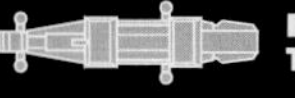
IMPERIAL TRANSPORT

REBEL TRANSPORT

BACTA TANK

TECH UPGRADE

MEDAL REQUIREMENTS

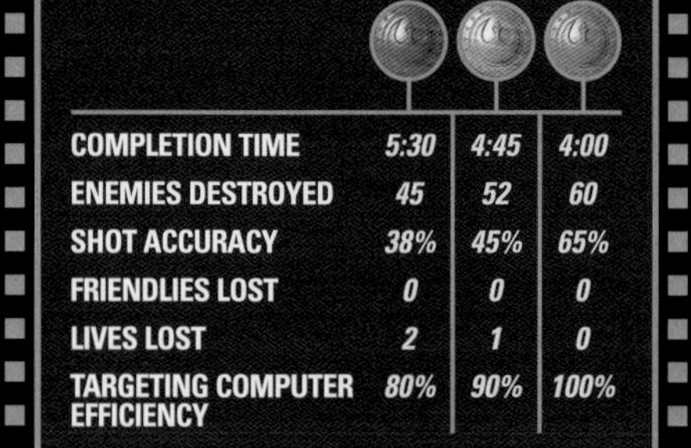

COMPLETION TIME	5:30	4:45	4:00
ENEMIES DESTROYED	45	52	60
SHOT ACCURACY	38%	45%	65%
FRIENDLIES LOST	0	0	0
LIVES LOST	2	1	0
TARGETING COMPUTER EFFICIENCY	80%	90%	100%

TECH UPGRADE: ADVANCED SHIELDS

The first group of Imperial transports is arranged in a line. Allow the last of the group to land and open its rear hatch. Reduce your speed and fly through the hatch to collect a shield-strengthening power-up.

1 DESTROY THE IMPERIAL TRANSPORTS

Imperial transports are heading for the surface. You must blow them to pieces before they empty their payloads. The large ships are easy targets. Start by firing on them from a distance and continue to lay on them until they explode.

The transports are large and slow, but well-armored. Use blasters and proton torpedoes to destroy them in a hurry and improve your time rating. The first group of ships is arranged in a line. After you and your wingmen destroy them, bank left to follow your radar display to the remaining targets.

2 DESTROY THE IMPERIAL LOADER SHUTTLES

Close your S-foils for a moment to zoom toward the first three Imperial loader shuttles as the second objective begins, then open the foils and hit the ships with blasters. The second group of shuttles may drop their cargo before you reach them. Fire on the falling containers.

3 DEFEND THE REBEL TRANSPORT

The Imperial loader shuttles were carrying AT-STs. Any containers that landed might have unloaded their walkers. Follow the scanner's wedge indicator and watch the ground for AT-STs. By destroying all of them, you'll give the Rebel transport *Luminous* a launch window.

4 FIND THE GENERAL

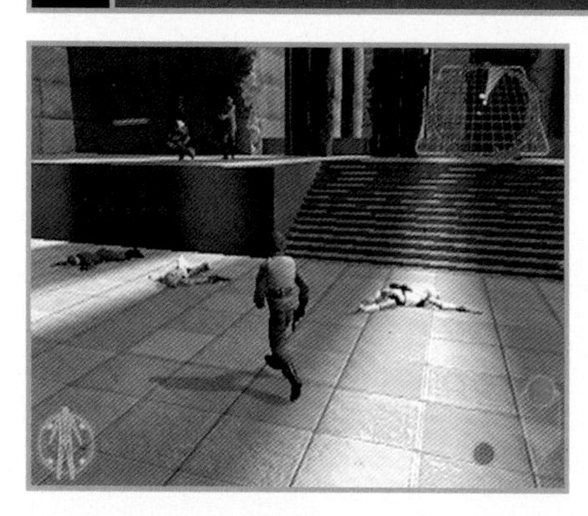

Enemies have infiltrated the base, chasing the general and his men into the ceremonial hall at the heart of the structure. You'll hop out of your ship and continue the mission on foot. To save time, you can reach the general's location at A9 without defeating all of the attackers in the halls. Use evasive maneuvers to avoid the blaster onslaught, collect the weapons of downed troopers and clear the hall of Imperials.

5 ESCAPE WITH THE GENERAL

nce you've defeated all of the eneies in the ceremonial hall, the radar splay will point you to an unlocked or at A7 that leads you back to the se's main hangar and another owdown with stormtroopers.

The hangar is crawling with agents of the Empire. You must defeat all of them to complete the mission. Hide behind obstacles when enemy fire overwhelms you, then come out fighting again. You can ensure that Wedge will help you defeat stormtroopers by directing him using support commands.

LUKE SKYWALKER'S CAMPAIGN

DEFIANCE ON DANTOOINE

Rebel informant Tycho Celchu is on the run from stormtroopers. You must travel to the remote planet of Dantooine, the site of an abandoned Rebel encampment, and track down Tycho. Hop onto a speeder bike and navigate Dantooine's river basin.

OBJECTIVES

1. REACH THE IMPERIAL LANDING ZONE BEFORE THE TRANSPORTS LIFT OFF
2. STOP THE GROUND TRANSPORT THAT'S CARRYING TYCHO
3. FOLLOW TYCHO BACK TO THE REBEL LANDING ZONE

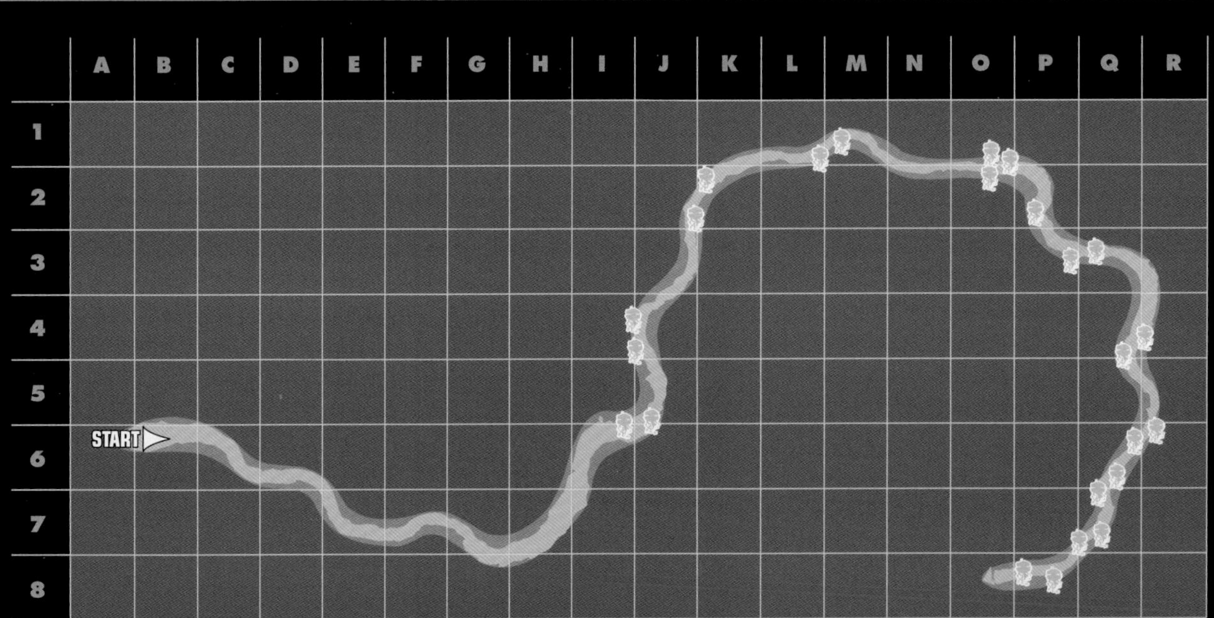

MAP KEY

 IMPERIAL PROBE DROID

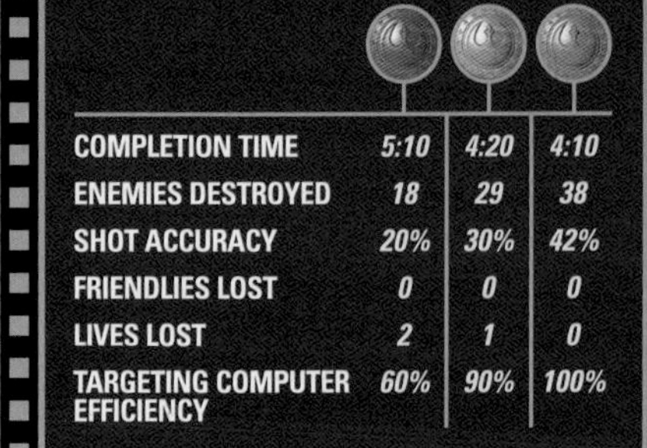

MEDAL REQUIREMENTS

COMPLETION TIME	5:10	4:20	4:10
ENEMIES DESTROYED	18	29	38
SHOT ACCURACY	20%	30%	42%
FRIENDLIES LOST	0	0	0
LIVES LOST	2	1	0
TARGETING COMPUTER EFFICIENCY	60%	90%	100%

TECH UPGRADE: ADVANCED LASERS

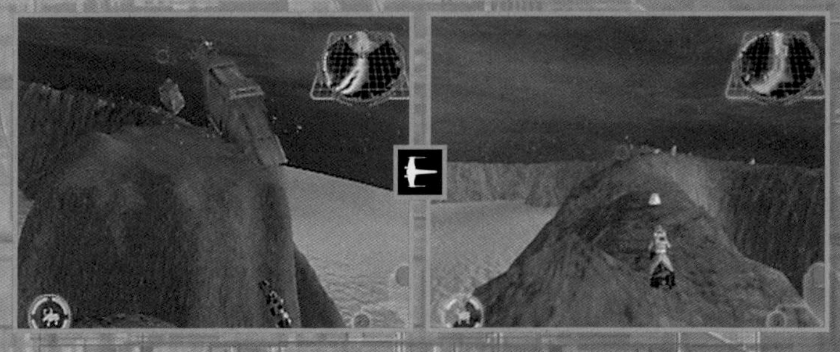

You'll skim over a mountain ridge on your way back to the landing zone with Tycho. After you've boosted to cross two long gaps, veer left at the fork in the path. You'll find the tech upgrade in the middle of the ridge (point R3 on page 33's map).

1 REACH THE IMPERIAL LANDING ZONE BEFORE THE TRANSPORTS LIFT OFF

SKIM THE RIVER AND WATCH THE WALLS

The river winds through a deep canyon. Stay near the middle of the path and avoid scraping against the canyon walls. You must also steer around the rock formations that protrude from the water. Direct impact with a formation will total your speeder bike. Slow down if you're losing control.

BLAST PROBES OR PASS THEM SAFELY

As you close in on the landing zone, you'll come across several Imperial probe droids that sport flashing lights. They will self-detonate if you get too close to them. Defeat them from a distance with quick laser bursts and either swing wide to avoid them or fly past them at high speed. If you destroy them, you'll rate higher in the Enemies Destroyed category for medal contention.

2 STOP THE GROUND TRANSPORT THAT'S CARRYING TYCHO

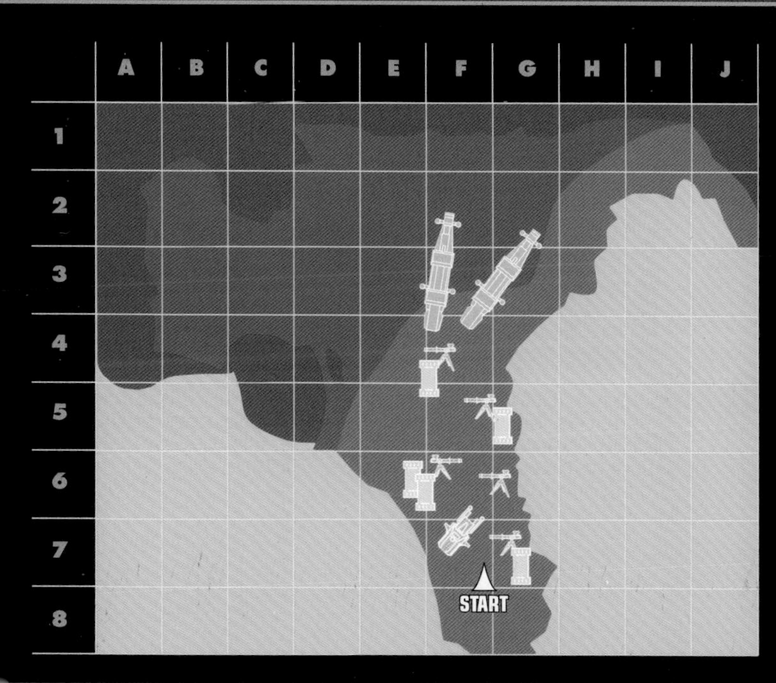

MAP KEY

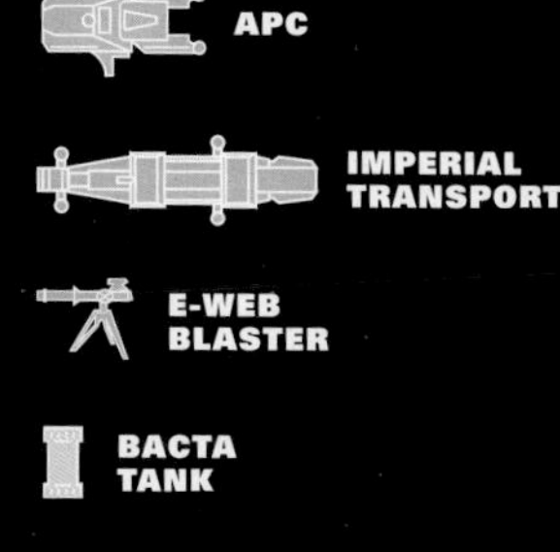

FIGHT FOR FIREPOWER

You'll dismount your bike and join the fight on hilly terrain. When you spot the soldier behind an E-Web blaster, defeat the Imperial pawn and take control over his weapon by tapping the C Stick.

TURN THE TABLES ON THE TRANSPORT

As soon as you have control over the blaster, lay into the troopers that will jump out of an APC, then concentrate your fire on the vehicle itself. It will begin to move. Keep firing at it until it is out of range, then step away from the blaster by pressing the B Button and run toward the craft.

GET ANOTHER GUN

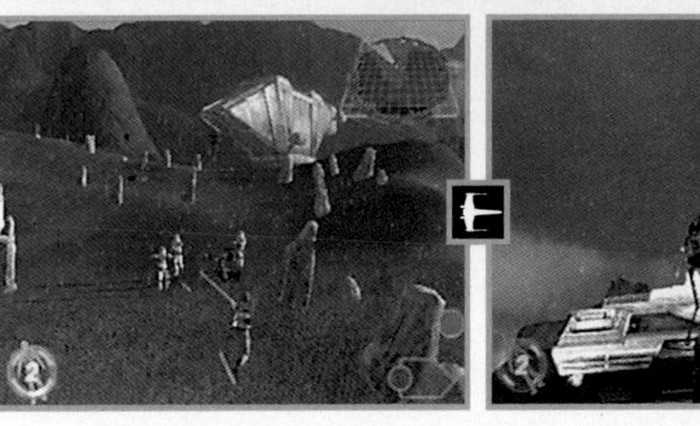

While you tail the APC, you'll come across another trooper behind an E-Web blaster. Defeat the trooper and his support forces, then take command over the gun and hit the APC with another round of stinging shots. After the APC starts moving again, let go of the tripod gun and follow the hovercraft.

CHAIN GUNS

Continue to follow the APC and hit it with shots from E-Web blasters until you run the ship into the ground. There are five blasters in all, but you may b able to finish off the APC with the third one, or on your way to the fourth. Once the hovercraft is down, Tycho will join you on a speeder bike ride over the mountain ridge.

3 FOLLOW TYCHO BACK TO THE REBEL LANDING ZONE

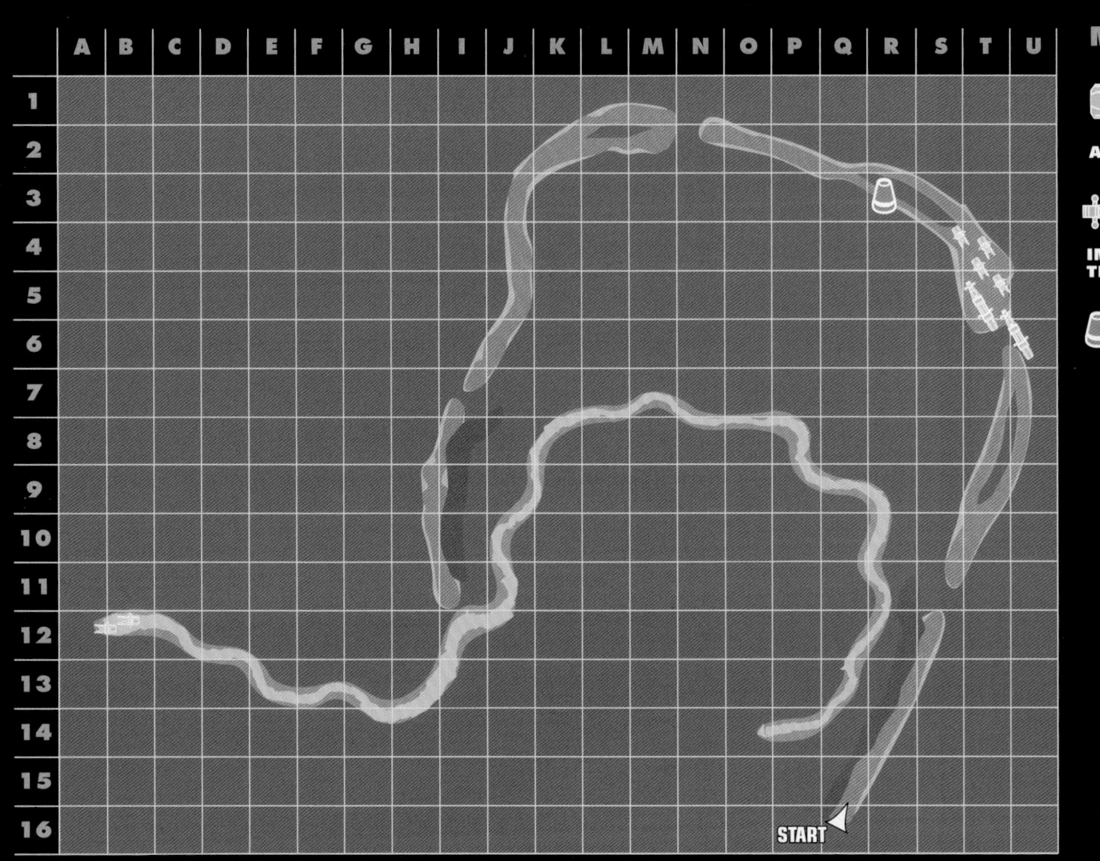

MAP KEY

APC

IMPERIAL TRANSPORT

TECH UPGRADE

HOVER HIGH OVER ROCK FORMATIONS

Your route back to the landing zone leads over a rocky ridge. Tycho will dart out into the lead and act as your guide. As you're flying over the narrow path, pull back on the Control Stick to soar over the rock formations that jut out from the ridge.

BLAST OFF OVER GAPS

Tycho will warn you about breaks in the ridge and instruct you when to boost over the gaps. As soon as Tycho gives you the word, press and hold the R Button to take off. While you're in the air, home in on the ridge on the other side of the gap and aim straight for it.

ROP TO THE RIVER RUN

As darkness falls on the ridge, you'll continue to accelerate over gaps and avoid collisions with rock formations. You'll lose altitude from one jump to the next and eventually reach the river's level. Follow the river path to the end. Some of its bends are quite sharp; you may have to decelerate to negotiate them safely. Also, watch for TIE bombers that drop explosive charges.

LUKE SKYWALKER'S CAMPAIGN

DEFENDERS OF RALLTIIR

Tycho Celchu's work behind the lines has led to the discovery of Rebel scientists on Ralltiir. Agents of the Empire will move in to stop your Ralltiir rescue efforts. Fight them off as they march toward the scientists' compound.

OBJECTIVE

1 DESTROY IMPERIALS THREATENING THE SHIELD GENERATOR

MAP KEY

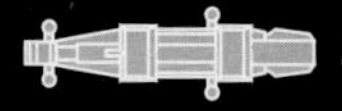
IMPERIAL TRANSPORT

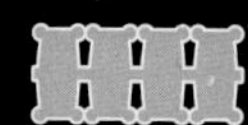
SHIELD GENERATOR

TECH UPGRADE

MEDAL REQUIREMENTS

COMPLETION TIME	5:00	4:05	3:30
ENEMIES DESTROYED	17	20	25
SHOT ACCURACY	25%	32%	48%
FRIENDLIES LOST	2	1	0
LIVES LOST	2	1	0
TARGETING COMPUTER EFFICIENCY	88%	95%	100%

TECH UPGRADE: ADVANCED TARGETING COMPUTER

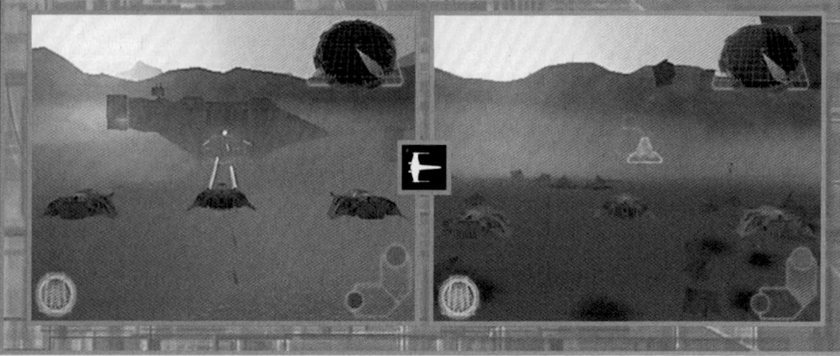

Bank left from the starting point and head for the bridge in the distance at L2. Look for and destroy an Imperial transport at the left end of the bridge. You'll discover the tech upgrade in the rubble.

1 DESTROY IMPERIALS THREATENING THE SHIELD GENERATOR

EXPLOSIVE EXTRACTION

The shield generator is surrounded by bombs, each one marked with a flashing red light. As you fly over a bomb, press the B Button to hook it with your tow cable. Once you have the explosive in tow, lift the speeder and let the device dangle from your ship. If you drag the bomb on the ground, it may explode.

BOMB THE BRIDGE

After you collect your first bomb, scan the horizon and head for either the bridge at F6 or the one at K7. When you reach the structure, let the bomb touch the span. A cut scene will show the bridge breaking into bits. By destroying two of the area's three bridges right away, you'll eliminate two-thirds of the invading forces.

SHIELD PROTECTION

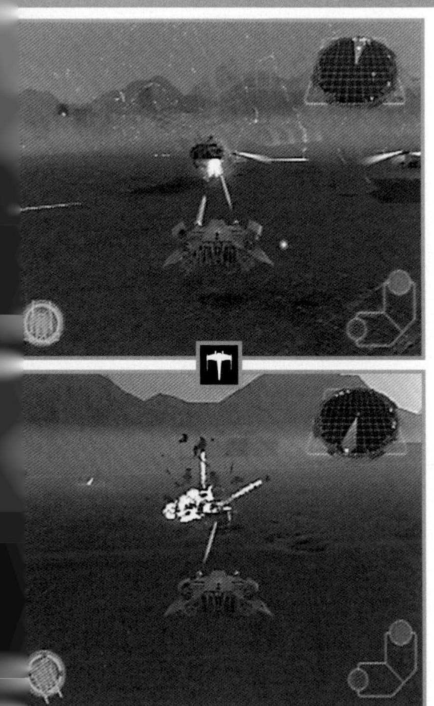

Imperials are attacking the shield generator. After you take care of the first two bridges, head for the generator and target the enemy units that surround the area. On your way to the generator, blast the APCs and AT-PTs on the fringe to pump up your Enemies Destroyed statistic, then clean up the units that pose an immediate threat to the Rebel facility. By hitting the units from behind, you'll avoid damage to your speeder's weak shields. AT-ATs also menace the generator. Either tie them up with your tow cable or use bombs to destroy them.

GOING FOR GOLD

ROCK THE WALKERS

As always, your completion time rating is crucial for earning a gold medal. To save time, use bombs to destroy the AT-ATs that threaten the shield generator. Pick up a bomb and approach a walker from the side. Reduce your speed to ensure that the bomb hangs straight down, and hit the AT-AT's cockpit with the device. The behemoth will fall on impact.

LUKE SKYWALKER'S CAMPAIGN

EXTRACTION FROM RALLTIIR

You've cut off the main invasion, but some Imperial forces remain on the ground and they have a hold on the compound's Blockade Runner. Your mission is to escort the scientists to the ship while piloting a hijacked AT-ST, then enter the ship and take control.

OBJECTIVES

1. CLEAR THE WAY TO THE BLOCKADE RUNNER
2. REGAIN CONTROL OF THE BLOCKADE RUNNER

TECH UPGRADE: HOMING PROTON TORPEDOES

The tech upgrade is easy to find, but you'll miss it if you're fixed on forward progress after the second turn. Once you've blasted the AT-STs at F5, turn to the right to find the upgrade on the ground.

MEDAL REQUIREMENTS

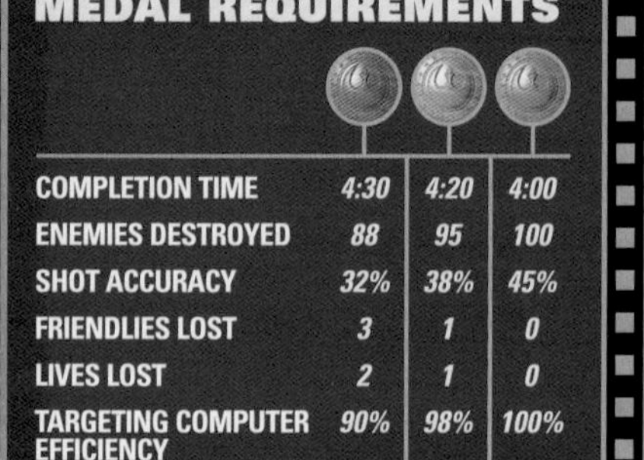

COMPLETION TIME	*4:30*	*4:20*	*4:00*
ENEMIES DESTROYED	*88*	*95*	*100*
SHOT ACCURACY	*32%*	*38%*	*45%*
FRIENDLIES LOST	*3*	*1*	*0*
LIVES LOST	*2*	*1*	*0*
TARGETING COMPUTER EFFICIENCY	*90%*	*98%*	*100%*

OBJECTIVE 1: RALLTIIR SURFACE

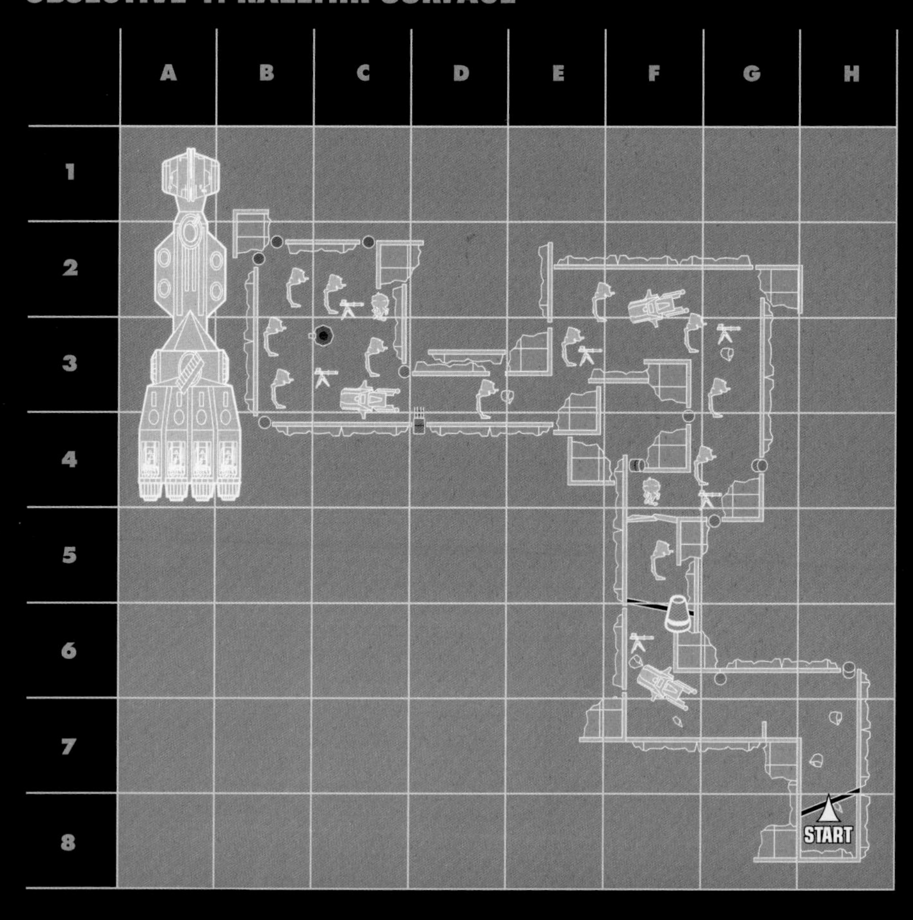

MAP KEY

AT-ST

APC

E-WEB BLASTER

BLOCKADE RUNNER

PROBE DROID

TECH UPGRADE

1 CLEAR THE WAY TO THE BLOCKADE RUNNER

STAY AHEAD OF THE PACK

Although the scientists' Rebel escorts are armed, you can provide much more powerful support by running ahead of the group and pounding the Imperials before they can hit your charges. As long as you are in the lead, most of the enemies will target your AT-ST instead of the Rebels on foot.

DANGER AROUND EVERY CORNER

Start moving as soon as the mission begins, and stride ahead of the scientists. As you round the first corner, you'll see a probe droid and an APC. Lay into the vehicle with everything you've got. If you take care of the APC quickly, the stormtroopers inside will have no chance to escape.

! WALK LIKE AN IMPERIAL

You'll crawl into the cockpit of an AT-ST chicken walker for the mission's first section. Controlling an AT-ST is a cross between guiding a human character and piloting a ship. Use the Control Stick to turn, and press R to move forward. When the AT-ST is damaged, stay behind cover to give its shields time to regenerate.

TURN THE TABLES

With an AT-ST under your control, you can use Imperial weapons against Imperial forces. The vehicle's lasers are strong enough to destroy another AT-ST with a few seconds of sustained fire to the cockpit. You'll have no trouble wiping out waves of stormtroopers, either. Employ the AT-ST's homing missiles when multiple large targets are bearing down on you.

RUN AND GUN WITH PINPOINT ACCURACY

Completion Time and Shot Accuracy are the medal categories that are most difficult to satisfy in the Extraction from Ralltiir mission. Run into each area ahead of the scientists and hit the most imposing enemies first, always lining up your shots before you fire. Use your homing missiles liberally to defeat enemies in a hurry. Your missile supply will replenish over time.

THE GOING GETS TOUGH

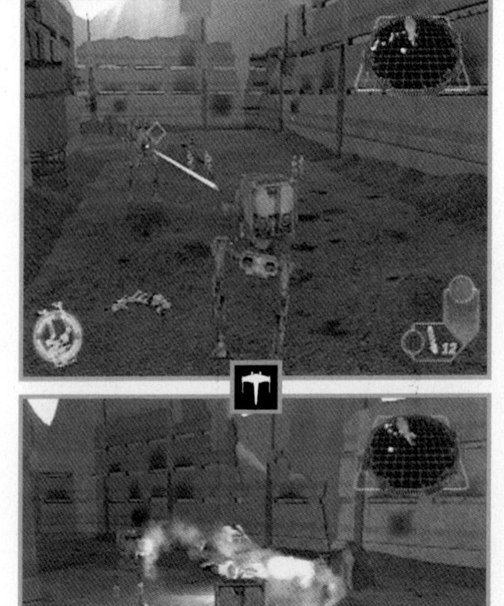

The Empire is well-represented in the corridors that lead to the Blockade Runner. When you reach G3, you'll face a platoon of stormtroopers and two AT-STs. Stop and hit the walkers, then strafe the troopers as you move forward. As you reach the next turn, an Imperial APC will appear. Clobber it before it releases more troopers. Next you'll face more AT-STs and a probe droid. Take care of them while the scientists are still out of their range.

THE BIG FINISH

As you close in on the Blockade Runner, you'll face one last APC, five AT-STs, a probe droid and two troopers stationed at E-Web blasters. Your best chance for success is to enter the last area slowly enough that you face the enemies one at a time. Bring down the transport first, then take on the AT-STs as you round the corner. Pick off the droid and trooper last. By staying ahead of the scientists you will ensure that few if any friendlies are lost, and you'll keep the mission-completion time to a minimum—both factors will figure into your chances for a gold medal. You'll satisfy the objective once you've destroyed the last Imperial.

2 REGAIN CONTROL OF THE BLOCKADE RUNNER

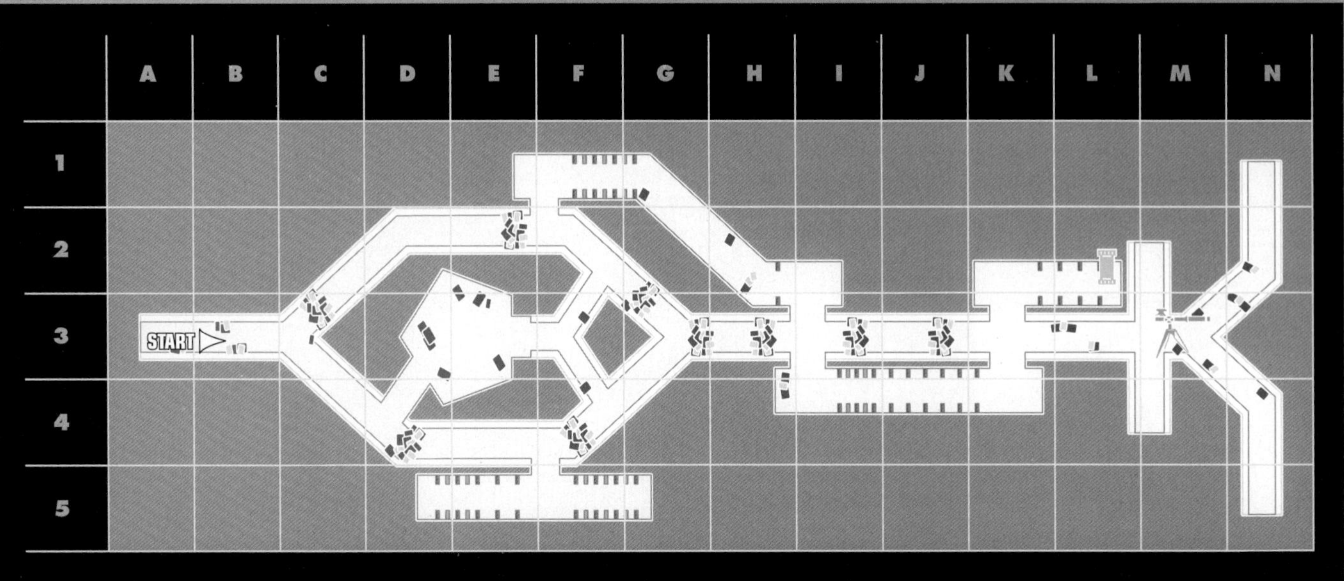

WATCH THE RADAR AND RUN

After you get out of the AT-ST and into the Blockade Runner, you will face a flock of stormtroopers on foot. Follow the radar wedge to forge into the most heavily infiltrated section of the ship, defeating all troopers along the way.

PICK A PATH

Debris blocks some sections of the main hallway. Continue to watch the wedge indicator and enter side-path detours to get around the blockage. Enemies hide behind cover. Run around the shields quickly and blast the troopers as soon as you have a clear shot.

TRIPOD GUN

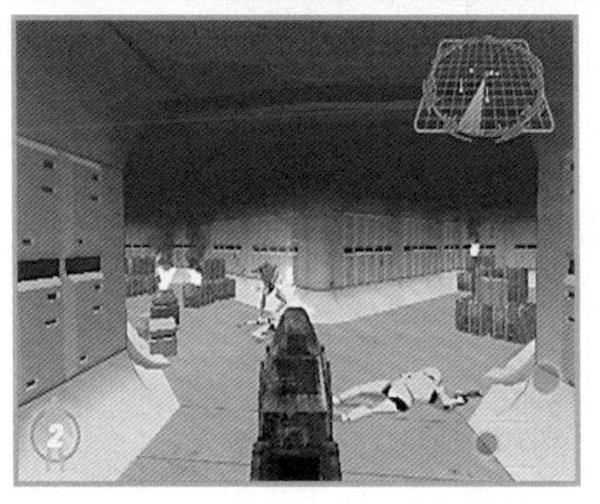

You'll find an E-Web blaster at M3. Tap the C Stick to commandeer the weapon, then use it to clear the hall of all remaining Imperials. You'll complete the objective when all enemies are gone.

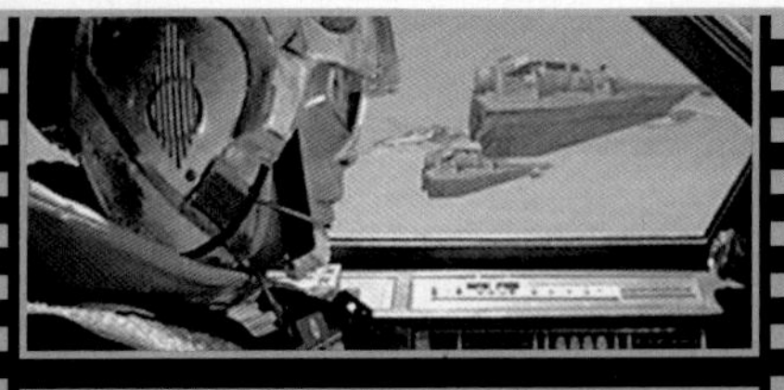

LUKE SKYWALKER'S CAMPAIGN

BATTLEFIELD HOTH

Picking up where Luke's story left off in the cooperative Battle of Hoth mission, Rebel Strike's Battlefield Hoth has Luke disabling AT-ATs with his lightsaber and riding a tauntaun across the snow and ice. The mission ends with an air battle for Echo Base.

OBJECTIVES

1. TAKE OUT THE TWO LEAD AT-ATS
2. GET TO THE TAUNTAUN
3. FOLLOW DERLIN BACK TO ECHO BASE
4. DESTROY THE THREE AT-STS
5. PROTECT THE THREE REBEL TRANSPORTS
6. DESTROY THE TIE BOMBERS

TECH UPGRADE: ADVANCED CLUSTER MISSILES

After three AT-STs emerge from Imperial loader shuttle containers, use the area's E-Web blaster to destroy the rightmost container and expose the mission's tech upgrade. Before you defeat all three walkers, step away from the E-Web blaster for a moment and grab the power-up from the rubble.

MEDAL REQUIREMENTS

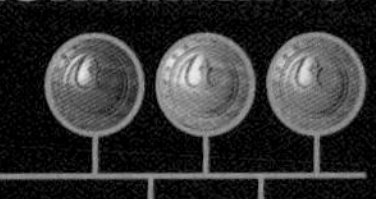

COMPLETION TIME	6:00	5:40	5:30
ENEMIES DESTROYED	40	50	60
SHOT ACCURACY	15%	17%	20%
FRIENDLIES LOST	2	1	0
LIVES LOST	2	1	0
TARGETING COMPUTER EFFICIENCY	70%	85%	90%

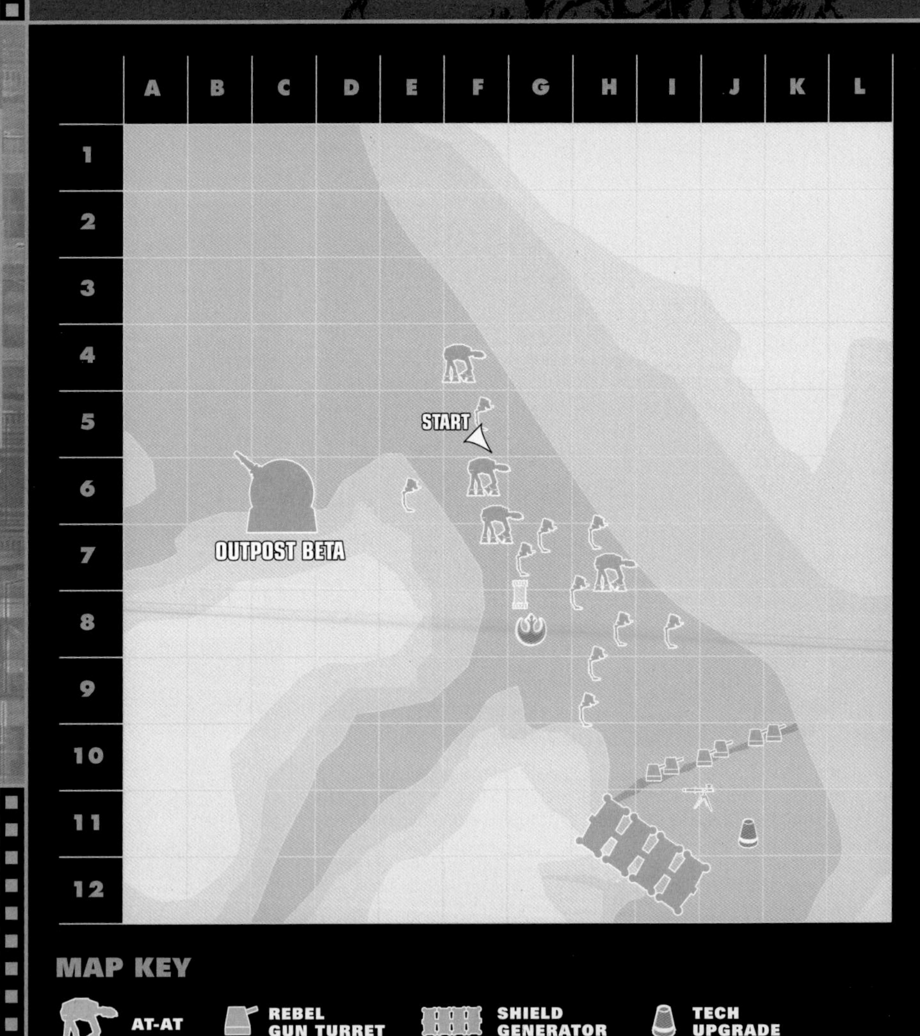

MAP KEY

 AT-AT
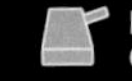 REBEL GUN TURRET
 SHIELD GENERATOR
 TECH UPGRADE
 AT-ST
 E-WEB BLASTER
 BACTA TANK
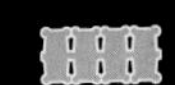 SWITCH TO TAUNTAUN

1 TAKE OUT THE TWO LEAD AT-ATS

Snowtroopers run alongside the Imperial walkers. If you ignore the soldiers, they'll cause a lot of damage. Clear them out, then run up to the downed troopers to collect their blaster rifles.

C IS FOR CABLE

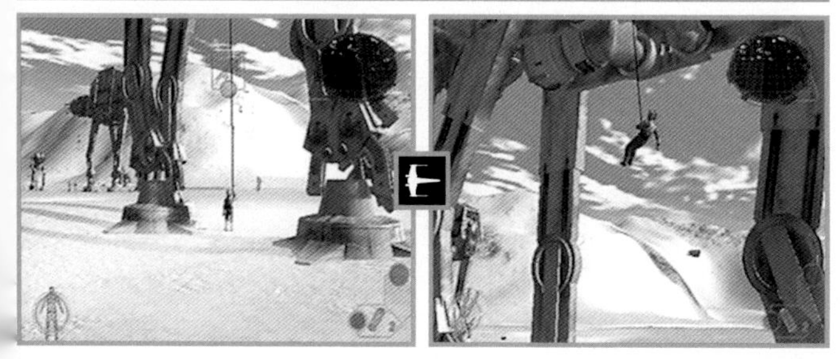

When you're directly under an AT-AT's midsection, a C-Stick icon will appear on the screen. Tap the C Stick in any direction to send a cable up to the underbelly of the beast, then press Up on the Control Stick to retract the cable and lift yourself to the walker's lower hatch.

A BOMB IN THE BELLY

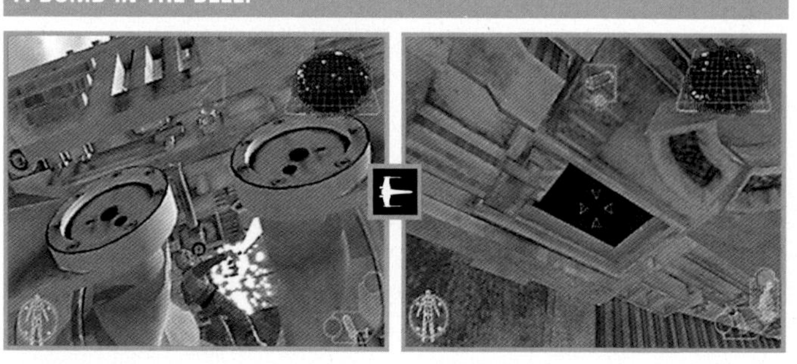

After you reach the AT-AT's torso, press A repeatedly to open a hatch using your lightsaber, then press B to switch to first-person perspective. Line up the aim indicator with the open hatch. The indicator will turn red when you're on target. Press B again to toss an explosive into the hatch. A successful throw will put an explosion inside the walker and send the view back to third-person perspective.

AVOID THE CRUSH

The disabled AT-AT will fall onto its left side. Run to the right or stay still as the walker crumbles. If you make the mistake of running left, the machine will crush you and you'll lose a life.

2 GET TO THE TAUNTAUN

Snowtroopers and probe droids surround Rebel soldier Derlin and two tauntauns. Eliminate the troopers from a distance, then target the probe droids. As soon as your aiming reticle centers on one of the droids, press and hold L to lock on to the droid, then fire away. After you've cleared away the enemies, grab a bacta tank near three crates on the ground to gain a health boost, then run to the Rebel symbol that accompanies one of the tauntauns and hitch a ride.

3 FOLLOW DERLIN BACK TO ECHO BASE

! TAUNTAUN

Tauntauns are camel-like creatures that run on two legs and are at home in the snow. As soon as you mount one of the beasts, you'll notice that it can run much faster than a person can. The tauntaun's weapon is also more powerful than a standard blaster. A single-shot direct hit will eliminate a snowtrooper.

FIRE FREELY

A C-Stick icon will appear above the tauntaun as you ride. Tap the C Stick to direct your blaster fire. The weapon will still lock on to targets, and the directed fire will allow you to eliminate enemies to your left and right.

REBEL RUN

Plow through the field on your tauntaun and blast snowtroopers on your way to boost your Enemies Destroyed rating. AT-ATs may collapse as you make your way to the goal on the far end of the field. Keep your distance to avoid a crushing blow.

4 DESTROY THE THREE AT-STS

TAKE OVER THE E-WEB BLASTER

After you hop off the tauntaun, head for the next group of snowtroopers and defeat them from a distance, locking on to each one by holding the L Button for better accuracy. Your fellow Rebels will provide assistance. Once all of the troopers are gone, run to the E-Web blaster and tap the C Stick to switch to first-person perspective. Shuttles will deliver three containers. While you're waiting for the containers to open, try to destroy the TIE fighters that buzz the landing site.

SURPRISE PACKAGE

AT-STs will pop out of each of the three cargo containers. Blast the walkers one at a time, starting with the one on the far right. It'll take about three seconds of direct fire to destroy each walker. While you're waiting for the next walker to approach, fire at the packs of snowtroopers—by doing so you'll pump up your Enemies Destroyed stat.

5 PROTECT THE THREE REBEL TRANSPORTS

The last three transports are attempting to leave Echo Base, but large squads of TIEs are making it difficult. Fly straight for the transports as soon as you're in the air. You'll soar right into a cloud of TIEs.

At least one of the transports must survive. Stay close to the huge cargo ships and concentrate your fire on the TIE bombers that are on attack runs. The more you can keep TIEs from firing on the transports, the longer the transports will survive.

6 DESTROY THE TIE BOMBERS

BATTLE BOMBERS IN GROUPS

TIE bombers travel in packs. Get behind a group of the slippery ships and adjust your speed to stay close to them. Destroy the bombers on the outside of the formation first, then target the leader. If you defeat the leader before you tag the wingmen, the formation will break up and you'll have a lot of stray enemies on your hands.

INTERRUPT THE INTERCEPTORS

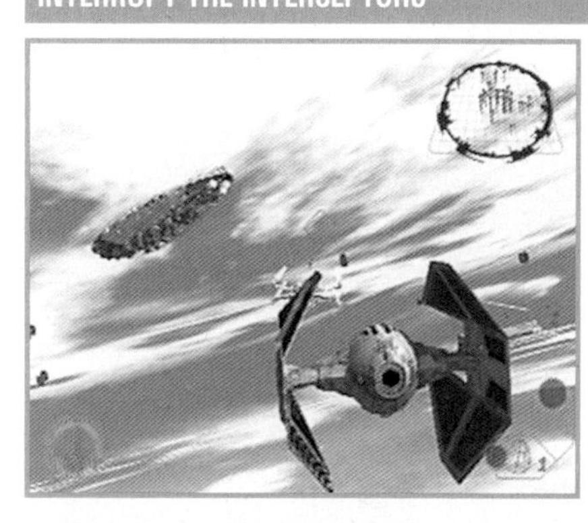

TIE interceptors will lock on to your ship and follow your flight pattern. You won't have to defeat the interceptors to satisfy the objective, but you should shake them off for the sake of your own survival. Execute hard turns and speed changes to get the TIEs to break away.

CLOUD CONTROL

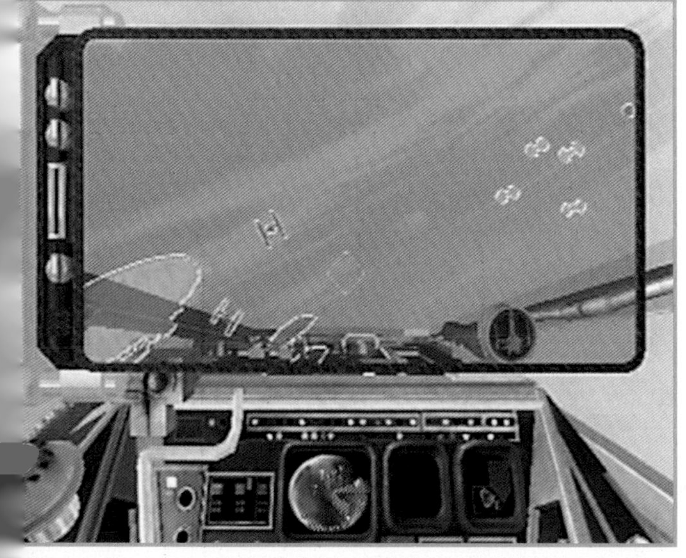

When you fly into the clouds, you'll have no alternative but to turn on your targeting computer. The TIE bombers will appear in yellow. Turn off the computer as soon as you're out of the clouds—you will need a high Targeting Computer Efficiency rating to earn any medals.

GOING FOR GOLD

RE-UP WITH UPGRADES

If you're having a hard time reaching the gold-medal plateau in the Battlefield Hoth mission, return to the mission once you have advanced blasters and advanced homing proton torpedoes. The battle against TIE bombers is the most difficult part of the mission. Once you have the right weapon upgrades, you'll be able to dispatch the bombers in less time and with more accuracy.

LUKE SKYWALKER'S CAMPAIGN

TRIALS OF A JEDI

"You seek Yoda! Take him to you I will!" The Dagobah Jedi training session teaches you the ways of double-jumping and blaster-deflecting. You'll complete the lesson by lifting your X-wing from the muck.

OBJECTIVES

1. FIND YOUR WAY TO THE STRANGE CREATURE'S HOME
2. COMPLETE YODA'S LIGHTSABER BLOCKING TUTORIAL
3. COMPLETE YODA'S DOUBLE-JUMP TUTORIAL
4. FOLLOW YODA BACK TO THE X-WING
5. USE THE FORCE TO RAISE YOUR X-WING FROM THE SWAMP

A B C D E F G H I J K
1 2 3 4 5 6 7 8 9 10
YODA'S HOME
START

MEDAL REQUIREMENTS

COMPLETION TIME	6:40	6:00	4:30
ENEMIES DESTROYED	15	18	22
SHOT ACCURACY	100%	100%	100%
FRIENDLIES LOST	0	0	0
LIVES LOST	2	1	0
TARGETING COMPUTER EFFICIENCY	70%	85%	100%

MAP KEY

X-WING

BACTA TANK

1 FIND YOUR WAY TO THE STRANGE CREATURE'S HOME

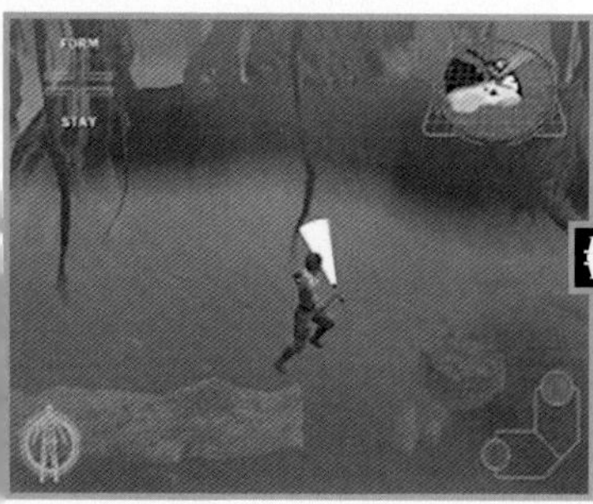

Follow the wedge indicator into the swamp by leaping from one log to the next. When you reach solid ground, destroy a spider's lair, then climb a short hill and drop into another swampy section. Hop from a sturdy log to the back of a moving water creature, then to a sinking log and dry land again. From there, you'll skip across two more logs to Yoda's home.

2•3 COMPLETE YODA'S TUTORIALS

Yoda will give you a pair of lessons before he challenges you to a test. You can deflect shots with your lightsaber by holding the B Button and facing the blasts. You can cross long gaps by double-jumping. Press X once to catch air, then tap X again when your character reaches the peak of his jump.

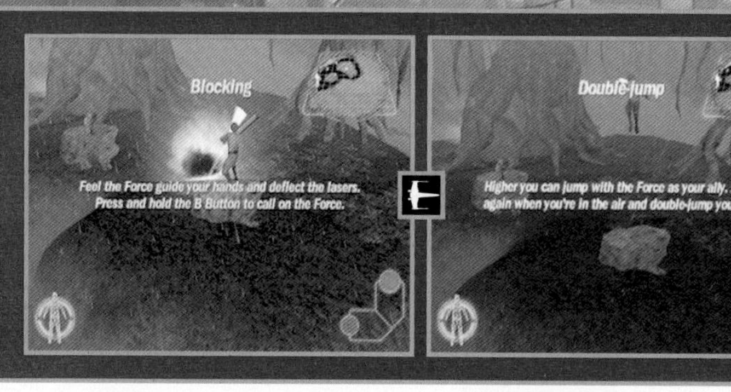

4 FOLLOW YODA BACK TO THE X-WING

JUMP AND DODGE ON YOUR WAY BACK TO THE SHIP

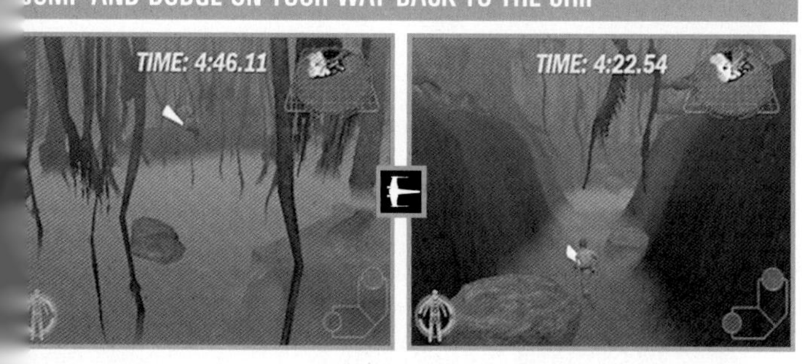

oda will give you five minutes to return to your sunken ship. You'll start by sing the double-jump technique to cross gaps between rocky platforms. Use our extra air time to adjust your trajectory and land perfectly. When you each the shallow valley, avoid contact with swiftly moving objects and continue to leap from rock to rock.

HOP ROCKS

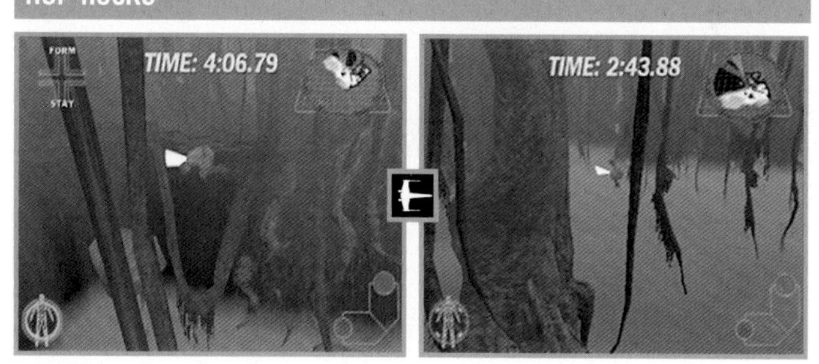

The jumping challenges toward the end of the obstacle course are tricky. There are stretches where several rocks in a row begin to sink as soon you land on them. In section B3 you must leap onto the backs of two water creatures. When the first creature is about to sink, double-jump to the left. You'll land on the second creature as it emerges from the water.

5 USE THE FORCE TO RAISE YOUR X-WING FROM THE SWAMP

On your final approach to the X-wing, you'll face several spiders that appear from two lairs. Destroy the lairs, then take on the stray spiders. After the spiders are gone, follow the wedge indicator to the edge of the water. If you're going for a gold medal, speed is key. You'll see Yoda in the distance. Double-jump across the water, toward the Jedi Master. He'll tell you to raise the X-wing and reset the clock to 20 seconds. Press the B Button quickly and repeatedly. If you manage to get the X-wing out of the water, a cut scene that tells the rest of the story will take over.

LUKE SKYWALKER'S CAMPAIGN

SARLACC PIT

Jabba's thirst for revenge doesn't compare to the monstrous Sarlacc's appetite. As Jabba's men prepare to throw Luke, Han, Chewie and Lando into the Sarlacc Pit, guide Luke to Jabba's barge and turn the tables on the guards. The mission features several clips from the famous *Return of the Jedi* scene.

MEDAL REQUIREMENTS

	Bronze	Silver	Gold
COMPLETION TIME	1:45	1:20	1:12
ENEMIES DESTROYED	12	14	16
SHOT ACCURACY	100%	100%	100%
FRIENDLIES LOST	0	0	0
LIVES LOST	2	1	0
TARGETING COMPUTER EFFICIENCY	95%	98%	100%

OBJECTIVES

1. GET TO JABBA'S SAIL BARGE
2. PROTECT LEIA UNTIL SHE GETS TO THE DECK GUN

1 GET TO JABBA'S SAIL BARGE

You'll use your newfound Jedi skills to reach and overtake Jabba's sail barge. After you defeat the first pair of guards, use the Force by holding the B Button to deflect laser shots while you wait for another guard ship to come around. When the ship is close, double-jump to it, then defeat more guards. Continue to hop ships until you reach the sail barge.

2 PROTECT LEIA UNTIL SHE GETS TO THE DECK GUN

Your Completion Time and Enemies Destroyed ratings are crucial if you're going for the gold medal. As soon as you reach the barge, go after the guards that pour out of the central hatch. The boar-like beasts will attack Leia. By defeating them, you will clear the princess's way to the deck gun. Once the guards are gone, take care of the gunners on the side of the barge.

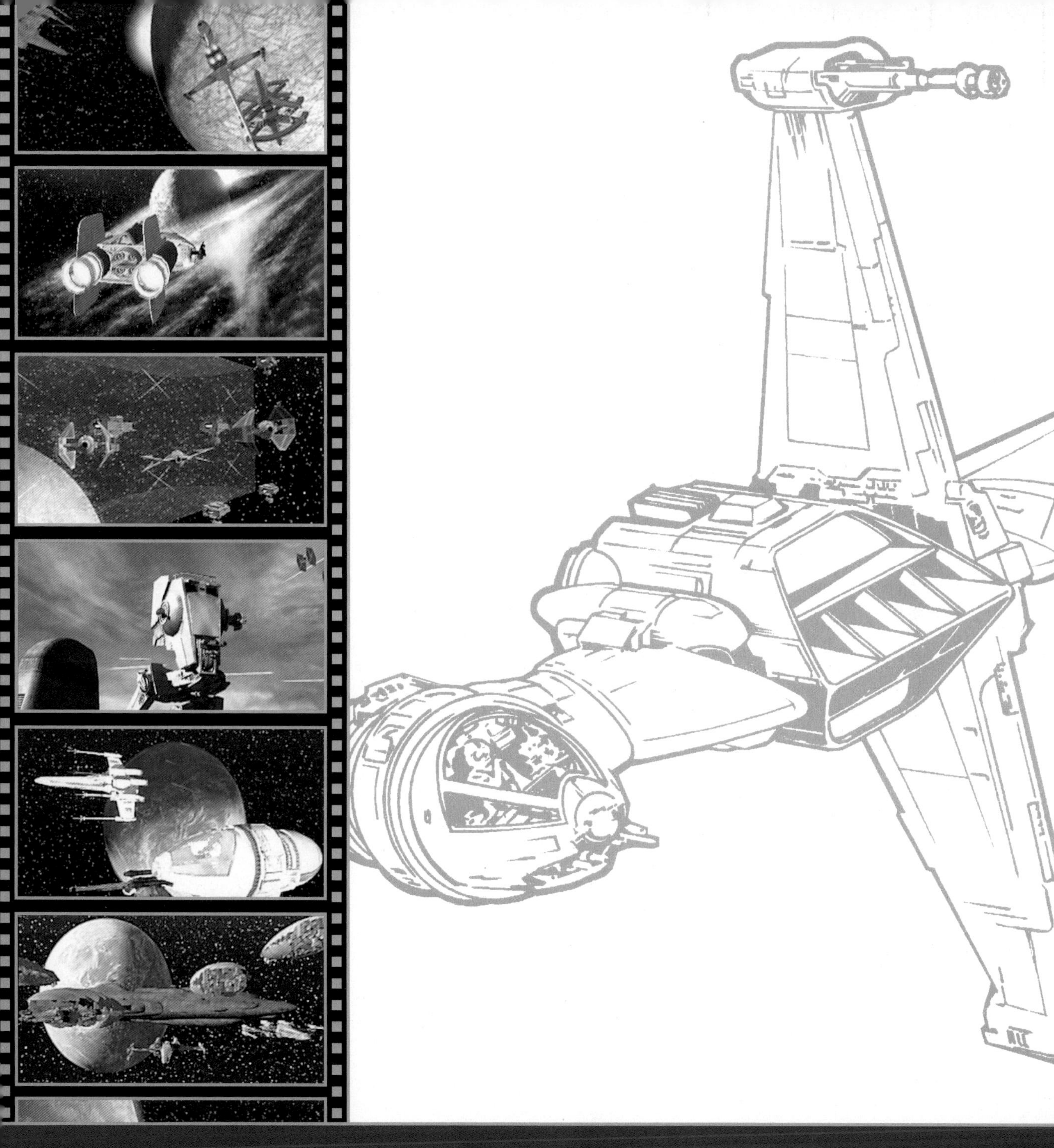

WEDGE ANTILLES' CAMPAIGN

Although he didn't play a big role in the classic film trilogy, Wedge Antilles is one of the Rebel Alliance's most accomplished pilots. His missions are almost exclusively space-based runs on important Imperial targets. You'll earn your flight-fighting chops after a few tours of duty with Wedge.

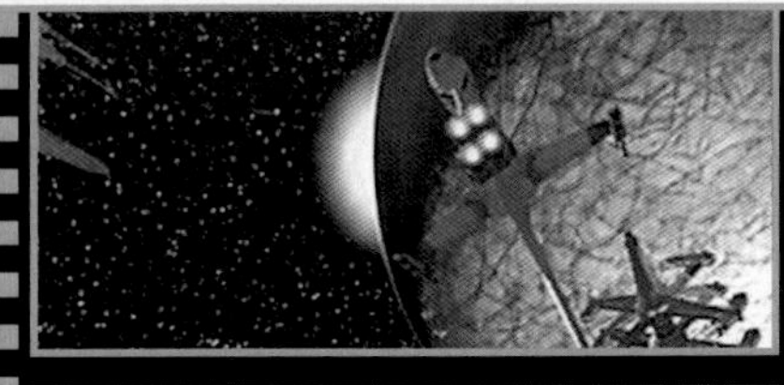

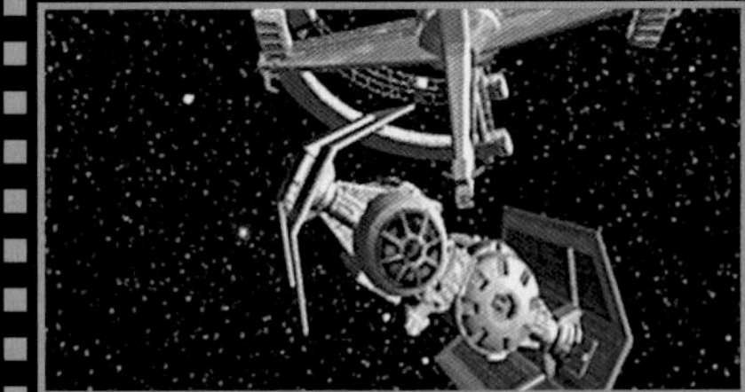

WEDGE ANTILLES' CAMPAIGN

RAID AT BAKURA

The Empire is holding Rebel prisoners on a space station above Bakura. Imperials will attempt to shuttle the captives to a new location. Stop the shuttles in their tracks and fight TIEs as Rebel transports save the prisoners. After you meet the silver medal requirements on the mission's first two objectives, the third objective will unlock.

OBJECTIVES

1. DISABLE ANY FLEEING IMPERIAL TRANSPORTS
2. PROVIDE COVER FOR THE REBEL RECOVERY CREWS
3. LOCATE AND RESCUE HOBBIE

OBJECTIVE 3: BAKURA SURFACE

A B C D E F G H I J K L M N O P Q R S T U V W X Y

1 2 3 4 5

START

HOBBIE

MAP KEY

FLOOR GUN TURRET

TECH UPGRADE

MEDAL REQUIREMENTS

	Bronze	Silver	Gold
COMPLETION TIME	15:00	13:20	8:30
ENEMIES DESTROYED	30	45	97
SHOT ACCURACY	1%	3%	28%
FRIENDLIES LOST	1	0	0
LIVES LOST	2	1	0
TARGETING COMPUTER EFFICIENCY	1%	3%	100%

TECH UPGRADE: ADVANCED PROTON BOMBS

The advanced proton bombs tech upgrade is on the surface of Bakura. You'll expose it by bombing the last domed tower. As soon as you see the power-up, swoop down to collect it, then continue your mission to rescue Hobbie.

1 DISABLE ANY FLEEING IMPERIAL TRANSPORTS

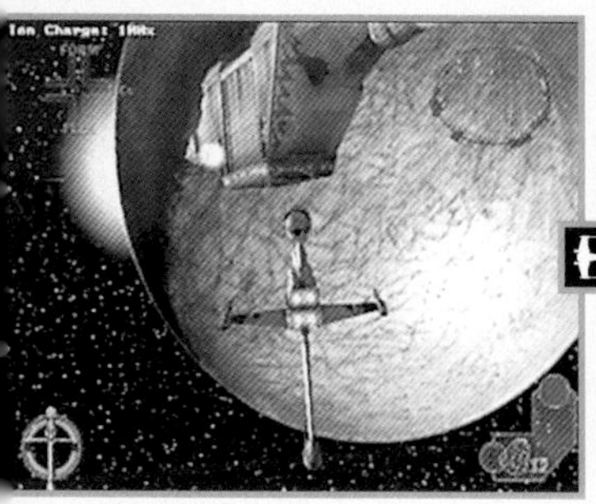

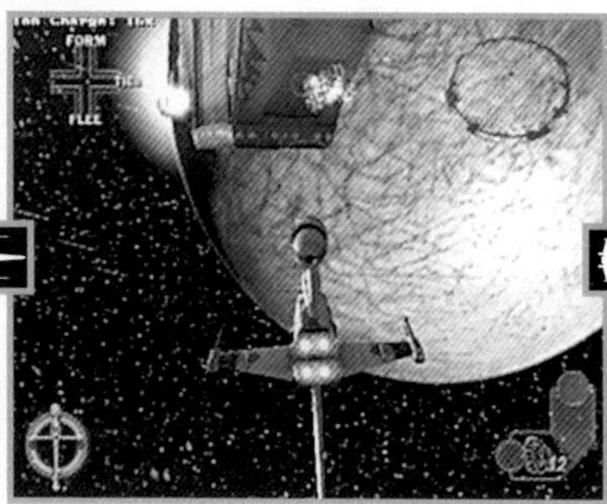

The B-wing is perfect for the first section of the mission. It's an underrated dogfighter and its ion cannons can disable the Imperial transports. Search the space station's perimeter for transports and listen for sound cues that indicate when they've launched. As you close in on a transport, hit it with three charged ion cannon shots to freeze it.

2 PROVIDE COVER FOR THE REBEL RECOVERY CREWS

TIE fighters patrol the area around the space station. Once you've disabled an Imperial transport, circle the ship and pick off the TIE groups in the area. The TIEs are relatively slow—you'll be able to rack up a lot of hits with minimal effort.

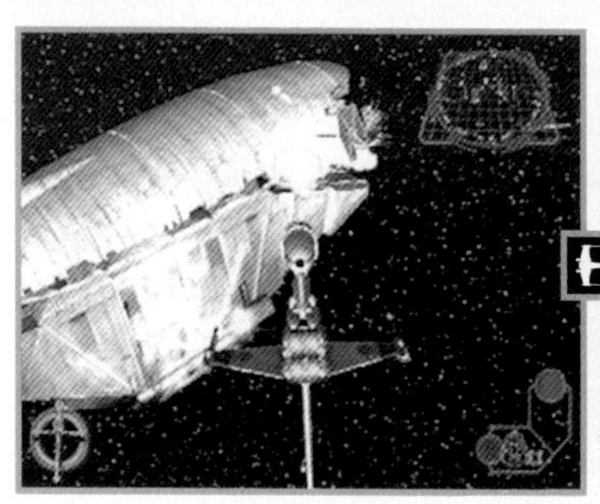

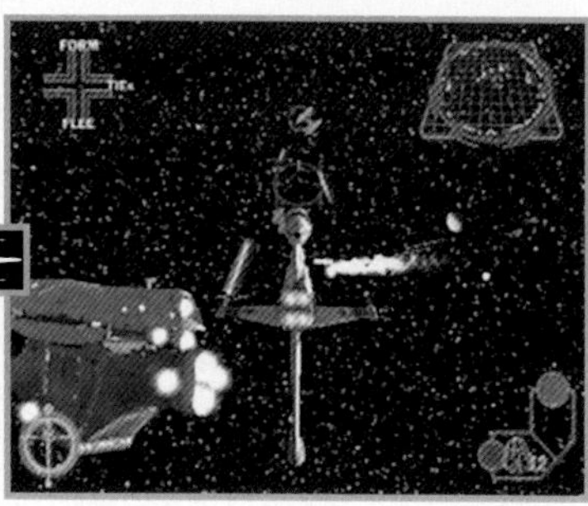

A Rebel rescue ship will dock with the disabled Imperial transport. While that's happening, keep TIEs out of the area by destroying them. Don't let stray shots hit the Imperial transports—they're vulnerable to friendly fire.

! FLY A TIE

Hobbie's rescue requires a ship that can accommodate two. You'll switch to the right vehicle—a TIE bomber—at the beginning of the third objective. The craft's lock-on missiles will take some getting used to, but once you learn to paint targets, you'll cause a lot of damage in the Bakura canyon.

The TIE bomber is equipped with proton bombs and lock-on missiles. You'll use the missiles to destroy multiple guard towers simultaneously and the bombs to blast the largest radar platforms.

3 LOCATE AND RESCUE HOBBIE

GO FOR THE GUN TURRETS

Press and hold the A Button and direct the TIE's targeting reticle over the gun turrets to lock on to them. Release the button to send out a missile barrage before the turrets are directly below your ship. The sooner you take out the towers, the less damage your craft will sustain.

CANYON CRAWL

Use missiles to destroy all of the gun turrets on the canyon floor, and bombs to take out as many of the radar platforms as you can in one pass. Stay low—you'll see turrets on the structures above your ship, but they won't bother you as long as you favor the canyon's lower reaches.

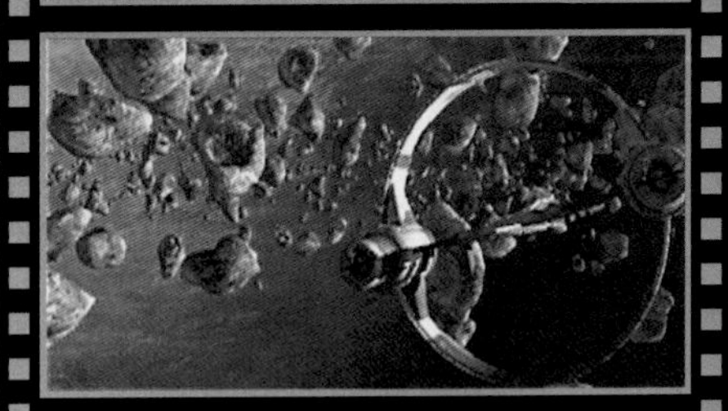

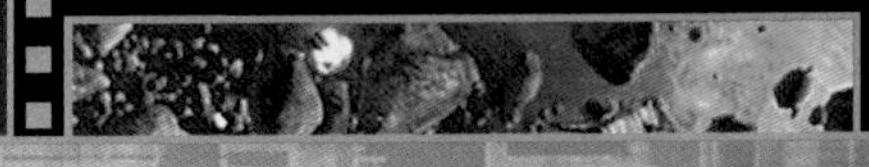

WEDGE ANTILLES' CAMPAIGN

RELICS OF GEONOSIS

Imperial transmissions have exposed three heavily armored escort carriers cutting through the asteroid field above Geonosis. After you destroy one ship and the others flee, you'll drop to the site of the initial battle of the Clone Wars and return to space in time to defeat the remaining escorts.

OBJECTIVES

1. FIND THE ESCORT CARRIER
2. DESTROY THE ESCORT CARRIER
3. PROTECT R5
4. DESTROY THE OLD REPUBLIC GUNSHIP
5. DESTROY BOTH ESCORT CARRIERS
6. PROTECT THE REBEL FRIGATE
7. FIND THE JEDI STARFIGHTER'S HYPERDRIVE BOOSTER RING

TECH UPGRADE: ADVANCED HOMING PROTON TORPEDOES

When you're on the surface of the planet, the third crashed escape pod that you see will be on its side with smoke pouring out of its exhaust port. Look for the tech upgrade at the source of the smoke.

OBJECTIVES 1-2: ASTEROID FIELD

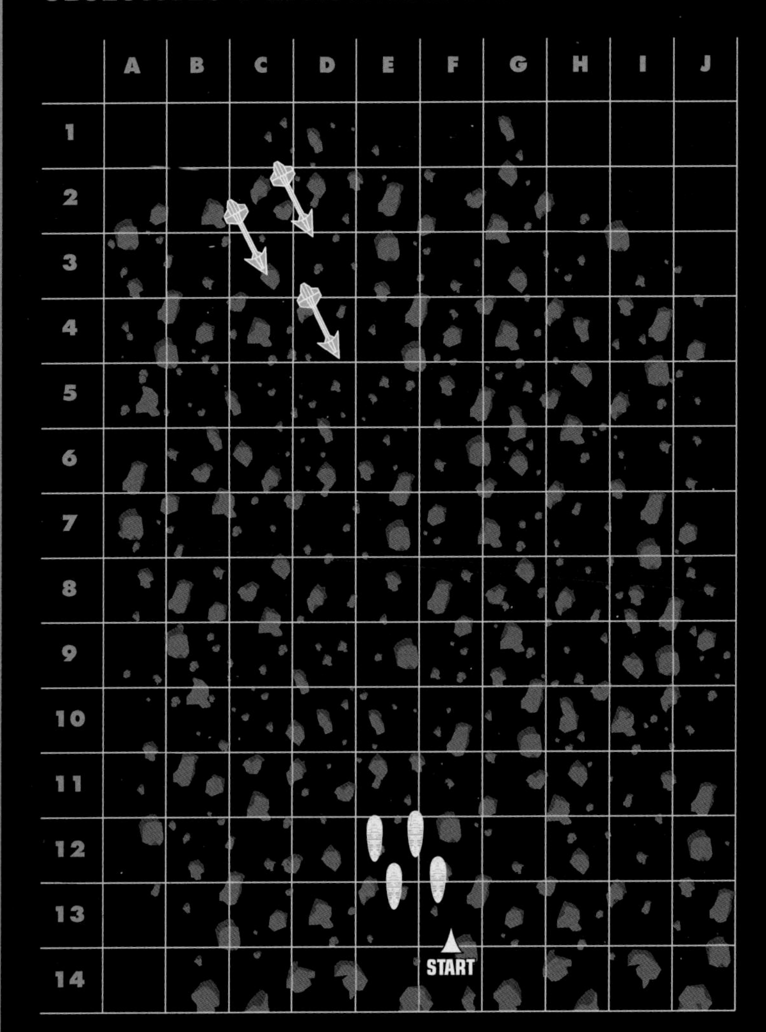

MAP KEY

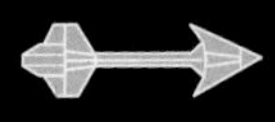

ESCORT CARRIER

REBEL TRANSPORT

MEDAL REQUIREMENTS

COMPLETION TIME	8:50	7:25	6:40
ENEMIES DESTROYED	115	126	135
SHOT ACCURACY	42%	53%	60%
FRIENDLIES LOST	1	1	0
LIVES LOST	2	1	0
TARGETING COMPUTER EFFICIENCY	86%	92%	100%

1 FIND THE ESCORT CARRIER

Rise above the asteroid field and follow the radar indicator to D4. Two of the escort carriers will turn tail and run. You'll find the other escort carrier by looking for the exploding asteroids that it is clearing out of the way. Approach the carrier from above and hold the L Button to slow as you pursue it. Your target is strong, but much slower than an X-wing.

2 DESTROY THE ESCORT CARRIER

UNLOAD PROTON TORPEDOES

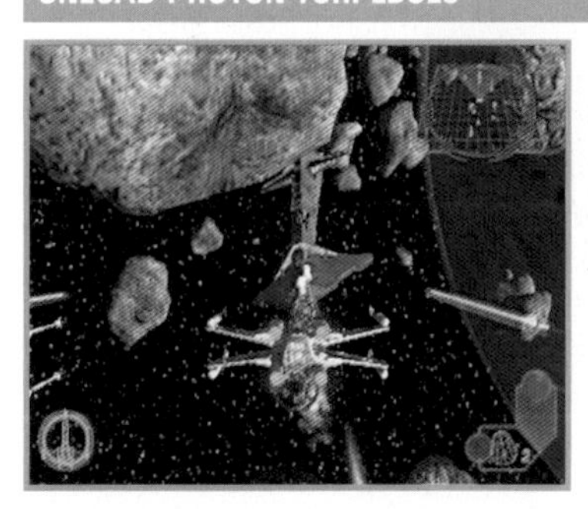

The escort carrier has a thick skin. Stay above it and target the ship's body using lasers and proton torpedoes. If you have advanced homing proton torpedoes, refrain from locking on to the ship's laser cannons. Hits to the body are the only shots that will contribute to the ship's demise. If you drop below the ship, its lower lasers will hit your craft. Rise, then continue your attack.

HOT PURSUIT AND HELP FROM THE WINGS

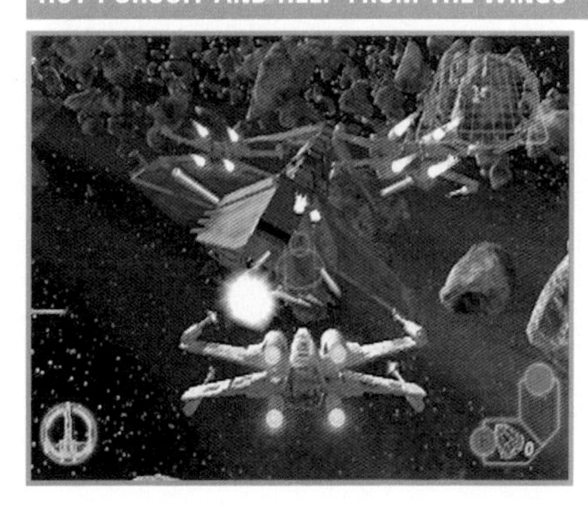

Position your ship behind (but still above) the escort carrier to hit the ship with everything you've got. If your X-wing crashes, you'll return with six more torpedoes. Launch them into the huge craft. When your wingmen ask you for commands, tell them to hit your target—the more firepower, the better.

3 PROTECT R5

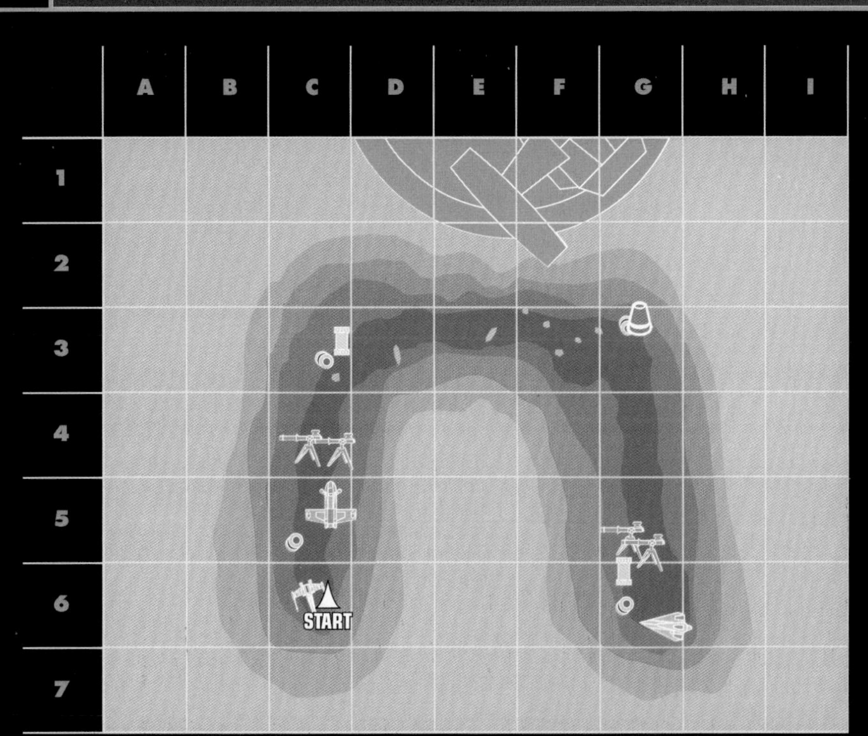

MAP KEY

E-WEB BLASTER

BACTA TANKS

JEDI STARFIGHTER

OLD REPUBLIC GUNSHIP

TECH UPGRADE

R5 IS ON A ROLL

After you crash on Geonosis, your R5 unit will go off in search of alternate transportation. Support your droid by targeting the stormtroopers and battle droids that surround it.

BATTLE-DROID BLAST

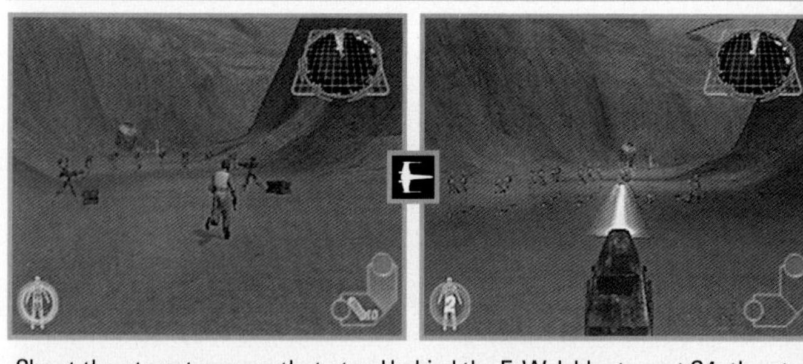

Shoot the stormtroopers that stand behind the E-Web blasters at C4, then tap the C Stick to take control of one of the powerful guns. Battle droids will attack in formation. Mow them down, but watch your accuracy. After all of the droids are down, step away from the blaster and resume your journey.

STOP AND REFRESH

Many of the stormtroopers and battle droids that you defeat will leave behind rapid-fire blasters. Pick them up to gain a significant firepower improvement. You can hold as many as 99 rapid-fire shots at once. If you're low on health, pick up the health-restoring bacta tank next to the escape pod at C3. If you don't need a health boost, leave the bacta tank for later. You'll find more next to an E-Web blaster at G5.

GUNSHIP GETAWAY

Once you reach G3, you'll draw heavy fire from an old Republic gunship that is equipped with superpowerful blasters and missiles. Move in a zigzag pattern and roll to avoid the gunship's shots. If you're low on health, grab the bacta tank at G5.

GOING FOR GOLD

LOB INTO THE MOB

Wedge is equipped with thermal detonators. You can use them to destroy several enemies at once. Practice will make perfect throws, helping your Completion Time and Shot Accuracy statistics.

4 DESTROY THE OLD REPUBLIC GUNSHIP

You must disable the gunship before you can leave Geonosis. As the ship patrols the area, get behind the E-Web blaster farthest from the starfighter and use it to blast your circling target. Aim for both blasters on each wing, then fire at the round features on either side of the cockpit and at the gunship's body.

SEARCH FOR A LIFT

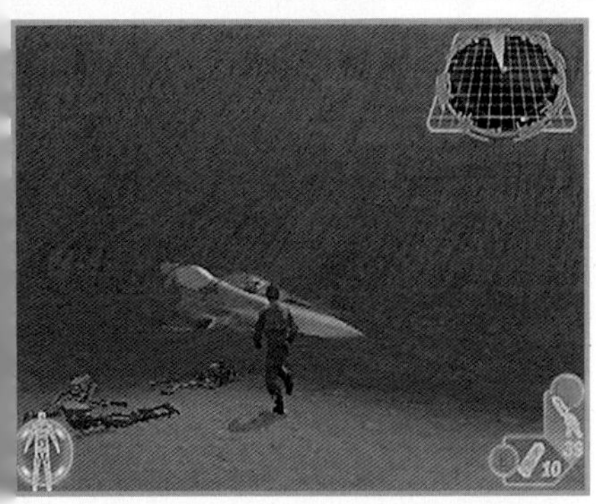

You'll discover a Jedi starfighter near a pair of E-Web blasters and a battle-droid platoon. The starfighter is your ticket off this rock, but before you can fire it up, you'll have to finish the fight. Take control over one of the blasters and fire away.

! THE JEDI STARFIGHTER

You'll discover a Jedi starfighter from the Clone Wars on the Geonosis battlefield. It's old, but it works. The ship is not unlike an A-wing—fast and agile but possessing relatively weak shields. You starfighter flight will pit you against swarms of TIEs and two escort carriers. Steer away from enemy fire whenever possible.

SONIC SILENCER

The Jedi starfighter's secondary weapon, the sonic mine, releases a tremendous energy wave that plows through everything in its way.

5 DESTROY BOTH ESCORT CARRIERS

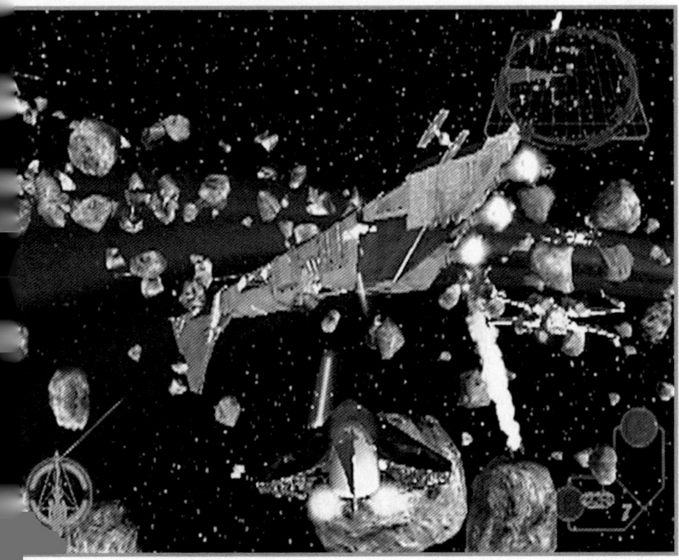

To demolish the two remaining heavily shielded ships, use the techniques that you used to down the first carrier. Attack them from above and hit their bodies with all of your firepower. Either arrange your wingmen behind you so they fight with you, or instruct them to attack your target directly.

6 PROTECT THE REBEL FRIGATE

TIE bombers pose a large threat on your ship and the Rebel frigate nearby. Locate the bomber groups and approach them from behind to minimize the chances that they will hit you with their homing missiles.

7 FIND THE JEDI STARFIGHTER'S HYPERDRIVE BOOSTER RING

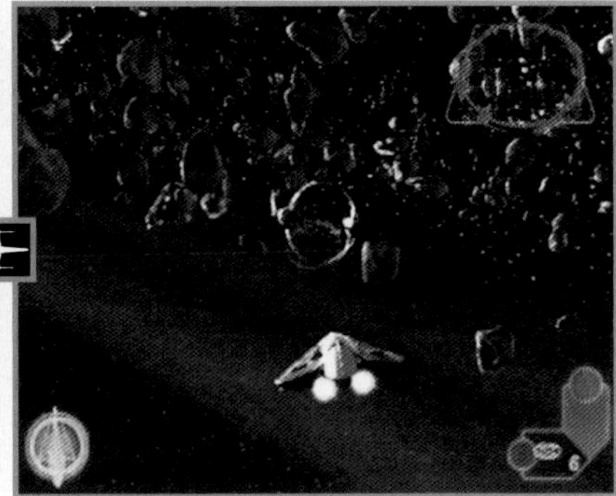

After the escort carriers are down and the Rebel frigate is safe, you'll finish the mission by hooking up with the hyperdrive booster ring. Follow the scanner's wedge indicator, then use the targeting computer to find the ring. When you get close to it, your ship will dock automatically.

WEDGE ANTILLES' CAMPAIGN

DECEPTION AT DESTRILLION

The Empire is conducting weapon-development research on Destrillion. The Alliance has singled out the facility as a prime target. By cutting through tunnels etched in Destrillion's energy field, you can reach the facility and identify targets for a Y-wing bombing run.

OBJECTIVES

1. FLY THROUGH THE ENERGY TUNNELS
2. DESTROY THE TIE HUNTERS INSIDE THE ENERGY FIELD
3. LOCATE THE IMPERIAL RESEARCH FACILITY
4. DESTROY THE TARGETING RELAYS

OBJECTIVE 2: ENERGY TUNNELS PART 1

OBJECTIVE 2: ENERGY TUNNELS PART 2

TUNNEL VISION

The map's callouts show laser arrangements, which will help you to plan your route through the tunnel. Thick lines represent the closest lasers.

MEDAL REQUIREMENTS

COMPLETION TIME	5:25	4:30	4:00
ENEMIES DESTROYED	18	25	27
SHOT ACCURACY	10%	22%	36%
FRIENDLIES LOST	1	0	0
LIVES LOST	2	1	0
TARGETING COMPUTER EFFICIENCY	86%	95%	100%

TECH UPGRADE: ADVANCED SPREAD PROTON BOMBS

During the bombing run at the end of the mission, you'll find the super laser inside a huge concrete bowl. Fly high above the bowl, then dive into it and look for a white dot. That's the tech upgrade.

1 FLY THROUGH THE ENERGY TUNNELS

GET SOME PERSPECTIVE

Navigating the energy tunnels will require fancy flying. Press the X Button to switch to first-person perspective. The from-the-cockpit view will allow you to thread tight sections more effectively.

AVOID ENERGY

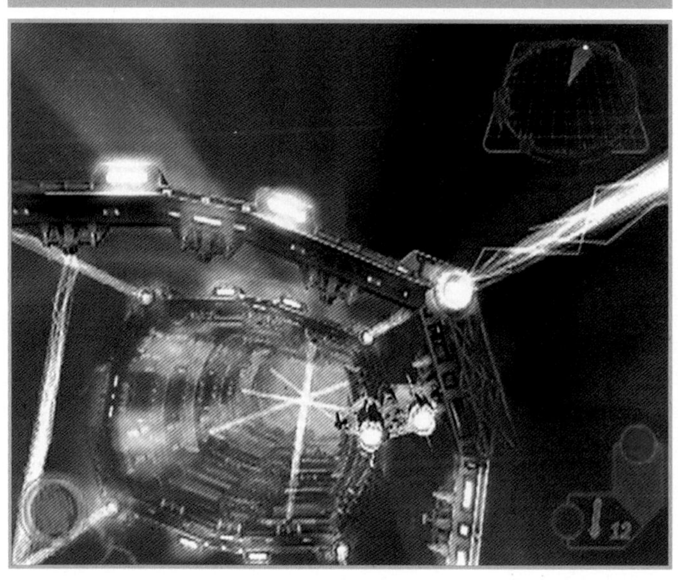

If your ship skims the tunnel's energy walls, it will sustain damage. If it hits a laser, it will blow up. Watch what's ahead and be ready to make aerial adjustments.

MOVE AND MANEUVER

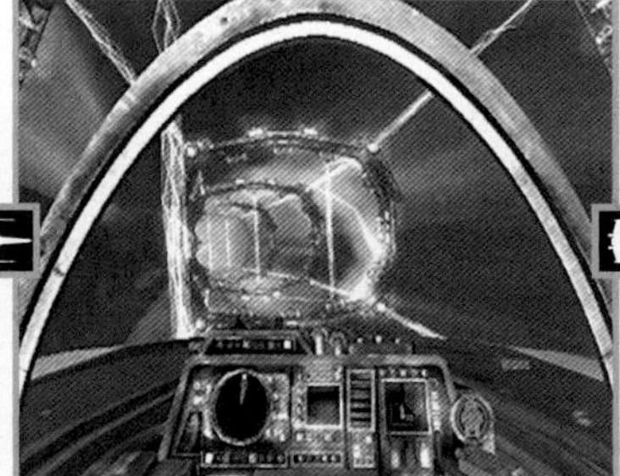

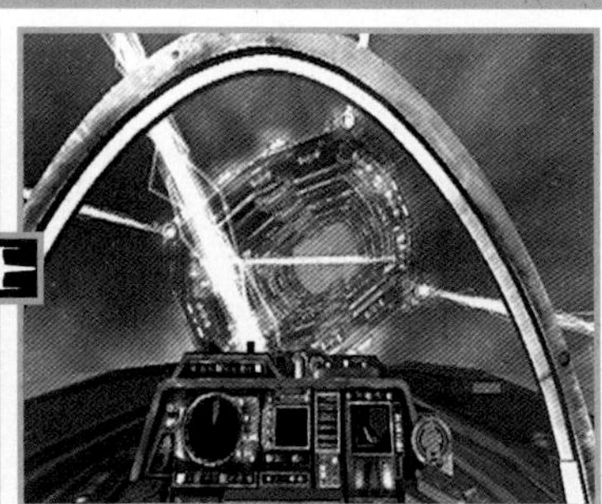

You'll need a plan to get through the tunnel in one piece. Study the map to prepare for the lasers deep in the tunnel. Keep your speed down as you navigate the trickiest areas.

GOING FOR GOLD

CUT TIME WITH SPEED

The A-wing is the fastest ship in the fleet. You can zip through the energy tunnel by engaging boost speed. Press R to boost through the tunnel's straight sections, but slow down on the turns and near the lasers unless you're confident in your ability to avoid obstacles with little notice.

2 DESTROY THE TIE HUNTERS INSIDE THE ENERGY FIELD

HUNT DOWN THE HUNTERS

Between energy tunnels, you'll encounter a TIE hunter squad. As you take on the hunters, a force field will keep you from continuing to the next section. Circle the platform in the center of the area and target TIEs. You must destroy all of the hunters to make the force field fall.

CONCUSSION DESTRUCTION

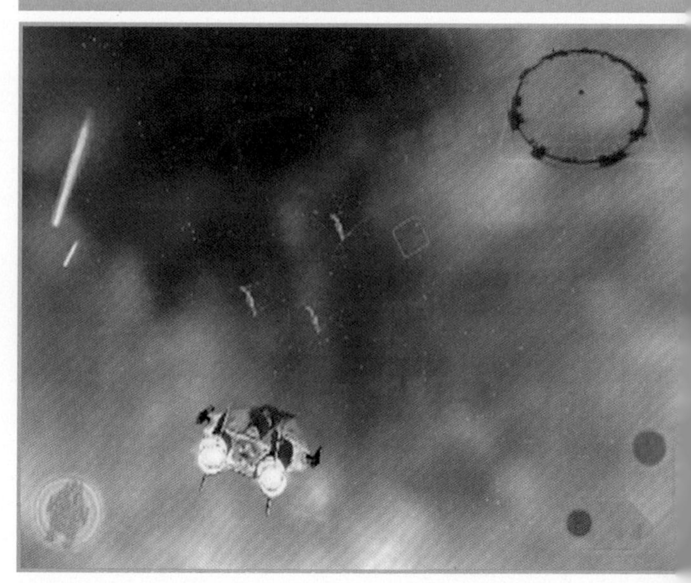

The TIE hunters are speedy. You can take them out with your blasters, but you'll have better luck using concussion missiles. The missiles can lock on to several targets at once, allowing you to destroy a cluster of TIEs in one fell swoop. While you're waiting for your missiles to replenish, execute evasive maneuvers and hit strays with your lasers.

3 LOCATE THE IMPERIAL RESEARCH FACILITY

A B C D E F G H I J K

1 2 3 4 5 6 7 8 9

START

MAP KEY

RELAY DISHES

TECH UPGRADE

RETURN TO THE TUNNEL

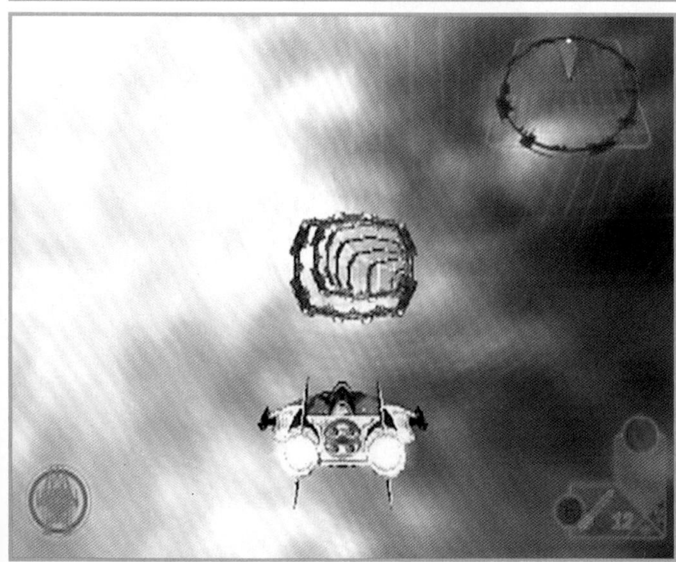

With the TIE hunters out of the picture, you'll be able to continue to the next tunnel. Consult the radar indicator to make sure you're heading for the correct opening. If you're not, turn around. Once you're oriented, hit the boost and speed toward the tunnel.

ALMOST THERE! USE CAUTION!

When Wedge says "Almost there!" you're close to the end of the tunnel. Decelerate and get ready for tight tunnel sections that are crowded with intersecting lasers. The first-person view will keep you in line with your ship, allowing you to negotiate the lasers easily.

4 DESTROY THE TARGETING RELAYS

BREAK THE DISHES

While you're emerging from the energy tunnels, your mission objective will switch to destroying the targeting relays via a bombing run on the planet's surface. A huge laser threatens a Rebel convoy. You'll use a Y-wing to bomb three radar dish relays and knock out the laser's targeting capabilities. Follow your radar indicator, use your ion cannon to blast the shields that cover each relay, then use bombs to destroy the relays.

TIES ON YOUR TAIL

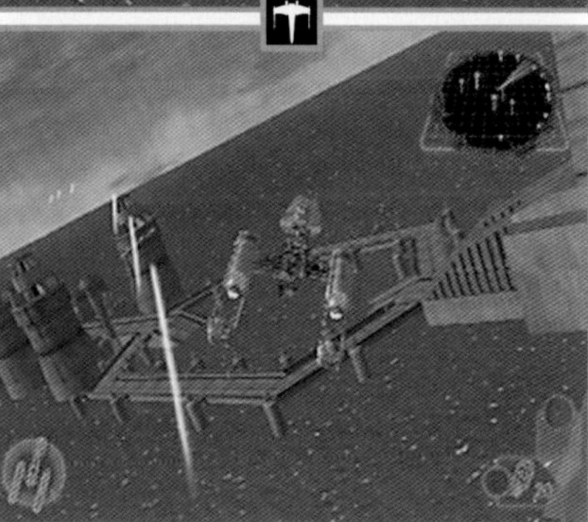

TIE fighters will buzz your slower Y-wing like bees around a picnic basket. Instruct your wingmen to go after the TIEs, and keep your eyes on the prize—the targeting relays. If a TIE fighter is locked on your tail, make speed adjustments and erratic moves to shake it, but don't waver from your course. The sooner you destroy all three targets, the sooner you'll be able to leave the area.

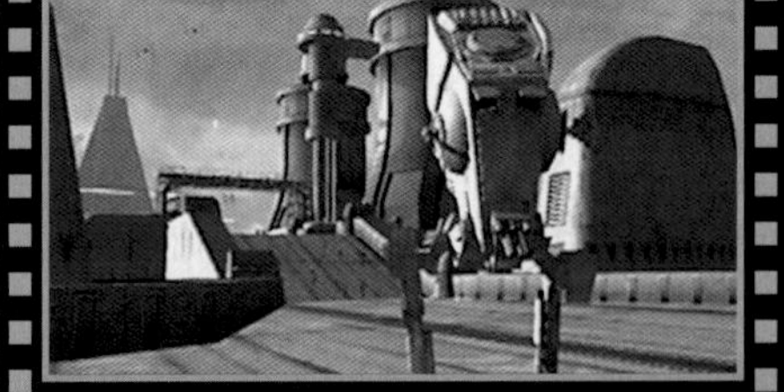

WEDGE ANTILLES' CAMPAIGN

GUNS OF DUBRILLION

An Imperial super laser is threatening Rebel Alliance targets. The laser's facility is well-protected from the air, making it a nearly impossible bombing target, but one willing hero could destroy the facility on the ground. The mission will require you to take control over an AT-ST and—for the final assault—an AT-AT Imperial walker.

OBJECTIVE

1 REACH THE SUPER LASER

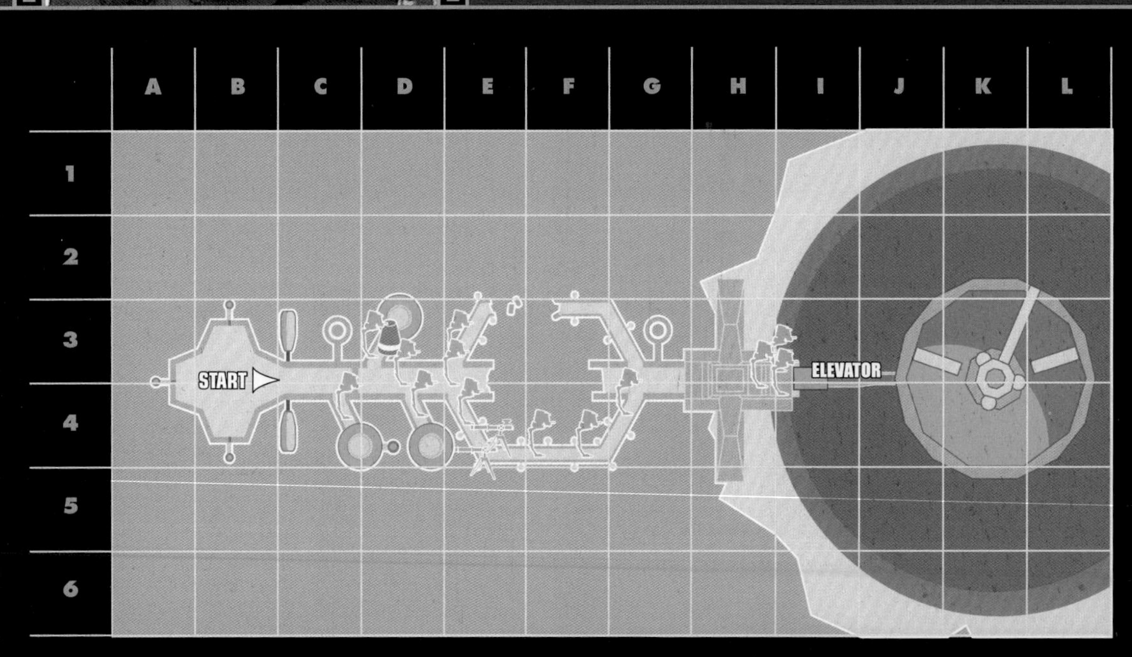

MAP KEY

AT-ST

E-WEB BLASTER

TECH UPGRADE

MEDAL REQUIREMENTS

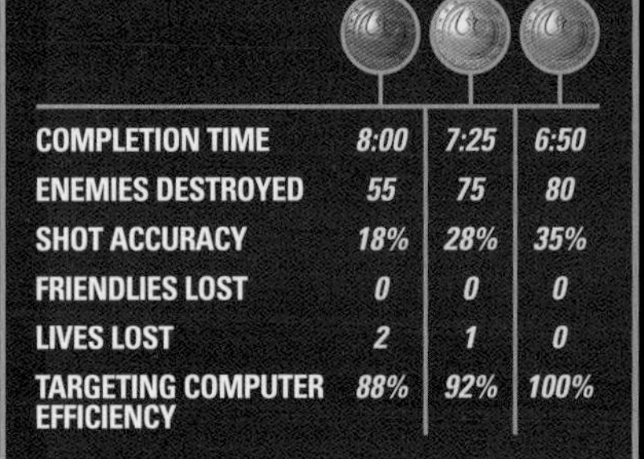

	Bronze	Silver	Gold
COMPLETION TIME	8:00	7:25	6:50
ENEMIES DESTROYED	55	75	80
SHOT ACCURACY	18%	28%	35%
FRIENDLIES LOST	0	0	0
LIVES LOST	2	1	0
TARGETING COMPUTER EFFICIENCY	88%	92%	100%

TECH UPGRADE: ADVANCED CONCUSSION MISSILES

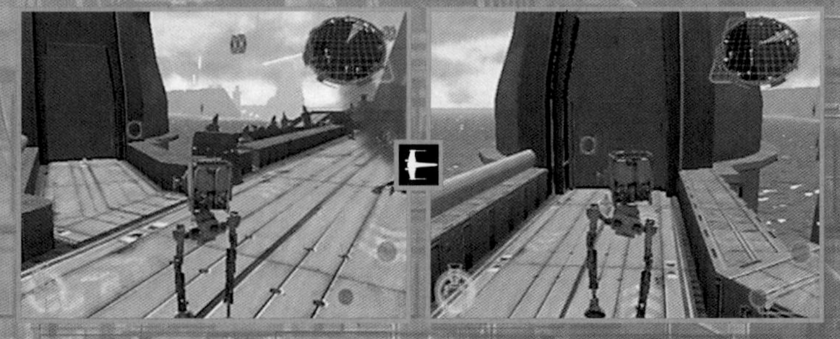

After you climb a ramp and take on a few AT-STs, turn left at the first opportunity to collect the area's tech upgrade. Mission success will give all of your concussion-missile-equipped ships a secondary weapon with a lot of bite.

1 REACH THE SUPER LASER

WAR OF THE WALKERS

The toughest, most persistent enemies that you will face in the mission's early stages are other AT-STs. They will target your chicken walker and never let up until you destroy them. Some walkers will arrive in landing shuttles. If you manage to destroy a shuttle cargo carrier before it drops, you'll have one less AT-ST to deal with.

GET THE GUNNERS AROUND THE CORNER

At the fork in the path, you'll see that the passage to the left has sunk. Turn right and target a pair of stormtroopers who are operating E-Web blasters. They can cause as much damage as AT-STs, but they have a lot less armor. As you proceed, landing shuttles will drop their cargo. First hit the AT-STs that emerge from the boxes, then target the crates.

TIE TRIALS

TIE fighters will occasionally take straight attack runs down the path. If you're not already targeting a more potentially damaging opponent, take a few shots at the approaching ship. Your Shot Accuracy rating may suffer, but you'll add to your Enemies Destroyed total. You'll also encounter groups of stormtroopers at C3 and G3 on the map. Hit them with carefully aimed shots to keep your accuracy up.

AT-ST TRIPLE THREAT

While you're approaching the elevator, you'll face a trio of AT-STs. Use homing missiles to target all three of the chicken walkers simultaneously.

SINK AND SHOOT

As soon as you reach the elevator, it will begin to descend automatically and floating probes will fire on your vehicle. Line up your laser shots and knock them out of the sky.

LONG-DISTANCE DESTRUCTION

After you reach the facility's lower level, turn left and start a counterclockwise run around the circular hall. AT-STs will walk toward you, but they won't fire until they are close. Lock on to the chicken walkers while they're still far away, and put them out of commission quickly.

TRACK DOWN THE TANKS

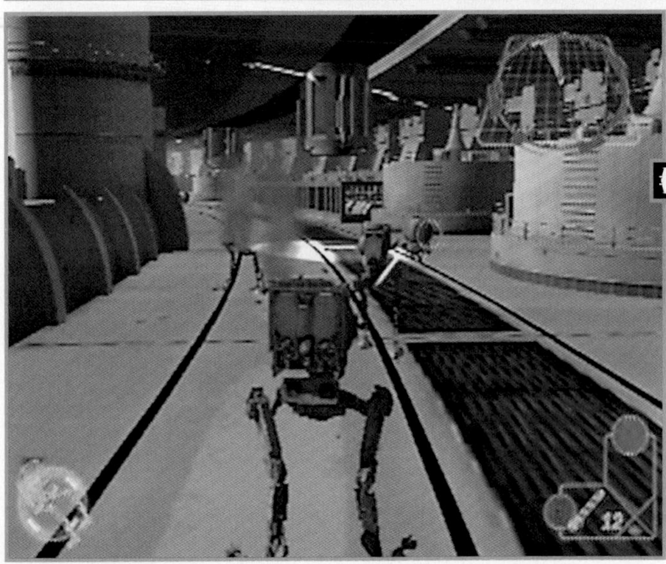

Tanks that carry a flammable substance will slide down the tracks at a good clip. If a tank hits your walker, the AT-ST will go up in flames. Target the tanks with your lasers while they're still a good distance away. If you hit a tank while it is close to an enemy walker, the explosion will destroy the tank and the walker.

! PILOT AN AT-AT

The AT-AT is the ground-combat equivalent of the Star Destroyer. It's imposing and immensely powerful, but it does have its weak points. Luckily, when you get behind the controls of an AT-AT, there won't be any speeders or lightsaber-equipped Jedi in the area. The Imperial walker will move forward automatically while you aim and fire its lasers. Press the L, R and A Buttons to release laser blasts.

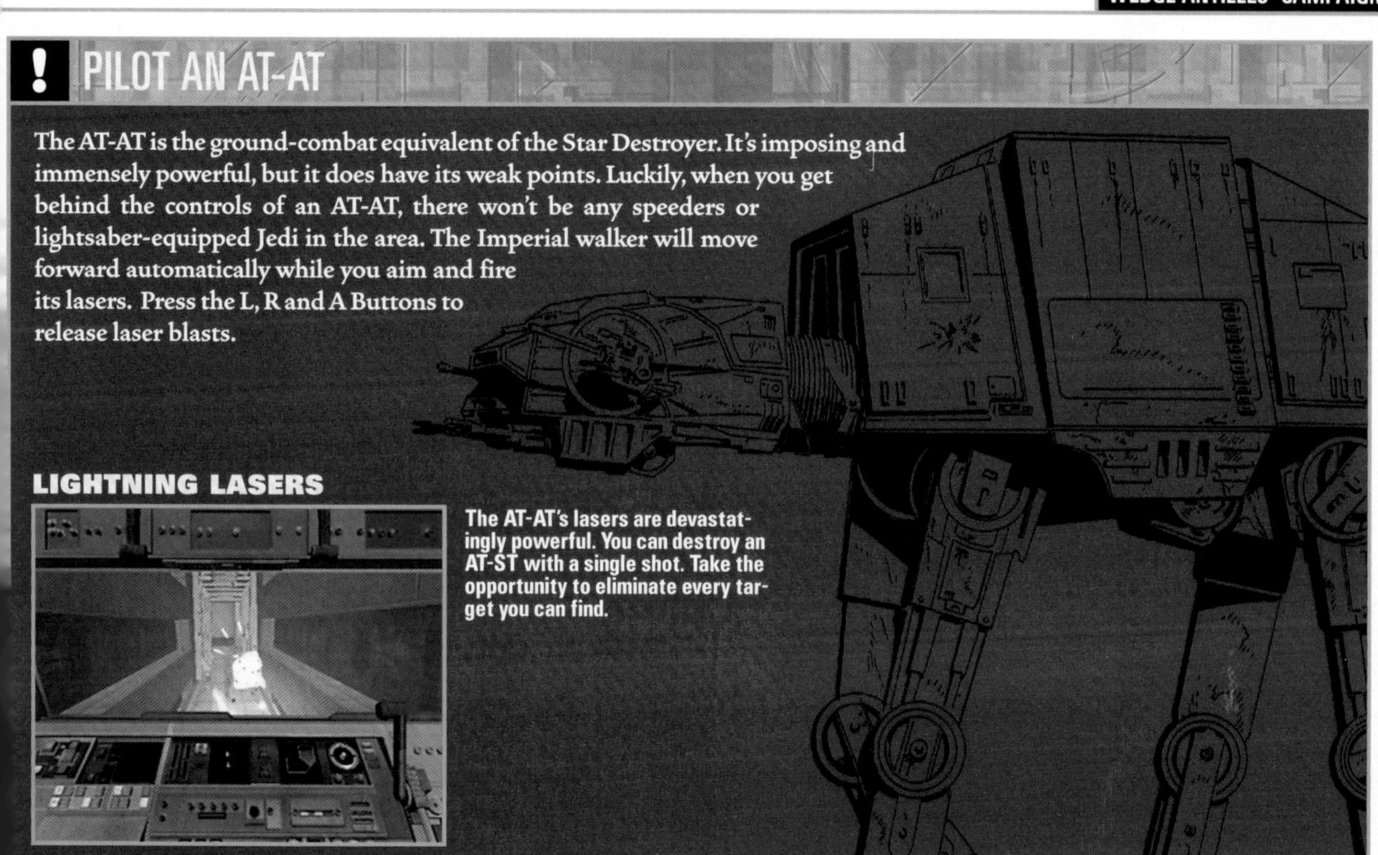

LIGHTNING LASERS

The AT-AT's lasers are devastatingly powerful. You can destroy an AT-ST with a single shot. Take the opportunity to eliminate every target you can find.

THREE WALKERS IN THREE SHOTS

he AT-AT will head straight for an elevator platform that three AT-STs guard. hey don't pose much of a threat to your walking tank, but eliminate them nyway. Line up each shot carefully and knock them out with one shot each to oost your Shot Accuracy rating.

THE HEART OF THE BEAST

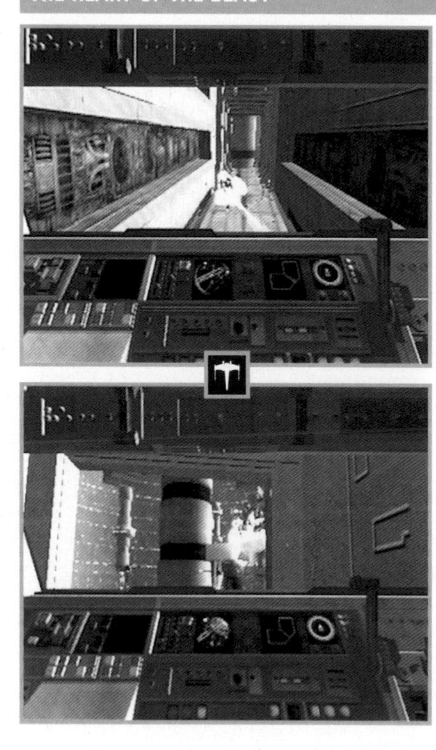

Once the elevator stops, you'll face more AT-STs on your way to the center of the super laser. After you blast the AT-STs, turn your attention toward the three turbines that rotate around the laser's central housing. You'll see only one of the turbines at first; the others will come into view as you get closer. In the interest of accuracy, don't fire unless you have a clean shot. The turbines are not incredibly strong. You'll knock all of them out before your walker comes to a stop.

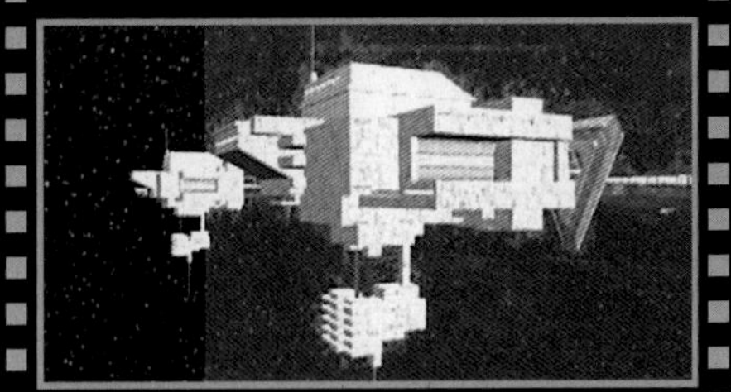
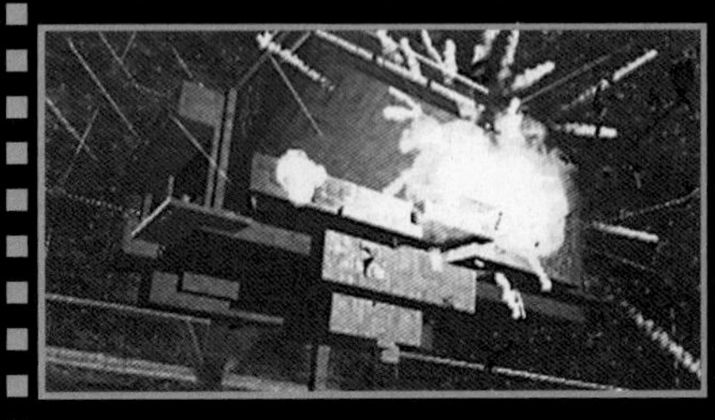

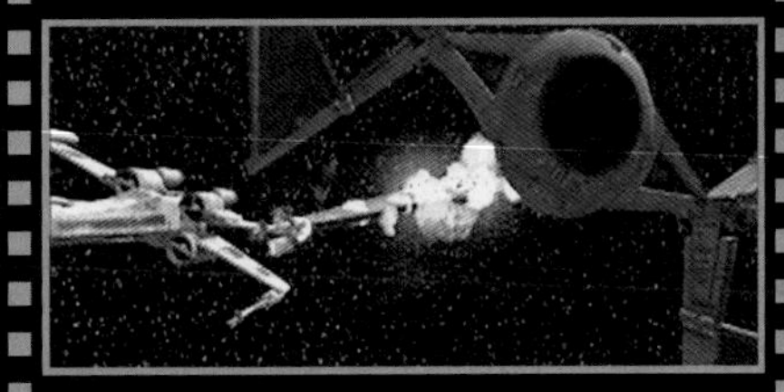

WEDGE ANTILLES' CAMPAIGN

FONDOR SHIPYARD ASSAULT

The Rebel Alliance has devised a variation of the Trojan Horse ploy. Posing as an Imperial pilot (in a TIE hunter), you will escort a booby-trapped transport ship to an Imperial target then attack an exposed shield generator. Note that the mission does not contain a tech upgrade.

OBJECTIVES

1. DEFEND THE REBEL TRANSPORT
2. USE ION CANNONS TO DISABLE THE HANGAR DOORS
3. DESTROY THE SHIELD GENERATOR BEFORE IMPERIAL REINFORCEMENTS ARRIVE
4. DESTROY ALL THREE CLOAKING DEVICES

MEDAL REQUIREMENTS

COMPLETION TIME	5:50	5:00	4:00
ENEMIES DESTROYED	28	43	50
SHOT ACCURACY	45%	50%	56%
FRIENDLIES LOST	2	1	0
LIVES LOST	2	1	0
TARGETING COMPUTER EFFICIENCY	88%	95%	100%

OBJECTIVE 1: DEFEND THE REBEL TRANSPORT

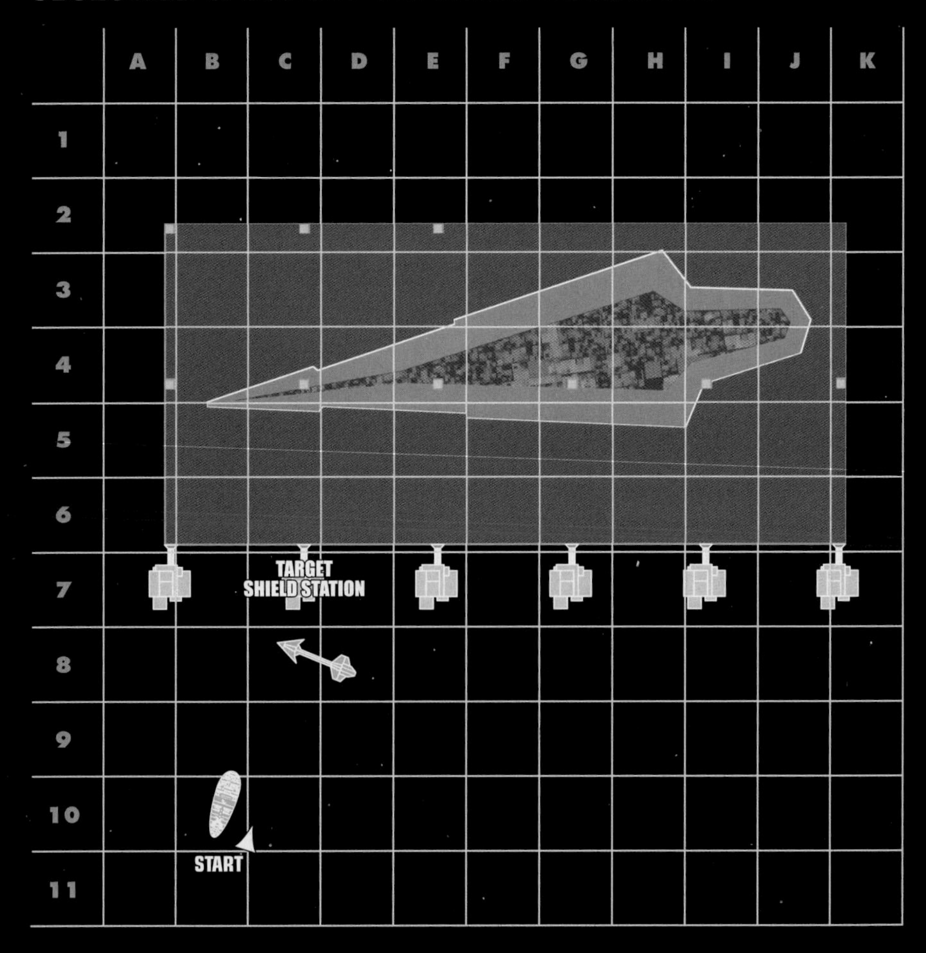

MAP KEY

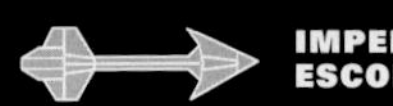
IMPERIAL ESCORT CARRIER

REBEL TRANSPORT

1 DEFEND THE REBEL TRANSPORT

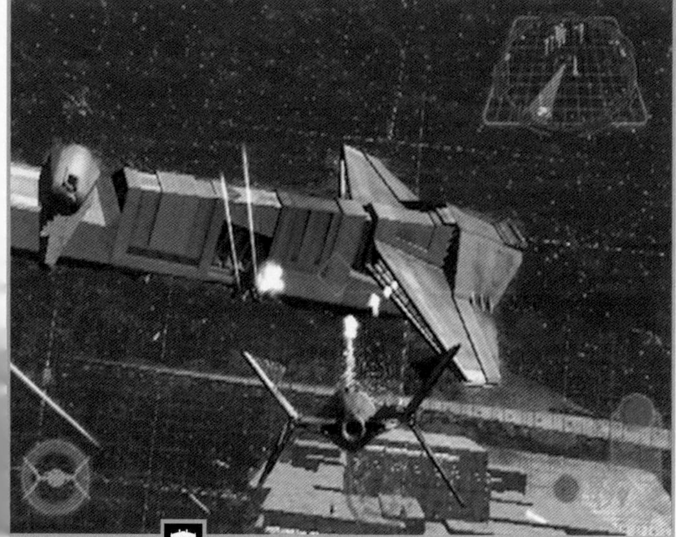

Your mission is to take down the Imperial ships that are attempting to destroy the booby-trapped transport. Start with the huge escort carrier by positioning your ship behind it and pumping it with proton torpedoes. Send your wingmen after the TIE fighters, then join them once the escort carrier is gone.

! THE TIE HUNTER

The TIE hunter is the Empire's answer to the X-wing. It's fast, durable and easy to maneuver. It even has X-wing-style S-foils that close when the pilot executes a speed boost. When the S-foils are closed, the ship is very fast and sleek, but it's unable to fire its weapons.

WEAPONS

The TIE hunter's advantage over the X-wing is in its two types of secondary weapons. You can fire proton torpedoes by tapping the B Button, or send out an ion cannon charge by holding the B Button then releasing the button after the reticle turns blue.

2 USE ION CANNONS TO DISABLE THE HANGAR DOORS

'he Rebel transport's collision with the shield station will cause a malfunction. As result, its hangar doors will open and close rapidly. To gain access to the shield enerator, you can freeze the shield station's doors in the open position by hitting hem with an ion cannon charge.

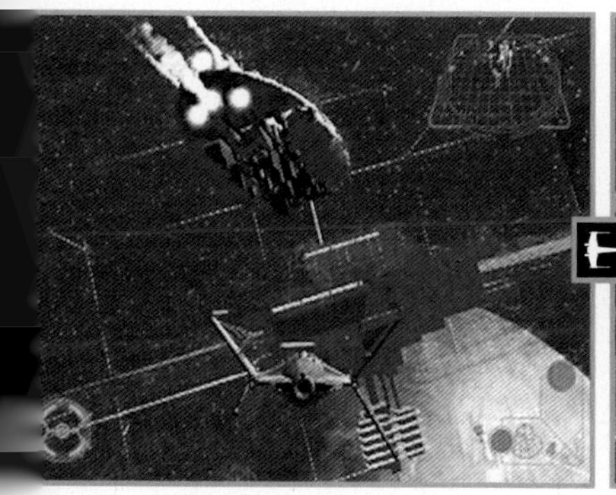

estroy the shield station's turrets on your approach, then charge your ion cannon and hit the doors when they're closed to make them freeze open for several seconds.

! AN A FOR EFFORT

Look for a Rebel symbol near the frigate and fly into the icon to switch to an A-wing. The new ship's homing concussion missiles will allow you to knock out Imperial ships with speed and accuracy. The last objective will be more of a challenge to execute with the A-wing, as the ship's shields are weaker than the TIE hunter's shields.

3 DESTROY THE SHIELD GENERATOR BEFORE IMPERIAL REINFORCEMENTS ARRIVE

The shield generator's weak point is the turbine in the middle of the hangar. Hit it with lasers and proton torpedoes. After you pass the turbine, fly to the hangar doors on the far side and use the TIE hunter's tight turning radius to pivot inside the hangar for another run at the turbine.

Stay inside the hangar to avoid exposure to enemy ships and lasers. Make an attack run on the turbine, then turn around when you reach the hangar doors on either side.

4 DESTROY ALL THREE CLOAKING DEVICES

DODGING THE SURFACE STRUCTURES

The only thing that's worse than a *Super*-class Star Destroyer is a *Super*-class Star Destroyer with cloaking capability. Your target has three cloaking devices. Follow the wedge indicator to the devices, stay low and hit them hard with everything you've got.

Look for red girder-based structures that look like buildings under construction and fly between the floors. While you're soaring through the structures, use your speed boost to save time and to fold your craft's S-foils so they don't graze the floors or ceilings.

TURRET TAKEDOWN

The *Super*-class Star Destroyer has plenty of turrets. Instruct your wingmen to go after the guns, and blast the turrets that are in your direct path. In the interest of your Shot Accuracy rating, be conservative with your blasts while targeting turrets.

DESTROY THE DEVICES

There are three cloaking devices aboard the ship, and your craft is equipped with 12 proton torpedoes. When you approach a cloaking device, hit it with four proton torpedoes, then finish it off with laser fire.

ENDOR CAMPAIGN

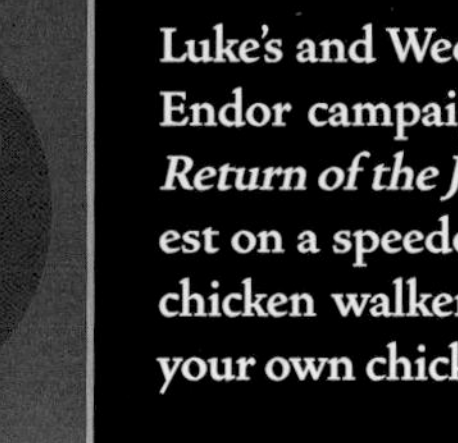

Luke's and Wedge's campaigns converge on Endor. The Endor campaign comprises two missions that follow *Return of the Jedi's* big finale. You'll fly through the forest on a speeder bike in the first mission, then destroy chicken walkers in the second mission with aid from your own chicken walker and the resourceful Ewoks.

ENDOR CAMPAIGN

SPEEDER BIKE PURSUIT

In one of *Return of the Jedi's* most memorable scenes, scout troopers piloting speeder bikes threaten to blow your cover on Endor. The biker scouts cannot survive a run through the forest path. You must mount a bike and knock the scouts off their bikes one by one.

OBJECTIVES

1. DESTROY ALL BIKER SCOUTS
2. DEFEAT THE LAST BIKER SCOUT

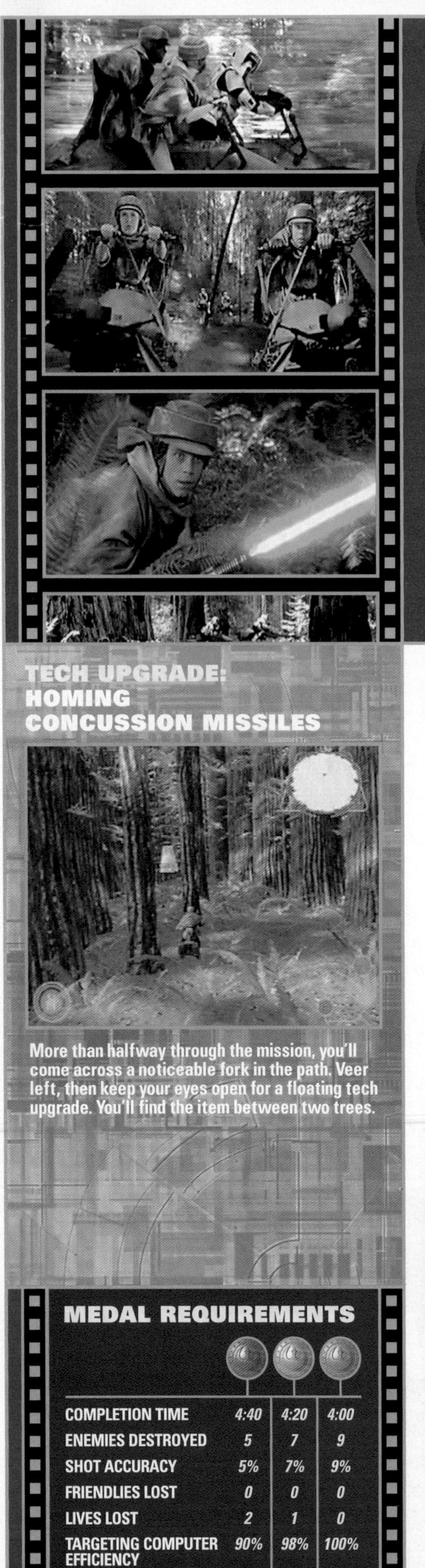

TECH UPGRADE: HOMING CONCUSSION MISSILES

More than halfway through the mission, you'll come across a noticeable fork in the path. Veer left, then keep your eyes open for a floating tech upgrade. You'll find the item between two trees.

MEDAL REQUIREMENTS

	Bronze	Silver	Gold
COMPLETION TIME	4:40	4:20	4:00
ENEMIES DESTROYED	5	7	9
SHOT ACCURACY	5%	7%	9%
FRIENDLIES LOST	0	0	0
LIVES LOST	2	1	0
TARGETING COMPUTER EFFICIENCY	90%	98%	100%

1 DESTROY ALL BIKER SCOUTS

The forest path is winding and packed with obstacles. You'll have to deal with scout troopers and avoid running into trees to survive the mission. Always keep an eye on what's ahead of you and determine early whether you will fly above, below, to the left or to the right of the forest debris. Even if you glance off a tree, you can still steer away from disaster. Use a speed boost in the rare moments when the path in front of you is clear. You can't run ahead of the biker scouts, but you can catch up to them.

BLAST BIKERS

Your speeder bike's blaster fires rapidly and with strong shots when it is fully charged, but its power will diminish if you hold the A Button for sustained firing. Let the auto aim line you up for your shots, and defeat the scouts ahead of you by using quick blaster bursts. You'll have a better chance o scoring accurate hits if you fire your weapon in clearings

SEND SCOUTS ON COLLISION COURSES

If a scout is next to you, the only way to knock him off his bike is to send him into the scenery. Either move very close to a tree to make your pursuer run into it, or ram into the scout while pressing the B Button to throw him off his course and have him turn wide into a tree.

GOING FOR GOLD

BEAT ALL BIKERS

You can beef up your Enemies Destroyed stat by dispatching biker scouts quickly. The faster you defeat them, the more of them you will encounter. Your Shot Accuracy stat will stay high as long as you fire when your enemies are in clear view and you hit them using short bursts.

2 DEFEAT THE LAST BIKER SCOUT

Vhen you reach the end of the ail, the final biker scout will close ı on you. You'll leap off your peeder in a cut scene, leaving you fight the scout on foot while he rcles you. Never fear—you have lightsaber on your side.

The biker scout is very fast. Study the radar display and wait for him to get close. When he's crossing into the shadowy area of the display that surrounds your character, face him and slash him with your lightsaber. If you hit the front of his bike, you'll win the battle.

ENDOR CAMPAIGN

TRIUMPH OF THE REBELLION

Han Solo and Chewbacca take the lead in a campaign-ending free-for-all battle against AT-STs and Imperial soldiers. Rebel forces are pinned outside the shield-generator bunker. Chewie must come to their rescue in a hijacked chicken walker.

OBJECTIVES

1. FIGHT YOUR WAY TO THE BUNKER BEFORE HAN AND LEIA ARE OVERWHELMED
2. FIGHT YOUR WAY TO THE BUNKER'S CONTROL ROOM
3. PLANT THE EXPLOSIVE CHARGES
4. FIGHT YOUR WAY OUT OF THE BUNKER BEFORE IT EXPLODES

TECH UPGRADE: HOMING CLUSTER MISSILES

Turn right into the first deep dead end and wander amongst the thick trees. You may not see the tech upgrade, but you'll hear a sound cue when you stumble upon it.

MEDAL REQUIREMENTS

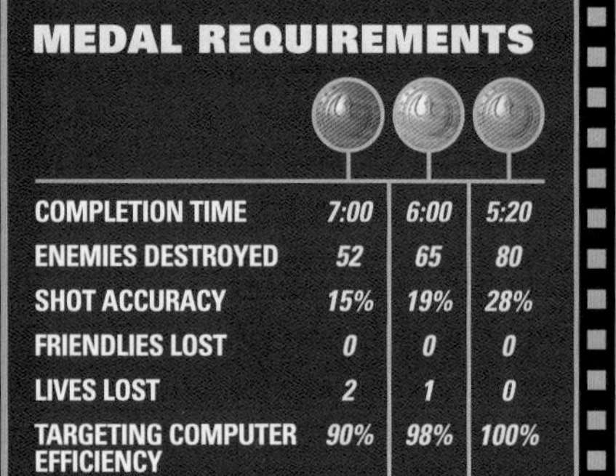

	Bronze	Silver	Gold
COMPLETION TIME	*7:00*	*6:00*	*5:20*
ENEMIES DESTROYED	*52*	*65*	*80*
SHOT ACCURACY	*15%*	*19%*	*28%*
FRIENDLIES LOST	*0*	*0*	*0*
LIVES LOST	*2*	*1*	*0*
TARGETING COMPUTER EFFICIENCY	*90%*	*98%*	*100%*

A B C D E F G H I J K L M

1 2 3 4 5 6 7 8 9 10 11 12 13

START

MAP KEY

 AT-ST

 E-WEB BLASTER

 LOG ROLL

 CATAPULT

LOG SWING

 TECH UPGRADE

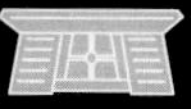

 BUNKER

1 FIGHT YOUR WAY TO THE BUNKER BEFORE HAN AND LEIA ARE OVERWHELMED

! THE EWOKS

The cuddly but fearless Ewoks are determined to save their forest by hook, crook or catapult. As you battle Imperials in your newly acquired AT-ST, you can instruct the Ewoks to fight the soldiers using three methods. Your timing will determine the effectiveness of the Ewoks' attacks.

LOG ROLL

The Ewoks have stacked logs in key locations. When you give them the word, they will let the logs roll downhill. You can roll out the logs by firing at them. Wait until you see an AT-ST near a woodpile, then release the lumber. Be careful. If you walk over the logs, you'll trip.

CATAPULTS

Several Ewok catapultists aim to protect their forest. You can use the spring-loaded weapons to weaken AT-STs and wipe out troopers. If you see any soldiers using E-Web blasters, hit them with your lasers to protect the catapult operators.

LOG SWING

The most spectacular Ewok attack requires the sharpest timing. Watch for an AT-ST to position itself between two suspended logs, then give the go-ahead for a smashing swing that will put the walking tank out of commission.

EXPLOSIVE SITUATION

The AT-ST is loaded with a self-replenishing supply of homing missiles. Use the missiles liberally to knock out the other AT-STs. By holding the B Button, painting multiple targets then releasing the button, you can hit several walkers at once. If you weaken the targets with catapult shots or laser blasts first, you can finish them off with one missile each.

GRIND AWAY AT GROUND TROOPS

By defeating large groups of scrambling stormtroopers, you'll increase your chances for survival and raise your Enemies Destroyed stat. If you don't single out the troopers, though, your Shot Accuracy statistic may suffer. Your first priority is to defeat the soldiers who are behind tripod guns.

2 FIGHT YOUR WAY TO THE BUNKER'S CONTROL ROOM

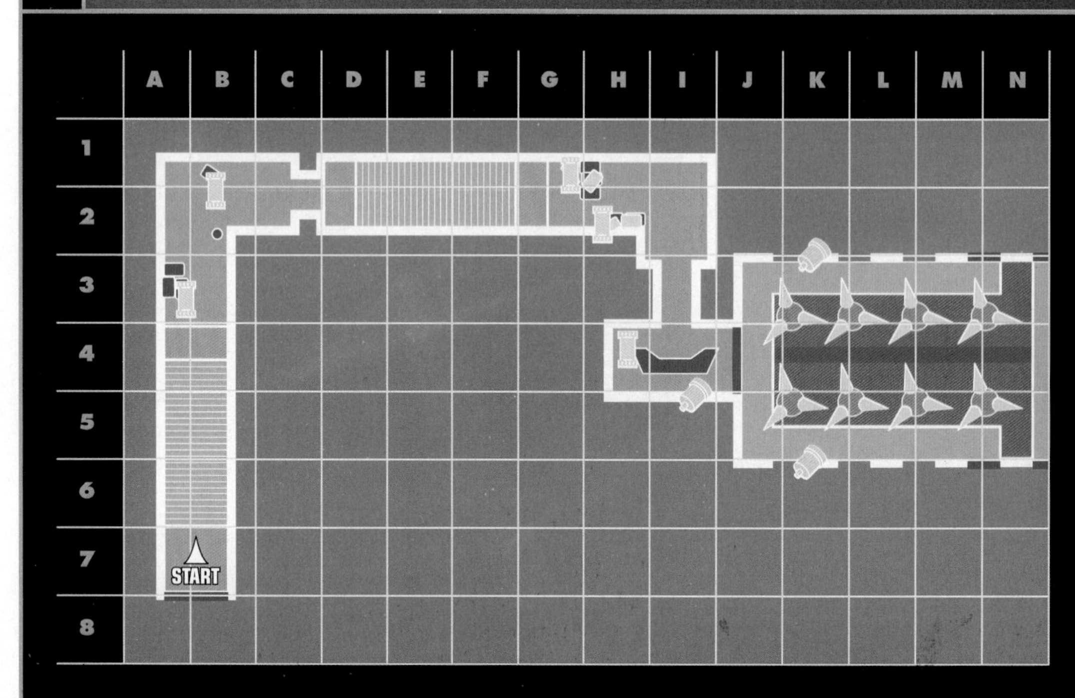

MAP KEY

EXPLOSIVE CHARGE PLACEMENT

BACTA TANKS

STOP, THEN DROP THE IMPERIALS

After Chewbacca's chicken-walker run through the forest, you'll guide Han in a heroic battle through the bunker. When you reach the bottom of the first set of stairs, stop for a moment behind the wall and wait for the Imperials to storm into the next room, then open fire on the entire unit at once.

USE CRATES FOR COVER

The enemies at the heart of the bunker are tough and quick. When you reach point H2, hide behind stacked crates and pick off the oncoming Imperials.

3 PLANT THE EXPLOSIVE CHARGES

BOOBY-TRAP THE CONTROL ROOM

When you reach the control room at I4, you'll find a place to set an explosive charge on the far side of the desk. Walk into the Rebel symbol, then tap the C Stick to plant a device. If you're gunning for a top medal, time is critical. Plant the charge quickly, then get ready to rejoin the battle.

CLEAR OUT THE TROOPERS FROM A SAFE POSITION

Before you enter the next room and experience a change in the camera positioning, stop near the open doorway for a few seconds and defeat all of the charging troops. When you reach the next area, you'll have fewer troopers to deal with.

DROP BOMBS AT DOORS AND CONTINUE THE FIGHT

The bunker's huge generator room has two walkways. You must plant a bomb along each walkway to complete the objective. Run down one path and take on troopers as you place the charge at the Rebel symbol, then backtrack and do the same on the other path.

4 FIGHT YOUR WAY OUT OF THE BUNKER BEFORE IT EXPLODES

Your last step is to escape the bunker. Retrace your steps while following the scanner's wedge indicator and run to the exit. Your escape will trigger a long piece of movie footage that shows the bunker exploding, the Death Star II's demise and the celebration on Endor.

The single-player campaigns end at the same place as *Return of the Jedi*, with Darth Vader gone and the Empire on the run. You can revisit campaign missions to relive the adventure and earn more medals. Medals will give you points to unlock single-player bonus missions.

THE END

BONUS MISSIONS

Some of the core campaign missions mirror scenes from the classic *Star Wars* films, but the real film tie-ins take place in the bonus missions. Return to Leia's Death Star rescue from *A New Hope*, escape from Hoth with Leia and Han, or run through Bespin's Cloud City. The missions' cut scenes are loaded with film clips.

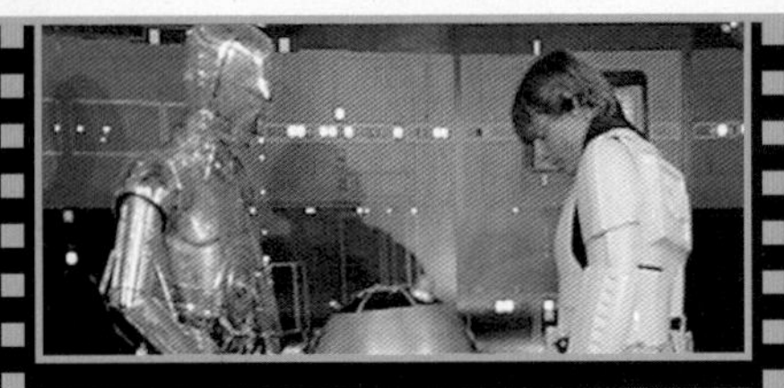

BONUS MISSIONS

DEATH STAR RESCUE

The game's earliest mission (chronologically speaking) recounts Luke, Han and Chewbacca's efforts to save Princess Leia from the Death Star. It includes extensive footage from the mission's companion scene in *A New Hope*.

OBJECTIVES

1. ACCESS THE SECURITY ELEVATOR
2. DEFEAT THE ENEMIES IN THE DETENTION CENTER
3. LOCATE PRINCESS LEIA
4. ESCAPE THE DETENTION AREA
5. FIND THE *MILLENNIUM FALCON* AND ESCAPE

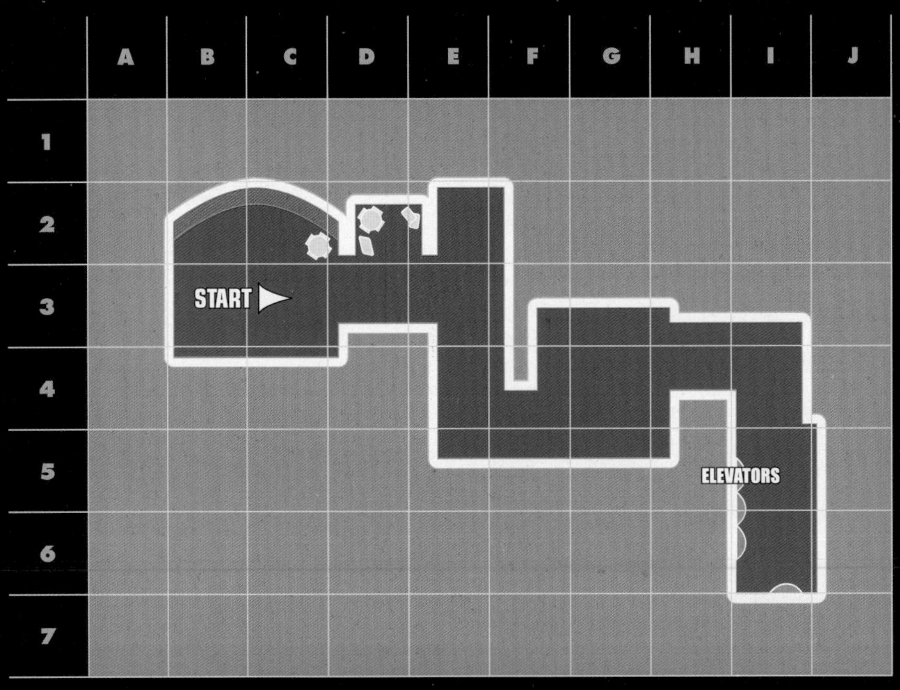

OBJECTIVES 2-3: DETENTION CENTER

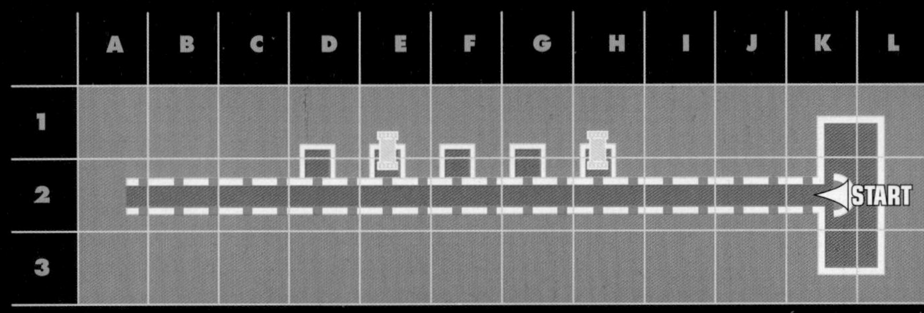

MAP KEY  BACTA TANK

MEDAL REQUIREMENTS

	Medal 1	Medal 2	Medal 3
COMPLETION TIME	4:20	3:40	3:20
ENEMIES DESTROYED	25	48	55
SHOT ACCURACY	19%	33%	45%
FRIENDLIES LOST	0	0	0
LIVES LOST	2	1	0
TARGETING COMPUTER EFFICIENCY	92%	98%	100%

1 ACCESS THE SECURITY ELEVATOR

You can reach the elevator at point 15 on the map without incident if you refrain from discharging your blaster on the way. Follow the scanner's wedge indicator to navigate the twisting halls, then enter the middle elevator. If you get into a firefight, the elevator's doors won't open until you defeat all of the stormtroopers in the area.

2 DEFEAT THE ENEMIES IN THE DETENTION CENTER

Once your cover is blown in the detention center, you'll have no option but to fight an onslaught of stormtroopers. Watch the green crosshairs to get an early signal of where they're coming from and to identify destructable surveillance cameras. By blasting the cameras, you'll reduce the number of enemies that flow into the room.

3 LOCATE PRINCESS LEIA

FIGHT YOUR WAY TO LEIA'S CELL

Troopers and guards will storm into the hall from the room at the end. Blast the enemies and floating probes and duck to avoid their return fire. Keep running and watch for a C-Stick icon that will appear when you are close to an unlockable door.

STOP AT THE CELL AND DIVE IN

Use the C Stick to open doors until you find Leia's cell. Your meeting with the princess will trigger a cut scene. Following the meeting, run back in the direction of the detention center's main desk. Before you reach the starting point, you'll reach a Rebel symbol at a closed vent. Fire at the vent to trigger another classic scene.

4 ESCAPE THE DETENTION AREA

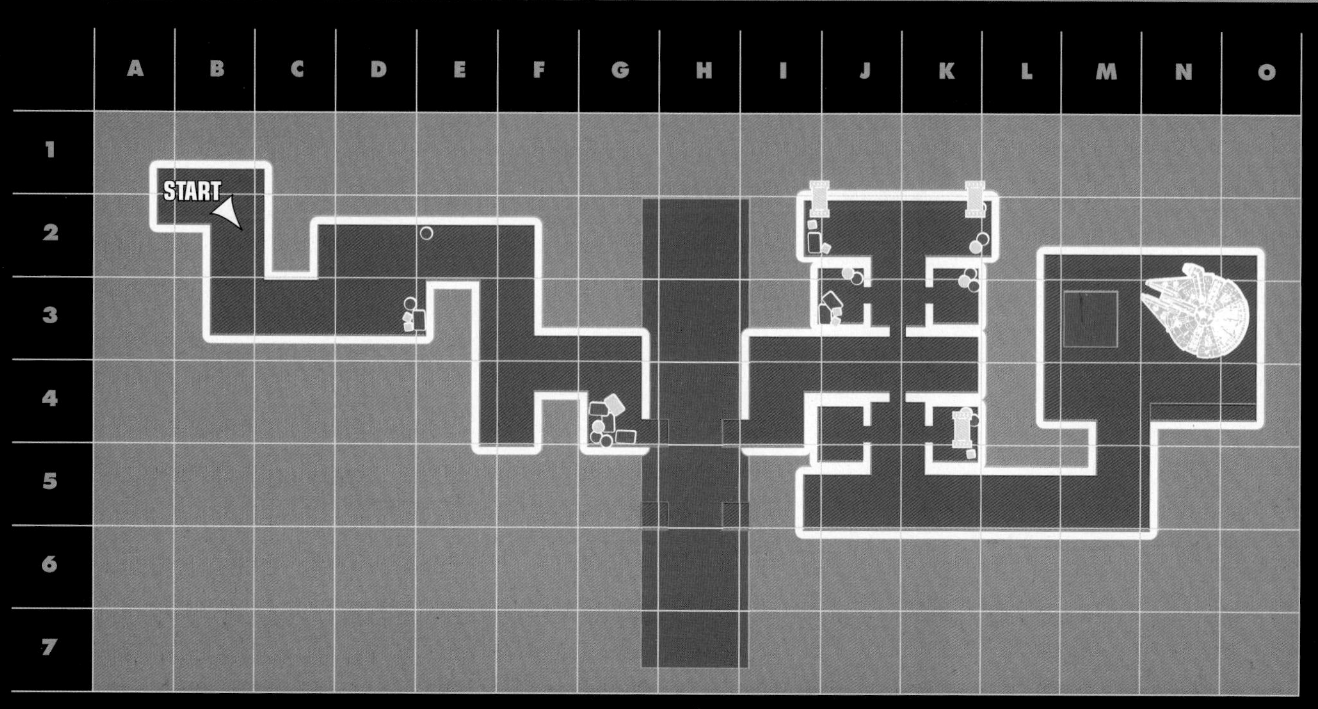

MAP KEY

BATTLE AND SWING

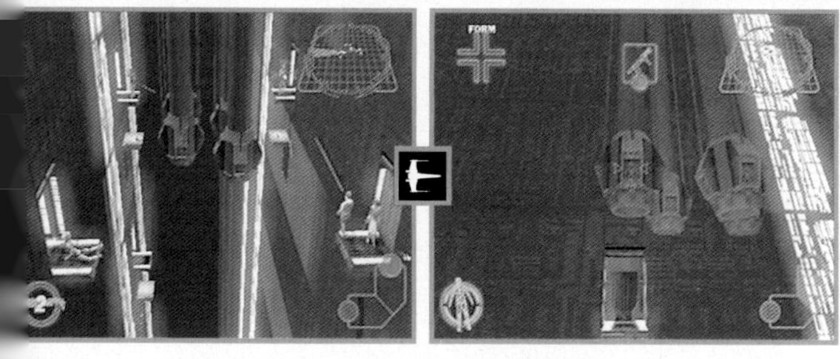

After Han creates a diversion, run to the ledge at point H4. Blast the stormtroopers that appear on the section's other ledges. After a C-Stick icon appears, tap the C Stick to switch to first-person perspective and use the Control Stick to aim for the latch point. Once you're locked on, press the A button to toss your cable. You'll fly over the wide gap with Leia in your arms.

CLEAR THE HALLS

Follow the wedge indicator to point N3 on the map, firing on targets as you acquire them. On your way there, check the rooms for rifles.

5 FIND THE *MILLENNIUM FALCON* AND ESCAPE

A pack of stormtroopers patrol the Death Star's vehicle bay. Keep moving, stay near the walls to avoid the crossfire and shoot on the run. After the enemies are gone, a Rebel symbol will appear, allowing you to board the *Millennium Falcon*.

Fire on the stormtrooper horde, then run to the *Millennium Falcon* after the Rebel symbol appears. You'll watch the *Falcon* make its escape in more film footage.

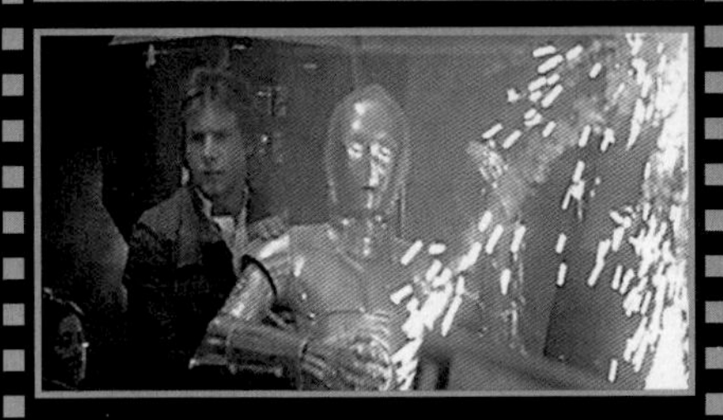

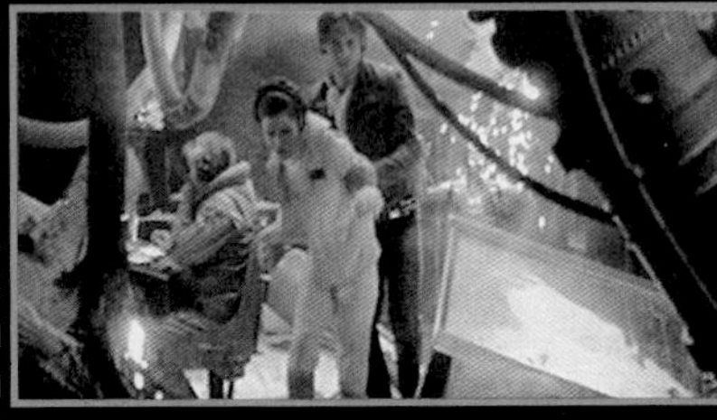

MEDAL REQUIREMENTS

COMPLETION TIME	*7:00*	*6:20*	*5:19*
ENEMIES DESTROYED	*49*	*56*	*69*
SHOT ACCURACY	*18%*	*25%*	*30%*
FRIENDLIES LOST	*0*	*0*	*0*
LIVES LOST	*2*	*1*	*0*
TARGETING COMPUTER EFFICIENCY	*85%*	*95%*	*100%*

BONUS MISSIONS

ESCAPE FROM HOTH

While Luke disables AT-ATs on Hoth's surface and protects transports from TIE bombers, Han and Leia escape from Echo Base in the bonus mission that branches off from Battlefield Hoth. Cut scenes cover key moments from *The Empire Strikes Back* and the mission ends with a dramatic flight in the *Millennium Falcon.*

OBJECTIVES

1. ESCORT PRINCESS LEIA TO HER COMMAND SHIP
2. REACH THE *MILLENNIUM FALCON*
3. PROTECT THE *MILLENNIUM FALCON*
4. DISABLE THE DAMAGED STAR DESTROYER AND ESCAPE

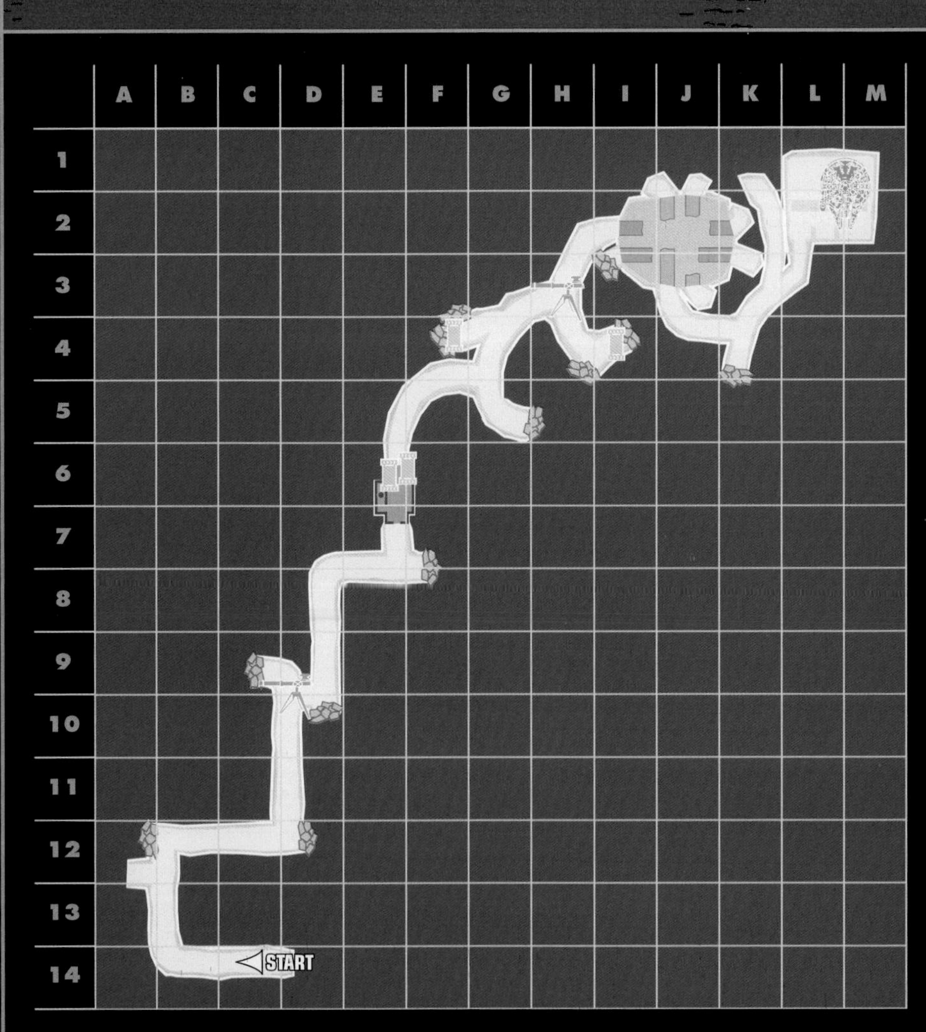

MAP KEY

E-WEB BLASTER

BACTA TANK

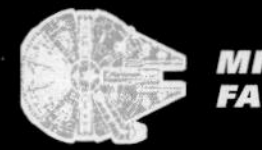
MILLENNIUM FALCON

1 ESCORT PRINCESS LEIA TO HER COMMAND SHIP

Although your objective is to take Leia to her ship, plans will change midmission and you will guide her to the *Millennium Falcon* instead. Run ahead of the princess, follow the wedge indicator and blast every snowtrooper in the path. When you reach the E-Web blaster at C10, take it over, then plow down a wave of approaching attackers.

GOING FOR GOLD

RUN AND GUN

You can cut down on your completion time by keeping to the path. Don't explore dead ends. By picking up rifles that downed troopers leave behind, you'll have rapid-firing capabilities that will help you clear the halls in a hurry.

2 REACH THE *MILLENNIUM FALCON*

TANKS FOR THE TAKING

Bacta tanks replenish lost health. Look for a pair of the shiny-green power-ups in the medical area (section E6 on the map). They'll take effect as soon as you collect them.

AMMO SUPPLY STOP

Rifle-equipped snowtroopers populate the dead end in section G5. If you can afford the time, veer off the main path, defeat the troopers and take their weapons.

FAST-FIRING SHOWDOWN

If you're stocked up on laser rifles when you reach point G3, you'll be able to defeat the oncoming surge of snowtroopers with ease and speed. You'll get a feel for the number of rapid-fire shots that it takes to down a trooper. Blast until the bad guy is gone, then stop firing and line yourself up with the next enemy.

RUN FOR YOUR LIFE

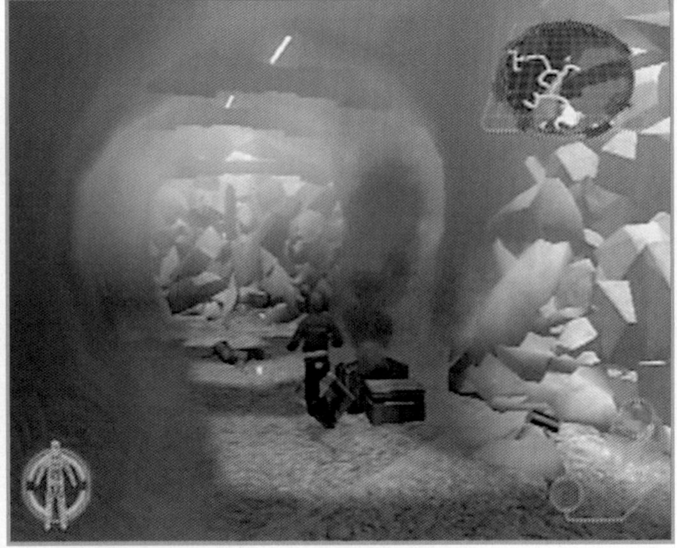

If you've got time and you need a health boost, pick up the bacta tanks at F4 and I4. Don't dillydally, though, and ignore the E-Web blaster at H3. You must reach the *Millennium Falcon* before the snowtroopers do, or you'll risk mission failure.

HOP OVER BRIDGE BREAKS

Chunks of rock and ice have pierced the the suspended bridges at I2, leaving wide gaps. Run to the first break, then jump to the right to access a parallel path. Jog along the new path until you reach another break, wait for the camera to pan, then hop across the gap to a path that leads to the area's exit. Princess Leia will follow you.

3 PROTECT THE *MILLENNIUM FALCON*

Troopers will flood the hangar as soon as you reach your ship. Fire at them from right to left and keep them from scurrying out of your cannon's range.

4 DISABLE THE DAMAGED STAR DESTROYER AND ESCAPE

DEAL WITH THE DOME

The only Star Destroyer that you must take on to fulfill the mission's final objective has already been damaged. Head straight for the first big ship that you see and fire on its remaining shield-generator dome. After your head-on run, turn around and bust the globe from behind.

FIRE DOWN BELOW

With both topside shield generators out of the way, you'll be able to concentrate on the bubble that protrudes from the Star Destroyer's belly. Hit it with rapid-fire laser blasts until it breaks.

! THE *MILLENNIUM FALCON*

The famously speedy and easily maneuverable *Millennium Falcon* is one of the galaxy's sweetest rides. It's a big target, so practice evasive moves when enemies are close. Use the ship's built-in concussion missiles to blast the big targets.

QUAD CANNON CONTROL

The *Falcon*'s quad cannon has rear-firing range. Use the C Stick to blast baddies in all directions. If you rely on the cannon too much, you'll risk a low Shot Accuracy rating. The weapon's main use should be picking off enemies that are directly behind your ship.

HIT IT WHERE IT COUNTS

The Star Destroyer will be vulnerable once its shields are down. The weak point is the shining blue bay window in the center of the bridge. Line up your shots with laser blasts, then add to your attack by unloading your remaining concussion missiles. If your ship is critically damaged, fly out of the fray for a moment to let its shields regenerate. Target TIEs if you want to increase your Enemies Destroyed tally.

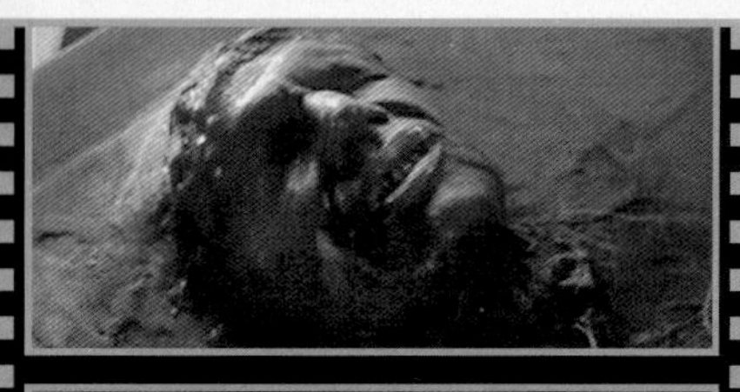

MEDAL REQUIREMENTS

COMPLETION TIME	*8:00*	*6:45*	*5:45*
ENEMIES DESTROYED	*38*	*45*	*48*
SHOT ACCURACY	*4%*	*6%*	*8%*
FRIENDLIES LOST	*0*	*0*	*0*
LIVES LOST	*2*	*1*	*0*
TARGETING COMPUTER EFFICIENCY	*90%*	*98%*	*100%*

BONUS MISSIONS

FLIGHT FROM BESPIN

With Han Solo frozen in carbonite and Boba Fett on the run, you can relive a key moment in *The Empire Strikes Back.* You're destined to let Han and Fett slip away, but you will catch up to Luke Skywalker later in the mission, fresh from his fight with Darth Vader.

OBJECTIVES

1. INTERCEPT BOBA FETT BEFORE HE CAN LEAVE THE CITY
2. LOCATE THE *MILLENNIUM FALCON*, AND ESCAPE
3. ELIMINATE THE TIE FIGHTER PATROLS
4. LOCATE AND RESCUE LUKE SKYWALKER
5. FLY TO THE ESCAPE POINT

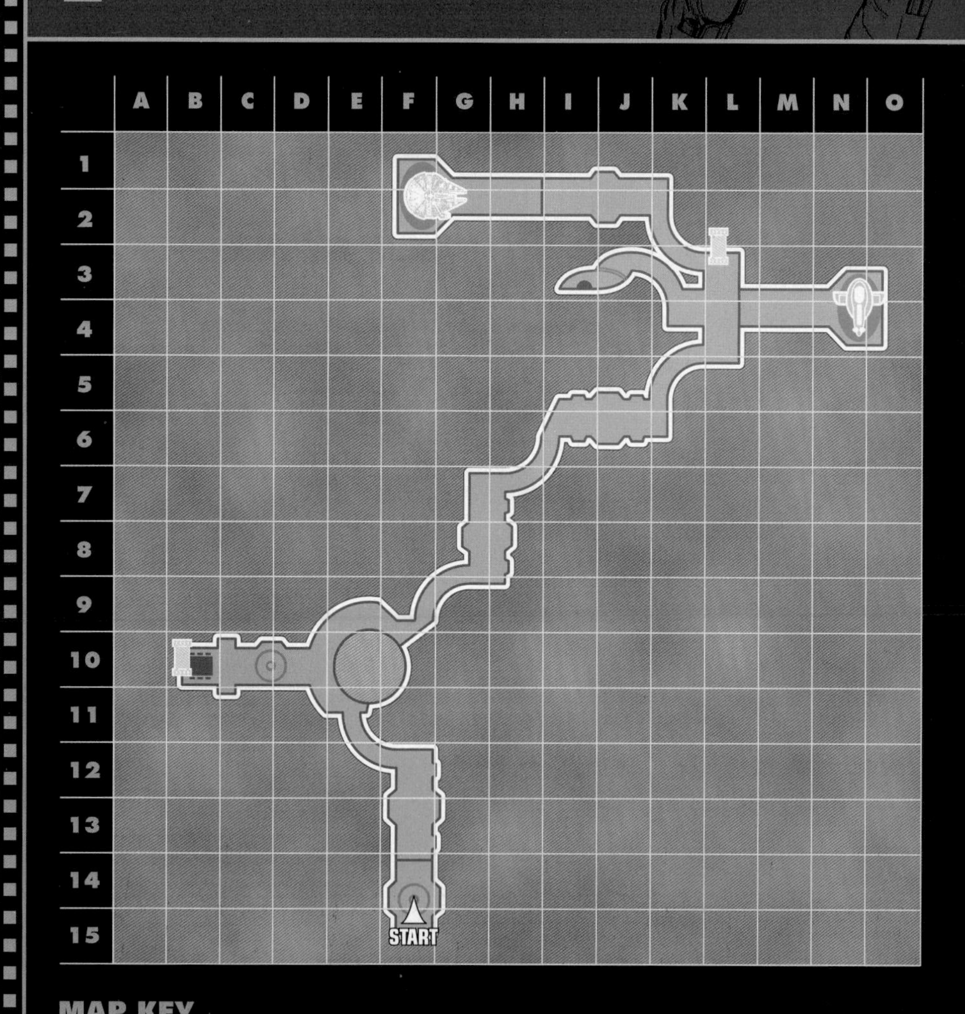

MAP KEY

 *SLAVE 1*

 *MILLENNIUM FALCON*

 BACTA TANK

1 INTERCEPT BOBA FETT BEFORE HE CAN LEAVE THE CITY

! ASSISTANCE FROM R2-D2

Princess Leia is the player-controlled character in the mission's opening section, but you'll get support from R2-D2, Chewbacca and Lando Calrissian. Artoo will provide assistance by tapping into the station's computer and unlocking doors.

When a door closes in front of you, a Rebel icon will appear. Walk into the icon, press the Comand Cross then step away. Artoo will interface with the computer and open the door.

IN PURSUIT OF THE BOUNTY HUNTER

The mission's initial objective is to chase Boba Fett. Have Artoo open the doors that Fett locks behind him, and follow the radar indicator to your goal. It's easy to get turned around at point D10 on the map. Follow the curved wall instead of taking an abrupt left turn. After you defeat the Imperial soldiers, collect the weapons they leave behind to gain temporary rapid-fire capability.

BOBA FETT BOLTS

Boba Fett willl volley laser blasts with you once you catch up to him on the platform, but he'll ultimately get away. You can relive scenes from the movies, but you can't change their effect on the story. After Fett leaves, turn around and take on a group of attacking troopers.

2 LOCATE THE *MILLENNIUM FALCON*, AND ESCAPE

Han is gone, but his ship remains. You'll find it at F2 on the map. From your meeting with Fett, backtrack to L4 and turn right. You'll reach a locked door and another Rebel symbol. Have Artoo open the door, then run to the *Millennium Falcon*.

3 ELIMINATE THE TIE FIGHTER PATROLS

The TIEs will come from all angles, and they'll be gunning for you. Don't spend time on fancy flying maneuvers in the battle's early stages. Pick a course and let the TIEs fly into your path. If you miss any of them, allow them to pass and continue to pick off the ships that are in your sights. You'll have to defeat all TIEs to satisfy the objective. When there are but a few enemies left, consult your radar display to single out the stragglers. If you're going for the gold medal, refrain from using the accuracy-damaging Quad cannon unless an enemy is right on your tail.

4 LOCATE AND RESCUE LUKE SKYWALKER

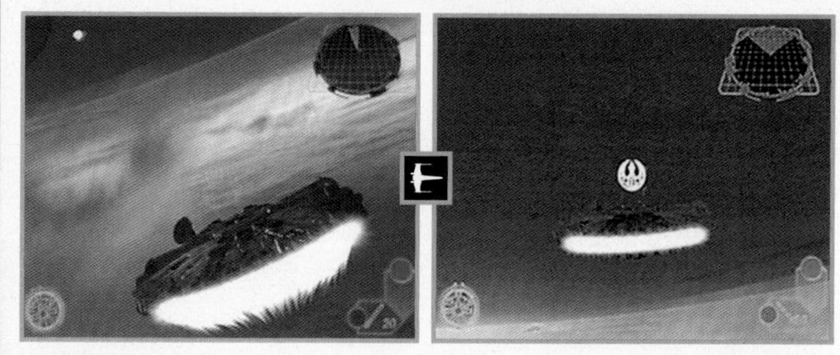

Once the first huge wave of TIEs is history, your mission objectives will point you to Luke's location. Follow the wedge indicator to a Rebel icon under the Cloud City's base. By flying into the icon, you'll trigger a cut scene that shows Lando taking Luke into the *Falcon*.

5 FLY TO THE ESCAPE POINT

The radar indicator will point to your escape route. Make a beeline for the area on the outskirts of the city. Don't bother battling the new TIE contingent unless you want to increase your Enemies Destroyed tally at the expense of Completion Time and Shot Accuracy.

BONUS MISSIONS

ATTACK ON THE EXECUTOR

A Rebel convoy endeavors to pass a group of Imperial capital ships led by *Super*-class Star Destroyer *Executor,* and they need your support. You'll start by disabling three Star Destroyers, then you'll target the *Executor's* bridge. Your A-wing isn't built to take heavy fire. Knock out enemy lasers before they target you.

MEDAL REQUIREMENTS

COMPLETION TIME	6:20	5:30	4:50
ENEMIES DESTROYED	33	46	55
SHOT ACCURACY	19%	24%	35%
FRIENDLIES LOST	2	1	0
LIVES LOST	2	1	0
TARGETING COMPUTER EFFICIENCY	88%	95%	100%

OBJECTIVES

1. DESTROY THE ION CANNONS THREATENING THE CALAMARI CRUISER
2. DESTROY THE EXECUTOR'S COMMAND DECK

1 DESTROY THE ION CANNONS THREATENING THE CALAMARI CRUISER

Although every Star Destroyer is equipped with eight ion cannons—four on each side—you need to target only the cannons that face the Rebel cruiser's path. Sweep over the first Star Destroyer and blast its four nearside ion cannons in one run, then zoom ahead to the next Imperial ship and demolish its four closest cannons. The Rebel cruiser will have exposure to both sides of the third Star Destroyer. Blast all eight of its cannons in two sweeps. If you have time after you hit the cannons, fire on nearby TIEs.

2 DESTROY THE EXECUTOR'S COMMAND DECK

The surface of the *Executor* is the size of a small city. Stay low, weave around the ship's structures and follow the radar indicator to the command deck. Hit the laser turrets with blaster fire on the way. When you reach the command deck, stay as low as you can and shower the central bay with lasers and missiles.

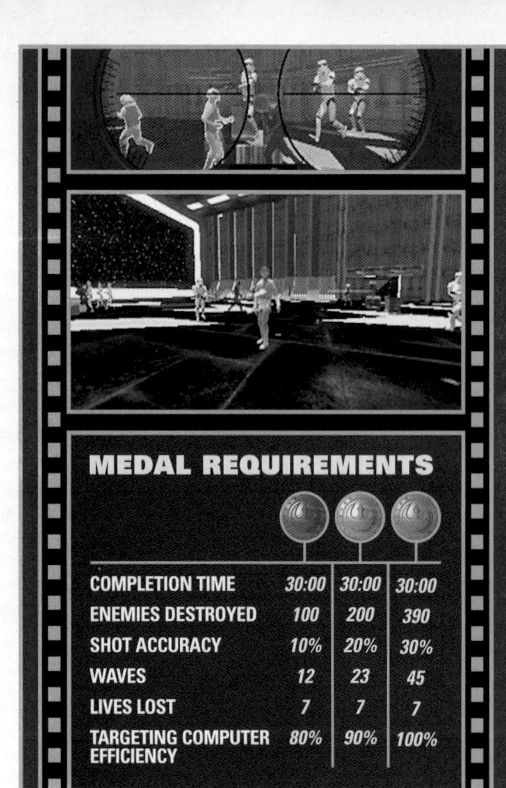

BONUS MISSIONS

REBEL ENDURANCE

The Rebel Endurance bonus mission is a no-holds-barred shootout against waves of enemies—soldiers of all stripes and Imperial probe droids. Your goal is to last as long as possible. Bear down on your targets and keep firing until they are history.

MEDAL REQUIREMENTS

COMPLETION TIME	30:00	30:00	30:00
ENEMIES DESTROYED	100	200	390
SHOT ACCURACY	10%	20%	30%
WAVES	12	23	45
LIVES LOST	7	7	7
TARGETING COMPUTER EFFICIENCY	80%	90%	100%

OBJECTIVE

1 DESTROY ALL IMPERIALS

1 DESTROY ALL IMPERIALS

STAY OUT OF THE CROSSFIRE

You'll be in a world of hurt if you run into the center of the mission area at the start and take enemy fire from all angles. Stay close to the wall until you've managed to blast at least half of the soldiers.

SHOOT SMART, GAIN WEAPONS

The enemies can withstand a lot of damage. Fire at each soldier until you are sure he is down for the count, then move on to the next target. Between waves of enemies, gather the discarded weapons from the floor and prepare for the next fight.

THE BEST OFFENSE IS A GOOD DEFENSE

The hardest part of the Rebel Endurance mission is staying alive. When new waves begin, large numbers of stormtroopers will surround you. Run from them and seek cover. By hiding behind stacks of crates that protect you on two sides, you can fire at enemies who have no chance of hurting you.

COOPERATIVE CAMPAIGN

You don't have to fight the Empire alone. Rebel Strike gives player pairs the chance to join forces for the Rebellion in 13 cooperative missions—it's a vehicle-based blaster-thon loaded with Imperial targets. You'll be glad that you have a partner when you see what challenges lie ahead.

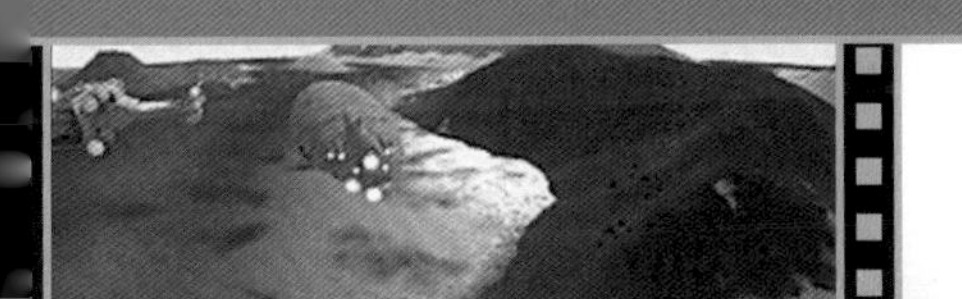

COOPERATIVE CAMPAIGN
ROGUE REBORN

Star Wars Rogue Squadron III: Rebel Strike contains Rogue Leader's 10 core missions and three of its bonus missions, all repurposed in a two-player cooperative campaign. The difficulty is higher than it was originally to make the campaign challenging for a team.

TEAM UP FOR THE REBEL ALLIANCE

DIVIDE AND CONQUER

Although two players function as a team, it often makes sense for the fliers to split up and approach the same objective from two angles or work on two different objectives at the same time. Communicate with your partner and try to stay on the same page. Time is always a key factor, and you'll save time as long as you both fight for a common goal.

PLAYER 1

The Razor Rendezvous mission exemplifies the payoff of having two players go separate ways. The player who selects the B-wing should concentrate on the Star Destroyer and leave the *Redemption* to the other player.

PLAYER 2

The X-wing is better equipped than the B-wing to take out TIEs. The player who selects the classic X-wing should concentrate on saving the *Redemption* from TIE attackers.

LOCK ON TO A SINGLE OBJECTIVE

Most missions have more enemies than they did in Rogue Leader, making it nearly impossible for a single pilot to complete enemy-quota objectives. In the Vengeance on Kothlis mission you have to protect a transport from tons of TIEs—a good example of an objective that two players must complete together.

FALL INTO A BACKUP POSITION

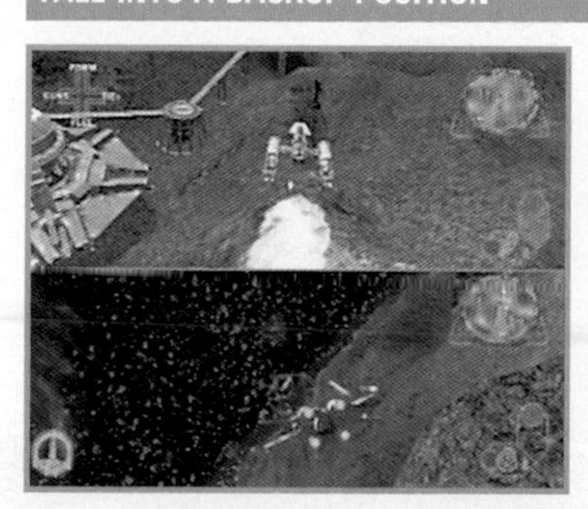

The Y-wing is perfect for the Prisons of Maw mission because of its ion cannons and its proton bombs. One player pilots a Y-wing, while the other player pilots an X-wing. While the Y-wing pilot completes mission objectives, the X-wing pilot mus provide support by destroying TI fighters.

EVERY STAT COUNTS

Medals are awarded for a team's performance in six categories. The Mission Complete screen shows the stats for the individual players, along with the combined stats, which determine medal qualifications. One player's performance may make up for the other player's lackluster efforts. The medal requirements are different from Rogue Leader's to reflect the mission's co-op adjustments.

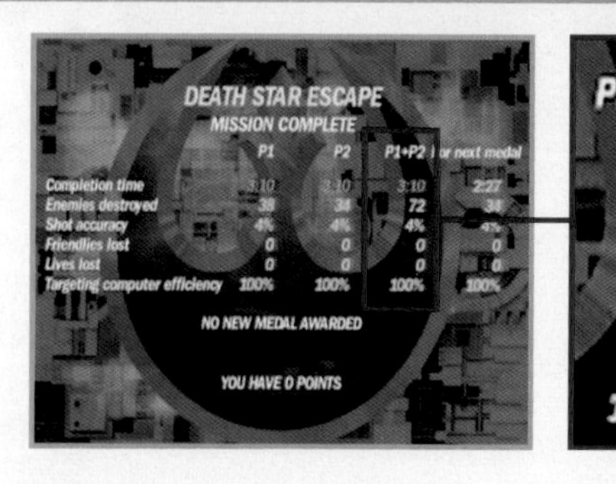

The game combines stats to dete mine the team's overall performance. The Completion Time and Friendlies Lost stats are the same for both players. The players' Enemies Destroyed and Lives Lost stats are added together. Shot Accuracy and Targeting Computer Efficiency are averaged between the two players' numbers.

COOPERATIVE CAMPAIGN FLOWCHART

If you've played through Rogue Leader, you'll be familiar with the overall mission flow of Rebel Strike's co-op missions. Missing are two of the original game's bonus missions (Triumph of the Empire and Revenge on Yavin). Three of the bonus missions remain, however, and the mission objectives are the same as before.

COOPERATIVE CAMPAIGN	PLAYABLE		
DEATH STAR ATTACK TECH UPGRADE: ADVANCED SHIELDS	X-WING Y-WING		
ISON CORRIDOR AMBUSH TECH UPGRADE: ADVANCED PROTON TORPEDOES	X-WING A-WING B-WING Y-WING	*MILLENNIUM FALCON* TIE ADVANCED NABOO STARFIGHTER JEDI STARFIGHTER	TIE FIGHTER *SLAVE I*
BATTLE OF HOTH TECH UPGRADE: ADVANCED LASERS	SPEEDER X-WING		
PRISONS OF THE MAW TECH UPGRADE: ADVANCED CLUSTER MISSILES	Y-WING X-WING		
RAZOR RENDEZVOUS TECH UPGRADE: ADVANCED PROTON BOMBS	B-WING A-WING X-WING Y-WING	*MILLENNIUM FALCON* TIE ADVANCED NABOO STARFIGHTER JEDI STARFIGHTER	TIE FIGHTER *SLAVE I*
VENGEANCE ON KOTHLIS TECH UPGRADE: HOMING PROTON TORPEDOES	X-WING A-WING SPEEDER Y-WING	B-WING *MILLENNIUM FALCON* TIE ADVANCED NABOO STARFIGHTER	JEDI STARFIGHTER TIE FIGHTER *SLAVE I*
IMPERIAL ACADEMY HEIST TECH UPGRADE: DAY: ADVANCED CONCUSSION MISSILES; NIGHT: SPREAD PROTON BOMBS	DAY: Y-WING NIGHT: SPEEDER IMPERIAL SHUTTLE		
RAID ON BESPIN TECH UPGRADE: HOMING CONCUSSION MISSILES	A-WING CLOUD CAR X-WING B-WING	Y-WING *MILLENNIUM FALCON* TIE ADVANCED NABOO STARFIGHTER	JEDI STARFIGHTER TIE FIGHTER *SLAVE I*
BATTLE OF ENDOR TECH UPGRADE: HOMING CLUSTER MISSILES	X-WING A-WING B-WING Y-WING	*MILLENNIUM FALCON* TIE ADVANCED NABOO STARFIGHTER JEDI STARFIGHTER	TIE FIGHTER *SLAVE I*
STRIKE AT THE CORE TECH UPGRADE: ADVANCED TARGETING COMPUTER	*MILLENNIUM FALCON* X-WING		

BONUS MISSION
UNLOCK WITH 15 POINTS
DEATH STAR ESCAPE
PLAYABLE
MILLENNIUM FALCON

BONUS MISSION
UNLOCK WITH 35 POINTS
THE ASTEROID FIELD
PLAYABLE
MILLENNIUM FALCON

BONUS MISSION
UNLOCK WITH 50 POINTS
ENDURANCE
PLAYABLE
X-WING
A-WING
B-WING
Y-WING
MILLENNIUM FALCON
TIE ADVANCED
NABOO STARFIGHTER
JEDI STARFIGHTER
TIE FIGHTER
SLAVE I

COOPERATIVE CAMPAIGN UNLOCKABLE STARFIGHTERS QUICK REFERENCE

The cooperative campaign follows the same ship-unlocking flow as Rogue Leader for the regular Rebel Alliance ships, though some ships are playable early to accommodate the second player. The campaign presents new ways to unlock most of the other ships. The Jedi starfighter, a ship from the era of the current *Star Wars* film trilogy, did not appear in Rogue Leader.

A-WING: Complete Ison Corridor Ambush.
Y-WING: Complete Prisons of the Maw.
B-WING: Complete Razor Renezvous.
TIE FIGHTER: Steal a TIE fighter during the daytime and nighttime in Imperial Academy Heist.
MILLENNIUM FALCON: Complete all standard cooperative missions.
TIE ADVANCED: Earn bronze on all standard cooperative missions.
NABOO STARFIGHTER: Earn silver on all standard cooperative missions.
JEDI STARFIGHTER: Earn gold on all cooperative missions, including bonus missions.
SLAVE I: Earn platinum on all cooperative missions, including bonus missions.

COOPERATIVE CAMPAIGN

DEATH STAR ATTACK

Star Wars lore begins with the Death Star, the planet-destroying space station. Thanks to two droids and a princess, the Rebels have discovered its weakness. After you soften the station's defenses, you'll take a harrowing ride through the Death Star's ditch and fire a torpedo into its center.

OBJECTIVES

1. DESTROY ALL DEFLECTION TOWERS
2. DESTROY ALL TIE FIGHTERS
3. SHOOT PROTON TORPEDOES INTO THE EXHAUST PORT

OBJECTIVE 1: DEFLECTION TOWERS

START

OBJECTIVE 2: TIE FIGHTER SQUADRONS

START

MAP KEY

DEFLECTION TOWER

GUN TURRET

TECH UPGRADE

RECOMMENDED SHIP SELECTION

PLAYER 1: X-WING

For speed, mobility and power, nothing beats the X-wing. You'll need all three attributes to take down the Death Star.

PLAYER 2: X-WING

Two X-wings are better than one. Join your partner by selecting the versatile fighter. You'll need the craft's proton torpedoes to deliver the final blow to the Death Star.

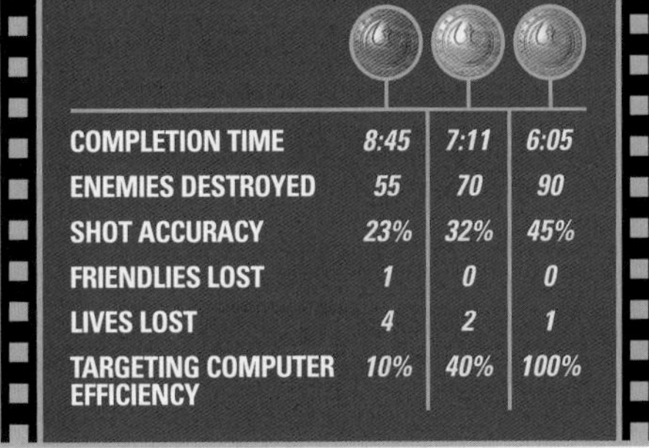

MEDAL REQUIREMENTS

COMPLETION TIME	8:45	7:11	6:05
ENEMIES DESTROYED	55	70	90
SHOT ACCURACY	23%	32%	45%
FRIENDLIES LOST	1	0	0
LIVES LOST	4	2	1
TARGETING COMPUTER EFFICIENCY	10%	40%	100%

TECH UPGRADE: ADVANCED SHIELDS

The tech upgrade that gives you advanced shields is yours for the taking in the mission's second section. As soon as the TIE-fighter battle begins, fly straight and low. You'll see the glowing power-up on the Death Star's surface. After you successfully complete the mission, the shields will take effect. A blue ring on the damage indicator represents the additional shields.

1 DESTROY ALL DEFLECTION TOWERS

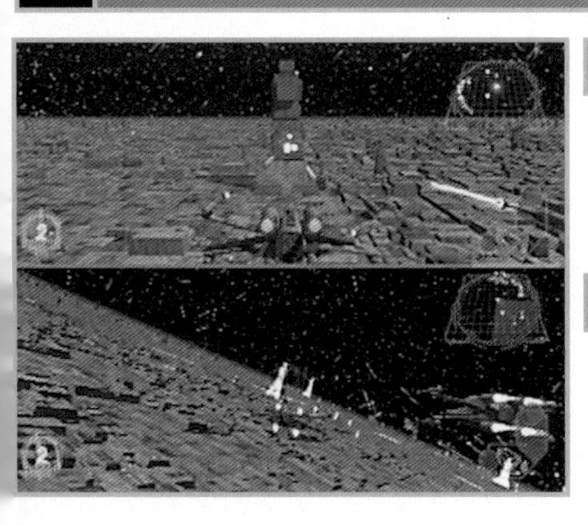

PLAYER 1

The towers are sturdier than their Rogue Leader counterparts. You may be tempted to run parallel with your partner for twice the power, but you'll save time by splitting up. Hit the tower at G14, then bank left and move up the map's right side.

PLAYER 2

Turn left immediately at the start of the mission and have your proton torpedoes at the ready to destroy the tower at B11, then continue to the towers on the left side of the map.

TOPPLE TOWERS WITH TORPEDOES

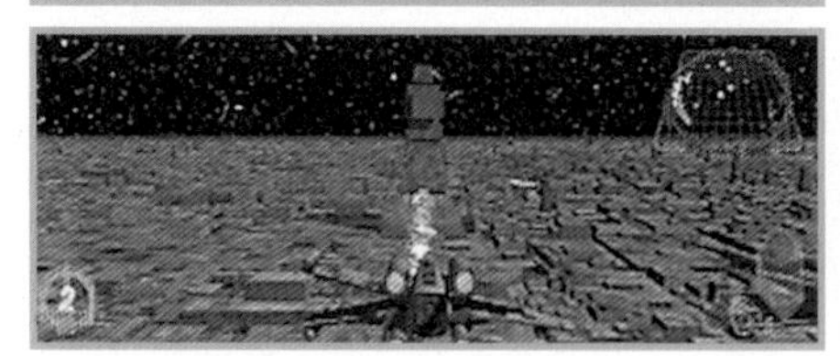

Each X-wing is equipped with six proton torpedoes. Since they aren't lock-on weapons, you'll do better by unloading the torpedoes on the stationary towers, rather than saving them for the nimble TIE fighters. You'll get a proton torpedo reload before you head for the Death Star's ditch.

2 DESTROY ALL TIE FIGHTERS

TIE FIGHTER FREE-FOR-ALL

After your run on the deflection towers, you'll fly into a cloud of TIE fighters. Split with your partner and take on the TIEs one formation at a time. When you attack a formation, destroy the wingmen first, then work your way in toward the leader. If you destroy the fighter in the middle of the pack, the rest of the ships will scatter.

GOING FOR GOLD

TURRET TAKEDOWN

While you're blasting deflection towers and tracking down TIE fighters, you can earn extra credit by targeting turrets. Use a single charged shot to hit each laser-firing turret. You'll get credit for a destroyed enemy and improve your shot accuracy at the same time.

3 SHOOT PROTON TORPEDOES INTO THE EXHAUST PORT

PLAYER 1

The Death Star's trench isn't wide enough for two X-wings flying side-by-side. Have Player 2 hang back a bit while you take the lead. Clear away the turrets that you can get to, but make speed your priority. Zip past obstacles and head for the port.

PLAYER 2

While Player 1 darts ahead of you, single out the remaining turrets and slide into a back-up position. TIE fighters will buzz the wing in the lead. Blast them before they can cause any damage.

FIRE IN THE HOLE

The exhaust port is at the end of the ditch. You'll see it as a green-glowing rectangle if you turn on your targeting computer. Fill it with proton torpedoes, then fly away. If Player 1 misses the port, mission success will be in Player 2's hands.

COOPERATIVE CAMPAIGN

ISON CORRIDOR AMBUSH

In a mission that takes place immediately after the Revenge of the Empire mission in the single-player campaign, Rebel transports shuttle from Yavin 4 to Hoth. The three-part battle pits you against squads of TIEs—turn on your targeting computer and go!

OBJECTIVES

1. DEFEND THE TRANSPORT AGAINST ANY REMAINING IMPERIAL FORCES
2. AT LEAST ONE TRANSPORT MUST SURVIVE
3. THE FRIGATE *REDEMPTION* MUST SURVIVE

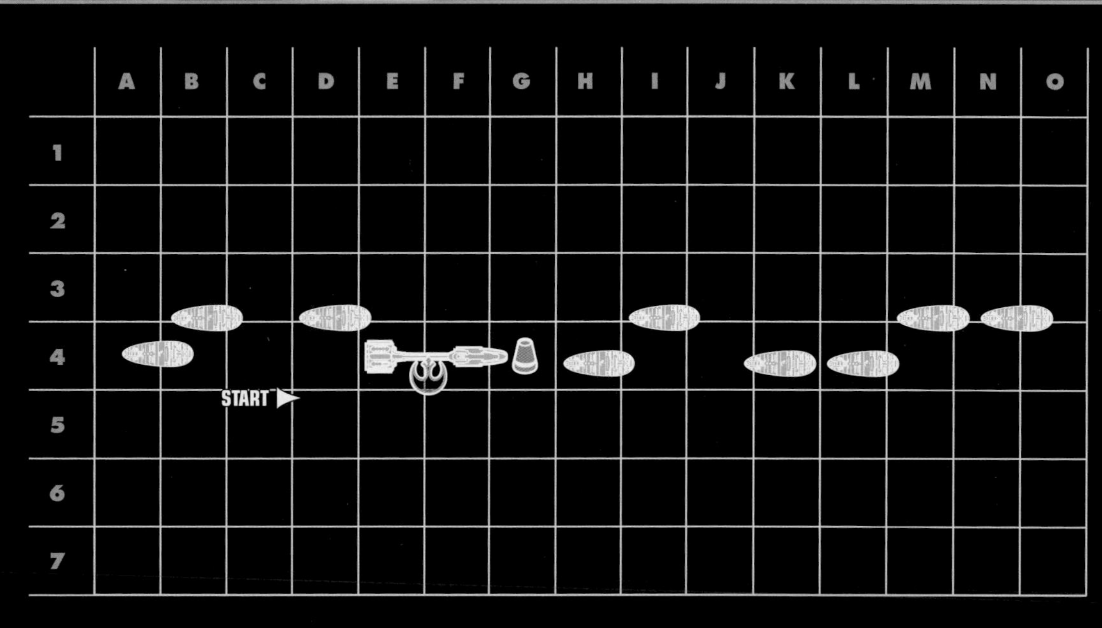

RECOMMENDED SHIP SELECTION

PLAYER 1: X-WING

PLAYER 2: X-WING

Start with your old standby, the X-wing, and pick off TIEs with your superior blasters as the Imperials close in on the Rebel fleet. You can switch to a faster A-wing midmission.

MAP KEY

 REBEL TRANSPORT

 FRIGATE *REDEMPTION*

 SHIP CHANGE: A-WING

 TECH UPGRADE

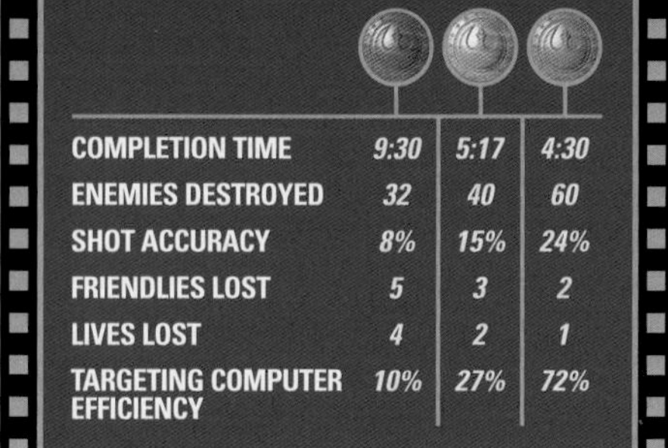

MEDAL REQUIREMENTS

	Medal 1	Medal 2	Medal 3
COMPLETION TIME	*9:30*	*5:17*	*4:30*
ENEMIES DESTROYED	*32*	*40*	*60*
SHOT ACCURACY	*8%*	*15%*	*24%*
FRIENDLIES LOST	*5*	*3*	*2*
LIVES LOST	*4*	*2*	*1*
TARGETING COMPUTER EFFICIENCY	*10%*	*27%*	*72%*

TECH UPGRADE: ADVANCED PROTON TORPEDOES

If you want more proton power, you'll have to exhibit expert flying maneuvers and wing your way through a chunk of debris. From your starting position, dive and look for a piece of space junk that has a wide rectangular opening. Fly through the hole and pick up the proton-torpedo upgrade as you make your way out the other side.

1 DEFEND THE TRANSPORT AGAINST ANY REMAINING IMPERIAL FORCES

PLAYER 1 DEFEND THE REAR FLANK

It's best to divide and conquer in the Ison Corridor Ambush. While Player 2 heads to the front of the pack, wait for stray TIEs to burn through the Rebel defenses and destroy the TIEs before they damage the rear transports.

PLAYER 2 PROTECT THE FRONT

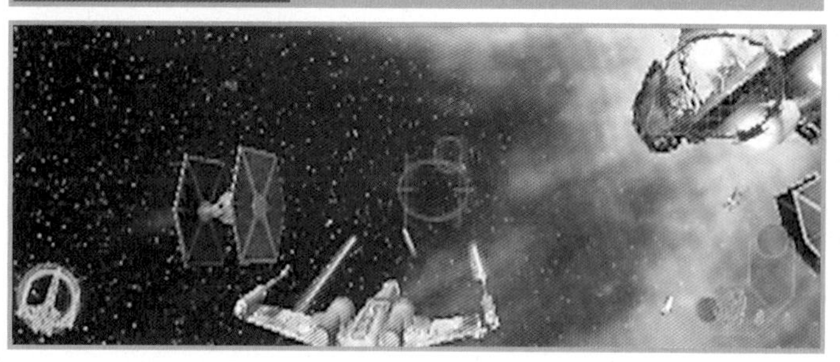

Let Player 1 stay back and attack the TIEs that swarm the transports while you take on the oncoming forces. After several TIEs slip past you, rejoin Player 1 at the transports.

2 AT LEAST ONE TRANSPORT MUST SURVIVE

One of the challenges of protecting the Rebel transports is to defeat the TIEs that are close to them without running into the massive ships themselves. Luckily, friendly fire does not damage the transports. Weave around the ships and concentrate your fire on the TIEs that are executing attack runs rather than on the strays that are leaving.

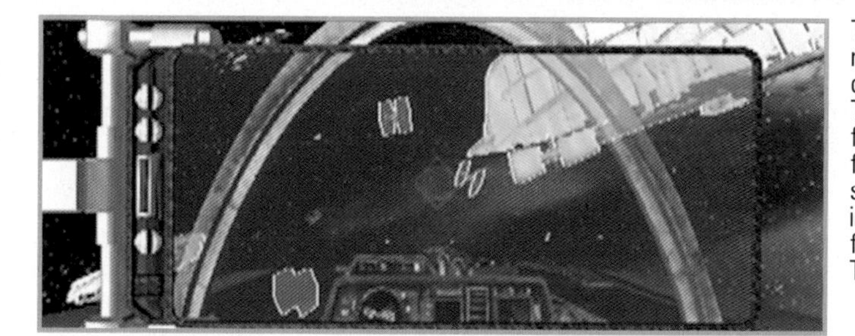

The targeting computer ranks the targets by priority. The yellow-shaded TIEs are on their way in for an attack on the freighters. The purple-shaded ones are not an immediate threat to the fleet. Attack the yellow TIEs first.

3 THE FRIGATE *REDEMPTION* MUST SURVIVE

In the third section of the mission, you'll fly into a nebula, where visibility is a major concern. You'll have no option but to rely on your targeting computer. If the TIEs manage to take down several transports, more attackers will concentrate on the *Redemption*. The frigate has stronger shields than the cargo ship, but it is still vulnerable.

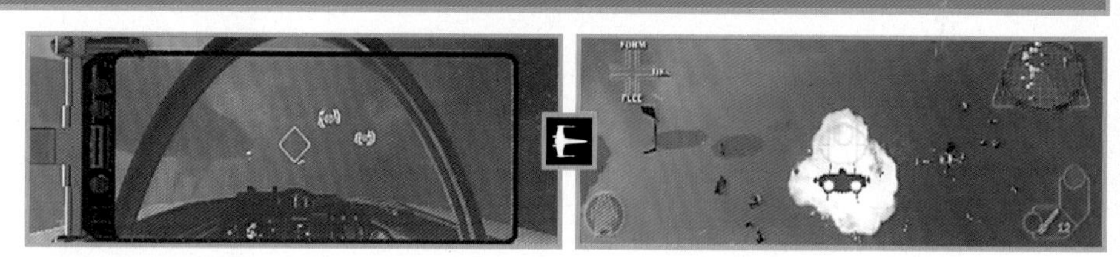

Your targeting computer is essential for spotting the TIE interceptors in the nebula. Knowing where you are in relation to the Rebel transports is also important. You can keep your targeting computer's efficiency high by using it to get behind the TIEs then switching it off when you're ready to attack.

GOING FOR GOLD

RETURN WITH TECH UPGRADES

Once you've collected key tech upgrades in advanced missions, return to the Ison Corridor Ambush mission for a gold-medal attempt. The advanced targeting computer will help you identify targets in the nebula without requiring you to hold the Y Button. Homing proton torpedoes will help you find TIEs in the X-wing without help from the targeting computer—and they'll increase your accuracy.

RETURN WITH MORE SPEED

Once you've honed your dogfighting skills, try using two A-wings. The ship's additional speed and homing concussion missiles will help you cut down on your Completion Time tally.

COOPERATIVE CAMPAIGN

BATTLE OF HOTH

Imperial forces have cast out a network of probe droids, and they have discovered the Rebel base on Hoth. You can't stop the Imperial invasion, but you can slow it down and guard Rebel transports as they take off for another planet-hopping journey.

OBJECTIVES

1. DEFEND THE REBEL FORCES AT OUTPOST BETA
2. SLOW THE ADVANCING IMPERIAL WALKERS
3. DEFEND THE FLEEING REBEL TRANSPORTS

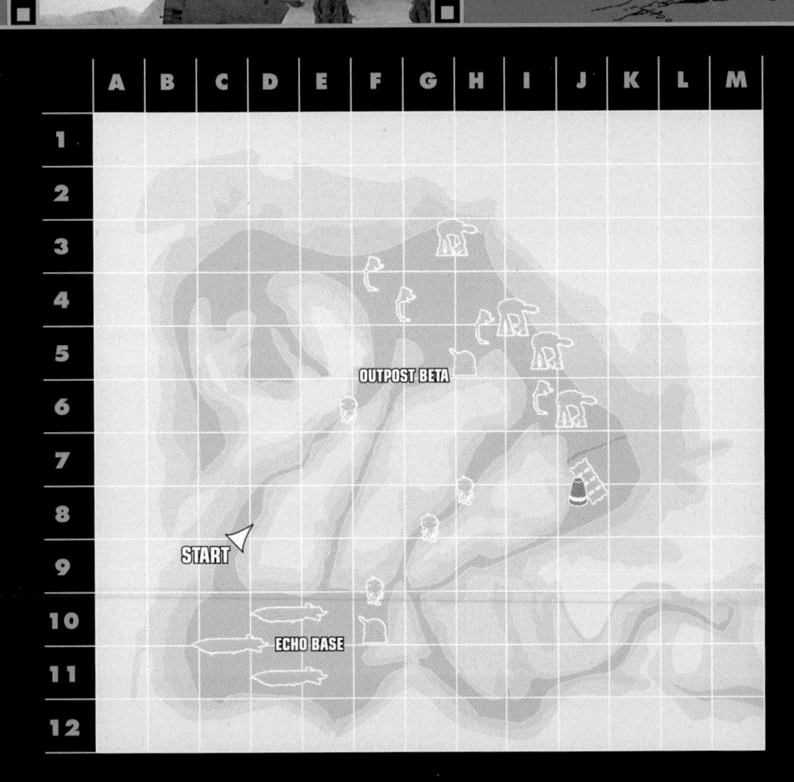

MAP KEY

 REBEL TRANSPORT

 ION CANNON

 SHIELD GENERATOR

 IMPERIAL PROBE DROIDS

AT-STS

 AT-AT

 TECH UPGRADE

RECOMMENDED SHIP SELECTION

PLAYER 1: SPEEDER

You'll start the mission in a snowspeeder, battling AT-STs and AT-ATs, then switch to an X-wing when the skies fill with TIEs.

PLAYER 2: SPEEDER

The snowspeeder is slightly faster than an X-wing and has the same handling. You can use its tow cable to tie up the Imperial walkers. The X-wing is a better dogfighting craft.

MEDAL REQUIREMENTS

	Bronze	Silver	Gold
COMPLETION TIME	9:55	7:10	5:00
ENEMIES DESTROYED	18	30	43
SHOT ACCURACY	14%	23%	30%
FRIENDLIES LOST	32	27	22
LIVES LOST	4	2	1
TARGETING COMPUTER EFFICIENCY	10%	55%	100%

TECH UPGRADE: ADVANCED BLASTERS

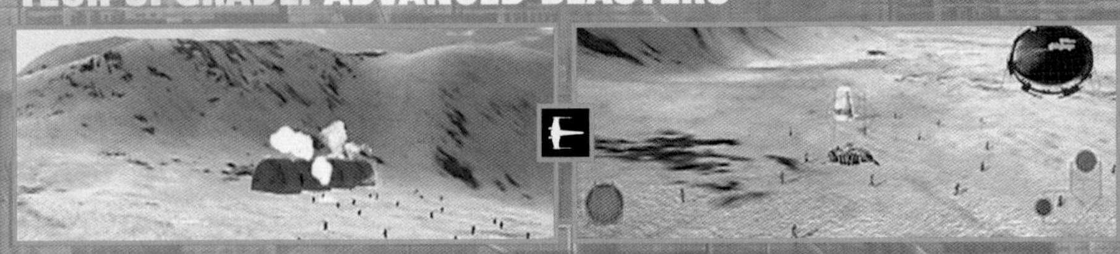

Between battles against AT-ATs and TIE fighters, you'll witness a cut scene that shows an AT-AT destroying a power generator. When play resumes, you'll be on your way to Echo Base. Turn around and head back to the leveled generator. You'll find a tech upgrade that will make the blasters on any Rebel craft more powerful once you've successfully completed the mission.

1 DEFEND THE REBEL FORCES AT OUTPOST BETA

PLAYER 1 — BLAST AT-STS IN THE OPEN FIELD

Following a quick ride through a canyon, you'll fly into the open battlefield. Bank left, fly to the far side of the battlefield at F3, turn around and hit the AT-STs from behind.

PLAYER 2 — PROTECT THE ION CANNON

While Player 1 flies left, you'll go right and take on the three lead AT-STs that pose an immediate threat to the ion cannon. Get behind your target, slow down and hit it with a blaster barrage. The ground troops under your command will want to help, but instruct them to flee to eliminate unnecessary casualties.

2 SLOW THE ADVANCING IMPERIAL WALKERS

PLAYER 1 — TIE UP THE WALKERS AND WATCH THEM TUMBLE

Rebels make due with what they have. You can stop AT-ATs with your speeder's tow cable. Head for the giant walker in the lead and press the B Button as you pass the machine. Your tow cable will snag onto one of the walker's legs. Circle the walker four times, staying close but avoiding a collision with the legs. After the walker trips and falls, move on to the next one in line.

PLAYER 2 — ELIMINATE THE AT-ST THREAT

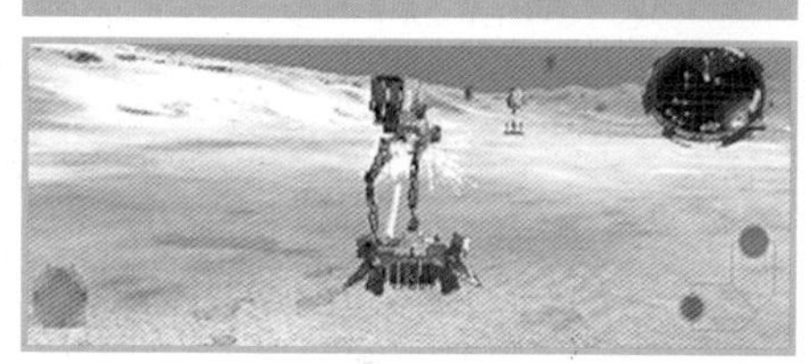

While your partner ropes AT-ATs, provide support on the field by taking out the smaller AT-STs and the Imperial shuttles that deliver more AT-STs. After you've eliminated the last cargo canister, tie up an AT-AT on your own.

3 DEFEND THE FLEEING REBEL TRANSPORTS

TIEs have descended on Echo Base. Look for the curved wings of the TIE bombers and attack the ships with a strong concerted effort. Once there are only a handful of bombers remaining, one of the players can target TIE fighters to increase your Enemies Destroyed rating.

GOING FOR GOLD

HOME ON THE BASE

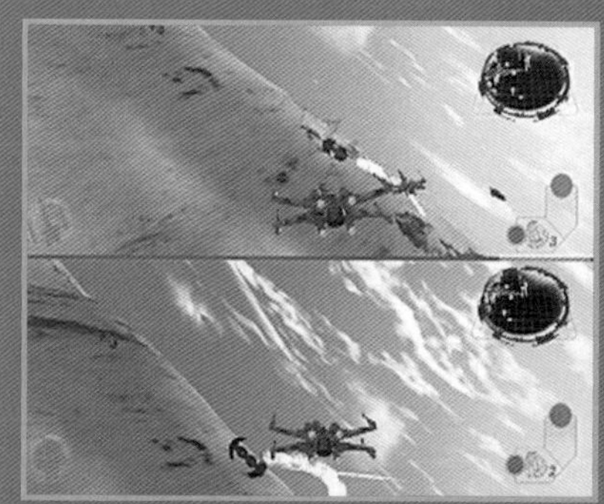

Your mission completion time and shot accuracy will suffer in the assault on Echo Base. Return to the Battle of Hoth mission after you've collected the homing proton torpedoes in the Vengeance on Kothlis mission. Then, when you switch to your X-wing, eliminate the bombers in style.

COOPERATIVE CAMPAIGN

PRISONS OF THE MAW

Not all of the Rebels have managed to run from the Empire. Your new mission takes you to a prison planetoid in a black hole cluster known as the Maw. After a run-in with asteroids, TIE fighters and an Imperial force field, the mission will really get tough.

OBJECTIVES

1. DISABLE THREE SHIELD PROJECTORS
2. DESTROY ALL OBJECTIVES MARKED BY THE PRISONERS
3. ESCORT THE TRAIN TO THE PLATFORM
4. ESCORT THE IMPERIAL LOADER OUT

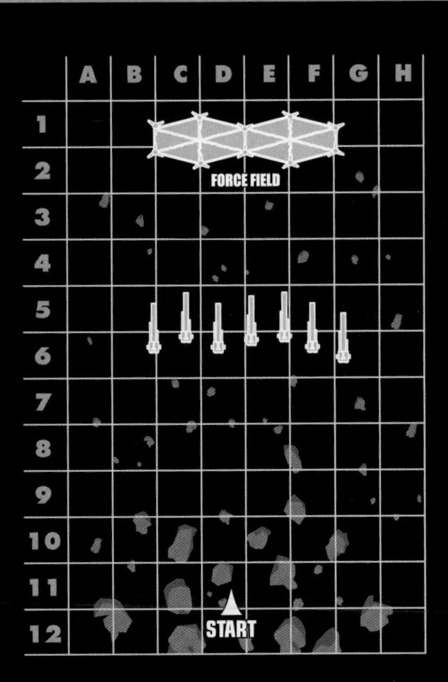

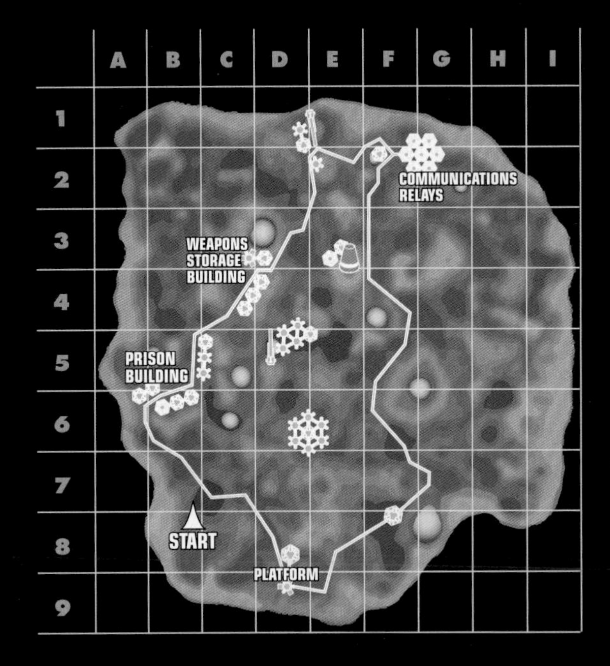

MAP KEY

 IMPERIAL TANKER

 TECH UPGRADE

RECOMMENDED SHIP SELECTION

PLAYER 1: Y-WING

The Y-wing was built for this mission. You'll use its ion cannon to disable the force field and its bombs to destroy surface targets at the prison.

PLAYER 2: X-WING

The more-capable dogfighter should pilot the X-wing. You'll protect your partner from TIEs in the asteroid field and take out surface targets with your blasters.

MEDAL REQUIREMENTS

COMPLETION TIME	12:15	10:45	9:20
ENEMIES DESTROYED	30	46	63
SHOT ACCURACY	24%	38%	47%
FRIENDLIES LOST	6	4	2
LIVES LOST	4	2	1
TARGETING COMPUTER EFFICIENCY	10%	38%	75%

TECH UPGRADE: ADVANCED CLUSTER MISSILES

Seek out an environmental dome in section E3 on the map. Drop bombs on the structure to blow it apart, then double back to look at the wreckage. You'll discover a tech upgrade that will equip the TIE Advanced and Naboo Starfighter (both bonus ships) with advanced cluster missiles.

1 DESTROY THREE SHIELD PROJECTORS

PLAYER 1

Fly straight from the start and make your way to the Imperial force field as quickly as you can, leaving the TIEs to your wingmen. Hit the force field's shield projectors with ion cannon blasts.

PLAYER 2

The X-wing is the Rebel Alliance's most capable dogfighter. Knock out TIEs on your way to the force field, then protect Player 1 by continuing to blast the Imperials.

UNRAVEL THE TIES

When a TIE is on your tail, you'll have to pull some evasive maneuvers to shake it off. Dive or bank abruptly and change your speed. If your pursuer persists, head for an asteroid and break away from it at the last moment. The TIE will likely collide with the rock.

2 DESTROY ALL OBJECTIVES MARKED BY THE PRISONERS

GET THE GUARDS

When you reach the prison, you'll start by destroying guard towers that the prisoners will point out to you. Use the X-wing's blasters and the Y-wing's ion cannon and bombs to knock out the towers.

PLAYER 1

After you take on the guard towers, you'll move on to the heftier communications relays. The Y-wing's bombs are essential for the job. After you make a bombing sweep of the relays, let your bombs recharge, then turn around and have another go.

PLAYER 2

Your X-wing's blaster will barely nick the communications relays. Leave the big munitions work to your partner and go after the turrets surrounding the communications relays and the Imperial ships that buzz the area.

3 ESCORT THE TRAIN TO THE PLATFORM

Although your objective in the mission's third section is to escort the prisoners' train, the real work is in destroying more guard towers. Fly where the radar display points and take down the towers with the X-wing's blasters and the Y-wing's bombs.

4 ESCORT THE IMPERIAL LOADER OUT

The prisoners have hijacked an Imperial loader. Your final objective is to protect the loader as it slowly escapes the planetoid. Circle the ship and pick off TIE interceptors as they come in for attack runs.

GOING FOR GOLD

COME BACK POWERED UP

Advanced weapons increase your ships' power and accuracy. With the right arsenal, you can save time and score big in offensive categories. For a run at the gold medal, return to the Prisons of the Maw mission after you have advanced spread proton bombs and advanced homing proton torpedoes.

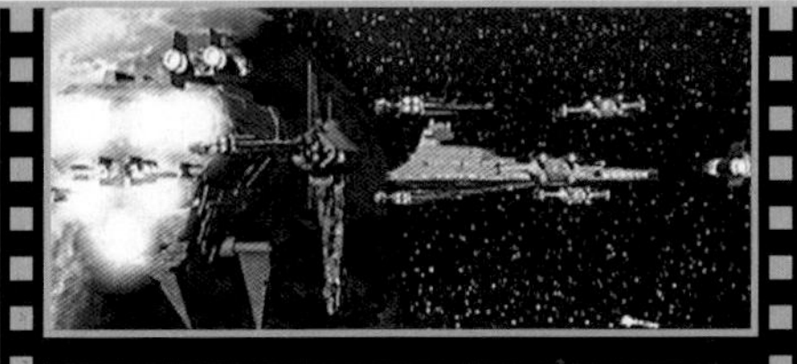

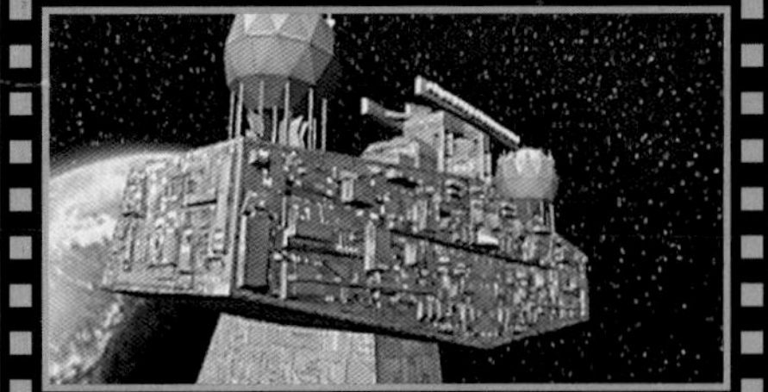

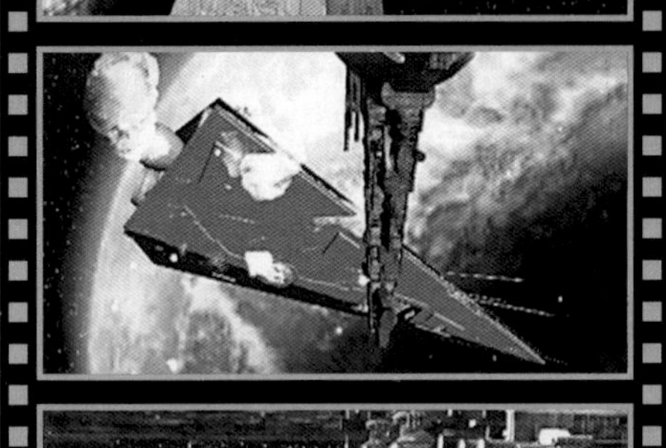

COOPERATIVE CAMPAIGN

RAZOR RENDEZVOUS

The Razor Rendezvous mission is perfect for co-op play, since it has simultaneous objectives. The frigate *Redemption* and a Rebel Blockade runner have had a run-in with a Star Destroyer. While one player protects the *Redemption*, the other one must take on the Imperial behemoth.

OBJECTIVES

1. PROTECT THE BLOCKADE RUNNER
2. PROTECT THE FRIGATE *REDEMPTION*
3. DESTROY THE IMPERIAL SHIELD GENERATORS
4. DESTROY THE IMPERIAL COMMAND DECK

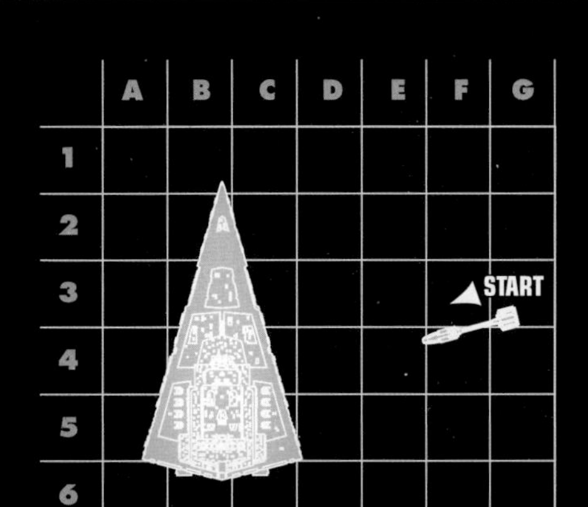

MAP KEY

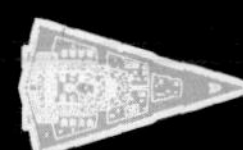
STAR DESTROYER

FRIGATE *REDEMPTION*

WEAK POINTS OF THE STAR DESTROYER

DEFLECTOR-SHIELD GENERATOR DOMES
CENTRAL COMMAND DECK
SHIELD GENERATOR
FRONT VIEW

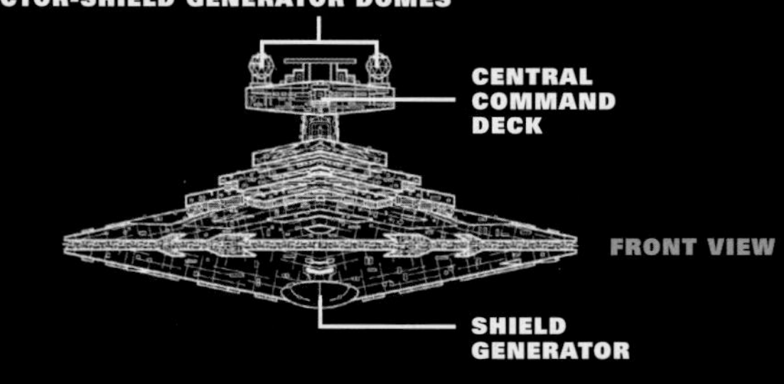

RECOMMENDED SHIP SELECTION

PLAYER 1: B-WING

The only way to make a dent in the Star Destroyer is to scramble its electronics with an ion cannon first—a job for the B-wing.

PLAYER 2: X-WING

The task of protecting the frigate requires advanced dogfighting skills. The X-wing has all of the right equipment to support a winning battle.

MEDAL REQUIREMENTS

	Bronze	Silver	Gold
COMPLETION TIME	4:30	3:00	1:15
ENEMIES DESTROYED	10	11	12
SHOT ACCURACY	15%	22%	25%
FRIENDLIES LOST	2	2	1
LIVES LOST	4	2	1
TARGETING COMPUTER EFFICIENCY	20%	40%	80%

TECH UPGRADE: ADVANCED PROTON BOMBS

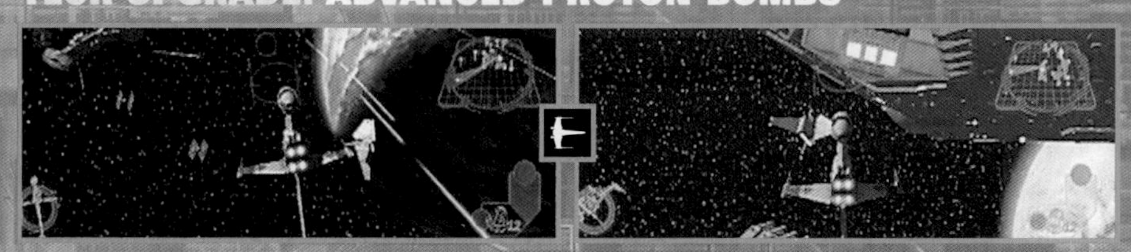

Use the X-wing (the faster ship of the pair) to track down and destroy an Imperial shuttle on the far side of the Star Destroyer at the beginning of the mission before the shuttle reaches the destroyer's docking bay. The shuttle will leave behind a tech upgrade that increases the power of the Y-wing's proton torpedoes.

1 PROTECT THE BLOCKADE RUNNER

The best way to save the Blockade Runner, *Razor*, is to defeat the Star Destroyer as quickly as possible. Let the *Razor* take care of itself in clashes with smaller targets, and concentrate your efforts on the big reward.

2 PROTECT THE FRIGATE *REDEMPTION*

PLAYER 2 LASER SURGERY

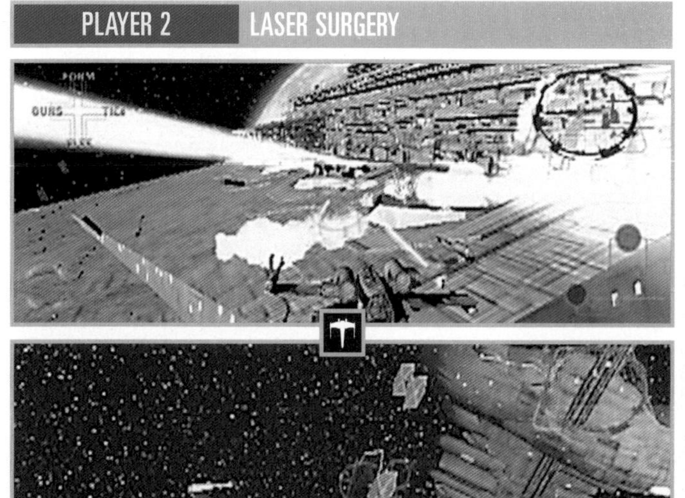

The Star Destroyer aims its laser turrets in the *Redemption*'s direction. The first step in saving the frigate is to unplug the turrets. Send your wingmen on a TIE-fighting mission while you concentrate on the lasers. After you've destroyed the turrets, set your course for the frigate and target the TIEs.

3 DESTROY THE IMPERIAL SHIELD GENERATORS

PLAYER 1 DESTROY THE DOMES

The key to the Star Destroyer's defenses is the shield generator, controlled by two domes atop the bridge. Head straight for the domes from the start and hit each one with multiple ion-cannon shots. While the domes are still glowing with blue electricity, finish them off by hitting them with lasers and proton torpedoes.

PLAYER 1 BATTLE OF THE BULGE

Once you've dealt with the domes, you can take on the shield generator, which protrudes from the belly of the Star Destroyer. Hit it with charged ion-cannon shots on your approach, then crush it with blaster fire and proton torpedoes.

4 DESTROY THE IMPERIAL COMMAND DECK

PLAYER 1 RIGHT BETWEEN THE EYES

The Star Destroyer's only weakness is its central command bay, exposed by the curved window in the upper deck. Make a run for the central command, hitting it with all of your firepower. Since you can lose one ship and still earn a gold medal, you could finish off the Star Destroyer by ramming the central command with your B-wing.

COOPERATIVE CAMPAIGN

VENGEANCE ON KOTHLIS

The Star Destroyer that you downed in the Razor Rendezvous mission is a rumpled wreck on Kothlis. You must race to the hull and hit it until it is beyond repair. You'll begin the mission by escorting a Rebel transport to the site.

OBJECTIVES

1. PROTECT THE TRANSPORT FROM THE TIES
2. DESTROY ALL AT-ATS
3. DEFEND THE COMMANDOS AS THEY RECAPTURE THE DATA
4. DESTROY ALL AT-PTS
5. BOMB A HOLE IN THE STAR DESTROYER FOR THE COMMANDOS

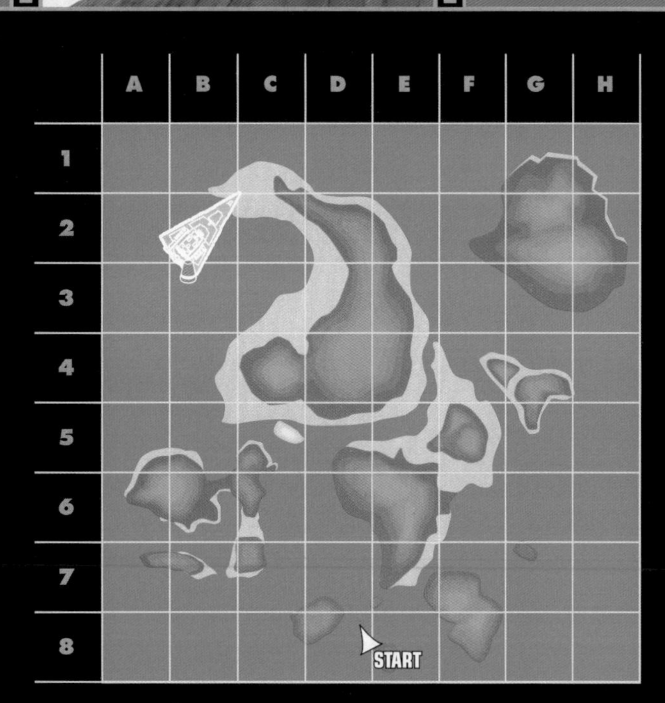

CRASH SITE CLOSE-UP

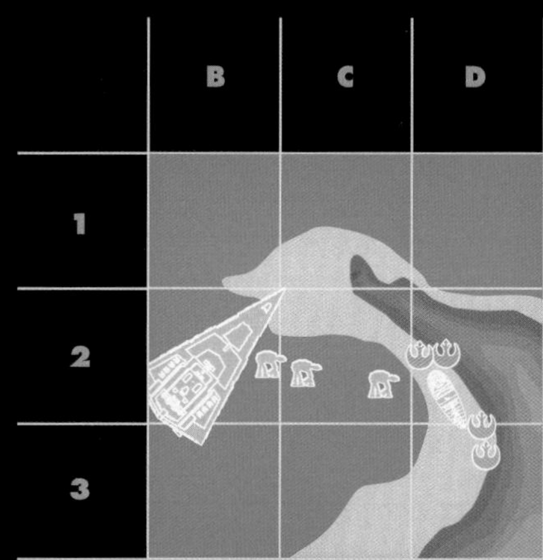

MAP KEY

 IMPERIAL STAR DESTROYER

 REBEL TRANSPORT

 AT-AT

 TECH UPGRADE

 SHIP CHANGE: Y-WING

 SHIP CHANGE: SPEEDER

RECOMMENDED SHIP SELECTION

PLAYER 1: A-WING
PLAYER 2: A-WING

The mission's first part has you fighting a large number of TIEs. The A-wing's homing concussion missiles will help you unravel the ships in a hurry.

MEDAL REQUIREMENTS

	Bronze	Silver	Gold
COMPLETION TIME	11:00	9:00	8:25
ENEMIES DESTROYED	75	100	135
SHOT ACCURACY	7%	14%	27%
FRIENDLIES LOST	4	3	2
LIVES LOST	4	2	1
TARGETING COMPUTER EFFICIENCY	12%	42%	85%

TECH UPGRADE: HOMING PROTON TORPEDOES

While the Rebel transport is landing, search for a small hole in the Star Destroyer's wrecked control deck. Blast turrets as you approach the deck, then fly through the hole. You'll collect the tech upgrade on your way out.

1 PROTECT THE TRANSPORT FROM THE TIES

STAY CLOSE TO HOME

The TIEs will concentrate on taking down the transport. Stay close to the Rebel ship and blast the enemies that are closing in on the craft for attack runs.

INTERCEPT THE INTERCEPTORS

TIE interceptors pose the biggest threat to your ship. Rank them as your top priority as you continue to thin out the enemy assault.

2 DESTROY ALL AT-ATS

A group of AT-ATs have survived the crash. When they become a problem, both players should switch to speeders. Communicate with your partner to ensure that you fly to different ship-change symbols. Attack the AT-ATs in the rear of the formation first to avoid laser fire from the others. Since the walkers are knee-deep in the water, you'll have little room to maneuver around the legs.

3 DEFEND THE COMMANDOS AS THEY RECAPTURE THE DATA

Your elimination of the AT-ATs will trigger another ship change. Switch to Y-wings and keep tabs on the Rebel commandos who make their way from the transport to the Star Destroyer. Use your Y-wing's bombs to blast the Imperial ground troops and hit the Star Destroyer's turrets with your lasers.

4 DESTROY ALL AT-PTS

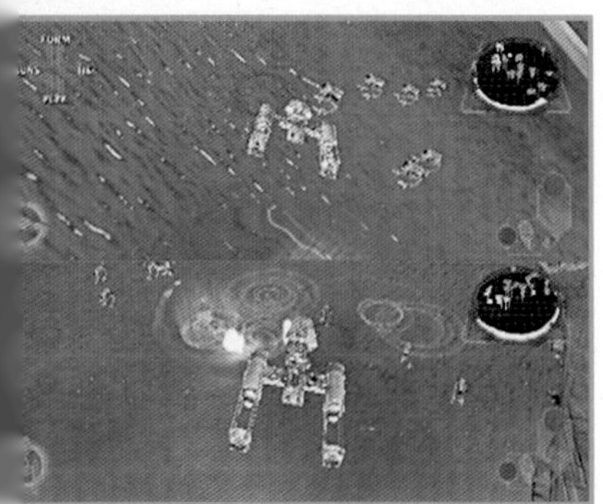

The AT-PTs that wade through the shallow water are a big threat to the commandos. If you temporarily run out of bombs, use lasers to attack the AT-PTs while you wait for your supply of explosive charges to replenish.

GOING FOR GOLD

ACCURACY ADVANTAGE

Your Shot Accuracy rating is a crucial component in your attempt to collect a gold medal. Return to the mission after you've collected advanced spread proton bombs to improve your accuracy in the Y-wing section. The wide spread of each bomb drop will make it more likely that you'll hit the targets. You'll also cut completion time along the way.

5 BOMB A HOLE IN THE STAR DESTROYER FOR THE COMMANDOS

A radio signal will prompt you to blast a hole into the Star Destroyer. By switching to your targeting computer for a moment, you'll find a large yellow-shaded rectangular target on the ship's hull. Rush to that spot and shower it with a handful of bombs. While one player is hitting the hull, the other player should continue to protect the commandos.

COOPERATIVE CAMPAIGN

IMPERIAL ACADEMY HEIST

A variable first objective makes Imperial Academy Heist a mission that you will want to check out in both the day and evening. You'll plow into the mission with sensor-disrupting Y-wings in the day and sneak in with speeders at night.

OBJECTIVES

1. DAY: DISABLE THE IMPERIAL SENSORS IN THE CANYONS
   NIGHT: EVADE THE IMPERIAL SENSORS IN THE CANYONS
2. STEAL AN IMPERIAL SHUTTLE
3. MEET AT THE RENDEZVOUS POINT

DAYTIME TECH UPGRADE: ADVANCED CONCUSSION MISSILES

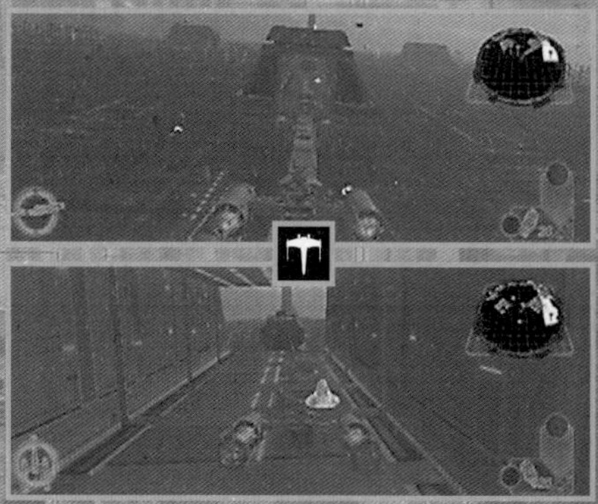

You'll find different tech upgrades during the mission's two times of day. Your daytime discovery will be advanced concussion missiles. Fly low through section E3 and line up for a straight approach into the area's hangar. You'll pick up the upgrade inside.

A B C D E F G H I

1 2 3 4 5 6 7 8

IMPERIAL ACADEMY

START

MAP KEY

- IMPERIAL SENSOR
- SHIP CHANGE: IMPERIAL SHUTTLE
- DAYTIME SHIP CHANGE: TIE FIGHTER
- NIGHTTIME SHIP CHANGE: TIE FIGHTER
- DAYTIME TECH UPGRADE
- NIGHTTIME TECH UPGRADE

MEDAL REQUIREMENTS

COMPLETION TIME	7:20	6:05	4:12
ENEMIES DESTROYED	15	29	55
SHOT ACCURACY	7%	25%	49%
FRIENDLIES LOST	0	0	0
LIVES LOST	4	2	1
TARGETING COMPUTER EFFICIENCY	15%	45%	100%

NIGHTTIME TECH UPGRADE: SPREAD PROTON BOMBS

The nighttime tech upgrade is in a hangar in section C3. Steer your speeder into the structure to collect an item that will turn each proton bomb into a cluster of explosives.

1 DAY: DISABLE THE IMPERIAL SENSORS IN THE CANYONS

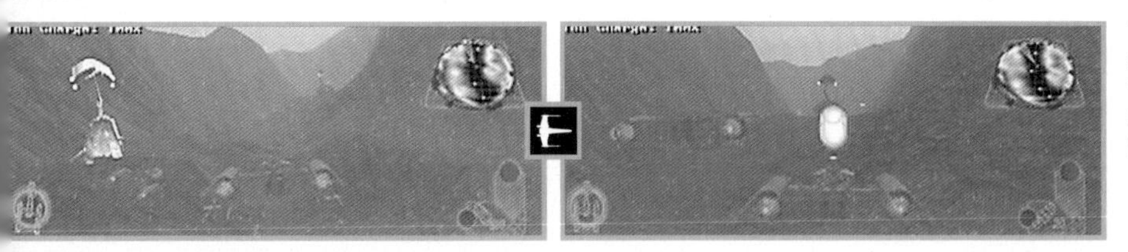

Team up for a double Y-wing attack on the canyon's sensors during the day. Fly low to avoid early detection and hit every sensor with a fully charged ion-cannon blast. If one pilot misses a sensor, the second pilot must be ready to disable the target.

1 NIGHT: EVADE THE IMPERIAL SENSORS IN THE CANYONS

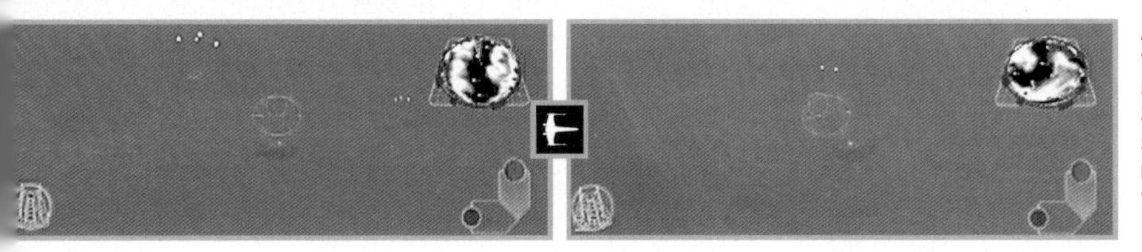

At night, both pilots will fly speeders, neither of which is equipped with ion cannons. Your only sensor-slipping solution is to avoid the detection devices. Stay low to the canyon floor and fly wide around the sensors. The trickiest section is the corner at D7. You may not detect the sensor around the corner until you're on top of it. Consult the map and be prepared.

2 STEAL AN IMPERIAL SHUTTLE

Stealing an Imperial shuttle is a two-player task. Both players must fly into the Rebel symbol at D1 before the shuttle takes off. The first player will pilot the ship while the second players takes control over the weapons.

Blast the four turrets around the landing zone to ensure a smooth shuttle takeoff.

! TAKE A TIE FIGHTER

By stealing one of the academy's TIE fighters, you can fly through the compound without tripping alarms. As soon as you start fighting, though, the Imperials will turn on you.

DAY

If you intend to steal a TIE during the day, you'll have to veer off the mission's main course. Bank right at C6 and fly to the clearing at F6. You'll find the ship-swapping Rebel icon near a radar dish.

NIGHT

Your nighttime TIE trek will take you through a path that begins at C8. Follow the canyon until you witness a cut scene, then discover the Rebel icon near an outpost. After you steal a TIE at both times of day, you'll have it for other missions.

GOING FOR GOLD

GET GROUND TARGETS

You can increase your Enemies Destroyed rating by demolishing parked TIE fighters. The bomb-equipped Y-wing is best suited to hitting ground targets, but you'll also be able to destroy your share of TIEs in a speeder or a hijacked TIE fighter. After you hit a TIE on the ground, neighboring TIEs will take off. Avoid the buzzing baddies and seek out sitting ducks.

3 MEET AT THE RENDEZVOUS POINT

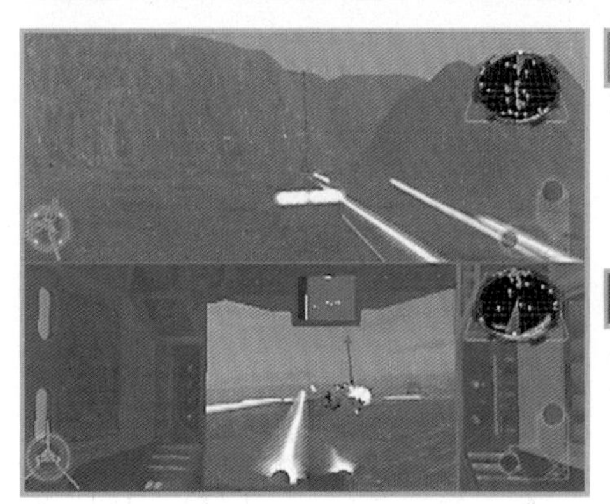

PLAYER 1

The first flier to reach the Imperial shuttle will steer the stolen craft. Follow the scanner's wedge indicator for directions to the rendezvous point and keep the ship steady to give your partner clean shots at enemy ships.

PLAYER 2

The second pilot into the shuttle will operate the craft's rear cannon. Don't jeopardize your Shot Accuracy rating by firing on far-off targets. Wait until the enemies are on your tail, then open fire.

COOPERATIVE CAMPAIGN

RAID ON BESPIN

The Empire has a stranglehold on Lando Calrissian's Bespin City and the Tibanna gas that it produces. Imperial forces would rather destroy the city's Tibanna gas platforms than let them fall into Rebel hands. It's up to you to save the platforms from destruction and to eliminate the Imperial presence in the city.

OBJECTIVES

1. SECURE THE TIBANNA GAS PLATFORMS
2. DESTROY THE CITY'S POWER GENERATORS
3. DEFEND THE TIBANNA GAS PLATFORMS FROM THE TIE BOMBERS

OBJECTIVE 1: GAS PLATFORMS

START

OBJECTIVES 2-3: CLOUD CITY

START

MAP KEY

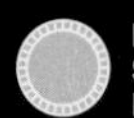
IMPERIAL SIEGE BALLOON

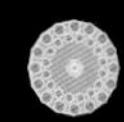
TIBANNA GAS PLATFORM

POWER GENERATOR

TECH UPGRADE

SHIP CHANGE: CLOUD CAR

RECOMMENDED SHIP SELECTION

PLAYER 1: A-WING
PLAYER 2: A-WING

The quickest, most agile ship in the fleet is great for the Raid on Bespin mission. A journey through the city's narrowest passages in the mission's second section will be a breeze with the masterfully maneuvering ship.

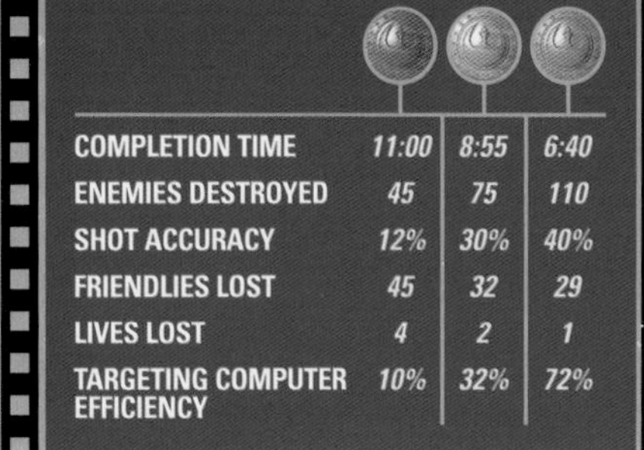

MEDAL REQUIREMENTS

	Bronze	Silver	Gold
COMPLETION TIME	11:00	8:55	6:40
ENEMIES DESTROYED	45	75	110
SHOT ACCURACY	12%	30%	40%
FRIENDLIES LOST	45	32	29
LIVES LOST	4	2	1
TARGETING COMPUTER EFFICIENCY	10%	32%	72%

TECH UPGRADE: HOMING CONCUSSION MISSILES

Although the first mission objective is to save the Tibanna gas platforms, you'll reveal the homing concussion missiles upgrade by destroying gas tanks (not a good move for a gold-medal run). Take off for the second gas platform from the start (C8 on the map) and target the Imperial tanker nearby. The explosion will set off a chain reaction on the platform, thereby revealing the upgrade.

1 SECURE THE TIBANNA GAS PLATFORMS

BLOW UP BALLOONS

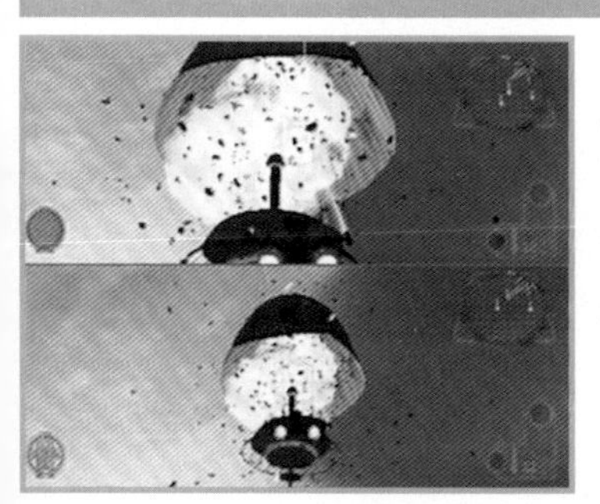

Imperial siege balloons surround the Tibanna gas platforms and target the tanks. Both players should go after the balloons to ensure a low Friendlies Lost mission rating. Approach each balloon from below and fire on one of its three gas jets, hidden under the canopy. The explosion will send the balloon to Bespin's surface.

TROUNCE THE TIES

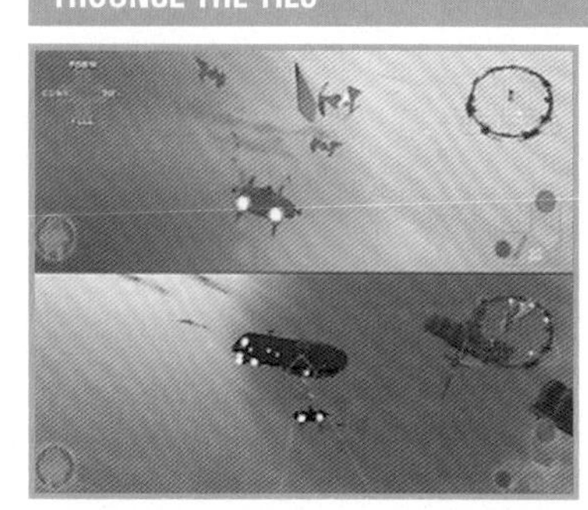

After you've saved a gas platform or a group of platforms from balloon interference, take on the TIE fighters that aim to cause more trouble for the platforms and Rebel transports. Since the clouds can get mighty thick, you'll do well by toggling on your targeting computer.

2 DESTROY THE CITY'S POWER GENERATORS

PLAYER 1

UNPLUG A PAIR OF GENERATORS

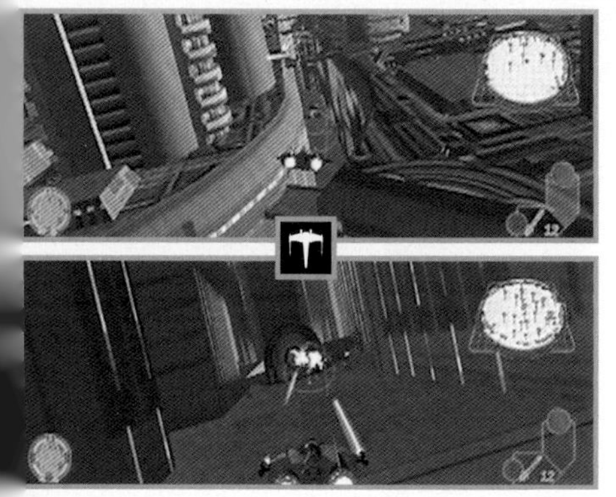

Power generators in Bespin City provide energy to Imperial forces. You'll find all three generators in the deep ditches that cut through the city—they're below laser cannons on bridges. Find and destroy generators in locations E2 and F6 on the map. Stay under enemy radar and fly out of one ditch only to duck into another one.

PLAYER 2

BLAST THE LAST GENERATOR AND A BUNCH OF BALLOONS

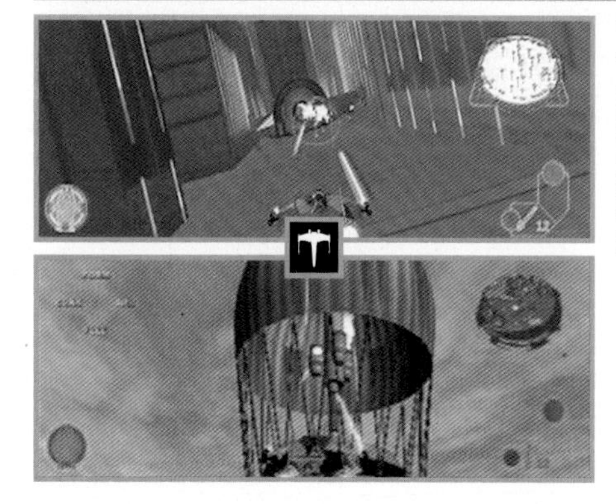

While Player 1 goes after two of the generators, provide support by destroying the generator in section C4. After the generator is gone, rise above the city and go after the balloons and TIE fighters.

3 DEFEND THE TIBANNA GAS PLATFORMS FROM THE TIE BOMBERS

FLOAT NO MORE

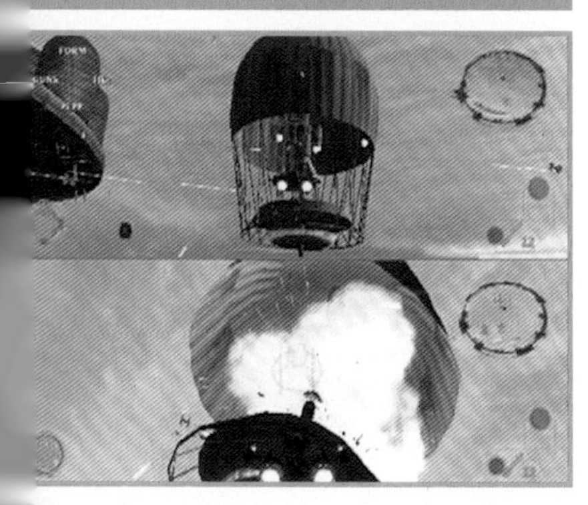

The mission's last objective is to protect more gas platforms from Imperial attackers. Both players should go after the balloons first. Player 2 can get an early start on the objective while Player 1 finishes off the power generators.

BLAST THE BOMBERS

Turn on your targeting computer and search for the yellow-shaded TIE bombers. You can avoid the fighters and the interceptors, but you must destroy the bombers to complete the objective. You'll be able to beat the bombers in a hurry using your homing missiles.

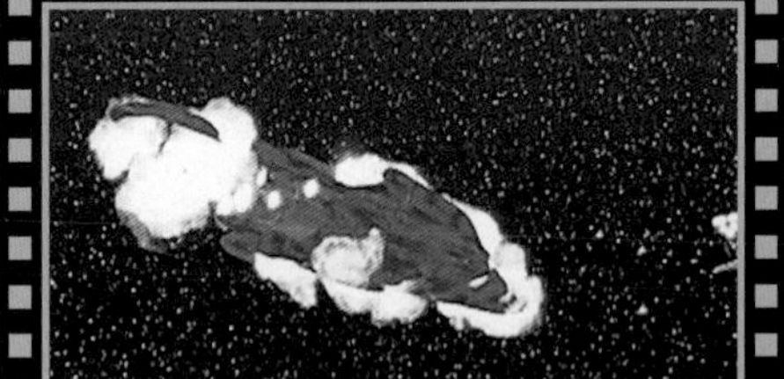

COOPERATIVE CAMPAIGN

BATTLE OF ENDOR

The Alliance's ultimate objective is to mount a strike on the Death Star's new incarnation. Before the Rebels can get the plan in motion, a long battle against TIEs of all varieties and two Star Destroyers will commence. Defend the Rebel fleet and clear the way for the ultimate attack.

OBJECTIVES

1. PROTECT THE FLEET
2. PROTECT THE MEDICAL FRIGATE
3. DESTROY ALL TIE BOMBERS
4. DESTROY BOTH STAR DESTROYERS

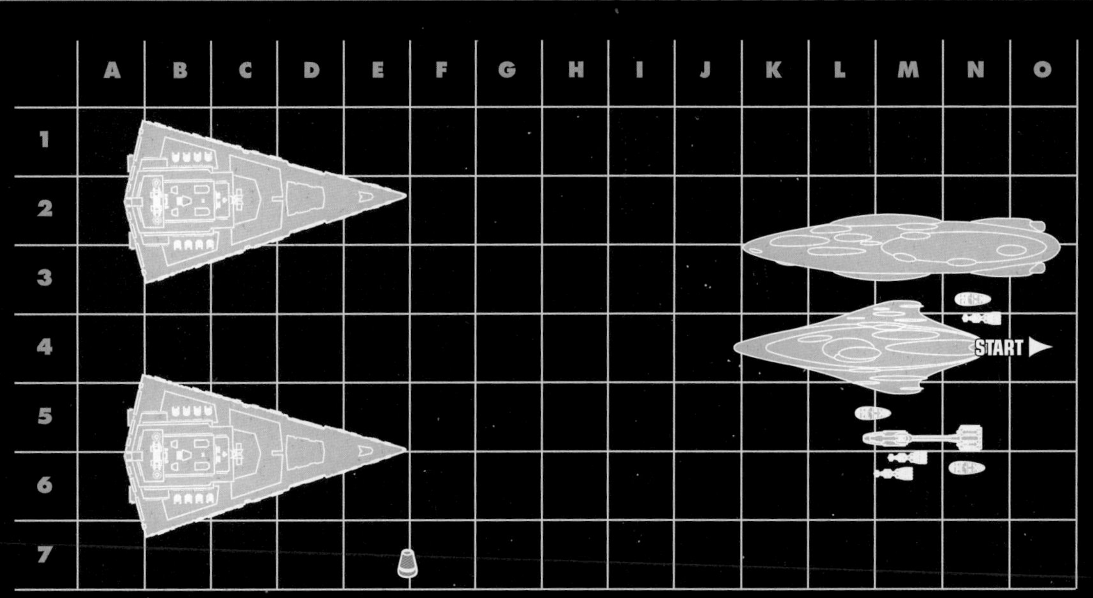

RECOMMENDED SHIP SELECTION

PLAYER 1: X-WING

Dogfighting skills are key for mission victory. The better dogfighter of the pair should board an X-wing.

PLAYER 2: A-WING

The A-wing is speedy, but its shields are weak. If you let the TIEs get behind you, your mission will end abruptly.

MAP KEY

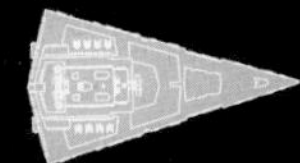
IMPERIAL STAR DESTROYER

HOME ONE

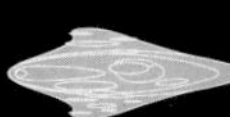
REBEL CRUISER

MEDICAL FRIGATE

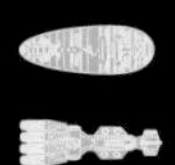
REBEL TRANSPORT
BLOCKADE RUNNER

TECH UPGRADE

MEDAL REQUIREMENTS

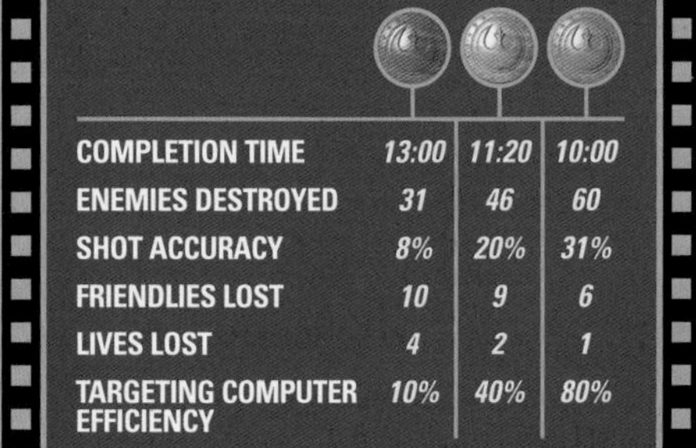

COMPLETION TIME	13:00	11:20	10:00
ENEMIES DESTROYED	31	46	60
SHOT ACCURACY	8%	20%	31%
FRIENDLIES LOST	10	9	6
LIVES LOST	4	2	1
TARGETING COMPUTER EFFICIENCY	10%	40%	80%

TECH UPGRADE: HOMING CLUSTER MISSILES

When you take on the fourth objective, veer to the left and down from the Imperial ship on the left, and look for a shimmering white dot against the planet's background—it's the tech upgrade. Another way to find the power-up is to wait until you've downed the Star Destroyer at C6. After the ship settles, you'll find the upgrade near its lower hatch.

1 PROTECT THE FLEET

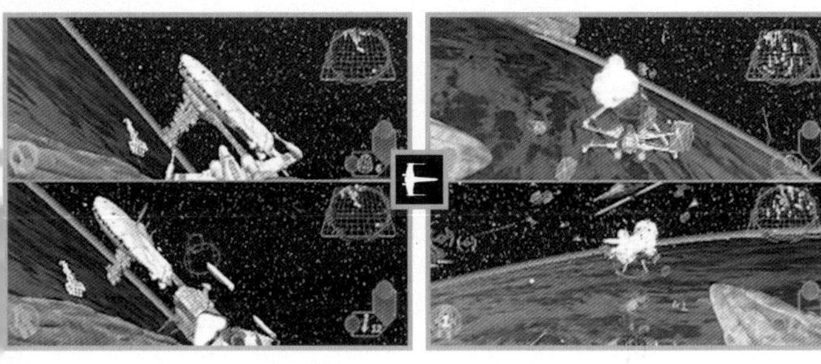

You'll begin with the Death Star II in view. Turn 180 degrees immediately and point your ship toward the Imperial fleet in the distance. Within seconds, your targeting computer will pick up dozens of TIEs. Fly into the fray and blast enemy ships left and right. Your primary targets are the TIEs that are starting attack runs on the Rebel fleet.

2 PROTECT THE MEDICAL FRIGATE

Several TIEs will concentrate their attacks on the medical frigate. If they destroy the ship, you'll lose the mission. Keep track of the frigate's location and target all TIEs in the area. The A-wing is equipped with homing concussion missiles. Use the enemy-seeking devices to boost your accuracy rating and cut your mission time.

3 DESTROY ALL TIE BOMBERS

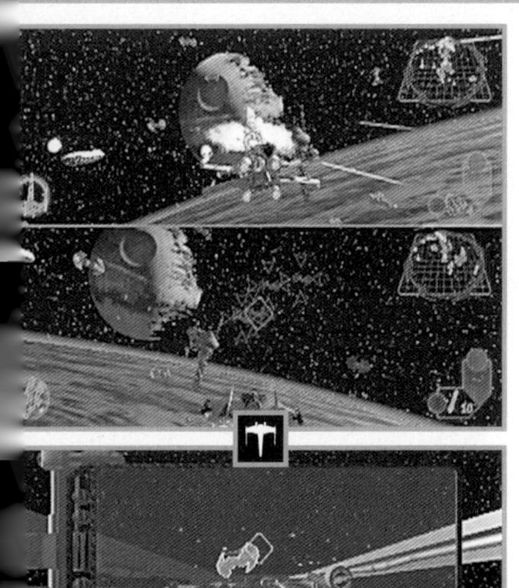

After one of your wingmen alerts you to the TIE bombers' approach, turn to face the Star Destroyers and race for the bombers before they reach your fleet. Your targets will be shaded yellow in the targeting computer's display. Avoid a head-on meeting with the bomber fleet and position your ship behind it. Use the A-wing's homing concussion missiles and the X-wing's blasters to take out the bombers.

4 DESTROY BOTH STAR DESTROYERS

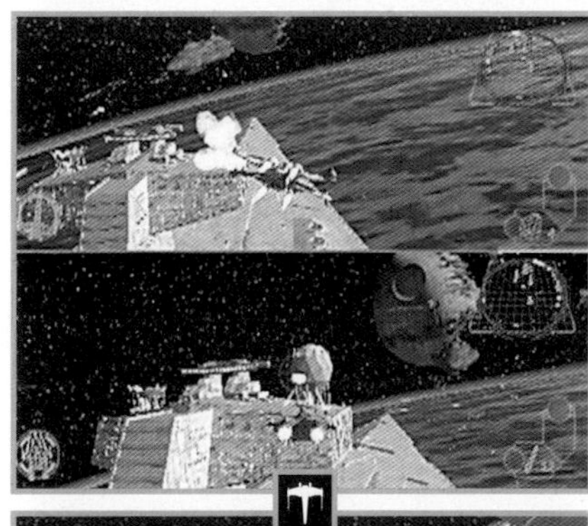

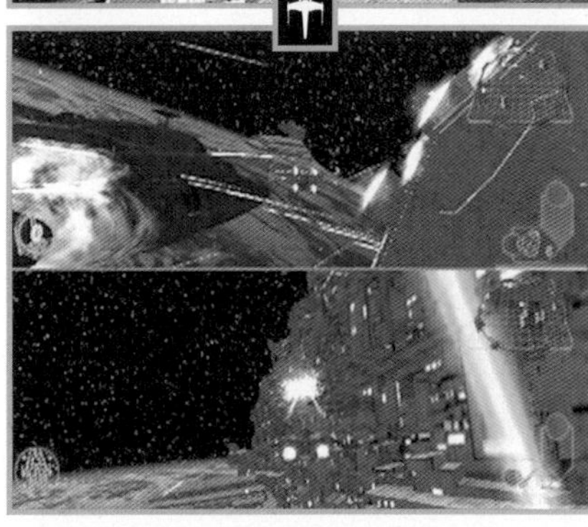

You've already destroyed one Star Destroyer, so you know what it takes—take out both globes on top of the bridge section, then target the shield generator at the bottom of the ship and finally go after the command bay on the front of the bridge section. You can split the objective with your partner and have each player target a Star Destroyer, or take on the Star Destroyers as a team. If you destroy the ships individually, you'll save time in the long run. If you choose the team approach, the Star Destoyer's lasers will attempt to target both of you, resulting in dispersed enemy fire.

GOING FOR GOLD

STAYING ALIVE

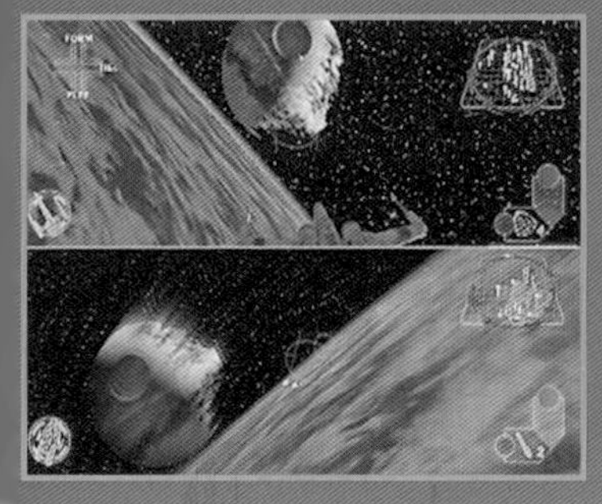

The most challenging aspect of winning a gold medal in the Battle of Endor mission is keeping down your Lives Lost stat. Watch your shield strength and peel off for a quick break if your energy is low. The X-wing's shields will regenerate over time. The A-wing must keep moving to avoid enemy fire.

BEAT THE CLOCK

You can save time during the TIE-bomber and Star-Destroyer attacks. Use the A-wing's endless supply of advanced weapons to home in on all targets, and employ the X-wing's limited supply of advanced homing torpedoes to demolish the Star Destroyers' shield generators and bridges.

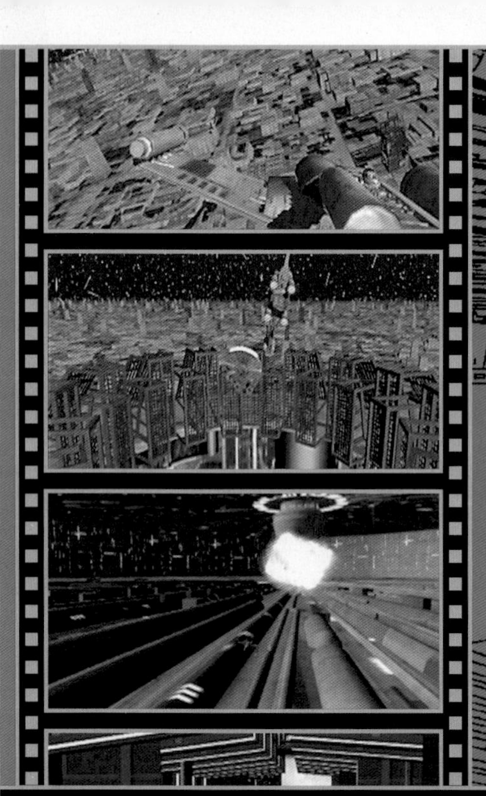

COOPERATIVE CAMPAIGN

STRIKE AT THE CORE

The Death Star II's shields are down, thanks to Han Solo and a Rebel commando team. While most of the Rebel fleet continues to deal with a TIE-fighter contingent, Lando Calrissian, piloting the the *Millennium Falcon*, and Wedge Antilles, behind the controls of an X-wing, head for the huge space station.

OBJECTIVES

1. REACH THE POWER CORE ENTRY
2. DESTROY THE POWER CORE

OBJECTIVE 2: PATH TO THE CORE

A B C D E F G H I J

1 2 3 4

START

POWER CORE

MAP KEY

 TECH UPGRADE

RECOMMENDED SHIP SELECTION

PLAYER 1: X-WING

The X-wing is responsible for the destruction of the first Death Star, but it's relegated to a support role in this mission.

PLAYER 2: *MILLENNIUM FALCON*

Superior speed and strong shields make Han Solo's famous fighter, flown by Lando in this mission, a good fit. The only drawback is that it may be hard to steer in the station's power core.

MEDAL REQUIREMENTS

	Bronze	Silver	Gold
COMPLETION TIME	7:00	6:15	5:05
ENEMIES DESTROYED	29	36	41
SHOT ACCURACY	10%	21%	32%
FRIENDLIES LOST	0	0	0
LIVES LOST	4	2	1
TARGETING COMPUTER EFFICIENCY	20%	45%	95%

TECH UPGRADE: ADVANCED TARGETING COMPUTER

On your way to the power core, you'll find the advanced targeting computer upgrade under a pipe, just before you reach the rib braces at the end of the tunnel. Use the X-wing to go after the power-up. Slow down, then squeeze into the tight space and grab the upgrade. It'll allow you to use the targeting computer without holding the Y Button.

1 REACH THE POWER CORE ENTRY

PLAYER 1 TARGET TURRETS

Unless you have your S-foils closed, you don't stand a chance of keeping up with the *Millennium Falcon*. Let Lando fend for himself and take out the Death Star II's turrets to boost your Enemies Destroyed stat.

PLAYER 2 SPEED AHEAD

Make a beeline for the power core entry from the beginning of the mission. Enemy turrets are a minor threat, so eliminate those and continue on your course. After you reach the entrance, the X-wing will catch up to you during a cut scene.

2 DESTROY THE POWER CORE

GET THE TIES OFF YOUR BACK

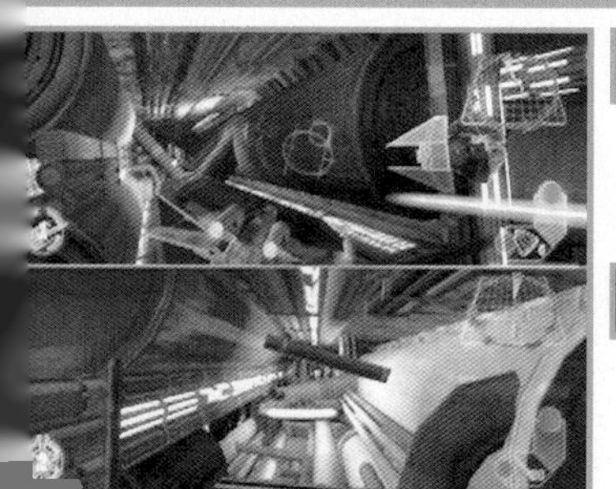

PLAYER 1

Your mission is to make sure that the *Millennium Falcon* reaches the core. Target the TIEs that threaten the *Falcon* first, hang back and wait for more TIEs to come in.

PLAYER 2

Hit the boost at the beginning of the tunnel and continue your course to the core. If any TIEs are trailing you, eliminate them using your C-Stick-controlled rear cannon.

TAKE THE TUNNEL TO THE CORE

PLAYER 1

Don't let the *Falcon* get too far ahead of you. Catch up if you can and target the TIEs that fly between your ship and Lando's craft.

PLAYER 2

The tunnel is tight and the *Millennium Falcon* is a bit bulky, but you will be able to negotiate all of the tunnel's obstacles without using the Z Button to barrel roll.

GOING FOR GOLD

RUN AND GUN

Completion Time is the toughest stat to master when going for the Strike at the Core gold medal. Try to memorize every obstacle, twist and turn, and boost through the power core tunnel, both on your way in and on your way out.

CONCENTRATE ON THE CORE

Both players should zero in on the core and fire away. The power core room is large. If you try to fire at it from too far away, your shots won't hit their target and your Shot Accuracy stat will suffer. Use advanced secondary weapons to lock on to the core and hit it with all of your might.

ESCAPE THE EXPLOSION

Once the core is gone, you'll have precious little time to get out before the Empire's second Death Star suffers the fate of the first. The X-wing will have an easier time of getting through the tunnel quickly. Let it lead. A single ship's escape will signal mission victory.

COOPERATIVE CAMPAIGN: BONUS MISSION

DEATH STAR ESCAPE

Tearing away from the Death Star's tractor beam, the crew of the *Millennium Falcon* faces a TIE fighter onslaught. You'll find the shooting-gallery-style bonus mission above Death Star Attack on the Mission Select screen.

MEDAL REQUIREMENTS

COMPLETION TIME	3:15	2:55	2:35
ENEMIES DESTROYED	65	68	72
SHOT ACCURACY	1%	2%	3%
FRIENDLIES LOST	0	0	0
LIVES LOST	0	0	0
TARGETING COMPUTER EFFICIENCY	100%	100%	100%

OBJECTIVE

1 DESTROY ALL THE TIE FIGHTERS

1 DESTROY ALL TIE FIGHTERS

COMMUNICATE WITH GROUPS OF TIES

PLAYER 1

You and your partner defend opposite sides of the *Millennium Falcon*. If a swarm of TIEs passes your station before you can shoot them down, they're headed to the other side. Give your partner a heads-up.

PLAYER 2

Communication with the other player is key in your quest to eliminate every TIE fighter. When you spot a wayward group leaving your area, let your partner know their number and flight path.

GOING FOR GOLD

STAY ON TARGET

Although the Shot Accuracy requirement is much lower than it is in most missions, you will have a difficult time reaching the gold-medal plateau. The *Falcon*'s guns don't have floating reticles, so you won't know exactly where you're firing until you pull the trigger. Try short bursts instead of sustained fire to keep the number of missed shots small.

SEE PATTERNS IN THE CHAOS

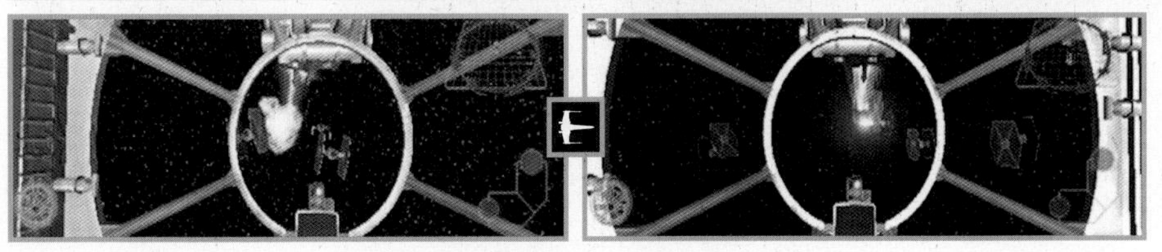

The TIEs fly in set patterns. The more you play the mission, the more you'll recognize the patterns and remember where the enemies will appear. Use your memory to anticipate the attack waves. You'll cut down on time and increase your accuracy. To get started, notice that the first wave of TIEs for each player appears down the middle. Player 1's TIEs veer right. Player 2's TIEs split.

COOPERATIVE CAMPAIGN: BONUS MISSION

THE ASTEROID FIELD

Recalling a scene from *The Empire Strikes Back*, the *Millennium Falcon* is surrounded by TIE fighters and asteroids, and the ship's hyperdrive is on the fritz. You have no alternative but to seek refuge as refuse attached to a Star Destroyer.

OBJECTIVES

1. ESCAPE THE TIE FIGHTERS
2. SECRETLY LAND ON AN IMPERIAL STAR DESTROYER

MEDAL REQUIREMENTS

	Bronze	Silver	Gold
COMPLETION TIME	*6:00*	*5:25*	*4:50*
ENEMIES DESTROYED	*25*	*37*	*45*
SHOT ACCURACY	*2%*	*5%*	*10%*
FRIENDLIES LOST	*0*	*0*	*0*
LIVES LOST	*3*	*2*	*1*
TARGETING COMPUTER EFFICIENCY	*10%*	*30%*	*75%*

1 ESCAPE THE TIE FIGHTERS

PLAYER 1 ROCKY RUN

While Player 2 guns for the TIEs behind the *Falcon*, you must navigate the asteroid field, avoid rocks and follow the course laid out by the wedge indicator. If you deviate from the course, you'll hit the edge of the mission area and turn around automatically. If you're following the pointer and still hitting the edge, you'll have to change your vertical angle. Fly closely past big asteroids to draw your pursuers into the rocks.

PLAYER 2 TAKE ON TIE FIGHTERS

Your part in the Asteroid Field mission is similar to your part in Death Star Escape. You must eliminate as many attacking TIEs as you can to defend the fleeing *Millennium Falcon*. To keep your Shot Accuracy rating high, use short bursts of fire to target the approaching ships and communicate with Player 1 when you need the *Falcon* to adjust its path and give you a better shot at the enemies.

PLAYER 1 STEADY AS YOU GO

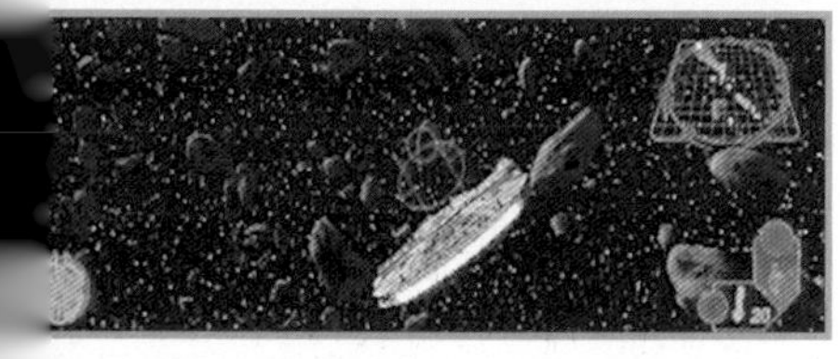

In the interest of staying on course and allowing your gunner to eliminate as many enemies as possible, avoid abrupt changes in your path and fly straight ahead. The only reason that you have for quick maneuvers is to avoid collisions with asteroids and large concentrations of enemy fire.

2 SECRETLY LAND ON AN IMPERIAL STAR DESTROYER

After you survive the first run through the asteroid field, you'll enter similar asteroid-and-TIE challenges. While Player 1 follows the wedge indicator and swerves around asteroids, Player 2 must eliminate trailing TIEs. Eventually, you'll exit the asteroid field and discover a Star Destroyer. Approach the Imperial craft from the rear and close in on the Rebel symbol behind the ship's bridge.

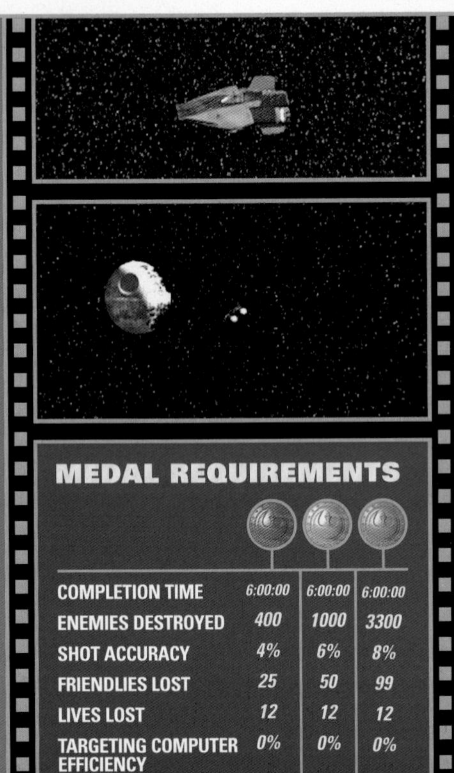

COOPERATIVE CAMPAIGN: BONUS MISSION

ENDURANCE

The ultimate cooperative bonus mission tests how long you can last in a seemingly endless battle over the Death Star. Waves of TIE fighters buzz the base. Blast them out of the sky and avoid scrapes with surface structures.

OBJECTIVE

1 DESTROY ALL IMPERIAL CRAFT

MEDAL REQUIREMENTS

COMPLETION TIME	6:00:00	6:00:00	6:00:00
ENEMIES DESTROYED	400	1000	3300
SHOT ACCURACY	4%	6%	8%
FRIENDLIES LOST	25	50	99
LIVES LOST	12	12	12
TARGETING COMPUTER EFFICIENCY	0%	0%	0%

1 DESTROY ALL IMPERIAL CRAFT

RETIRE TIE FIGHTERS

The object of the mission is to last as long as you can, making shield preservation an important factor. Whenever possible, attack the TIE-fighter squadrons from behind to avoid their forward-firing lasers and use your homing concussion missiles to hit them four at a time. If you face a group of TIEs head on, blast them with missiles and lasers, then veer off their course before they get too close. Once the wave has turned into a trickle, use your targeting computer to pick off the stragglers to save time.

RECOMMENDED SHIP SELECTION

PLAYER 1: A-WING PLAYER 2: A-WING

The A-wing's weak shields are a concern, but its homing concussion missiles will let you whittle away at the TIEs in bunches. If you've upgraded to homing proton torpedoes, the X-wing will be a worthy alternative.

SHUTTLE DISCOVERY

Imperial shuttles comprise every tenth wave of enemy ships. By clearing away the passive ships, you can earn an extra craft in reserve. You'll need the backups if you expect to endure.

GREEN MEANS GO FARTHER

Look for floating green power-ups near the Death Star's surface. The items replenish your ship's secondary weapons or shields. If you're doing fine but your partner's craft is not shipshape, share power-up loactions. Several seconds after you've collected a power-up, it will reappear.

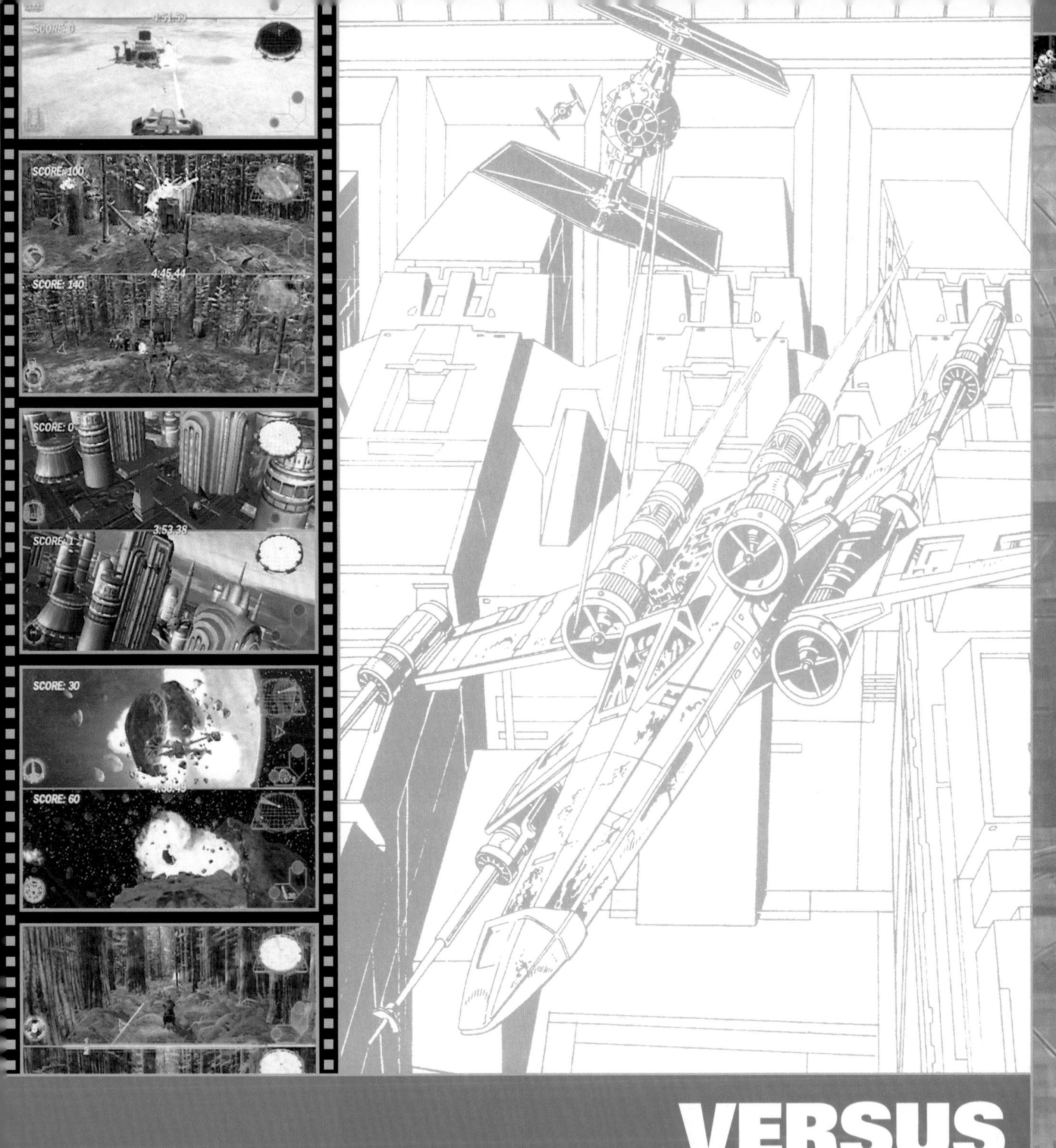

VERSUS MODE

Who's the best pilot in the galaxy? Rebel Strike offers dozens of unlockable competitive scenarios to help you answer the question. Race another ace through Beggar's Canyon, clash over Geonosis, claim control of bases on Kothlis and find out who deserves to receive honors in Yavin 4's ceremonial hall.

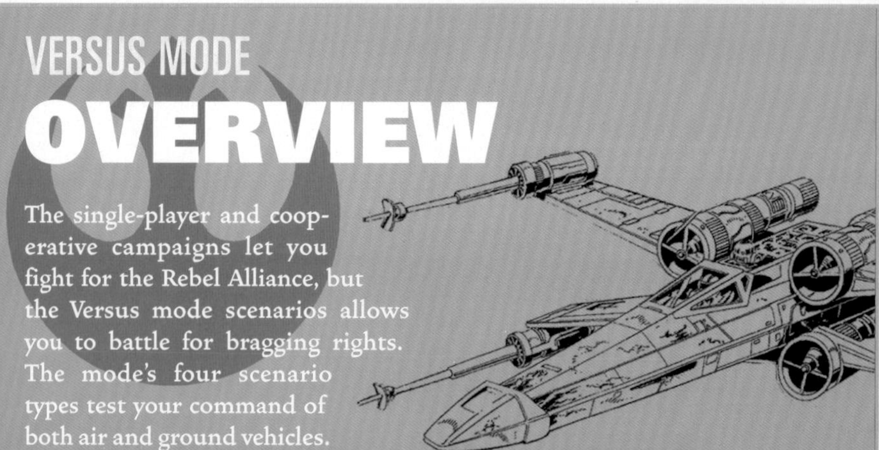

VERSUS MODE
OVERVIEW

The single-player and cooperative campaigns let you fight for the Rebel Alliance, but the Versus mode scenarios allows you to battle for bragging rights. The mode's four scenario types test your command of both air and ground vehicles.

VERSUS OPTIONS

Customize your Versus-mode session to your liking by adjusting elements within each scenario and making changes to scenario-ending conditions.

TIME LIMIT

Adjust the time limit from 1 to 20 minutes or eliminate the limit altogether.

TARGET SCORE

Set a target score to allow for victory before the time limit is up.

NUMBER OF LIVES

Make the scenario a battle of endurance by limiting ships in reserve.

WINGMEN

Toggle on the Wingmen option to give each player a single computer-controlled squadmate. You can direct the allied craft to fire its secondary weapon, attack your target, attack your competitor's craft or return to formation behind your ship. If you lose a wingman, the support craft will not return until you fly into a Wingman power-up.

POWER-UPS

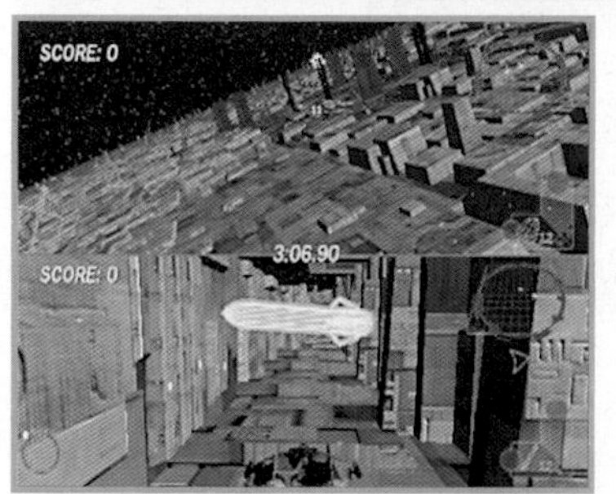

Easily visible floating symbols appear on the landscape when the Power-Up option is on. By collecting a power-up, you can restore your shields, replenish your secondary weapon supply or bring back your lost wingman. After you collect a power-up, it will take several seconds to reappear.

ADDITIONAL AI ATTACKERS

By adding computer-controlled enemies to Dogfight and Tag-and-Defend scenarios, you can create more excitement. You won't increase your score by destroying an AI target, but you will receive a five-percent shield restoration. Most Rampage scenarios already have AI targets that you can destroy to add to your score.

CRAFT CONSTRUCTION

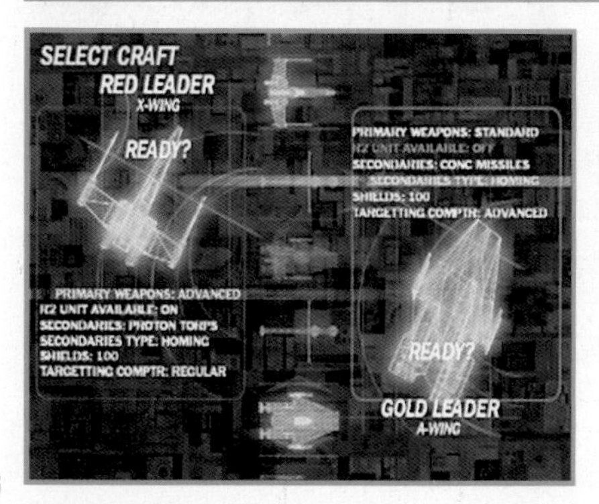

You can outfit your ship with a secondary weapon that it does not traditionally carry (for example, cluster missiles on an X-wing). If one player is more experienced than the other, you can offset weapon, shield and targeting-computer options to even the playing field.

! NEW SHIPS JOIN THE PARTY

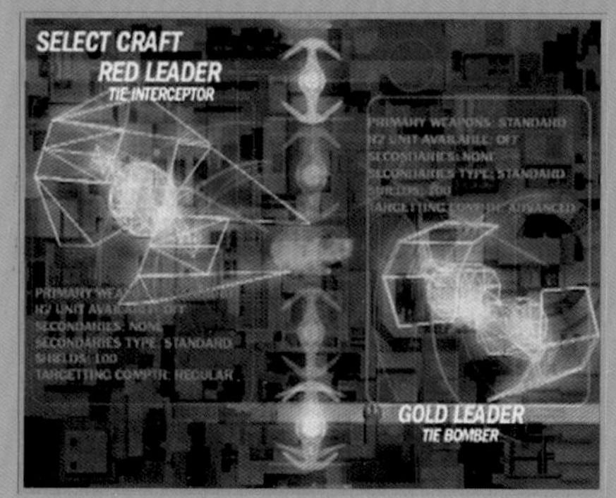

When you unlock ships in the single-player campaign, they become available in Versus mode. See pages 9-13 for ship-unlocking conditions. The descriptions of Versus-mode scenarios on the following pages include lists of ships that are selectable for each type of scenario.

VERSUS MODE

DOGFIGHT

Dogfight scenarios are battles of wits and courage. They break fighting strategy down to its essence. Some pointers in the following pages will help you win in specific dogfight locations while others will aid you in any one-on-one scenario.

PRIMARY TARGET LOCATION

'he wedge indicator on your canner points to the opposing player's craft, as does a yellow arrow on the screen. If your primary target is in view, homing crosshairs will help you locate it n the darkness of space. By knowing where your competitor s at all times, you'll be able to orm effective attack strategies.

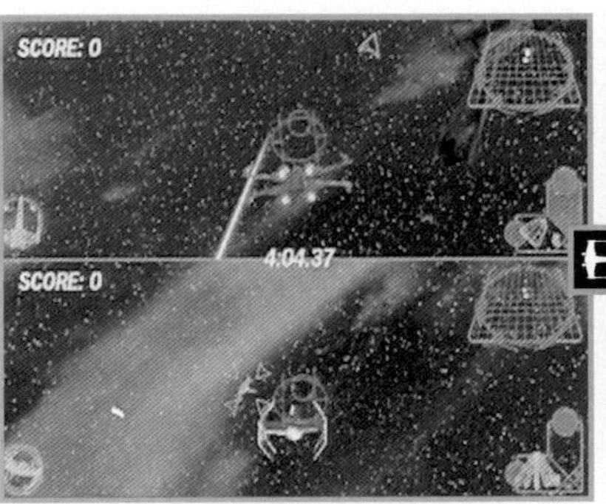

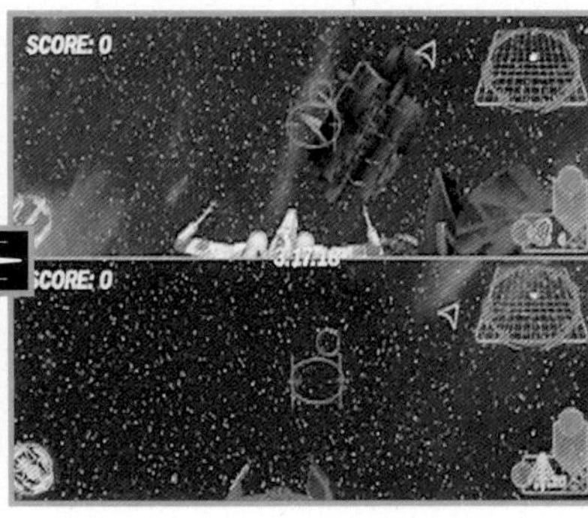

An arrow on each split-screen view points to the opposing fighter. If the crafts are close and both players are following their arrows, they may lock into a continuous circle around each other. When you break out of the circle, try to position your craft behind your target.

DEATH STAR DOGFIGHT

'he planet-destroying station's gray landscape provides an ominous backdrop for a thrilling ght. Compared to other locations, the Death Star is a fairly open battleground. You can ngage with your target without paying much attention to your surroundings.

PLAYABLE VEHICLES

A-WING	NABOO STARFIGHTER	TIE HUNTER
B-WING	*MILLENNIUM FALCON*	TIE INTERCEPTOR
SLAVE I	TIE ADVANCED	X-WING
IMPERIAL SHUTTLE	TIE BOMBER	Y-WING
JEDI STARFIGHTER	TIE FIGHTER	

'AKE REFUGE IN THE TRENCH

If you're confident of your flight skills in tight places, dive into a Death Star trench section to shake your opponent or a locked-on weapon. The trench section is very short—watch for dead ends.

TROUBLE FROM TURRETS

If you're skimming the surface, the Death Star's turrets will target your craft, even if the Additional AI Attackers option is off. Turrets fire damaging lasers, but their shots are not very accurate. As long as you keep up a good speed, you'll avoid stray laser fire from the surface.

GEONOSIS DOGFIGHT

The scanner display and crosshairs will prove to be invaluable while you search for your opponent in the asteroid belt above Geonosis. If you turn off the navigational aids by way of the Game Settings menu, you'll spend a lot of time in the dark.

PLAYABLE VEHICLES		
A-WING	NABOO STARFIGHTER	TIE HUNTER
B-WING	*MILLENNIUM FALCON*	TIE INTERCEPTOR
SLAVE I	TIE ADVANCED	X-WING
IMPERIAL SHUTTLE	TIE BOMBER	Y-WING
JEDI STARFIGHTER	TIE FIGHTER	

GEONOSIS GEOLOGY

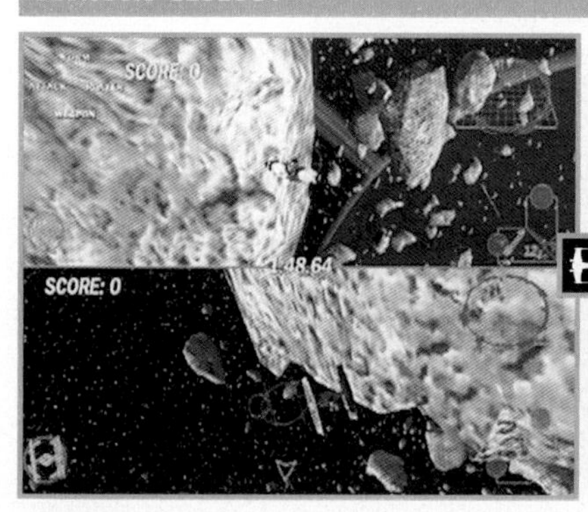

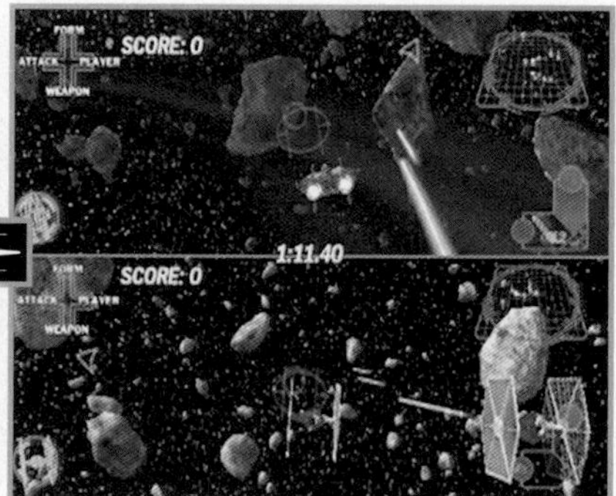

The atmosphere is thick with floating rocks. You can clear away the small- and medium-sized asteroids, but the larges ones are indestructible. If your opponent is hot on your tail, you can shake the pursuer by playing a game of chicken. Head for one of the big rocks and break away from it at the last moment. Your opponent will either collide with the large moving obstacle or likely break off in a different direction and lose you in the process.

BESPIN DOGFIGHT

You can engage in a pure one-on-one clash with little, if any, outside influence in the Cloud City's bright and open sky. Keep the scanner and crosshairs on, or you may lose your opponent in the sunlight.

PLAYABLE VEHICLES		
A-WING	NABOO STARFIGHTER	TIE FIGHTER
B-WING	*MILLENNIUM FALCON*	TIE HUNTER
CLOUD CAR	SPEEDER	TIE INTERCEPTOR
SLAVE I	T-16 SKYHOPPER	X-WING
IMPERIAL SHUTTLE	TIE ADVANCED	Y-WING
JEDI STARFIGHTER	TIE BOMBER	

URBAN WARFARE

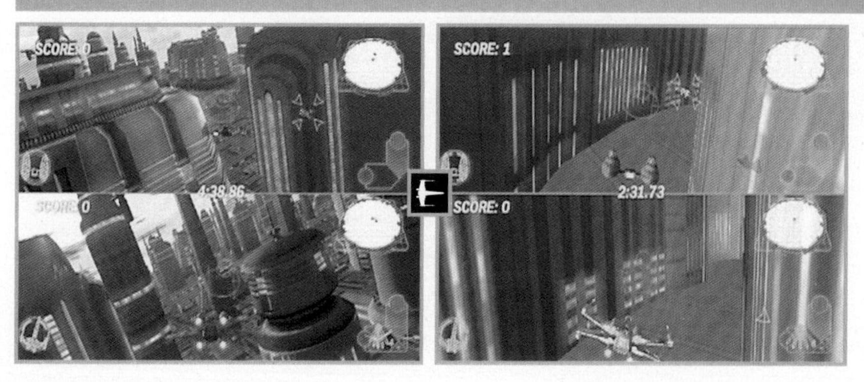

If you bring the action down to the level of the buildings anc ditches, you'll experience a fight that is quite different fron the battle in the open sky. Small craft and ships with stron shields have the advantage in tight city locations. Dive into urban pathways to shake your enemy and locked weapons from your tail.

DOGFIGHT OVER HOTH

Blue skies, wispy clouds and a snow-covered landscape provide a beautiful scene for a dogfight. Scan the horizon for the ion cannon's blasts and close in on the huge turret to find a power-up. Shots from the cannon will not affect your ship.

PLAYABLE VEHICLES

A-WING
B-WING
CLOUD CAR
SLAVE I
IMPERIAL SHUTTLE
JEDI STARFIGHTER
NABOO STARFIGHTER
MILLENNIUM FALCON
T-16 SKYHOPPER
TIE ADVANCED
TIE BOMBER
TIE FIGHTER
TIE HUNTER
TIE INTERCEPTOR
X-WING
Y-WING

FLY SKY-HIGH

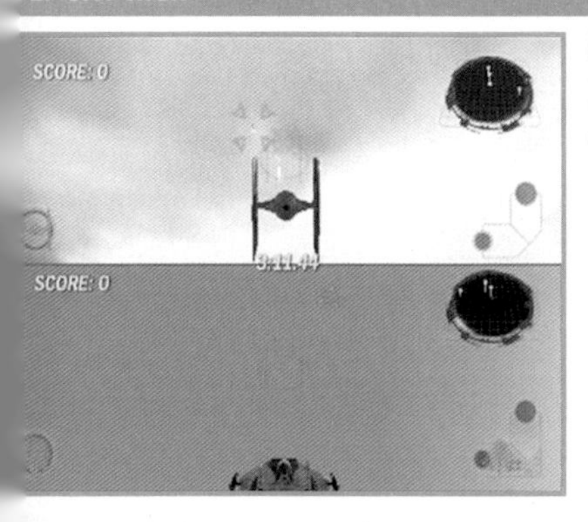

Hoth's flight ceiling is well above the clouds. You can rise into the wild blue yonder for quite a while without having to head back toward the ground. You'll be completely free from obstacles.

AI ATTRACTION

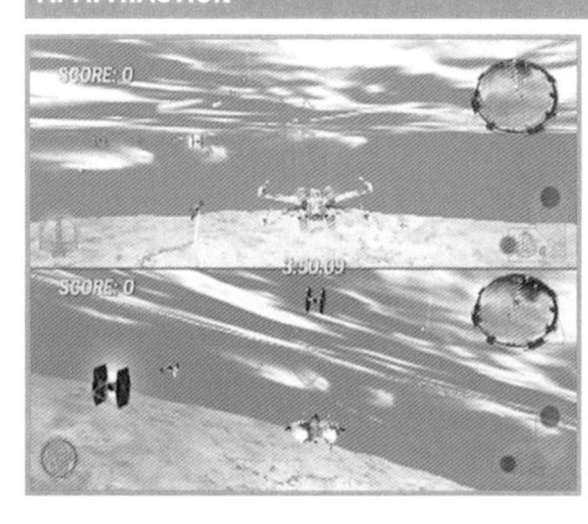

If you find open-air battles against a single opponent dull, you can add excitement to the Dogfight over Hoth scenario by turning on the Additional AI Attackers option. Tag the TIEs to replenish your ship's shields.

ISON CORRIDOR DOGFIGHT

The obstacles of the Ison Corridor are not as tightly packed as the asteroids over Geonosis, but some of the chunks of space debris do blend into the background, making them difficult to see. Keep an eye on what's ahead while you scan the area for your enemy.

PLAYABLE VEHICLES

A-WING
B-WING
SLAVE I
IMPERIAL SHUTTLE
JEDI STARFIGHTER
NABOO STARFIGHTER
MILLENNIUM FALCON
SPEEDER
TIE ADVANCED
TIE BOMBER
TIE FIGHTER
TIE HUNTER
TIE INTERCEPTOR
X-WING
Y-WING

DIVE FOR DEBRIS

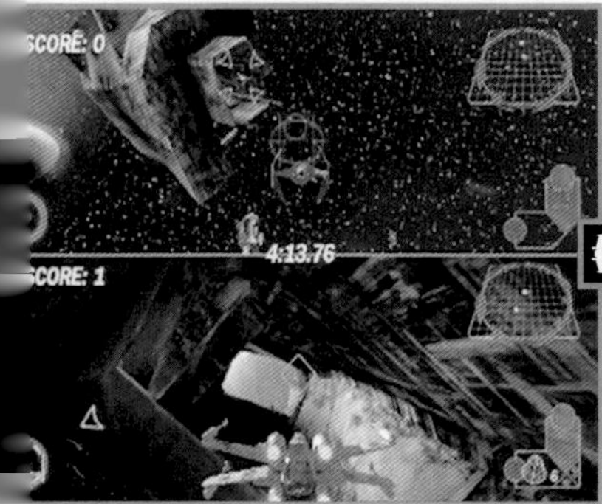

You can use the indestructible space junk of the Ison Corridor to your advantage, as long as you are confident in your ship's shields and its turning radius. Fly close to the debris while your opponent is following you or locked-on weapons are headed your way, and veer out of the path of destruction at the last moment. If computer-controlled ships are part of the scenario, use your targeting computer to find them. TIE fighters are hard to see against the star-filled background.

DOGFIGHT OVER ENDOR

It's unusual to see Rebel Alliance vehicles fight each other in the company of Star Destroyers, but that's part of the fun in the Dogfight over Endor scenario. Use the big ships as cover from your enemy's fire.

PLAYABLE VEHICLES

A-WING	NABOO STARFIGHTER	TIE HUNTER
B-WING	*MILLENNIUM FALCON*	TIE INTERCEPTOR
SLAVE I	TIE ADVANCED	X-WING
IMPERIAL SHUTTLE	TIE BOMBER	Y-WING
JEDI STARFIGHTER	TIE FIGHTER	

DESTROYERS BRING THE PAIN

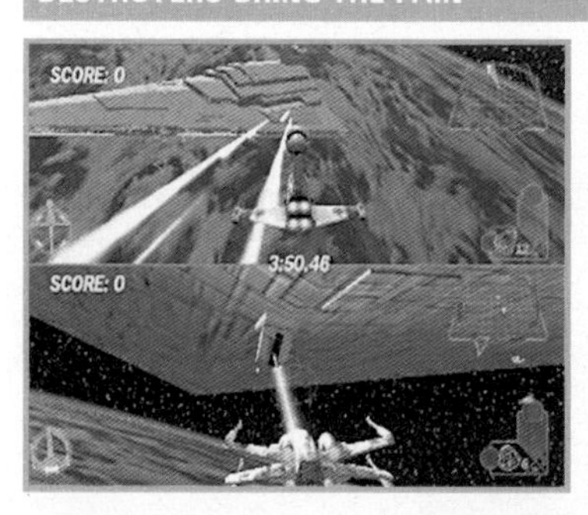

The ion cannon blasts on the topside of the Star Destroyers are harmless, but the green lasers that emanate from the belly of the beasts are directed and damaging. Stay out of their way.

IMPERIAL ASSISTANCE

You'll find power-ups above the Star Destroyers' bridges and in their cargo bays. Collect the items in long, tough battles, but fly carefully as you approach them to avoid collisions with the monstrous ships.

VERSUS MODE
RAMPAGE

When it comes to pure destruction, Rampage scenarios have no equal. Targets are plentiful. Line them up and shoot them down. The player who causes the most destruction will win. The Rampage strategies in the following pages are specific to each scenario.

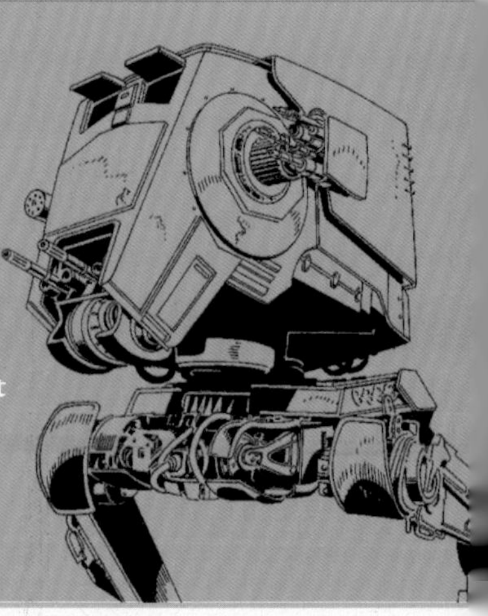

MOVING TARGETS

In addition to destroying computer-controlled enemies and obstacles, it's always a good idea to target your opponent. A finishing blow will earn you 100 points and you'll be able to profit from destroying the targets that your opponent has already weakened.

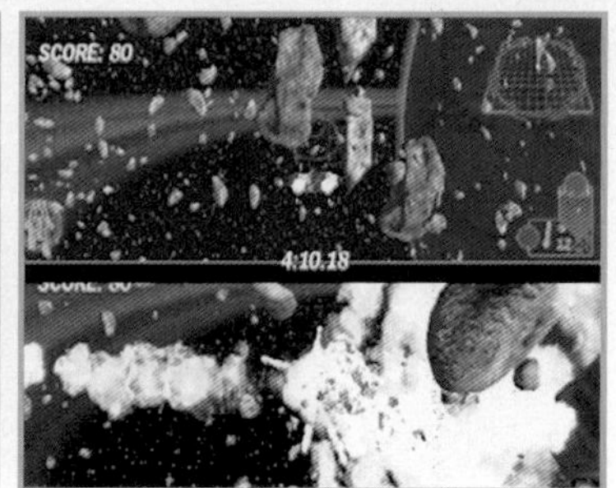

You'll earn 100 points for destroying your opponent's craft, but you'll lose 100 points if you destroy your own craft by crashing into an obstacle.

GAS PLATFORM RAMPAGE

They're not part of the fray in the Bespin Dogfight scenario, but the gas platforms and balloons of Bespin figure big in Bespin's Rampage session. Keep your opponent away from the big targets and practice a concentrated attack strategy.

POINTS	
GAS CONTAINER	5 POINTS
BALLOON TURRET	25 POINTS
IMPERIAL TANKER	100 POINTS
OPPOSING PLAYER	100 POINTS
BALLOON	500 POINTS

PLAYABLE VEHICLES

A-WING
B-WING
CLOUD CAR
SLAVE I
IMPERIAL SHUTTLE
JEDI STARFIGHTER
NABOO STARFIGHTER
MILLENNIUM FALCON
T-16 SKYHOPPER
TIE ADVANCED
TIE BOMBER
TIE FIGHTER
TIE HUNTER
TIE INTERCEPTOR
X-WING
Y-WING

STRAFING BONANZA

The only destructible parts of a gas platform are the 40 tanks that line the main deck and tower. Approach a platform from slightly above the main deck, cut your speed and hit the tanks with a wash of laser fire. After the deck is clear, knock out the tanks on the tower to earn a total of 200 points for the entire platform.

APPROACH BALLOONS FROM BELOW

The only way to destroy a balloon is to target the burners that fill the gas bag. If you're at the same level as the target balloon, take a dive, position your ship below the balloon, identify one of the burners and blast it.

DEATH STAR RAMPAGE

The Death Star Rampage scenario is similar to the first section of the Death Star Attack mission in the Cooperative campaign—it's packed with deflection towers and turrets. Look for power-ups between the deflection tower pairs.

POINTS	
TIE FIGHTER	25 POINTS
TURRET	25 POINTS
DEFLECTION TOWER	100 POINTS
OPPOSING PLAYER	100 POINTS

PLAYABLE VEHICLES

A-WING
B-WING
SLAVE I
IMPERIAL SHUTTLE
JEDI STARFIGHTER
NABOO STARFIGHTER
MILLENNIUM FALCON
TIE ADVANCED
TIE BOMBER
TIE FIGHTER
TIE HUNTER
TIE INTERCEPTOR
X-WING
Y-WING

SEEK TARGETING ASSISTANCE

It can be difficult to see TIE fighters against the black sky and turrets against the Death Star's gray surface. Use your targeting computer to single out the small targets. Since targeting-computer efficiency is not a factor in Versus mode, you can keep the computer on the screen for as long as you like.

TOWER POWER

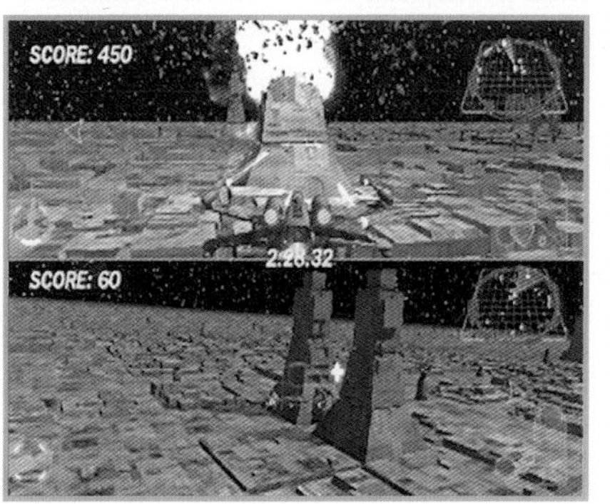

The scenario's deflection towers are stronger than the ones in the Death Star Attack mission. It will require several passes to destroy a single tower. If you see your competitor attempting to destroy a tower, target the opposing ship to earn 100 points, then attack the weakened tower for 100 additional points.

GEONOSIS ASTEROID RAMPAGE

TIE fighters and small asteroids are worth the same number of points in Geonosis Asteroid Rampage, but the rocks are much better targets. There are plenty of them, they move slowly and they don't return fire. Clear them away, but avoid the larger indestructible rocks.

POINTS	
TIE FIGHTER	25 POINTS
ASTEROID	25 POINTS
OPPOSING PLAYER	100 POINTS
IMPERIAL ESCORT	500 POINTS

PLAYABLE VEHICLES

A-WING
B-WING
SLAVE I
IMPERIAL SHUTTLE
JEDI STARFIGHTER
NABOO STARFIGHTER
MILLENNIUM FALCON
TIE ADVANCED
TIE BOMBER
TIE FIGHTER
TIE HUNTER
TIE INTERCEPTOR
X-WING
Y-WING

LEAN ON THE TRIGGER

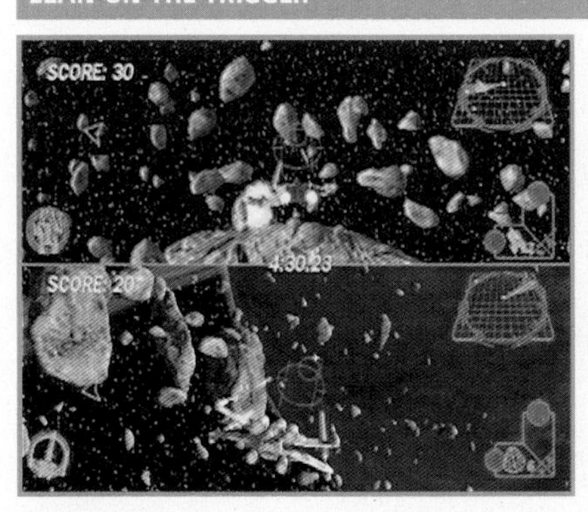

Although your lasers will be more powerful if you allow them to recharge between shots, sustained fire works best in a target-rich environment. Hold the A Button and never let up. You'll destroy some rocks without intentionally targeting them.

RACE FOR THE CARRIER

Imperial escort carriers come onto the scene one at a time. It's likely that your opponent will zone in on a carrier as soon as it arrives. Try to beat your competitor to the punch and hit the carrier with everything you've got—constant laser fire and secondary weapons. If you deal the final blow, you'll earn 500 points.

RAMPAGE OVER HOTH

The sky over Hoth is big, but it's riddled with TIE fighters and larger Imperial ships. The scenario is built for players who can outrun fast-moving targets and get to larger targets in a hurry. Select a ship that is quick and strong.

POINTS	
TIE FIGHTER	25 POINTS
OPPOSING PLAYER	100 POINTS
IMPERIAL SHUTTLE	200 POINTS
IMPERIAL TRANSPORT	500 POINTS

PLAYABLE VEHICLES

A-WING
B-WING
CLOUD CAR
SLAVE I
IMPERIAL SHUTTLE
JEDI STARFIGHTER
NABOO STARFIGHTER
MILLENNIUM FALCON
T-16 SKYHOPPER
TIE ADVANCED
TIE BOMBER
TIE FIGHTER
TIE HUNTER
TIE INTERCEPTOR
X-WING
Y-WING

CENTER ON LARGE SHIPS

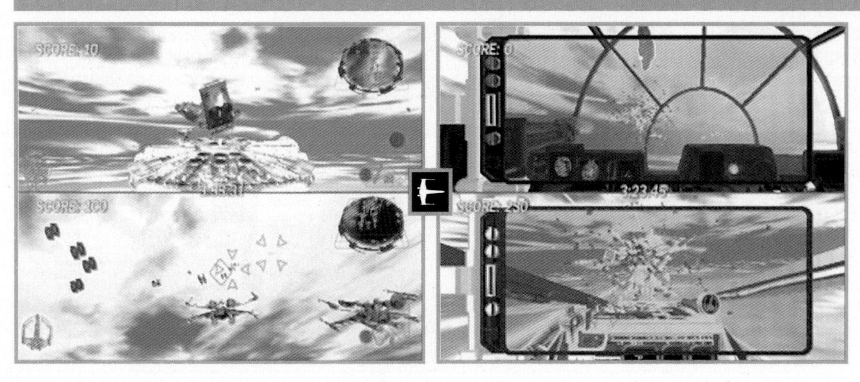

Head for the clouds from the start and take down TIE fighters while you wait for the big targets. Imperial transports and Imperial shuttles will appear as yellow-shaded targets in your targeting computer display. While a shuttle is not worth as many points as a transport, destroying one is a much easier way to earn 200 points than destroying a group of eight TIE fighters.

KOTHLIS RAMPAGE

The fight to demolish the targets of Kothlis will take you low to the ground and water. At first glance, it may seem that stationary targets are few and far between, but upon closer inspection you will find plenty of turrets and bases.

POINTS	
TIE FIGHTER	25 POINTS
TURRET	25 POINTS
SENSOR RELAY	25 POINTS
OPPOSING PLAYER	100 POINTS
BASE	100 POINTS
OUTPOST	100 POINTS
IMPERIAL SHUTTLE	200 POINTS

PLAYABLE VEHICLES

A-WING	NABOO STARFIGHTER	TIE HUNTER
B-WING	*MILLENNIUM FALCON*	TIE INTERCEPTOR
CLOUD CAR	T-16 SKYHOPPER	X-WING
SLAVE I	TIE ADVANCED	Y-WING
IMPERIAL SHUTTLE	TIE BOMBER	
JEDI STARFIGHTER	TIE FIGHTER	

SKIM AND SCORE

You'll find several bases on the water's surface. Drop to sea level and approach the big targets from a distance. Hit the bases' turrets first (for 25 points each) to avoid a firefight, then knock out the bases for 100 points a pop.

TRACK DOWN TARGETS

Shuttles land on open platforms. Keep track of the platform locations and return to them often to look for shuttles. You'll earn 200 points for every shuttle that you destroy. Also, search the hills for turrets. You'll find them amongst the trees by using your targeting computer.

HOTH SPEEDER RAMPAGE

'he first section of the Battle of Hoth mission in the cooperative ampaign will prepare you for the Hoth Speeder Rampage sce- ario. You may find some stray TIEs, but the most points are in round targets. Fly slow and low in heavily populated areas and estroy every target you see.

PLAYABLE VEHICLE

SPEEDER

POINTS	
AT-ST	100 POINTS
OPPOSING PLAYER	100 POINTS
IMPERIAL SHUTTLE	200 POINTS
IMPERIAL TRANSPORT	300 POINTS
AT-AT	500 POINTS

OPE WALKERS FOR BIG POINTS

AT-ATs are worth 500 points each. Your blasters won't work on them, but your tow cable will. Press B while passing an Imperial walker to snag one of its legs with your cable, then fly around all four legs three times to trip up the machine. If your opponent is trying to trip a walker, target the opposing speeder first, then take down the walker yourself.

KEEP AN EYE ON ARRIVALS

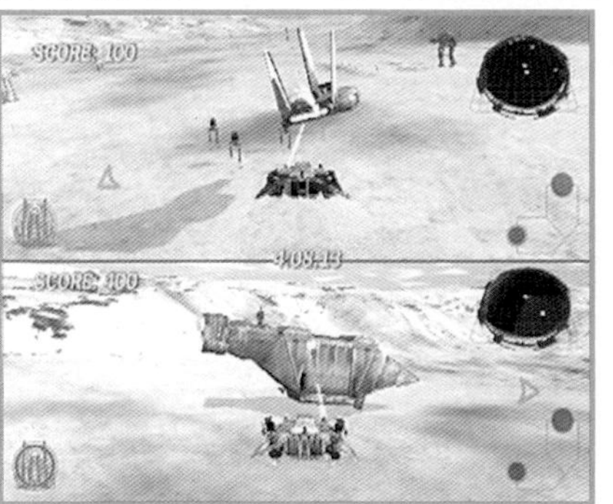

Scan the horizon for large Imperial ships. They're easy to defeat and worth a lot of points. When the ships arrive on the scene, they'll be well above your speeder's flight ceiling. Wait for them to touch down before you target them.

TAG AND DEFEND

Tag and Defend scenarios provide a mix of pure destruction and dogfighting. The test is to capture and keep bases and outposts. You'll find that a strategy that works well in one Tag and Defend level will be effective on any other level.

FORCEFUL TAG

The only way to claim a property is to fire at it until it gives up. Destroy the turrets on your approach, then target the structure itself. A Rebel symbol will appear above a defeated property. Fly through the symbol to take possession of the base.

After you capture a base, the structure and the turrets will repair themselves slowly. The turrets will target your opponent's ship, but they won't go after you. The longer you hold a base or an outpost, the more points you will earn.

PREFSBELT IV TAG AND DEFEND

Attacking under the cover of night, you'll take Prefsbelt IV by storm and swoop down on its bases. Keep track of your rival's progress and steal bases that he or she has been targeting whenever possible.

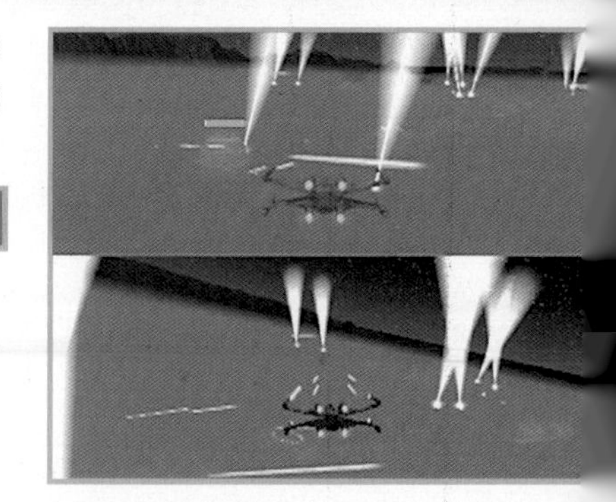

PLAYABLE VEHICLES		
A-WING	JEDI STARFIGHTER	TIE FIGHTER
B-WING	NABOO STARFIGHTER	TIE HUNTER
CLOUD CAR	*MILLENNIUM FALCON*	TIE INTERCEPTOR
SLAVE I	TIE ADVANCED	X-WING
IMPERIAL SHUTTLE	TIE BOMBER	Y-WING

CUT THROUGH THE FOG

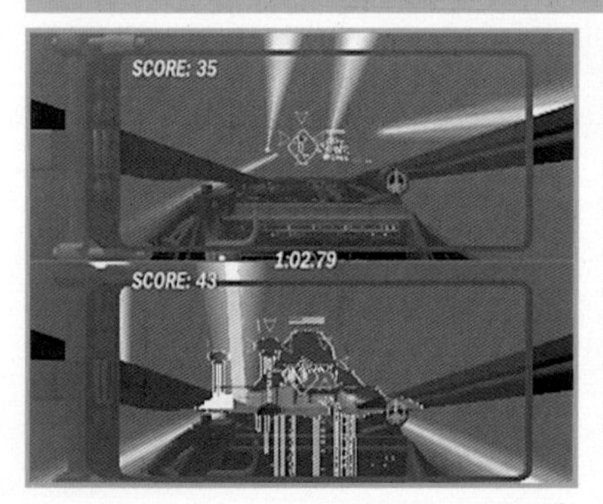

The dark and fog make visibility very limited. Select advanced targeting computers while you're setting up the scenario and use your computer for the length of the mission. If you are piloting a Y-wing, use of the targeting computer is less important than it is with other ships. You don't have to see through the fog to bomb targets.

FLY IN FOR RECOVERY

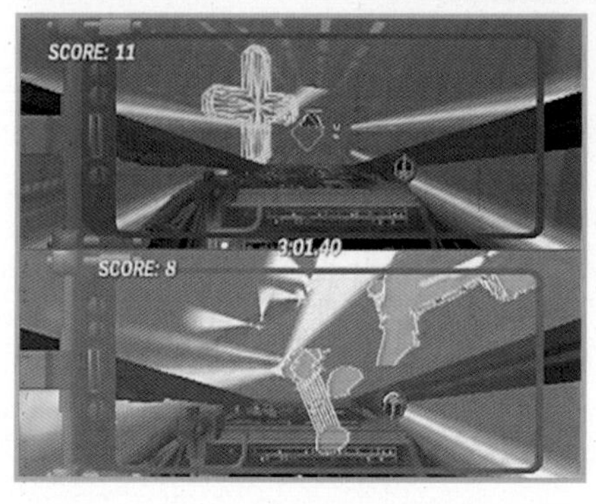

The area's hangars hold power-ups. Swoop down on the bases near the hangars and capture then then head for the hangars to replenish your shields and secondary weapon supply.

ASTEROID TAG AND DEFEND

Large, immobile and indestructible asteroids serve as platforms for the bases in the Asteroid Tag and Defend scenario above Geonosis. Computer-controlled ships aren't a problem, but stray asteroids are a big concern. Keep blasting to clear your way through the field.

PLAYABLE VEHICLES

A-WING	NABOO STARFIGHTER	TIE HUNTER
B-WING	*MILLENNIUM FALCON*	TIE INTERCEPTOR
SLAVE I	TIE ADVANCED	X-WING
IMPERIAL SHUTTLE	TIE BOMBER	Y-WING
JEDI STARFIGHTER	TIE FIGHTER	

360-DEGREE PROTECTION

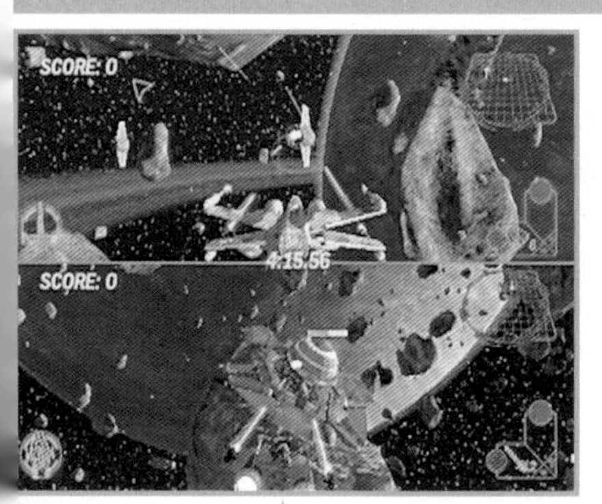

Turrets above and below the massive stationary rocks protect the base on top of the rocks from all angles. If you approach a base from a low angle, target the turrets below the base's rock before you take on the complex atop the rock.

SNEAK IN FOR A STEAL

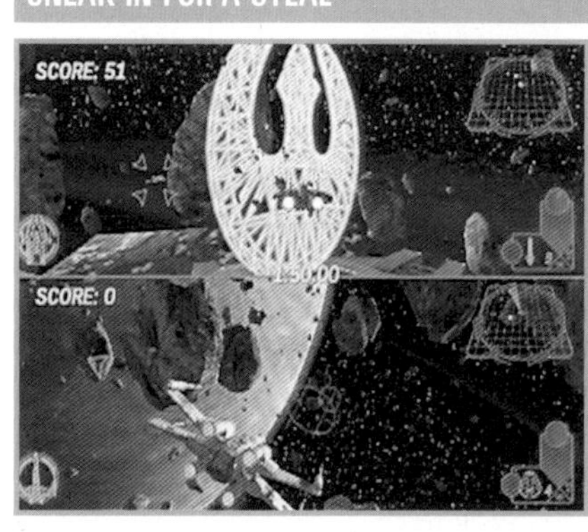

Watch your opponent carefully throughout all Tag and Defend scenarios. After the opposing player destroys a base then flies into the Rebel symbol to claim it, the base will remain vulnerable until its shields regenerate. You can take advantage of the base's weak position by attacking it and capturing it in one run.

KOTHLIS TAG AND DEFEND

The island chain on Kothlis is a beautiful place for a battle. The same types of structures that you can destroy in the Kothlis Rampage scenario act as bases in the Tag and Defend scenario. You'll find them on the water, just off shore.

PLAYABLE VEHICLES

A-WING	NABOO STARFIGHTER	TIE FIGHTER
B-WING	*MILLENNIUM FALCON*	TIE HUNTER
CLOUD CAR	SPEEDER	TIE INTERCEPTOR
SLAVE I	T-16 SKYHOPPER	X-WING
IMPERIAL SHUTTLE	TIE ADVANCED	Y-WING
JEDI STARFIGHTER	TIE BOMBER	

MOUNTAIN MISSILES

Missile turrets top some of the mountains of Kothlis. If you see a structure as you approach a mountaintop on your way to a power-up, hit it with a laser barrage before it can release one of its homing missiles.

Y-WING ADVANTAGE

The Y-wing is the vehicle of choice for most Tag and Defend scenarios. By using the craft's bombs, you can attack the bases from far above them, defeating them quickly and avoiding damage from the turrets. The only danger is that a faster craft could move in before you have a chance to dive into the Rebel symbol and claim the base.

MAW TAG AND DEFEND

Bases and outposts are few and far between on Maw. Most of the structures are surrounded by bare mountains. Since the structures are far apart, you may find that it is difficult to hold on to several properties at once.

PLAYABLE VEHICLES		
A-WING	NABOO STARFIGHTER	TIE HUNTER
B-WING	*MILLENNIUM FALCON*	TIE INTERCEPTOR
SLAVE I	TIE ADVANCED	X-WING
IMPERIAL SHUTTLE	TIE BOMBER	Y-WING
JEDI STARFIGHTER	TIE FIGHTER	

THE BEST DEFENSE IS A GOOD OFFENSE

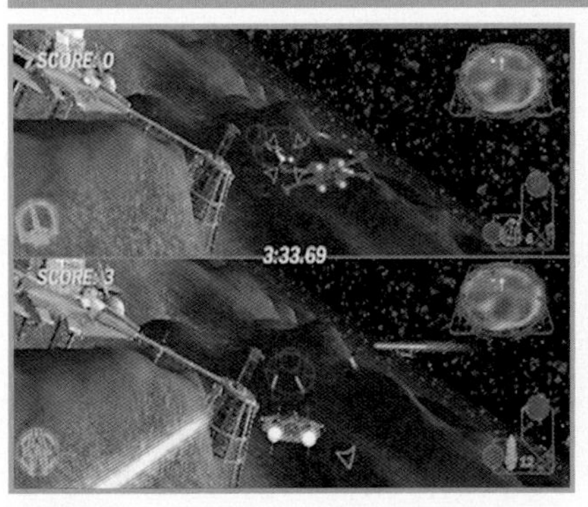

Your opponent will have a hard time getting through your bases' defenses with a damaged ship. Once you have a few bases of your own, seek out and battle the opposing player's craft. You need not destroy it, but every hit that you score will reduce the likelihood that the ship will survive an attack on one of your properties.

CAPTURE HOME BASE

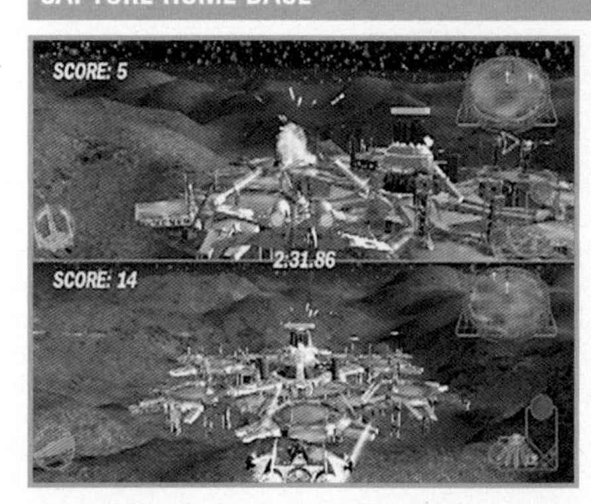

Maw has one full-fledged base and several outposts. The base has twice as much protection as the outposts, and it is worth many more points once it's in your possession. Capture it early and hold onto it. You'll be well on your way to victory.

TATOOINE TAG AND DEFEND

The Tatooine Tag and Defend scenario has very similar terrain to the Maw scenario—the main difference being that Tatooine has light sand and a blue sky, making visibility a little better than it is on Maw.

PLAYABLE VEHICLES		
A-WING	NABOO STARFIGHTER	TIE HUNTER
B-WING	*MILLENNIUM FALCON*	TIE INTERCEPTOR
CLOUD CAR	T-16 SKYHOPPER	X-WING
SLAVE I	TIE ADVANCED	Y-WING
IMPERIAL SHUTTLE	TIE BOMBER	
JEDI STARFIGHTER	TIE FIGHTER	

GROUND-TO-AIR COMBAT

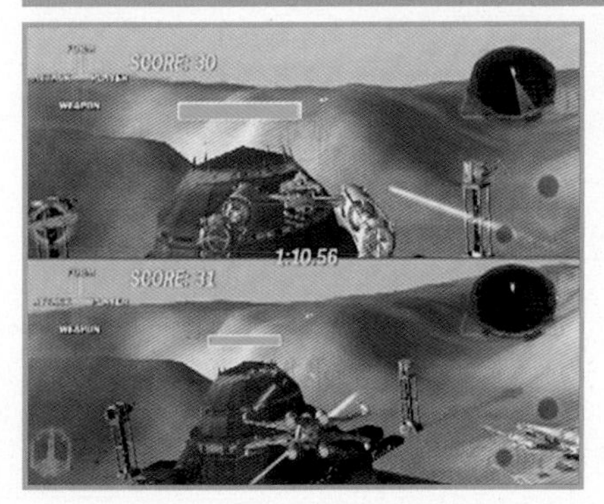

If your opponent is on your tail, fly toward your closest base or outpost and stay low. When you near your property, your turrets will turn on the opposing player and do their best to shake the opponent off your tail.

NATURAL PROTECTION

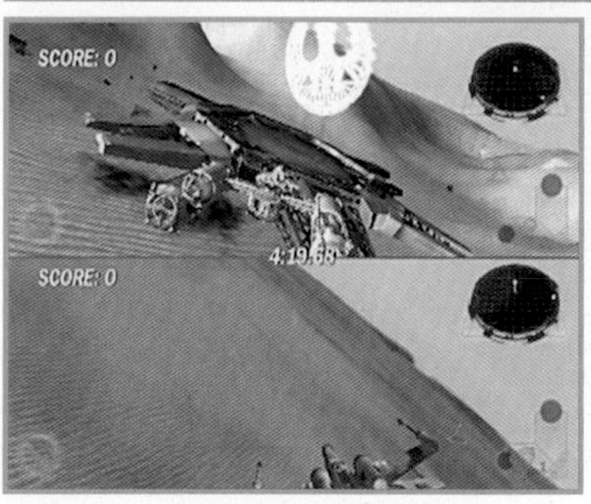

One of the Tatooine outposts is located in a shallow canyon and is naturally protected by the surrounding hills. If you take control over the outpost, you'll stand a good chance of keeping it for the duration of the scenario. Look for a power-up close by.

HOTH TAG AND DEFEND

The Hoth scenario may be the most competitive Tag and Defend scenario of the bunch. Players can choose only speeders, and there is only one base to capture. You'll spend the entire time locked in battle with your opponent.

PLAYABLE VEHICLE
SPEEDER

ONE BASE TO RULE THEM ALL

Both players will go after the area's single base from the start of the scenario. If your opponent captures the base, be ready to swoop in and attack it before the shields regenerate.

HOLD ON TO WHAT YOU'VE GOT

Once you have possession of the base, all you have to do is keep it. Circle the base, collect power-ups on neighboring platforms when they become available and target your opponent at every opportunity.

VERSUS MODE
SPECIAL

One pair of scenarios are ground-bound Rampage runs with chicken walkers. The other two Special scenarios are two-player races with a single adjustable option—the number of available lives.

READ YOUR RACING POSITION

A graphic in the middle of the screen shows the relative position of the two competitors and their proximity to the finish line. If you're close behind your competitor, the more important graphic to view is the yellow crosshair that surrounds the opposing vehicle. Watch it to know which route to take around obstacles.

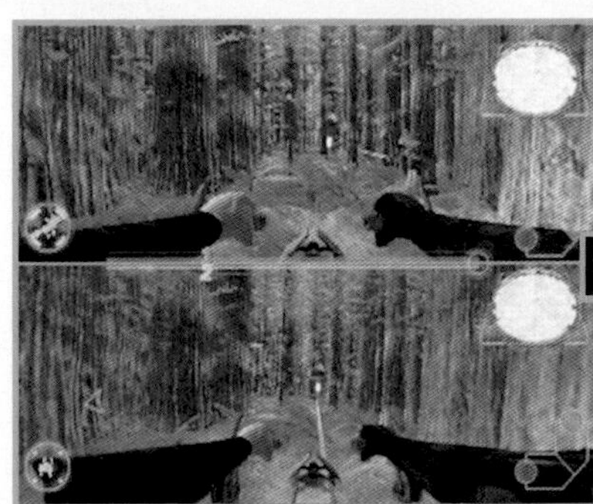

If you get far ahead of your opponent, it's your race to win or lose. Slow down and practice extreme caution. If you don't make any big mistakes, your opponent won't be able to catch up to you.

ENDOR WALKER RAMPAGE

The Endor Walker Rampage scenario is a showdown of Imperial vehicles and troops. There's not a piece of Alliance equipment to be found, except for the Ewoks' stacked logs. Although you won't get any points for knocking down trees, forest destruction will help you clear the way to hidden troopers and AT-STs.

PLAYABLE VEHICLES
AT-PT
AT-ST

POINTS	
STORMTROOPER	25 POINTS
IMPERIAL PROBE DROID	50 POINTS
WALKER	200 POINTS
SPEEDER BIKE	300 POINTS

BATTLE OF THE CHICKEN WALKERS

The AT-ST can pick off enemies with lasers and homing missiles, and hold its own with powerful shields. The AT-PT doesn't carry missiles, but its laser is more powerful than the AT-ST's primary weapon. The AT-PT is also faster than the AT-ST, and it's a slightly smaller target.

SEEING THE ENEMIES FOR THE TREES

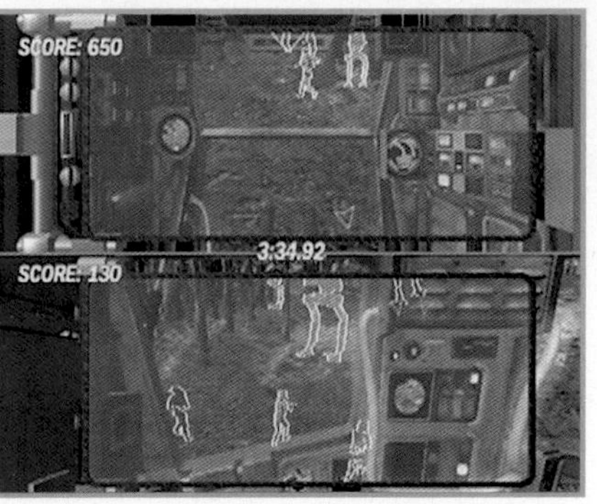

The forest is dark and thick with trees. Use your targeting computer to uncover targets on the other side of the brush and plow your way into the trees to root out the Imperials.

TATOOINE WALKER RAMPAGE

The AT-ST exercise in the Tatooine Training mission is tame compared to the fast and frenzied Tatooine Walker Rampage. You won't have time to think as you run around a small sunken section of the desert and pick off one Imperial after the next.

POINTS	
STORMTROOPER	25 POINTS
IMPERIAL PROBE DROID	50 POINTS
WALKER	200 POINTS

PLAYABLE VEHICLES

AT-PT
AT-ST

HEATED BATTLE UNDER THE HOT SUN

The battle is intense from the beginning, with enemies attacking from all sides. Stay mobile and try to use the big rocks for cover.

TAKE ON TROOPERS TOO

You may be compelled to concentrate on the chicken walkers for the sake of racking up monster points, but if you don't devote some attention to the stormtroopers, they'll whittle away at your shields and cause you a lot of trouble. Strafe the groups of troopers between walker attacks.

DEATH STAR TRENCH RACE

ou'll get a new look at the setting for *A New Hope*'s finale by racing another X-wing through e Death Star's trench. It can be difficult to distinguish the open path from the obstacles. The est way to ensure victory is to memorize the course and fly through it at maximum speed.

PLAYABLE VEHICLES

X-WING	TIE INTERCEPTOR	NABOO STARFIGHTER
A-WING	TIE BOMBER	JEDI STARFIGHTER
Y-WING	TIE HUNTER	
TIE FIGHTER	TIE ADVANCED	

TAY ON TARGET

If you're in a tight race, and you still have a good distance to go before you reach the finish line, fall back and let your opponent take a short lead. You'll be able to plot out a course around the obstacles by following the other racer, and you'll also be able to weaken your opponent's shields by firing at the vehicle.

DITCH THE LASERS

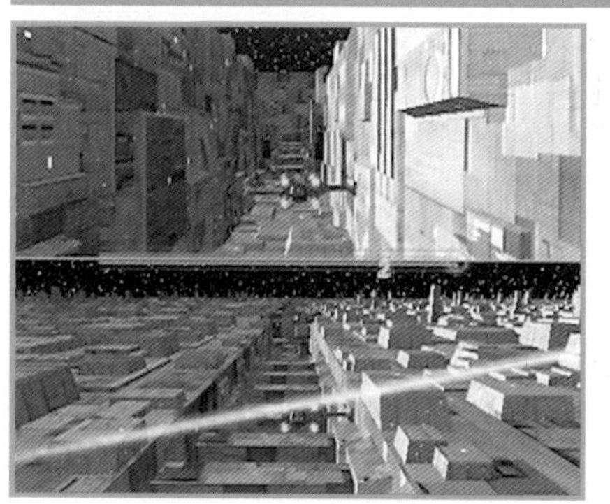

Although the Death Star ditch may not seem like a safe haven while you're in it, you'll realize how safe it is if you rise above the walls. As soon as you clear the edge, multiple lasers will target your ship. Dive back into the ditch while you still have a chance.

ENDOR SPEEDER BIKE RACE

The setting for one of the most exciting scenes of *Return of the Jedi* and one of the final stages of the single-player campaign also serves as the setting for a two-player race. The path is tight and winding. Watch what's ahead and make your decisions quickly.

PLAYABLE VEHICLE
SPEEDER BIKE

TAG THE LEADER

It's not always a good idea to be in the lead, unless you're close to the end or far ahead of your opponent. Drop back in a close race and hit your opponent with bursts from your blaster. Your shots will be more effective if you let your weapons charge between blasts.

BOOST AT YOUR OWN RISK

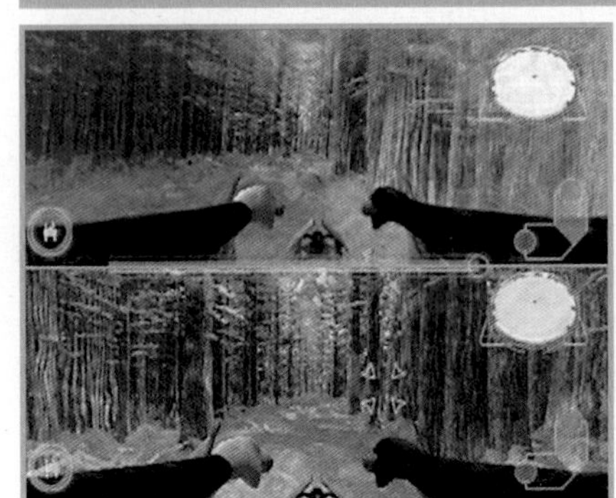

Trees and logs appear with minimal notice on the Endor forest trail. Your speeder bike is capable of boosting, but you should use boosts only if you are far behind your opponent and you have nothing to lose, or if you are on a straight section of the path.

! KEEP TRACK OF THE TALLY

By selecting the Change Pilots option in the Versus Game Select menu, you'll go to a table that keeps track of your wins, losses and draws. It separates the Special scenarios to let you see the best overall time on each track.

MAY THE FORCE BE WITH YOU.